ALL THE DEMONS ARE HERE

ALL THE
DEMONS
ARE HERE

A NOVEL

JAKE
TAPPER

Little, Brown and Company

New York   Boston   London

Little, Brown and Company
Hachette Book Group
1290 Avenue of the Americas, New York, NY 10104
littlebrown.com

First Edition: July 2023

Little, Brown and Company is a division of Hachette Book Group, Inc. The Little, Brown name and logo are trademarks of Hachette Book Group, Inc.

The publisher is not responsible for websites (or their content) that are not owned by the publisher.

The Hachette Speakers Bureau provides a wide range of authors for speaking events. To find out more, go to hachettespeakersbureau.com or email hachettespeakers@hbgusa.com.

Little, Brown and Company books may be purchased in bulk for business, educational, or promotional use. For information, please contact your local bookseller or the Hachette Book Group Special Markets Department at special.markets@hbgusa.com.

ISBN 9780316424387
LCCN 2022948738

Printing 1, 2023

LSC-C

Printed in the United States of America

To Daryl, Alana, Max, and Milo

I created the character called Evel Knievel, and he sort of got away from me.
  —Robert "Evel" Knievel, June 1998

ALL THE DEMONS ARE HERE

CHAPTER ONE

IKE

Butte, Montana

June 1977

So I slept in the hobo jungles
Roamed a thousand miles of track

—Elvis Presley, "Guitar Man"

THE TOUGHEST TAVERN in Big Sky Country wasn't the legendary Jimtown Bar near Lame Deer, with its acre of spent beer cans under which a corpse or two were likely buried. It wasn't Al's Tavern near the Billings sugar plant, with its buckshot-scarred front door and concrete floor stained with blood and brains.

No, that honor belonged to the Dead Canary, a dive outside Butte where the shot glasses once used to throw whiskey down the coal-dusted throats of dying miners were now clasped by Hells Angels and truck-stop hookers, poachers, and drug dealers from the Flathead Indian Reservation. Plus the gang of circus freaks more formally known as the pit crew of legendary daredevil Evel Knievel.

I was one of those freaks.

That Saturday night, I was hanging out at the bar staring down the dozens of elk-head trophy mounts hung without rhyme or reason, as if customers paid their bar tabs with taxidermy. The effect was bizarre, like the beasts were stampeding right at me.

I was sitting beneath a sign that announced POWDER: NO CANDLES OR LIGHTED PIPES ALLOWED IN THIS DRIFT PER ORDER, a relic from the Montana Mining Company's hunt for silver and gold and a warning that seemed a little too on the nose—for the bar and for me. This place was always one lit match away from disaster; it was squat and dim, with no windows for an easy escape. A cover band jammed in the far corner. Drunks crashed into each other on the makeshift dance floor.

I was tossing back whiskey and trying to make the bartender, Rachel Two Bears, laugh. She was tall and lean and hailed from the Crow Rez at the Wyoming border, though now she lived above this bar. She told me she was just there to help out a friend and planned to leave once Labor Day came around, but it seemed like she'd made herself at home, and I was glad about that. I wasn't sure if we liked each other or just hated the same people. Okay, I'm full of shit—I was crazy about her.

"Big push to spring Patty Hearst for good," I said, reading the front page of the *Montana Standard*. The kidnapped heiress turned bank robber was out on bail while she appealed her conviction, and newspaper columnists fed us daily dollops of details about how hard life had been for her when she was criming.

"Carter's going to commute her sentence, mark my words," she practically spat.

"You really think so?"

"The best 'justice' system money can buy," she said. She mockingly assumed the voice of a bleeding heart: "Oh, poor girl, she was only nineteen when it started."

"The Marines got me when I was seventeen. Where's my sympathy?"

"Right here," she said and refilled my shot glass.

Rachel's politics were interesting; she seemed to have sympathy for Native American and other civil rights causes, but generally speaking, she was pretty hard-core law-and-order. Especially when it came to rich white folks gaming the system.

There were bikers in the house, big, ugly, hairy dudes. Some of those guys were freedom-loving rebels; others were actual fascists. There were also cowboys and Indians, students and farmers—and I wondered which way the night would go.

As if she'd read my mind, Rachel said, "Cantina scene tonight." A few days before, Rachel and I had gone to see *Star Wars*.

"Lotta weirdos," I agreed. "Not sure this means we're at the start of an epic adventure, though."

She smiled. "You're not getting Leia'ed, if that's what you mean."

"Solo again," I grumbled.

She winked at me, then went down the bar to pour a shot for a short, stocky biker in a black leather jacket.

Rachel was an enigma, a conundrum, a paradox—all those vocab words Mom made me study (for naught, since I bypassed college for the Marines). Anytime I tried to find out more about her—about life on the rez or where her family was or how she'd ended up here, of all places, in this rotten saloon in Butte—I hit a wall. She wasn't a good liar, didn't have a prepared story about who she was. Anytime I pried, she just closed up, flicked her attention past my shoulder, and waited for the conversation to move on. I had secrets too, of course, and sometimes I wondered who had more to hide.

The biker grunted his thanks. He was about as wide as a refrigerator, and on the back of his leather jacket, a German iron cross was painted in red. He downed his drink and signaled for another. Rachel told him to pay for the first two. He dug into the pocket of his jeans, dropped the change on the bar, and slowly counted his pennies and dimes.

Behind him, a smelly, greasy-haired cowboy mocked the biker in a dumb-guy voice: "One nickel…two nickels…der…I lost count."

The biker turned to the grinning cowboy. "Why don't you fuck off and—"

Rachel interrupted. "Kindly excuse Bitch Cassidy here," she said, referring to the cowboy. "He's just stoned. Fact is, he's gonna pay for your drinks as compensation for his rudeness as long as you walk away and don't cause no trouble. Okay, handsome?"

The biker stared into her dark eyes, possibly getting lost in them the way I frequently did. Cowboy started to complain, but Rachel's scowl shut him down. The biker scraped up his change and walked back over to the corner where his buddies were emptying pitchers.

"All right, Midnight Cowpie," Rachel said. "What are you buying other than two shots for the fifth column?"

The cowboy wasn't happy, and Rachel's quickness didn't endear her to him. Not that he was going to do anything about it. Rachel had a shotgun behind the bar and a Model 19 Combat Magnum handgun on her hip, and if her little show-and-tell didn't keep him in line, I was ready to. I had a couple years in the Corps and forty pounds on him and would've been happy to shut his mouth.

Wild Turkey on the rocks, he said. Rachel obliged, and as he walked off, she poured me one too. Wild Turkey was what my boss drank. If Evel caught you with anything else, he'd give you shit for being disloyal or soft, depending on the beverage.

"Motley crew," she said.

"Motleyest in a while," I said.

"I don't think that's a word."

"Maybe not. Woulda been had Webster ever visited Montana."

"Bikers and miners and drunks, oh my!" she said.

"And he's talkin' with Davy, who's still in the navy and probably will be for life," I sang.

She spritzed carbonated water from the soda gun into a glass and raised it. "May we be who our dogs think we are." Mac, her black-and-white mutt behind the bar, grunted.

I racked my brain for a decent toast that wouldn't offend her, but nothing I'd picked up in prep school or the Marines qualified. Not that she was paying attention. She, along with a couple of the bar creeps, had turned toward the door. So I looked too.

A young blond woman wearing the kind of gray tailored suit you'd see on the streets of Manhattan—not in rural Montana—had just entered. I must have been drunker than I thought, because she looked exactly like my sister. But she couldn't be my sister. My sister had no idea where I was. My sister was in DC, and I was hiding here, where she'd never find me. I squinted, and the woman locked eyes with me and gave me my sister's goofy grin.

"Holy fucking shit," I said.

"Ike!" She ran across the room, flung herself into my arms, and squeezed the breath out of me. I hugged her too, pretending I was happy she was here. I was, in a way.

She leaned back to get a better look at me and tugged at the beard I'd grown. "Not Marine Corps regulation."

"How the fuck did you find me?"

Her nose wrinkled at the curse, then she smiled. "I'm a reporter, stupid."

I guided Lucy to a corner table between the bar and the door, away from everybody, then went back and got her a beer and myself a whiskey rocks. "You can't leave a military hospital in the middle of the night and expect no one to worry," she said when I came back. "I thought Mom and Dad were overreacting, but seeing you now, I'm not so sure."

"The Marines know where I am," I said. This wasn't exactly true, but I hadn't been officially declared AWOL.

"That's not what the Corps told Dad. He and Mom are freaking out."

Lucy didn't know the whole story, and I wasn't about to burden her with it. She was only two years older than me, but you'd think she was my mom. "How are they?"

"Worried about you," Lucy said, "but keeping busy." She looked down at her beer, caressing the lip of the glass. "Mom's been dragging Dad to every Shakespeare play at the Folger. Last week was *The Tempest*."

"Dad must fucking hate it."

"He's fine. Okay, he's not totally fine. He's drinking again." She looked pointedly at the glass in my hand.

I glanced away. Her eyes always were a little too sharp. "And how's he dealing with the new administration?" Dad was a moderate Republican senator from New York; his respect for Carter, shall we say, knew bounds. Vice President Rockefeller had been a mentor of his, and he'd adored President Ford. I didn't give a damn about any of this, but Lucy loved talking politics, and it got her out of my grille.

"He feels guilty, I think," Lucy said. "By coming out against Nixon so early, he worries he undermined Ford and set the stage for his defeat."

"How's work at the paper?" The previous summer, right out of Yale, Lucy had been hired as an intern at the national desk of the *Washington Evening Star*.

"I left the *Star*, I quit," she said. "I have a new job. Long story, but I'd rather hear about you. How did you end up…" She looked around the room as if she smelled something foul. Lucy had been a protective older sister—always looking out for me, comforting me when I got suspended for fighting in high school, supportive when I enlisted before graduation. "Like, what do you talk about with this…gathering of the Cro-Magnon Society?"

"Work," I said. "Bikes. Trucks. I've heard you and your friends yammering, and that's not exactly the fucking Algonquin."

"That's true," she said, laughing. She raised her glass to me. "Do you still watch TV? Back home, everyone's talking about *Roots*."

"I don't have a TV." My digs consisted of a bed in a room the size of a closet in what was essentially a flophouse for the pit crew. "But I read the book. And a lot of other stuff. Don't really miss TV, except Carson."

The band took a break. Rachel stepped out from behind the bar—cowboy boots, tight blue jeans, black sleeveless top. I liked watching her move. She went over to the jukebox. The first guitar bursts of Led Zeppelin's "All the Demons Are Here" ricocheted around the room.

Ev'ryone gettin' crazy
Desperation in the air
The storm made the trip and crashed the ship
We were all in deep despair

Ferdinand saw the evil
Knew from whence it came
The cursed love, the gods above,
The ship consumed by flame

Helllllllllll is emmmmmmpty
And all the demons are here

Hellllllllllll is emmmmmmpty
And all the demons are here

Somewhere in the midst of one of Robert Plant's more orgasmic vocals, the bar door opened and a whiff of gasoline from a motorcycle that was obviously jetting way too rich punched me in the face. A man by the door lit a cigarette, and in the lighter's flare, his facial features were sharp, hawklike. When I blinked, the man's face filled out, became chubby. To those who haven't had them, flashbacks are difficult to explain, especially when they're from combat, but for a moment in time, the sensory overload of rhythm and odor and harsh sounds pushed me out and away from Lucy and into a sweaty heart-pounding oblivion.

Lucy reined me in. "I didn't know Zeppelin had made it to the wilds of Montana."

It took me a second to get my bearings. "Oh, sure. We have the wheel now too."

She shrugged. "I figured your jukes would be chock-full o' Nitty Gritty Dirt Band."

I looked at her. I'd been mad at Lucy. Growing up, I was closer to her than anyone, then she went off to college and lived her life and created a vacuum in mine and everything changed. I began spinning out of control; I got in trouble at school, and by the time I enlisted, I'd been drinking and fighting for so long, I figured I might as well get paid for it. Of course, Mom and Dad begged me not to do it, but that just made me want to get away more. I knew it wasn't logical to blame any of this on Lucy, but I did anyway. I also wanted to tell her everything, like what had happened to me in Lebanon. But I couldn't talk about it. Not even to her.

"Bathroom," I said, standing. "Be right back."

* * *

Swaying at the urinal, I read for the five hundredth time the September 9, 1974, *New York Daily News* front page that some-one had tacked on the wall years before. Although the headline read "Nixon Gets Full Pardon," most of the page was about my boss: "Evel Fails, Chutes into Canyon; He Is Unhurt in 600-Ft. Drop." It was the story of Knievel's ill-fated but spectacular jump over Snake River Canyon in a rocket that looked like some-thing Wile E. Coyote had ordered from the Acme Corporation. That crazy stunt shared billing with a moment of actual historic import. I couldn't help smiling, thinking of that crazy daredevil. Standing there looking at the photo of his broken rocket slowed everything down in my mind and calmed me, got me out of my fight-or-flight zone and gave me back some perspective. Evel Knievel! People couldn't get enough.

I'd joined his pit crew seven months before. Evel had seen me on a TV news segment about my so-called heroics in Lebanon, an urban battle and urban legend in which I'd taken part, and it included some stunts I'd pulled on the back of an old motor-cycle. The Pentagon was only too excited to sell to the American public via *60 Minutes* its (redacted) version of my story to cloak the more important narrative of our disastrous mission and the larger problem of the dying American empire flailing and failing abroad.

If you're lookin' for trouble, Elvis sang from the jukebox out in the bar, *you came to the right place*. The King's words relaxed me.

After seeing the *60 Minutes* segment, Evel had sent a message to me at the Bethesda Naval Hospital via the Montana grapevine to look him up if I ever made it to Butte. When I got out here, he was impressed with my work ethic and the way I handled a motorcycle; he hired me to work on V-twin engines and ride like

I had nothing to lose. A world-famous celebrity was shining his affection on me, and I got to bask in it—for a while, anyway. He was a moody guy, and he was currently blaming me for his latest near-fatal crash, which placed me atop a short list of people he wanted to murder. I was hoping to make my way off that list and back to the light.

I felt calmer now. The bathroom was spinning less, and my heart rate had returned to normal. I would go out there and show Lucy that everything was okay, that I was doing just great, so she could get on that plane to DC and tell the folks to stop worrying. I'd go home when I was ready.

That was the plan, anyway.

Back out at the bar, I nudged past some low-level pot dealers from the Flathead Reservation (Damon, Adam, and Paul Yellowmountain; cousins, they said) and asked Rachel for another round of drinks. "The beer's for my sister."

She glanced over, and one eyebrow went up. "That's the famous Lucy?"

"Come say hi when you get a minute."

"Corporal," Paul said to me.

"Lance corporal," Damon said.

"Lance boil," said Adam; his giggle and pink eyes revealed how stoned he was.

"I'm a lowly sergeant," I said. "How's business, gentlemen?"

Adam tucked his long dark locks behind his ears. "We're all good, *kemo sabe*."

"Yo, man, that ain't cool," Damon said. Damon was always trying to stir up shit. "*Kemo sabe* means 'idiot' in Apache."

"No, no, it just means 'white boy,'" Adam told him.

The three—obviously smoking away their profits—giggled hysterically.

As I headed back to my table, I noticed a big biker guy leaning over Lucy, his right boot propped up on my chair—a run-of-the-mill Montana dirtbag. I went over, handed Lucy her beer, and pulled my chair out from under his foot. He almost fell but caught himself.

"I was handling this," Lucy said calmly.

"I thought you were with the redskin slut," the guy said.

This guy wasn't worth breaking my hand on. Bar fights were stupid, and it'd be even stupider to fight in front of Lucy, who was there to ensure I wasn't beating up dirtbags in a bar in Montana. I told myself all these things, but I was drunk and riled up. I took a breath. Maybe this would resolve itself.

Then he gestured to Lucy and said, "Or is *this* your slut?" and I punched him in the face.

He hit the floor but quickly got up, rubbing his chin and smiling.

"Ike, stop!" Lucy said.

The band had come back from break and was blasting a cover of AC/DC's "Dirty Deeds Done Dirt Cheap." Out of the corner of my eye, I caught Rachel shucking her pump-action shotgun. Usually, that sound was enough to stop anyone in his tracks. And in this part of the world, few would judge her for the bullet.

This guy must have figured she was bluffing and pulled a knife. A dirty, rusty switchblade. He lunged at me. I felt a sting as the knife nicked me under the rib. He came at me again and I lifted him like a duffel and slammed him into the wall. A two-top and a pitcher of beer crashed to the floor. I grabbed his wrist and twisted it, and the blade fell. He went for it and I got on top of him and pummeled his face with my fist.

I can't pretend I didn't know what I was doing. I was venting frustrations that had nothing to do with this miscreant. I was enjoying beating him up. Hell yes, it was fun. Facts I couldn't acknowledge to Mom and Dad and Lucy: Fighting was fun, and winning was immensely satisfying.

He covered his face with his bloody hands, but I kept hitting him. Even after his hands dropped and he lay there, not moving, I kept hitting him.

The Yellowmountain boys dragged me off him. Rachel checked for a pulse. I realized the band had stopped playing, and Lucy was watching everything, terrified. I thought it was just a typical Saturday-night bar fight in Butte, but then I realized she'd never seen me fight and was horrified by what I'd done to the man now unconscious on the floor. Shame crawled up my neck. I felt like I was breaking my sister's heart. I could see that she was revolted by me.

Rachel pulled up the guy's bloodied T-shirt, looking for any wounds, as they teach in first aid. The band resumed playing. Folks picked up the tables and put them back in place. The rumble of conversations started up again. Rachel got up from the unconscious guy and came my way.

Lucy glared at me. "Ike, what the hell—"

"Listen, both of you," Rachel interrupted. "He's covered with prison tats—swastikas. SS. Hitler. He's an Idaho Nazi. The sheriff's in with them."

"The sheriff?" Lucy went pale. "What does that mean?"

"You need to go right now, both of you, before you get killed."

CHAPTER TWO

LUCY

Washington, DC

May 1977

TWO *WASHINGTON POST* reporters were regaling Dad with a tale about Barry Goldwater. I was fifteen minutes late to our lunch, and somehow the dashing super-journos had managed to talk their way into the Senate Dining Room and sidle up to Pop. I took them in from a few feet away, Woodward and Bernstein, two journalism gods, in all their rumpled chic. The film version of their Pulitzer Prize–earning, history-making Watergate reportage, in which they were played by heartthrobs Robert Redford and Dustin Hoffman, had come out the previous spring, enhancing the legend of their work exposing Tricky Dick. Since then, they had not slowed down; their bestselling follow-up, *The Final Days*, had recently been published to critical acclaim and commercial success.

They were at my dad's corner table, out of the way but with a good view of the room, which was elegant and expansive, with golden wallpaper, burgundy curtains, and a regal chandelier. Only senators and their guests—and celebrity journalists, apparently—were permitted in the dining room. Dad had been coming here since he'd left the House and been elected to the Senate in 1974.

My pop cut quite the figure with his swanky tweed suit (which Mom bought) and tousled mop of graying hair. These days he also had bags under his eyes like Walter Matthau, but all my girlfriends still loved him. However, it was the glow of the two dashing, ink-stained saviors of our democracy that drew the room's attention. Bernstein was shorter, with a feathered bouffant that could rival that of any of Charlie's Angels; Woodward was tall and lanky with a chiseled jaw and dimples you could lose your purse in.

I braced myself and walked up to the table. They both smiled at me as Dad patted the seat beside him.

Woodward went on. "So Goldwater invites us up to his apartment to read his diary—"

"And pours himself a big tumbler of whiskey," Bernstein continued. "And a big tumbler for each of us. Reaches into a cabinet and pulls out his diary of the last days of Nixon's presidency and says, 'I'm going to read this to you.'"

Bernstein was the duo's primary raconteur, and Woodward seemed to be enjoying himself. Dad was smiling too, but his feelings about Watergate were deep and conflicted.

"And he reads this scene," Bernstein continued, "where he and the leaders of the House and Senate, the Republican leaders, marched to the Oval Office and met with Richard Nixon. By then Nixon knew he was going to be impeached by the House, but he thought he would be acquitted in the Senate trial. And the president looked at Goldwater and said, 'Barry, how many votes do I have?'—fully expecting Goldwater to tell him, *You have enough to prevail, Mr. President.* And Goldwater is reading this to us. 'How many votes, Barry?' And Goldwater looks him in the eye and says, 'Mr. President, right now you may have half a dozen votes—*and you don't have mine.*'"

Woodward laughed. "And Nixon announced his resignation the next day."

My dad smiled politely, but I knew the subject was painful.

For years, he'd been the lone voice among his Republican colleagues in the Senate arguing that Nixon had no regard for the Constitution or the law or common decency, that he was unsuited for the presidency and was a dangerous man. Dad was happy that Goldwater and the others ultimately landed back in the land of basic civility and principle, but he'd been there by himself for a while and he'd been quite lonely.

"I don't know that what Goldwater said—to you or to the president—was true," my dad said. "But it's a great story."

The jovial expressions of the brash young reporters lost a glint of sparkle with my dad's comments, but their smiles remained.

"Well," said Woodward, though nothing followed.

"In any case, gentlemen, this is my daughter, Lucy, a journalist herself, at the *Star*, and I'm sure you'll excuse us."

"The *Star*?" said Woodward, feigning offense. "Why not the *Post*?"

I shrugged. "I sent your editors my clips from the *Yale Daily News*." I knew Woodward had gone to Yale, so I'd also sent my résumé and clips directly to him, but I knew better than to bring that up. His inbox no doubt looked like Santa's.

"Wouldn't be the first time our editors screwed up!" Bernstein said with characteristic bombast. "I started at the *Star*, was a copyboy there! At fifteen! Rose quickly through the ranks!"

"But he didn't stay, since the *Star* requires its reporters to have a college degree," Woodward said. Bernstein raised an eyebrow, and Woodward added: "Much to the paper's eternal regret, I'm certain!"

"We'll get you to the *Post* before you know it!" Bernstein told me with a smile. And with that, they excused themselves and moved on. (Later I saw them at Senator Church's table, and when our lunch ended, they were still working the room.)

Before I could look at the menu, Dad asked whether I'd heard from Ike. I hadn't. Then he asked whether I knew how to reach him, and I said no. I wasn't lying exactly, but I couldn't tell Dad all I knew, which made me feel a vicious pang of guilt. He seemed so vulnerable in his concern.

There was nothing more important than truth, no virtue I found more compelling than honesty, and I loved my parents more than I loved anyone on earth. Except one person: my baby brother, who couldn't bring himself to tell me what had happened to him in Lebanon. Whatever it was, I suspected it was why he had flown the coop.

"I've told you everything I know," I said. "Last time I saw him, in the hospital, he was vaguely contemplating how nice it would be to hit the road for a bit. I'm sure he'll call soon."

The truth was that I'd been worried for a while.

"Okay, Cindy-Lou,"[1] he said. "It's just that your mother and I are kind of in the bell jar about this."

"Yes, but you know how he gets when he wants to be alone with his motorcycle."

Fact: My brother loved his bike the way some guys loved women. Another fact: I wouldn't have minded being adored by a guy even half as much as Ike loved his motorcycle. Third fact: The last guy I dated, Skylar—a White House speechwriter—fell short on the cherish-and-love scale. I hadn't admitted this to anyone, especially Ike. I didn't want to give him the satisfaction, since early on, he'd called Skylar a snake in an alligator shirt.

---

1   Dr. Seuss's *How the Grinch Stole Christmas* was published when I was three and almost immediately became my favorite book. Cindy-Lou Who, a minor character who is all that is pure and good in Who-ville, whence the Grinch steals the holiday, became an obsession of mine; I dressed as her for four Halloweens straight. Dad made it a point to call me by that name at least once a conversation; even if I was rushing off, he'd slip in a quick "Toodle-oo, Cindy-Lou." Dads.

"I just wish," Dad said sadly, "that he and I had the kind of relationship you and I have."

I felt sad too. "He loves you a lot."

Ike had never belonged in a four-story town house on Dent Place NW in Georgetown. He liked to ride his bike to the gas station on the way to Dupont Circle and ask the guys to teach him how to work on cars. He fixed his mini-bikes in our garage, almost killed himself a few times popping wheelies, hung out with smelly wrench heads, and sat down to dinner smeared in grease and reeking of oil. He was in trouble a lot and got suspended for fighting; he was smarter than anyone but he hated school. He was more like Grandpa, a former Rough Rider, than like Dad. Though he revered Dad.

Our waiter, Samson, approached our table in his formal white jacket. "Miss Lucy! We haven't had the pleasure of your company in far too long!"

"Samson!" I smiled. "I've been busy with my new job."

"Your father mentioned you were working at the *Star*," he said. "I have no doubt they'll be making movies about your journalistic exploits before long." He turned back to my father. "Have you and Miss Lucy made a decision?"

My dad laughed. "You know we get the same thing every time, Samson," he said.

"The day I don't ask will be the day you no longer desire our famous bean soup and a steak, medium rare." Samson grinned. He looked at me. "Caesar salad, dressing on the side, Miss Lucy?"

"Yes, sir." I nodded.

"I'll be right back with your iced teas," Samson said. Dad gave Samson a subtle wink. I knew that when Dad was in dire straits, he calmed his nerves with prescriptions from Dr. Jack Daniel's, so I suspected that meant Samson was sneaking whiskey into his iced tea.

"You ask me why I'm still a Republican?" Dad said, though I hadn't. He motioned to the entrance of the Senate Dining Room, where Tennessee GOP senator Howard Baker was walking in with two freshman senators. "That's my party's Senate leader. Baker. The one who asked, 'What did the president know and when did he know it?'"

I paused and pondered the accuracy of what he'd just said. I didn't think Baker was quite the hero Dad thought he was, though I knew the lore was part of the GOP's current efforts at revisionism about Nixon.

Dad motioned with his head toward the far corner where the Senate majority leader, Robert Byrd of West Virginia, was laughing with some aides. "And look, that's the leader of the Democrats." Dad screwed his face up as if we were driving past one of those North Jersey refineries on I-95. "A former exalted cyclops in the Klan! Absolutely disgusting. And most of those Democrats from the South—Eastland, Sparkman, Stennis—they're hideous bigots."

"What about Nixon?" I asked. "Not exalted, not a cyclops. He has two eyes, but is he any better?"[2]

"Nixon is no longer the head of the party."

It wasn't easy for Dad. From New York City, he saw himself in the mold of his former commanding general Dwight Eisenhower. He and Congressman Larry Hogan Sr. of Maryland had been the only Republicans on the House Judiciary Committee to vote

---

2 Nixon's 1968 "law and order" campaign; his continuous attacks on forced busing; the code words he used; the images of civil rights marches he interspersed with scenes of riots in his TV ads; his statements to Southern audiences that he would not enforce judicial desegregation orders "with all deliberate speed"—all of this was rooted in the same rank soil. Dad had told me this himself before Nixon resigned.

for all three articles of impeachment against Nixon. This hurt Hogan in Maryland[3] but it helped Dad when he ran for Senate in New York against a Democrat who had a troubled ethics history. His longtime lack of support for the disaster in Vietnam also helped sway voters. I was proud of Dad. I'm not certain his party was.

Samson slid Dad's iced tea by his side as if he were an MI6 operative slipping an envelope into a Berlin dead drop. Mine was placed less stealthily.

When Samson was out of earshot, Dad said in a low voice, "I will confess, I ran into these absolute cretins at a Pennsylvania fundraiser last month. House guys, deranged about Nixon."

My antenna went up. Story idea? "How so, Dad?"

"Saying stuff like 'The party didn't fight for him,' 'He didn't do anything wrong,' 'Liberals and Jews in the media set him up,' dreck[4] like that," he said. "Bunch of dead-enders."

"You don't mind if I look into it? Not the event, but the sentiment? I haven't heard that expressed since Nixon flashed us the peace signs and hopped on the chopper."

Dad let out a long-suffering sigh. "Cindy-Lou, assume that we are always off the record. Our lunches are not...what do you call them? Pitch meetings?"

Chastened, I turned to my iced tea, then saw Senator Baker heading our way with two men in their forties who looked

---

3   Hogan was courageous and a hero, so naturally the voters punished him for it. He ran for governor but lost in the GOP primary. The *Baltimore Sun*, September 1974: "No sooner had the early returns arrived than the analysts, including Hogan himself, were blaming his failure on his early stand against Nixon before the Judiciary Committee began its public impeachment hearings...Some maintain further that the judgment against him should be a warning to other Republicans out there not to treat the former president too harshly, lest the voters retaliate." Don't judge a crook too harshly, folks!

4   You pick up a *schtickle* of Yiddish when you live in New York City.

vaguely familiar. One was unusually tall and lanky, the other short and elfin. Mutt and Jeff came to mind.

Senator Baker introduced the men, both of whom were newly elected senators: Jack Danforth from Missouri and Dick Lugar from Indiana. Dad didn't seem to know them well, but he'd followed their races and he told them he'd donated to each of their campaigns to make sure that this time around, they didn't lose. Dad had never lost an election in his life, and it was so like him to bring up the previous failures of his colleagues. But it made both new senators laugh. Or maybe they were faking it. I was lost without my Politi-Speak-to-English dictionary.[5]

"Did you see the interviews?" Dad asked them.

Nobody had to ask what interviews he was talking about. They had shocked the world and roiled Capitol Hill, and my dad had been ranting about them for days: the interviews British journalist David Frost had done with Nixon (who was paid a fee of six hundred thousand dollars). I'd watched, like everyone else, to make some sense of the nightmare Nixon had put us through and to see if he'd reflected and now realized that his paranoia and narcissism and delusions had hurt us all, damaged the nation.

I wanted an apology, really. So did the country.

We didn't get one.

"The most dishonest man I've ever known!" shouted a white-haired, bespectacled old man walking toward our table.

"Hiya, Barry," said Dad. As in Goldwater, the conservative Arizona senator and 1964 GOP presidential nominee. Baker, Danforth, and Lugar all extended their hands in greeting, but Goldwater didn't seem interested in niceties; he was fired up.

---

5   Ike and I made one for Dad one Christmas. Sample: *I will certainly take that under advisement* means "Go F yourself."

"No Republican in his right mind should do anything to help that man rehabilitate himself!" Goldwater ranted. "His actions have destroyed the political party to which I've dedicated my life."

My dad was nodding vaguely but not looking at Goldwater. I watched as his expression changed, softened, and I knew: Mom had entered the room.

My hero, my mom. Margaret Marder, zoologist, loving wife, nurturing mother, a feminist ahead of her time. Her blond hair was cut in an impeccably stylish bob, and as usual, her clothes—today, a fashionable striped blouse and brown maxiskirt—appeared effortlessly perfect. Trust me, it wasn't an easy look to pull off; my whole life, I'd been trying to achieve it.

"Hey, everyone!" she said, plunking a thick manila folder down on the table. Samson appeared, grabbed a chair from a neighboring table, and held it out for her, and she sat as if they'd performed this ritual a few hundred times, which I suppose they had.

"Nothing for me, Samson, my old friend," Mom said. He smiled and walked away.

"Margaret, you're a vision, as always," said Baker in his charming Tennessee drawl. He introduced her to the freshman senators. Goldwater grabbed her hand, kissed it, then strode off, muttering to himself.

"You're all discussing Mr. Nixon's latest passion play?" Mom's mistrust of Nixon dated back to her arrival in DC in 1953. Vietnam, Cambodia, the '72 election, the Watergate break-in, the tapes, the impeachment hearings, and Nixon's attempts at pathos had made her loathe him. "What did he tell Frost—'When the president does it, that means it's not illegal'? That comment alone is an impeachable offense!"

"Well, now, Margaret," said Baker, "truth is, I'm not sure there's any way to know whether President Nixon committed an impeachable offense because the Senate didn't actually hold an impeachment trial."

"You have got to be kidding me," Mom said.

I loved Mom so much. What a complete badass.

After an incredibly awkward silence, Baker bade the three of us adieu and extricated himself and the freshman senators from the conversation, avoiding any further discussion of their least favorite topic.

"They hate discussing him like they hated discussing Mc-Carthy, but they never did a goddamned thing to stop either of them," Mom said.

Samson delivered a bread basket, and Dad put a warm roll on his plate, tore off a piece, and slathered butter on it. "You could be slightly less obvious about how much you're relishing this, honey."

"I've been tearing through Sam Dash's new book," Mom said, referring to *Chief Counsel,* Dash's account of his experiences as the top lawyer on Senator Sam Ervin's Watergate Committee.

"How do you have time to read actual books when Jackie keeps sending you manuscripts?" I asked, picking up the manila folder Mom had dropped on the table. Back in the 1950s, Mom had befriended a neighbor named Jackie Kennedy, then a senator's wife and now, all these years later, a book editor at Viking. I opened the folder and perused the manuscripts the former First Lady had sent Mom.

"And let me tell you, Charlie," Mom said, not answering my question, "your Howard Baker is full of bear scat. Dash says Baker was doing Nixon's bidding the whole time. Says he was meeting with Nixon, Haldeman, and Ehrlichman in private while acting like Perry Mason in public."

"Bad pop-culture ref, Mom. Perry Mason's a defense attorney," I said.

Mom turned a smug smile my way. "Even better, then."

I glanced at the first manuscript, a memoir by a Soviet dissident. Looked interesting.

"C'mon, honey," Dad said. "What about 'What did the president know and when did he know it?'"

"Dash says Baker was trying to separate Nixon from the actions of his lackeys. He wanted to establish that Nixon did *not* know anything until much later. Baker asked what the president knew and when he knew it because he hoped the answer would be *exculpatory*."

Dad pointed his butter knife at her. "One could argue that Sam Dash is a very partisan Democrat trying to sell books."

"Nothing wrong with selling books," I said without looking up. "Ask your friends Woodward and Bernstein." The second manuscript Jackie had sent Mom was an unauthorized biography of Chicago mayor Richard J. Daley, one of Dad's least favorite Democrats.

"You can judge whom you find more credible, Dash or Nixon," Mom said.

"I'm not defending Nixon! I'm talking about Baker." He finished his spiked iced tea, and Samson, now channeling Doug Henning instead of George Smiley, made another one magically appear.

I couldn't tell whether it was Dad's obvious day-drinking or this talk of Nixon and Baker that made my mother's face flush. She was discreet, though. She did not air personal grievances in public spaces such as the Senate Dining Room.

"Charlie, you're acting as if these guys care about Watergate," Mom said. "As if anything matters to them except that he got caught."

"And ushered a ton of Democrats into Congress," I added, to which Mom touched her nose: *Bingo*.

Dad smiled at Samson as he delivered our food. When he left, Dad said, "I think you're being a bit tough on them, sweetie. Goldwater is still pretty peeved. Those freshmen seem fine." Dad could swivel like a weather vane on this stuff; he was tough on the GOP when Woodstein offered harrowing tales, more forgiving of the party when Mom attempted to lump them all together. In this case, that he admired much of Nixon's agenda—the creation of the EPA, minimum tax on the wealthy, guaranteed income for the poor—added to his pivot.

"Tell Mom about the House gremlins, Pop," I said excitedly. "The dead-enders."

Dad lifted his hands in a helpless gesture. "I thought we were having a family lunch."

"Dad says there's a House caucus of Nixon Nuts," I said. "They want to bring Nixon back. They're saying the whole Watergate thing was a liberal plot."

"Your father's party is about to descend into oophagy,"[6] she said, using one of her obscure zoologist insults. Dad was usually grateful that her barbs were so esoteric, since, in public, it helped hide her disdain for his colleagues.

"Oh, Mom," I said, remembering, "speaking of bodies of water—sort of—a new Poirot film is coming out next year. Ustinov again. *Death on the Nile*." Mom and I were Agatha

---

6   Mom constantly dropped zoological references, most of which we had to press her to explain. This one Dad and I knew because she'd been using it since Watergate. *Oophagy* ("oh-AHF-ah-jee") refers to embryos in the uterus feeding on eggs produced by the ovary; it's common in most sharks, and it's even more revolting in gray nurse sharks, who practice embryophagy—essentially intrauterine cannibalism: the first developed gray nurse shark embryo consumes not just eggs but other embryos. Most people would have just used the term *backstabbing*, but Mom likes her zoological metaphors.

Christie enthusiasts and we'd loved his performance in *Murder on the Orient Express*.

"That's nice—we'll go. It's a date," she said. "But more important, how's the *Star*, darling?"

"Oophagous. Paper stole my scoop about Carter's DOJ planning to clear Wayne Hays.[7] They just handed it over on a platter to a different reporter."

"What?" Dad said, outraged. "They can do that?"

I shrugged as if I didn't care, even though I burned. "Editors can do anything. They're omnipotent."

"Like department chairs," Mom said.

"And appropriators," added Dad.

"Was it because you're an intern?" Mom asked. "Or because you're a woman?"

"Yes," I said. "And this isn't the first time it's happened. Usually, they just fold my mini-scoops into other larger stories, but this one was so big, it was an act of outright theft. D. B. Cooper." I was trying to play it off as no biggie, but the truth was it incensed me. My whole life, males—first teachers and boys, then professors and college men, now reporters and fossilized editors—had downplayed my intellect, my accomplishments, my worth. The clever catch-22 men had constructed: Women who protested being treated as inferiors were regarded as whiny or shrill, thus proving we were inferior or didn't belong and that the misogyny was justified, rational. I smiled.

Mom reached across the table and squeezed my arm; the corners

---

7   In 1976, the *Washington Post* broke the story that Congressman Wayne Hays, Democrat from Ohio, the chair of the powerful House Administration Committee, employed as his secretary a woman with whom he was having an affair, Elizabeth Ray, who admitted to reporters: "I can't type. I can't file. I can't even answer the phone." Ray let a reporter listen in on a phone call where Hays insisted to her that his marriage to a different office assistant wouldn't affect her standing as "Mistress Number 1."

of her mouth turned down in regret. Mom wasn't one for hollow consolations, and she didn't try to shovel any at me now. Nothing she could say would change one darn thing. We both knew that.

But at least I had someone in my life who got it, who understood a woman's work was often stolen and dismissed. She nodded along when I said that I'd been told to get coffee instead of working on the story and that none of my bosses could see past my face and gams to recognize how good I was. And I *was* good; I was born for this darn job. If only someone would give me a real chance.

I looked down at the manuscripts again. The third one looked like something Ike would like. I set it aside.

A tall woman stopped by our table. She had a model's face and silky blond hair, and her power pantsuit was straight out of *The Woman's Dress for Success Book*[8] with its sculpted jacket and flared trousers. I was digging her vibe before she even opened her mouth.

"I am sorry for interrupting," she began. She had a warm voice with an upper-class British accent. (Admittedly, I didn't know much about the class distinctions of British accents beyond what I'd picked up at the movies, but she sounded more Mary Poppins than chimney sweep.) She introduced herself as Danielle Lyon, daughter of Maximillian Lyon, and we all knew who he was—the British media magnate known as the "Mighty Knight of Fleet Street." His recent arrival to conquer the American news-media market had everyone in my newsroom talking. Earlier that year, the Lyons had launched a tabloid, the *Washington Sentinel,* a newspaper that was supposed to be "fairer to the beliefs and principles of the majority of the country," or

---

8 The book didn't come out until later that year, but I'd been gifted an early draft via Mom via Jackie O.

so Maximillian Lyon told the *Wall Street Journal*. The *Journal* had treated his foray into publishing as a business story, a mere curiosity, but it was proving to be far more than that.

Now she was in the exclusive dining room for senators. I assumed she was here to befriend Republican senators like Dad. I inched to the edge of my chair. But no, she was actually talking to me. "Terrible etiquette, I know, but aren't you Lucy Marder of the *Star*?"

"Um, yes. Yes, I am!"

"I heard you broke the Hays story," Danielle said. "And I also heard your editors cheated you out of the byline."

"How did you…where did you hear that?" I asked.

She smiled. "We're hiring some of your colleagues. I'll tell you this, at the *Sentinel*, we don't cheat reporters out of their bylines. We don't oppress our women reporters—we celebrate them. And I think we should celebrate you."

"Are you…are you offering me a job?" I asked, feigning calm. My insides were fizzing with excitement.

"Absolutely." Danielle reached into her Kelly bag, took out a business card, and handed it to me as if it were the key to the castle. The card was made of heavy stock and had DANIELLE LYON, EXECUTIVE EDITOR, WASHINGTON SENTINEL embossed on it in gold lettering. Eek, she was so glamorous.

"Stop by the office tomorrow after lunch." Turning her radiant smile on my parents, she said, "Forgive my bad manners! Not saying hi to the legendary Senator Charlie and Dr. Margaret Marder! What must you think of me?"

"We love it when people appreciate Lucy's brilliance," Dad said with sincerity.

Mom was cooler. She told Danielle that it was nice to meet her, but her tone suggested otherwise. I thought I knew why.

"Our address is on my card," Danielle said, pointing it out.

"The new office in Georgetown was featured in the *Times*' architecture section just last Sunday! Come see it—and me!" With a wave, she left.

"Okay, Willard Scott, what's with the cold front?"[9] Dad asked Mom.

Mom lifted one elegant shoulder. "Not a fan of the *Sentinel*. You may appreciate whatever ideological diversity the Lyons are bringing to DC, but they're also dragging Fleet Street scuzz into this city."

"You mean the Callahan story?"[10] I asked.

"Yes. They're just reckless," Mom said.

I didn't mind the paper revealing hypocrites and liars like Callahan. "He pretends to respect women but he's out there carousing like a Rat Packer."

Mom shot Dad an amused, knowing look, then turned to me. "I don't care that Callahan's sins have been exposed, though I do feel sorry for his poor wife. But would the *Sentinel* run the same story about a Republican? I don't think they would."

"Couldn't you say the same thing about a Democrat and the *Post* or the *Times*?" Dad asked. "I mean, remember what Earl Butz said about the liberal press."[11]

---

9   Scott was a very popular weatherman on our local NBC affiliate, WRC-TV.

10   Relying on European paparazzi employed by the Lyon media empire, the *Sentinel* had published photographs of Senator Roderick Callahan on a yacht in the Mediterranean in flagrante delicto with a young woman decidedly not his wife. The headline: "Demo-Cad." The subhead: "That's Not Your Wife, Senator Callahan!" The photo caption: *Liberal Democrat apparently changes position on offshore drilling.*

11   In 1976, former Nixon White House counsel turned Watergate witness John Dean wrote an article on the Republican National Convention for *Rolling Stone* in which he quoted an unnamed Ford cabinet secretary saying the GOP was having trouble attracting black voters because "coloreds" only want "three things: first, a tight pussy; second, loose shoes; and third, a warm place to shit." The teller of the "joke" was outed as Agriculture Secretary Earl Butz, who soon resigned. Many GOP officials reacted by bemoaning the lack of safe places to tell such jokes.

"Oh, c'mon, Dad, you don't think that," I said. "Earl Butz is a pig."

"I agree that Butz is a racist and a pig, and good riddance," Dad said. "But I confess, I wonder whether he would have been outed for that joke had he been in the Carter administration. Do you think reporters were as aggressive with JFK and LBJ as they were with Nixon?"

"Is this a joke, Charles?" Mom asked. "Have you observed the news media being particularly protective of"—she motioned toward me—"Wayne Hays? Or Teddy Kennedy? Or Wilbur Mills?"[12]

"Or Bob Leggett?"[13] I added.

"Or John Young?"[14] said Mom.

"Let us not forget Allan Howe,"[15] Dad said.

We all dissolved into laughter, the litany of congressional Democrats sleazing their way around the Capitol was so preposterous.

"It's like Caligula's palace," Mom said.

I nodded. "A place like this deserves a newspaper that will cover it aggressively."

"There's a lot more to cover in DC than sex scandals," Dad observed. "And those stories have all been reported!"

---

12 In 1974, the limo of Arkansas congressman Wilbur Mills, the Democratic chairman of the House Ways and Means Committee, was stopped by police near the Washington Mall. Mills was drunk and cavorting with an Argentinean stripper who ran out of the limo and into the Tidal Basin.

13 In 1976, the *Post* broke the story that Rep. Bob Leggett (D-CA) had been cheating on his wife with a congressional secretary with whom he had two children, and that he was also having an affair with an aide to the House Speaker.

14 In 1974, a congressional aide named Colleen Gardner claimed that her boss, Rep. John Young (D-TX), had hired her only for sexual favors.

15 In 1976, Rep. Allan Howe (D-UT), a married father of five, was arrested for soliciting a prostitute who turned out to be an undercover policewoman. Police released the transcript of the conversation in which the officer and Howe discussed prices.

"And that's *my* point," Mom said. "I just don't believe the *Sentinel* has any actual values, journalistic or otherwise. The paper seems entirely defined by its hatred of liberals and the rest of the news media."

To be honest, shining a light on the dirty laundry of politicians' personal lives was not at the top of my list of priorities. It wasn't ultimately as important as real corruption and malfeasance; it wasn't what Woodward and Bernstein focused on. And while maybe I should've been more put off by a newspaper defined by a hatred of liberals, what excited me most at that moment was Danielle knowing and appreciating my work. But I changed the subject to Dad's legislative work and Mom's newest zoological interests. Over the years I had learned the great art of dodging and deflecting, for me and for Ike.

As they chattered, I glanced at Dad's glass, now empty, and saw the frown lines between Mom's eyebrows when Samson brought him another. She clearly knew Dad was pounding spiked iced teas, and I wondered if all this unspoken tension was about Ike or Captain Jack or something else.

It made me sad.

Although the *Sentinel* had yet to prove itself in Washington in any commercial or journalistic sense, the Lyons' offices in Georgetown conveyed success. Their newsroom took up the top three floors of a new building on the Potomac that had a glorious view of the river and the Virginia shoreline.

Around noon the next day, I left my silver VW Beetle with the valet—I'd never known a newspaper to have valet parking—and walked into the lobby, the walls of which were lined with blow-ups of front pages of the family's newspapers from all over the English-speaking world: the UK, Australia, New Zealand,

Canada, Ireland. Even the Caribbean, where the Lyons owned resorts as well. These headlines were all newsworthy—Bloody Sunday, Australia's constitutional crisis—the kind of serious stories my mother couldn't criticize. I wondered how accurately these articles reflected the overall output of the papers; I had no way of knowing. The Lyons had a reputation for owning tabloids that focused on bloody murders and embarrassing sex scandals. But maybe that was unfair?

At the tap of stilettos on the Formica floor, I turned. Danielle crossed the lobby and hugged me like a sister. "I'm so glad you came. This is going to be great." She said it as if I'd accepted the job she hadn't officially offered.

We took the elevator up and got off on the top floor—the fourteenth (really the thirteenth[16])—and went into a buzzing newsroom. I loved the hustle of newsrooms, the phones constantly ringing, the editors shouting, the mesmerizing clatter of typewriters and teletype machines. I loved it at the *Star* and I immediately loved it more in this brand-new building with its walls of windows and its posh view of the river, the scent of freshly ground coffee beans in the air, the pastry stations sprinkled generously throughout.

"Not just a perk," Danielle said when she saw me eyeing the pastries. The *Star*, like every newspaper, had its share of coffeemakers, and if you were hungry and had the correct change, you could get a candy bar from the vending machine near the men's room. But the *Sentinel*'s freshly ground coffee

---

16 The refusal to label thirteenth floors as what they are is truly the stupidest thing in the world. Thinking of luck as a force you can control—by, say, avoiding the number thirteen—is contradictory, for one thing. For another, even if you call the thirteenth floor the fourteenth floor, it's still the thirteenth floor. This superstition is rooted in Judas Iscariot being the thirteenth guest to arrive at the Last Supper, which even the worst sufferer of triskaidekaphobia would have to grant had nothing to do with his betrayal of Jesus.

and croissants were unheard-of newsroom luxuries. "These little stations keep everyone full of caffeine and sugar. More important, it keeps people here, not interrupting their work to run around outside looking for better coffee and nourishment."

She walked me to the far side of the sunny room, where several people stood around the desk of a husky middle-aged man with salt-and-pepper hair in a pin-striped suit. He was reading the *Evening Star* with his feet up on the double-pedestal mahogany desk, which was enormous and had the kind of intricate carvings I'd noticed on the Resolute Desk when Dad snuck me into the Oval Office. (That was during a Christmas party President Johnson threw for senators who'd supported his civil and voting rights laws, if memory serves.)

The guy in the chair was Max Lyon. Standing next to him was the most handsome man I had ever seen in my life. He was in his late twenties and tall and lean and tanned, with a face like a movie star's—bright blue eyes, cleft chin, all that delicious dark hair. He raised his eyebrows at me as if to say *Why, hello there* and held my stare for a long breathless moment.

"Go with the cancer baby and vitamin B-seventeen," Max Lyon said. "Maybe the mainstream papers wouldn't dream of challenging so-called medical experts, but there's no harm in continuing to take up the cause. Also, I want more on Carter seeing UFOs."

"What's that?" My brain was still a little sex-fogged. "*President* Carter?"

"We got confirmation from—from what?" the beautiful man asked a young bow-tied guy holding a notepad.

The guy turned back a few pages in his notepad. "We got on-the-record confirmation from, um, both the International UFO Bureau in Oklahoma and the National Investigations Committee on Aerial Phenomena in Maryland. He filed two reports."

"I knew this guy was a flake," said Max.

It was like walking into the last two minutes of a movie and asking people about the plot. "Are you saying President Carter saw a UFO?" I said.

The beautiful man was now grinning at me. Jesus Christ. Whatever brain cells hadn't sizzled out before were now gone, *poof*, obliterated by that smile.

"Where are we on that senator with the boy?" Max asked.

"Legal's still sussing it out. I had them take a hard look," said the handsome guy.

"Argh!" grunted Max. "To quote the Bard: 'The first thing we do, let's kill all the lawyers'!"

Guffaw, guffaw—everyone laughed. Except me.

"Perhaps the most misunderstood Shakespeare quote of all time," I said.

"Pardon?" said Max.

"That line," I said. "It's from *Henry the Sixth* and it's said by Dick the Butcher, a brute." I paused, realizing the effrontery of correcting the boss but also wanting to show off. Danielle and the handsome man looked at me warily. "Everyone quotes that line as if it's a great goal to kill lawyers. But Dick the Butcher wants to get rid of them because they're all that stands between civilization and anarchy. Shakespeare is saying lawyers are the last line of defense against mob rule."

There was a tense silence.

Then a smile spread across Max's face.

Phew.

Danielle gestured my way and introduced me to her father and the Greek god in the bespoke suit—who, it turned out, was her older brother, Harry Lyon.

"Ah, the star to be born, the supernova!" Max said. "I should have known! Welcome to a real newspaper!"

"A supernova is a *dying* star, Dad," Danielle said.

Max put his newspaper down and smiled again. "It is lovely to see all that money I spent on your education kicking me in the nethers." He waved at me and added, "I can see why you two hit it off!"

The editors laughed in harmony.

"What are you all still doing here?" Max shouted. "Cancer baby is our wood, go get it!" (*Wood* is newspaper slang for the front page of a tabloid—the story, the splashy headline and images, the works.) Dismissed, his minions departed. He turned to me. "So, you want to work here? You get the kind of stories we want, and we'll give you your own byline! That sound good?"

I was surprised he knew even that little bit about me. "Well, Danielle only asked me to come by—"

"Harry just talked to Bellows," Max said, referring to Jim Bellows, the legendary editor of the *Star*. My boss. Whom I'd never actually met.

Harry gave me that look again, the one that made me forget everyone else in the room. "I told him we were stealing one of his best reporters. I named you, of course. Bellows said, 'Who?' I couldn't believe he didn't know who broke the Hays story. Brilliant work, stunningly well done."

My cheeks got hot. "Oh, um, thank you." Jesus.

"Then I said, 'Come on, Jim. That was a dirty trick you pulled. You know who really broke the Hays story, and so do I. Lucy Marder.' Still, he had no idea who you were. When I said *Senator Marder's daughter*, it finally jogged his memory. So daft."

What was worse than having your work stolen? Having an editor who knew you only because of who your father was.

"Harry!" Danielle said. "What a hurtful thing to say!"

"Yes, Harry," agreed her father, "you can't talk to journalists the way you belittle tuppers who spill gobbo."[17] Max turned to me. "I'm sorry, Lucy. You can take the boy out of the rugby scrum and all that."

A confused look crossed Harry's beautiful face.

"Harry's been more focused on the…less refined parts of our family business," Danielle explained.

A middle-aged white guy—beer gut, glasses, sleeves rolled up, thinning hair—approached the desk. He looked like an egg. (I would later find out this was managing editor Oliver "Ollie" Baniczak.) "Boss, they found Jeannie Beanie."

"Dead, I presume?" Max asked.

"Body dumped off a trail in Rock Creek Park," Baniczak said.

"Who?" I asked Danielle quietly.

"Missing woman, some suburb in Virginia," she murmured. "Manassas, I think?"

"Oh, do you mean Jeannie *McBean*?" I asked. I'd heard someone at the *Star*'s Northern Virginia desk note her rather memorable name.

Danielle nodded. "We stay atop all local crime stories."

"Especially ones that involve beautiful young women like Jeannie McBean," Max added, as if there were something virtuous about that.

"We did this in New Zealand," Harry said, "and it brought our paper there from nothing to first in circulation, second in subscriptions."

"Horrible case." Danielle grimaced. "Serial murderer who preyed on kids."

"What are you waiting for?" Max thumped his fist on the desk.

---

17   Harry later translated that for me: A *tupper* carries the hod—the V-shaped open trough—for bricklayers; *gobbo* is mortar. The Lyons made their first fortune in construction.

"Get a reporter on the scene already. I want someone to follow every development until the thug who did this gets the chair."

"What about sending Miss Marder here?" Harry said.

Danielle smiled at Harry in approval. Max gave me an up-and-down look. "Fine idea, Harry. Send her."

"But, sir, while I appreciate your faith in me," I said, flustered, "I don't actually work for you."

"Sometimes opportunity doesn't knock, young lady—it barrels into you like a freight train," Max said, making an impatient gesture toward the phone on his desk. "Call Bellows. Tell him you want to work for a real paper. Then go break this damn story for us."

I couldn't say no. I was too scared and excited and there was a momentum I couldn't stop. Danielle showed me to an office where I could make a private call. "No pressure," she said. Jim Bellows kept me on hold for five minutes. While I sat there, someone brought me a book about my new bosses: *Pride of Lyons: The British Family Reinventing the News*. I flipped through it—lots of photos—until Bellows came on the line. I gave him my name, and, sure enough, I had to remind him who I was. He said, "Charlie Marder's daughter?"

I told him I'd gotten an offer to work at the *Sentinel*, and he said, "Well, good luck with that place, um, Lucy," and that was that. I was now employed by Max Lyon. My new story? The murder of twenty-five-year-old Jeannie McBean.

In my short time at the *Star*, I'd helped cover at least a dozen crime stories. The assignment usually meant me scribbling notes while listening to the police's public information officer feed tidbits to local TV reporters—who needed something new every afternoon for their evening shows—then feeding the key information to the man who actually got the byline. But maybe the *Sentinel* would be different. Max didn't seem to want what everyone else was being fed by the spokesperson. He sensed in me a real hunger, a desire to get more. Or so I told myself. I put aside my uneasiness about how comfortable Max seemed to be with pursuing sensational stories to sell papers and tried not to think of the fact that I might not have a choice; I wasn't sure any other place would have me. I leaned into the headiness of the moment. I embraced the praise and recognition of my work, the acceptance into this fancy family, the air of opportunity. It was a risk, it was a gamble, but I was excited.

Don't get me wrong. It was tragic that a woman only three years older than I was—or anyone, really—had been murdered. The little I knew about the case so far—young woman, body dumped in a national park—was shocking.

But I won't lie: There was something thrilling about being a crime reporter trying to right an injustice and find facts and truth when the police were holding back details, about setting your will to reveal the killer against the desire of the murderer to remain hidden. I already had fantasies of cracking the case, putting away a very bad person so he would never harm another woman again...

All of this was in my head half an hour later as I steered my VW into a parking lot in Rock Creek Park and wended my way among the police cruisers. I chose a spot next to the morgue van and crossed the lot with my camera slung around my neck, the heels of my shoes sinking into the gravel.

In this part of the park, the trees were tall, and the sun had already dipped behind them. Lights from the tops of the TV cameras guided me to the area where the body had been found. A group of reporters jostled for position outside the yellow police tape. I was told we were waiting for a briefing from the DC Police's public information officer. "What are you hearing?" I asked Dean Berman, a veteran reporter for Channel 4 News. Then a photographer shouted, "PIO's coming out!"

A female officer ducked beneath the yellow crime scene tape. When she straightened up, I saw who it was: tanned, petite, disdainful Mimi Spanjian, who I'd heard was a new PIO but whom I hadn't yet encountered. We'd been classmates in high school. She'd absolutely loathed me. I'd never fully understood why, though in retrospect, I think it might have been because she was a scholarship kid whose father, a cop, had been killed in the line of duty, and I was a girl who, despite how much Mom and Dad lectured us about humility and humanity, projected privilege. But that was years ago; she wouldn't still hate me, would she? God, I hoped not.

Mimi turned to the cameras and said in a professional tone: "Today at approximately four forty p.m., the Metropolitan Police Department responded to a call from a local resident who had been walking his dog and discovered a woman's body off the trail. A unit from the Third District was dispatched, and homicide investigators were called to the scene. The victim's family has been notified. The victim is twenty-five-year-old Jeannie McBean of Manassas, Virginia. It appears, preliminarily, that Mrs. McBean died of strangulation. We are asking for the public's help. If you have any information about Mrs. McBean's disappearance, please call the Metropolitan Police."

As she continued, three technicians from the medical examiner's transport team wheeled Jeannie's body out of the woods. I elbowed my way free of the scrum, jostled for a spot with a clear view of the body, and lifted my camera. I got a moody photo of the gurney coming out of the woods, a good shot of the body being loaded into the morgue van, and another good shot of the morgue van driving off. I hated the circumstances, of course, but I was thrilled beyond belief to have this job. At long last, I was on my way.

CHAPTER THREE

IKE

Butte, Montana

December 1976

Come along, come along,
there's a full moon shining bright

—Elvis Presley, "Come Along"

THE 1974 BESTSELLING novel *Jaws* had spawned the 1975 blockbuster movie *Jaws,* the highest-grossing film of all time, and this made a light bulb go on in Evel's always-operating brain. I had joined Evel's team late in the fall of 1976 and was getting used to life as a glorified grease monkey when I heard that his next stunt would involve a motorcycle jump over a tank of man-eating sharks. Shark chic, I guess.

That afternoon, I was standing in the machine shop honing the front jug of one of Evel's XR-750s. It was fancier than it sounded; the machine shop was in his expansive garage next to his mansion overlooking the sixteenth hole at the Butte Country Club. Six of us were toiling among an assortment of Harley-Davidson motorcycles and several cars—a Maserati, a Dodge, a Chevy, a Mark IV, a Buick, a Cadillac Eldorado, and two Ferraris, one gold with a horn that played "La Cucaracha" and one silver with a horn that squeaked a few notes from the *Bridge on the River Kwai* theme.

"What do you think'll happen if I land in the tank?" Evel asked us.

He was a big guy, nearly as tall as I was but lankier, with a mop of dirty-blond hair and a showman's strut that told you he didn't give a shit about anyone or anything, maybe not even himself. Thirty-eight at the time, he wore alligator boots and several fifty-five-thousand-dollar fuck-you-all diamond rings. He had ice-blue eyes and no sense of boundaries, both of which were unnerving.

"If you land in a tank with man-eating sharks?" I asked. You didn't need a mom who was a zoologist to figure that one out.

"You'd be surrounded by thirteen Knievel-eating sharks," observed the crew chief, Huckleberry Jennings, the best mechanic in the state and a chunky good ol' boy with thick muttonchops like a nineteenth-century general. He was meticulously cleaning a 36 mm Mikuni carburetor.

Evel leaned back with his feet up on a weather-beaten oak desk, a *Playboy* calendar tacked on the wall behind him. He had an eye for women and it never blinked. A combination of Elvis, Dirty Harry, and Billy the Kid, Evel was an actual outlaw turned self-made millionaire, and his love of the ladies was far from unrequited. Maybe he wasn't as lean as when I'd first started following his jumps—gravity, hard living, and rough landings all knew his address—but he'd come by his legend authentically, if not honestly.

He was really hopped up on himself that month. He'd finished shooting a movie that was coming out in June, *Viva Knievel!*, starring Evel as himself, Gene Kelly as his alcoholic mechanic, and a Revlon model named Lauren Hutton as a photojournalist sent to cover Evel's big jump. I couldn't really follow the plot as Evel described it, but it sounded fun and full of capers and stunts, and I could see why he was so excited.

"What do you think I'd do if one of those hammerheads came at me?" Evel asked. "I'd punch that motherfucker in the face."

I had to laugh; we all did. He was just so utterly, preposterously, charmingly cocksure. He unscrewed the top of his diamond-encrusted cane and poured Wild Turkey from its hidden compartment into a coffee cup. He downed the caramel-colored whiskey in one big cheek-puffing swallow, then poured another. We were all ensuring that his three favorite bikes were in impeccable condition, but Evel didn't seem that concerned about being in top form himself.

Usually I kept my mouth shut, but for some reason—maybe it was the sharks—I piped up. "So, before a jump, you're not like a prizefighter getting into shape?" I asked him.

Someone snickered; perhaps I was overstepping my bounds. It was hard to know in this place that was so far from my hometown, with its drawing rooms and dinner parties. I needed to watch myself; I needed this to work out. I didn't want to go back to DC, and right now I couldn't think of any other place that would have me.

"Before a jump, I drink *more* booze," Evel said. "Spend *more* money. I mean, I'm gonna do the same thing Jesus Christ did at the Last Supper: I'm gonna invite a bunch of friends and have a real feast, have a good time! I want to live!"

"Jumping over sharks is just the natural next step, I'd think," I said.

His ice-blue eyes narrowed. "How so?" He wasn't sure what I was driving at, maybe thought I was insulting him somehow.

"From your first jump. Rattlesnakes and mountain lions!"

"Holy crap, that's right!" he said, laughing. When Evel was happy, man, you felt like you were having a gorgeous day out on the Snake River landing rainbow trout—just fun and good times. We all stared at him, hanging on every word. "Was that a jump! Little Moses Lake, Washington, they had a racetrack and a big halftime show. This was, oh, I don't know—1965? They said, 'Knievel's gonna jump these mountain lions and rattlesnakes.' The guy that owned the mountain lions was afraid I was going to kill them, so he put them close to the takeoff ramp. What was it—fifty, maybe a hundred rattlesnakes in that twenty-foot-long cage? Sure as shit, I jumped over them, and when I landed, my back tire knocked the cage apart and the damn snakes got out."

He laughed again, and so did we, although I was probably the only one who hadn't heard him narrate this story before—he had a tendency to recycle anecdotes.

"There weren't no grandstands there, and the snake wrangler was running around trying to catch all these damn snakes that were slithering through the crowd. People were screaming and running every which way. It was funnier than hell! A real crowd-pleaser, you might say!"

"Ike, whatchu call a group of rattlesnakes?" Huck asked me. The guys were always making fun of me for being, in their view, brainy. They got a particular kick out of quizzing me on terms for various groups of animals—a murder of crows and whatnot. I'd learned them from my zoologist mom, and Dad knew them too. Apparently, when Mom and Dad met, their nerdy knowledge of these classifications had created quite a spark.

I smiled and turned to Evel. "A group of snakes or a group of rattlesnakes?"

"The dangerous ones," he said with a gleam in his cool eyes. "Rattlesnakes."

"A rhumba."

Evel pounded on the desk like I'd said the funniest thing

he'd ever heard. "A rhumba!" he yelled. Then he poured me a drink. What can I say? When he was happy with me, it felt amazing.

In buttoned-up Washington, DC, certain things were expected of me: Getting straight As at Georgetown Prep. Knowing American history and learning the Constitution so I could answer my dad's questions in detail. Understanding world politics and all that other stuff in the news. Remembering all the fun trivia Mom taught me about kingdom, phylum, class, order, family, genus, species. Most people I knew back there found Evel's brand of homegrown Americana inexplicably silly, like *Hee Haw* or the Miss America Pageant. They regarded everything about him as laughable and stupid. *Most people* included my parents and sister. But as a teenager, I lay on the floor of our den watching him do his jumps on *ABC's Wide World of Sports*—dozens of amazing, dangerous, and, above all, *successful* jumps between the summers of '72 and '74 without one single crash—and I was hooked.

Right before I started basic training, in August '74, Evel attempted his biggest stunt ever, an ill-fated attempt to jump the Snake River. It landed him on the cover of *Sports Illustrated*, although typically he was treated with snobbery by the hip magazines; *Rolling Stone* had put Evel on its cover, but mockingly, with a caricature of him atop a star-spangled phallus-like rocket next to the words *King of the Goons*.

The Snake River debacle was followed by another spectacular failure: Evel jumped thirteen buses at Wembley Stadium in the UK, but when he tried to land, he was tossed off the speeding motorcycle like a rag doll. The crash fractured his pelvis, crushed two of his vertebrae, busted his right hand, and knocked him unconscious. Although nothing was hurt as badly as his ego, it seemed, because after coming to, he hobbled to the microphone and announced his immediate retirement. "You are the last people in the world who will see me jump," he told the crowd. "Because I will never, ever, ever jump again. I'm through."

He retracted all that a few days later from his hospital bed, natch.

I had entered his life during the transition period of his career. Most of those who reach the big stage don't become rich and famous and then die. They become rich and famous, then less rich and less famous, and then they die. *ABC's Wide World of Sports* now seemed ambivalent about covering him; the producers likely thought his best days—and his successful jumps—were behind him. The planned shark jump would be part of the lower-rent *CBS Sports Spectacular*. It was the television-sports version of all those *Jaws* knockoff movies trying to capitalize on the original film's success: *Mako: The Jaws of Death* and *Grizzly* and the upcoming *Tentacles*, which was about an octopus terrorizing a beach town and starred Henry Fonda and Shelley Winters.

But, hey—Evel was right at home in that shameless, cheesy knockoff sweet spot, with his brazen charm and crazy risks with gutsy stunts. Millions of people thought of him as a folk hero. They loved him for his spectacle. Maybe he wasn't the best cycle jockey—I'm a motorcycle snob—but he was the best damn showman since P. T. Barnum.

What was it about Evel that moved me? That still moved me even after everything I came to know about him? The dime-store psychology answer is that I traded a father for a father figure, but that doesn't get at it, not really. Dad was a legitimate war hero and a loving, moral man; Evel was the Bizarro Planet version of him. So why did I care?

Later that night, we ended up where we always did, the Dead Canary. We sat at the corner table reserved for Evel and his crew.

Rachel brought us pitcher after pitcher of Montana Marys—an evil concoction of beer, vodka, Wild Turkey, and tomato juice.

Elvis's "Moody Blue" came on the juke. I was a diehard fan and kept up with him on the radio whenever I could—in both DC and Montana there were late-night Elvis radio shows—so I knew that this particular song had been recorded in the Jungle Room at Graceland a year before. One of the DJs noted that he'd performed that song fully only once, at a concert in Charlotte. He said *fully* because Elvis had tried it the night before but forgot the words, so the next night he returned to the stage with the lyrics in hand. The King was slipping, but he was still the King. I'd seen him live a few times, and I looked forward to seeing him perform again soon; Rachel and I had talked about road-tripping to see him in South Dakota or Nebraska in June.

We all got really pickled that night, more than usual. Something in that brine brought back Lebanon—the rubble and the dust and how it clogged my throat. I smelled the kerosene from the Middle East, an olfactory hallucination, and other things that were worse to smell, and death came close, breathing hot down my neck. After half a dozen whiskeys that night, I told everyone I was going to the parking lot for some fresh air and a smoke and I got the hell out of that bar. This sort of disorientation happened pretty much every night to different degrees. That night, it was close to the third degree.

The Dead Canary was outside of downtown, across from the brand-new Silver Bow drive-in movie theater, which that night was showing a trailer for *Tentacles*. (Yes, it was cold, but the Silver Bow was open year-round; Montanans are a hardy bunch.) The octopus was "turning the beach…into a buffet!" the drive-in's marquee teased. I could hear the dialogue from across German Gulch Road, and it sounded just awful. I think the filmmakers even had the aforementioned octopus growling

at one point. I'm nowhere near as smart as my mom the zoologist, but I'm fairly certain octopi don't growl. For that matter,
octopi don't even *have* tentacles—they have arms. When you
grow up around politicians in Washington, DC, you quickly
learn there's a big difference between truth and marketing. Dad
wasn't like that—the Venn diagram of Dad's real self and Dad's
image was pretty much a circle. But most of the pols in town
were so phony, they'd summon your inner Holden Caulfield
tout de suite.

From across German Gulch Road came the rapid firing of a
machine gun. The damn filmmakers must have had a character
sniping at the octopus. *Not real,* I told myself. But adrenaline
shot through me. I took a deep breath and exhaled, slowly.
I closed my eyes and rested my head against the outside of
the bar.

This was Montana, not Lebanon.

That was a film, not an ill-fated mission in Beirut.

I opened my eyes and saw that, surprisingly, Evel had followed
me outside. He pulled out a pack of Luckys, handed me one,
and lit it with an old silver Ronson. In the lighter's flame, his
features changed—became devilish for a moment—then the
flame went out, and he was Evel again.

"I've been thinking, jarhead," he said. "It's pretty surprising
to meet a fancy-pants senator's son who's also a Marine. Not to
mention one who can actually ride."

I didn't want to talk about being anybody's son or a badass
Marine, not when the cool night air was calming me, and the
cigarette was clearing my head. I made myself focus on the upcoming jump. "Let me ask *you* a question," I said. "How many
people do you think are buying tickets to the Chicago show
because they're hoping to see sharks eat you?"

"There's always a percentage who go to the Indy Five

Hundred to see a crash," he said, "but sixty or seventy percent of your fans are there to pull for a guy. They don't want to see anybody get killed or hurt. I know I don't."

He lit a Lucky for himself. I told him about some of my broken bones, and he told me about some of his. He'd had more than his fair share and made it all sound like a great adventure. Then he turned those cold laser-beam-like eyes on me. My boyhood hero was taking an interest, wondering when I'd come the closest to death, no doubt fishing for a story about my time in combat, which I didn't want to think about and didn't feel like giving him. We talked for a while. I needed the wall to help me stand up, and the rest of that night was a blur.

The closest I'd ever come to death, besides Lebanon, was when I was ten years old. I don't think I said anything about this to Evel. It was 1966, and Lucy and I had Grandma staying with us while Mom and Dad were out on the campaign trail or hobnobbing with movie stars and fat-cat donors or off God-knows-where. They were always away on adventures, saving the world and whatnot. Don't get me wrong, they were great parents, but they often weren't around, which sometimes made me feel like an afterthought.

One spring afternoon when I was in fifth grade, I started feeling really sick. At the time, I just thought, *Gosh, what a weird flu I've got.* But the fatigue lingered for weeks, and when summer came, I didn't feel like doing much and couldn't catch my breath for anything. Grandma was of a generation where you didn't go to the doctor unless you were at death's door, so I just stayed home. She seemed to think I was a weak boy. It got worse, and in August, I barely left my bed, which should have been a clue that something was very wrong, since I'd always been an active little dude.

When my skin turned snow white and my nose started to

bleed, Lucy told Grandma she had to take me to a doctor. Lucy even gave up her long-anticipated trip with her Camp Fire Girls troop to see the wild ponies of Nanticoke and Susquehannock Islands so that she could watch over me. One morning when I got out of bed, I was so dizzy, I fell. I hit my head, and the bruise quickly bloomed purplish blue, discoloring half my face. That was it for Lucy. She called Dad's congressional office, got the number of the hotel they were staying at while they solved whatever mystery it was, and ordered them, like a commanding general, to come home at once.

My parents were back in DC the next day, and they rushed me to our family physician, Dr. Thomas Boswell. He pricked my finger to get a blood sample. Whatever the results were—I remember something about a low hemoglobin level, but truly, I was in such a fog, I'm not sure—they were dire enough that he came into the exam room and told my parents to take me to the hospital immediately.

This I distinctly remember: Mom pushed Dr. Boswell to tell her what this could be, worst-case scenario. He was reluctant, but Mom pressed, and then I heard it, loud as the voice of God from the burning bush: "Leukemia."

Mom left the room. When she came back fifteen minutes later, her eye makeup was smudged. The next twenty-four hours were a distressing fuss of doctors and nurses at the pediatric hospital in DC, injections and blood draws, poking and prodding, and the Marder family got a crash course in the importance of a sufficient number of functioning red blood cells, which I did not have. The concerned faces of so many experts terrified me—oncologists, pediatricians, hematologists, all of them trying to figure out what was wrong. My parents pretended to be stoic, but I could tell they were terrified.

Lucy didn't leave my side. She held my hand the whole time

except when she fell asleep on the floor. Even at twelve years old, she had fortitude. She was rock solid. She was *there*.

On day two of hospital hell, the doctors told my parents that I had one of three possible conditions, none of which were good. One was lymphocytic leukemia, cancer of the blood and bone marrow, which was a death sentence in 1966. Another was a type of anemia in which my body failed to produce enough red blood cells. The third was a different type of anemia in which my body destroyed its red blood cells faster than it made them. Both anemias could also be fatal.

On hell day three (or maybe it was four; who kept count?), Lucy was telling me a story while tickling my forearm, annoying me (typical Lucy) to distract me from my misery (also typical), when she suddenly stopped. She turned to the adults—the doctor was yammering on about something to my parents and Grandma—and said, "Say that again." When the adults ignored her, she repeated herself, louder: "Say that again!"

Dad always talked to Lucy as if she were almost a peer. "The doctor was just asking us if Ike has been on any medication, honey."

"He hasn't," Mom told the doctor.

"That's not true," Lucy said.

Most memories fade into the ether as if they never happened, but some are so memorable, you can place yourself in that precise moment decades later.

The doctor cocked his head, intrigued.

"Grandma was putting an ointment on him for his bubbles," Lucy said.

My "bubbles" were tiny bumps on my arms and legs, some sort of rash that made my skin rough. Months earlier, Grandma had started rubbing some cream on them. "A topical ointment I've used for years," Grandma said.

The doctor asked for the name or at least the brand of the medication, but Grandma couldn't remember.

Lucy piped up again. "It's called Skincleer, with two *e*'s."

Turned out, Skincleer contained a chemical compound that health authorities were realizing had serious side effects. The ointment in fact was causing the aplastic anemia, which quite possibly could have killed me. Armed with that knowledge, the doctor started me on blood transfusions and prescribed plenty of rest and recuperation. A few weeks later, I was good as new.

Lucy saved my life. From then on, she thought of herself as my protector whether I wanted her to or not.

That was the story I should've told Evel that night at the Dead Canary.

The next morning, I woke up with that uneasy feeling I got sometimes with a very bad hangover, that maybe I'd said or done something I shouldn't have but couldn't remember what. The more I fretted, the more a dark fear wove through my gut. The Marine Corps had lied to the nation and pinned a medal on my chest for both my valor and my silence. And yeah, I'd been hammered out of my mind, and yeah, when I was a kid, Evel had been a hero of mine, and he'd come into my life when I needed help, but still, I had to keep my trap shut. I wouldn't have been stupid enough to tell Evel Knievel, the most ruthless, mercurial man I knew, my other near-death story, no matter how much I craved his approval. Would I? But what had we talked about the previous night outside the bar? It was all a black hole.

Later that day, a sliver of memory cut through my worries: Evel leaning against the wall, long and lean with those ice-blue eyes focused on me, me telling him he'd been the hero of my youth. I was starstruck still; I wanted to make him happy. I might even have said (ugh) how cool it was to have a hero talk to me. All that was in response to...what exactly? That fear slithered through me again, and with it an image of Evel lighting another smoke and handing it to me, me staring back and seeing two of him.

That's how drunk I was. Before me stood two heroes, both wanting to know how I'd ended up in Bethesda Naval Hospital. They'd both called me, lovingly, "jarhead."

I'm pretty sure I answered them. The two Evels, I mean. An answer I'd regret.

In January 1977, the pit crew and I temporarily relocated to Chicago. A few weeks had passed since that night outside the bar. Even when we were just days away from the premiere of CBS's *Evel Knievel's Death Defiers*, Evel was still in Fort Lauderdale, fifteen hundred miles away. I overheard some of the guys saying that Evel was super-bummed because *Viva Knievel!* was getting blasted by Hollywood critics and would have only a limited release. Supposedly he was living on his yacht, marinating in bourbon. No one knew when he would show up. Everyone was getting antsy.

We were all set in terms of equipment, so out of boredom and curiosity, I sneaked into the show's press conference, hoping one of Evel's PR guys would shed some light on when he'd be here. I hung out in the back, avoiding the cameras. Last thing I needed was a video telling the Marines and my parents where I was. The show's producer, Marty Pasetta, was standing with the PR guy next to a placard that read CHALLENGING THE JAWS OF DEATH; in front of them was a scaled-down model of the ninety-by-fifty-by-four-foot shark tank, this one filled with a few gallons of water and thirteen dime-store rubber shark toys. The PR guy told the assembled reporters that he hadn't been able to contact Evel the previous night.

Pasetta tried to hype the other acts that would fill most of the ninety-minute extravaganza, including Jumpin' Joe Gerlach, who would dive from the top of the arena into a large foam-filled pit, and Orval Kisselburg, "the Daredevil Clown," who would light four sticks of dynamite under his chair.

The reporters in the room snorted.

"You laugh, but these are all professionals!" Pasetta said, fuming. "I hope you're not making light of this!"

Pasetta opened the floor to questions, most of which he answered: Knievel would be making five hundred thousand dollars from the event. From CBS. No, not from floor tickets, which were $6.50 to $7.50 apiece. Yes, the event would still be hosted by Telly Savalas and Jill St. John. Yes, they were prepared for the worst-case scenario; paramedics and ambulances would be on hand, as would scuba divers, and—so you wouldn't miss even one chomp—the tank was equipped with underwater cameras.

Suddenly, as if in a movie, a messenger burst into the hotel conference room and delivered a note to Pasetta, who unfolded it with a staged urgency. Pasetta waved the paper in the air and said, "This is from the man himself."

He read the message aloud: "'This is a more dangerous jump than Snake River Canyon or any of my other jumps! Signed, Evel Knievel.'"

It was hard not to laugh. The claim was such an obvious lie, fueled by pure defensiveness and delivered with the most narcissistic self-regard. But his ego was also so amusing. In my brief time on the pit crew, I'd come to see Knievel as primarily a performer. He held up a mirror to the country, revealing our national need for spectacle, the brutality of powerful men, and the sycophancy of their followers. He was utterly shameless, tethered to neither decorum nor facts, and there was something refreshing about that, about his admissions of infidelity and his petty grievances. The country was waking up with a hangover from years of being lied to by presidents and generals, but I couldn't tell if that realization was propelling us into a world of truth or a world where the truth had no value.

The morning of the jump, I had a terrible sense of impending catastrophe, as sharp as the cold wind assaulting me on the walk from the hotel to Canaryville.

"*Well, the south side of Chicago,*" I sang to distract myself from both my nerves and the windchill, "*is the baddest part of town . . .*"

The International Amphitheatre, across from the Union Stock Yards, had originally been built for cattle exhibitions. Elvis had performed there, and so had the Beatles, and the theater had housed the infamous 1968 Democratic National Convention, which I'd watched at home with my dad. When Senator Ribicoff condemned the Chicago police's "Gestapo tactics," the camera cut to Mayor Daley, and I lip-read his fury: *Fuck you, you Jew son of a bitch, you lousy motherfucker, go home!*

I crossed Halsted, flashed my pass to a lone security guard, and walked into the building. Dirty, dank. I saw rusted pipes, wires sprawling like intestines from a gutted deer—it was all coming apart at the seams. Place was a dump. There had always been something a bit bargain-bin about Evel. That might have been part of his charm for his fans; they prayed that he'd be able to pull off these crazy stunts that were seemingly improvised at the last minute and held together with chewing gum and safety pins. Frankly, for America, the entire decade was like a once-glossy Polaroid fading in the sun, all that had been vibrant proven ephemeral.

The floor of the arena was crowded with red, white, and blue ramps that looked as if they'd been swiped from an aging amusement park. The stadium itself was an odd pick—it wasn't long enough to contain the runway Evel needed to get lift-off, the shark tank, and the landing ramp. Since the landing was the most important thing, the workmen had to assemble the jump ramp starting in the tunnel that went from back-stage to the floor of the coliseum. The crowd would hear Evel rev his motor, but they wouldn't see him until several seconds into his ride, just a few yards before he launched his bike over the tank.

The sharks, Huckleberry told me, had been caught off the Florida Keys and transported north, and I'd watched as a forklift operator moved each shark in its coffin-size box from back-stage to the ninety-foot-long saltwater tank between the ramps. Those sharks didn't evoke the one from *Jaws* in any real way. I wasn't sure if they even fit the definition of *man-eaters*. The fishing crew down south had told Evel that they were hoping for lemon sharks but would settle for anything with a dorsal fin. We were lucky, I suppose, that they hadn't brought us a pod of dolphins.

I went over to Huck, who was chatting with the two Tommys, Evel's mechanics from the Wichita Harley-Davidson dealer. Tommy M. had a mess of black hair, a mustache, and a beer gut. Tommy R. was lean, with Elvis sideburns and a perpetually furrowed brow.

"One of the sharks didn't survive the trip," Huck told Side-burns Tommy as he tinkered on the motorcycle he'd brought with him from Butte.

"I'm amazed any of them did," I said, studying the boxes containing those poor creatures. "When were they last fed?"

"Fish food isn't our department," said Beer Gut Tommy.

"We better hope our boss isn't the fish food," I said.

Huck gestured toward a patriotically painted XR-750 Harley a few yards away. "Would you give Evel's bike a lap or two?"

"Sure," I said. "Why?"

"Huck thinks there might be a flat spot just above idle," said Sideburns Tommy. "We might have to drop the needles."

The other Tommy tugged at the waistband struggling against his beer gut. "Kindly disabuse Huck of that notion."

I mounted the Harley. She was a good bike, a bit beat up, but like all XRs, she was built for flat-track racing. None of the motorcycles Evel used were intended for anything remotely like his stunts. This one had a Ceriani fork and Girling shocks with four or five inches of travel—half as much as a motocross bike designed to handle jumps. Evel never used a speedometer or a tachometer and he never made any calculations accounting for wind speed or other variables. He went by feel, by instinct. It's one of the reasons he crashed so much. That and his fundamental lack of skill when it came to operating a motorized vehicle with prescience and precision, which he tried to compensate for with his showmanship and willingness to defy death in the most spectacular ways.

XRs were intended for race use; a kick-starter was just extra weight and another part to break, so I pushed the bike for a few quick strides and hopped down on it, giving the throttle a little gas as I released the clutch. For a moment the bike hesitated, but then it came to life. I started off slow. Nothing felt unusual. I took a spin around the edge of the arena floor, speeding up, enjoying the ride. I would always rather be on a bike.

When I was thirteen, my dad bought a Hudson Valley estate with the money he inherited from his father, my grandfather, the legendary Winston Marder, Rough Rider and deity of my childhood. The estate was one of a number of grand properties owned by a member of the British royal family, a duke who'd fled the United Kingdom in 1957 after the Eisenhower administration released the Marburg Files, revealing his (and others') dalliance with the Third Reich. When the duke died, Dad bought his New York property and everything in it for a song; none of the royals wanted to be associated with the Marburg stink. Mom got the duke's rare furniture and china; Dad spent days in his library with its collection of historical tomes; Lucy gushed over the art.

None of it meant a damn thing to me. Then I found that bike.

It was like discovering the Rosetta stone. The AJS 500 cc Model 18 motorcycle was stuck behind some plywood in the back of the garage; it was black and chrome with the signature *AJS* stenciled in gold across the fuel tank and the most beautiful lines, and I knew my parents would never let me ride it.

If they found out about it, that is.

I'd picked up a lot at the neighborhood gas station, so I knew I had to remove the gas tank and flush it, change the oil, and put in new plugs. Most of the work was dismantling and cleaning the varnish out of the carb. The first couple of times I tried to kick-start it, it kicked me back twice as hard, but eventually I learned to slowly push down on the kick-starter until I found top dead center. At that point, I dropped on it with all my teenage weight, and it thumped to life with an idle so slow that I could hear each firing in that one cavernous cylinder.

Whenever I had a chance, I'd announce that I was going for a walk—which seemed to please my parents, who wanted their privileged urban scion to enjoy the countryside—and I'd head out on the bike and roar around for hours, going down narrow roads, getting lost in the speed and the solitude. The thump of that big single beneath me, the sun on my face, the infinite possibilities in front of me—it was practically a religious experience. When I finished, I'd hide the bike back under its tarp in a broken-down shed behind the barn where the tractors were kept and return home with color in my face and my hair mussed. My folks were happy with my new outdoorsy-ness.

It took a few years for my parents to figure out what I was doing, but by then, I was old enough to ride and I rode well. Mom handed me a helmet, and Dad mandated that I had to wear it, but other than that, there was little for them to object to.

And when I think back to how and why I ended up in Butte with Knievel, I see there was a purity to it, as odd as it might be to use that word in relation to Evel. We both loved to ride; we loved the freedom of it, the rebelliousness, the solitude. And the truth is, I rode better than Evel, and I think he knew that.

Before I could complete the second lap on the patriotic Harley that Huck needed me to check out, and only hours before his shark jump, Evel stepped into the path of the bike. I had to crunch the brakes, drop it into first, and swerve around him. He looked like a furious matador who knew the bull would back off.

"You son of a bitch, what are you doing on my bike?" he snarled.

Was he joking? I read his face. Nope, he was furious.

This was a side of him I'd witnessed at the Dead Canary and the Freeway and the Elmar and the Acoma and the Met and at Mal's. It was a rage I'd read about in *Rolling Stone* and heard other members of the pit crew discuss, but he'd never directed it at me before.

I felt like a kid being reprimanded by Daddy. "The fellas told me to give it a ride, see if the carbs were jetted right."

Evel looked at Huck and the Tommys, who weren't even trying to suppress their laughter. Clearly, I'd been set up.

"It's bad luck for anyone but me to ride my bike on jump day,"

Evel growled. "Everyone knows that. I won't ride that now. You might as well sell it for parts."

"So sorry, Evel, I had no idea," I said. "I was just trying to help."

I thought about telling him exactly what Huck and the Tommys had said, but Evel wouldn't have cared. All that mattered was that his bike was "ruined." That I'd gotten hoodwinked into this dumbfuckery was hardly an excuse. I hopped off the bike and began to walk it back to the guys. Evel only seemed to get angrier.

"Hold on a second there, jarhead," Evel said. "About-face. Follow me."

I turned the XR and followed him past the jump ramp and through the circular white stone tunnel that led backstage. He stopped and pivoted. He had a wild look on his face. I could smell the Wild Turkey on his breath.

"You think you're such hot shit?" He motioned down the tunnel, toward the tank. "Give it a go."

I laughed. What? He had to be kidding.

"I'm serious," he said. "Jump."

"I d-don't understand," I stammered.

"Make my jump, big shot."

I thought of the sharks, the ninety-foot length of the tank, my lack of preparation and training. Evel was a mercurial man, but this seemed especially deranged.

"Do it," he said, "or I'll tell reporters about your whole fucked-up mission in the Root and most especially about you going AWOL."

The blood left my face. If he knew we called Beirut "the Root," then I had clearly talked way too much that night. "You'll what?"

"I only employ patriots," he sneered. "Not *deserters*."

He would tell journalists about what happened in Lebanon? About the utter goatfuck there? About the Pentagon cover-up? So I *had* confided in him. Drunkenly. Unwisely. In an attempt to ingratiate myself, I had handed him my secrets, and he was going to use them to destroy me? And my dad...Jesus Christ, what the hell would my dad think? Would it create a scandal back home for him? Why the hell had I opened my big mouth?

"Evel, what? No, please—"

"We're in Chicago now, not Butte," Evel said. "Lots of press who'd love to hear about a senator's son who's disloyal, disobedient. Who I had to kick off my team after I learned what he was part of in the Middle East."

Christ.

A million times since that moment, I've reflected on whether he wanted me to attempt that jump because he thought it would kill me. He'd seen me ride, but only in a limited capacity, showing off for the fellas. I didn't impress them by spinning doughnuts or pulling big wheelies—they all did that—but I could keep the bike balanced almost vertically while coasting to a nearly complete stop; I did lurid power slides around gravel corners, showering them with roost; and sometimes I'd jam the throttle, climb right up to stand on the seat and tank, and steer my bike like a surfboard. One of the guys called that a "Christ." Not as in "Christ, did you see that?" but because he thought I looked like Christ on the cross, I guess. (This wasn't a particularly pious group.) We did stuff like that for each other in the garage and the parking lot and on those empty Montana roads.

Evel didn't think I could do this jump, here, in the Chicago arena—I read it in those ice-blue eyes.

He was dooming me to be a fireball. Or chum.

Maybe he didn't think I had the guts to ride that hog one hundred miles an hour up and off a ramp, that I couldn't, oh

God, stick that back tire on the giant X. As Evel always said, anybody could jump; the trouble began when you tried to land. It was tough to get into his head. I suspected he wanted me to cower, to bow down to his genius, like the rest of the pit crew, like everyone in Butte, everyone in Montana. Like his poor abused wife.

I suddenly thought of Mom. She always said that the folly of leadership was that men succeeded to the point that they inevitably removed from their circle anyone who kept them from self-destruction. She had been talking about Nixon, LBJ, McCarthy, but Evel too surrounded himself with yes-men. He was accustomed to trembling and cowering.

I was trembling, all right, but I would not cower. I was sick of it, frankly.

So I got back on the Harley, stood up straight. I hopped down on it, once again twisting the throttle. This time was no time for caution, though. As I accelerated up the ramp and toward the arena, I saw a shark handler adding another beast to the tank.

Could I land it?

I had it wide open. Speed was safety. The more I thought about what I was doing, the likelier it was that I would err. I would need to outrace my brain.

I thundered up the ramp. Everything was a blur.

Then I was in the air, soaring, filled with lightness and joy. I was defying gravity, maybe even death; I stood up on the foot pegs, ready to absorb the shock of landing with my legs.

I muscled the front tire upward, so I would land on the rear...

And then — *bang* — I was on the other side, the rear tire hitting the ramp, the shocks bottoming and rattling my bones. I landed on the giant X put there for my aiming pleasure.

The front end of the bike hit next. I eased on the brakes and slammed in a couple of downshifts, kept steering straight.

The ramps were white with a thick red stripe on the left, a blue one on the right. The landing ramp curved up, which slowed me down.

The bike wobbled, but I regained control. We came to a stop.

Exhale. Relief.

Applause!

Holy shit, I'd made it!

Huck and the Tommys were clapping. Evel glowered at them, and they stopped.

I shook my head, thinking to myself: *Wow, I made it. I survived. I was not eaten by sharks.*

But also: *Oh my God, that was truly stupid.*

Really fucking stupid.

Not only because I'd done that idiotic stunt but also because I realized now he hadn't wanted me to do it; he had wanted me to cower, and that would have been much smarter.

As I wheeled the bike off the landing ramp and onto the arena floor, that characteristic *potato-potato* sound of an open-piped hog echoed through the amphitheater, building in tempo to a lopsided *vroom!* Suddenly Evel himself was speeding up the jump ramp on one of his spare bikes, and then he was in the air, soaring high, always the great showman.

I noticed him getting slightly crossed up, turning the handlebars in midair. Not a good idea if you plan to run straight upon your return to Earth.

He landed on the *X*. Hard.

And he landed wrong.

He veered sharply to the right, and he and his bike fell to the left and skidded like a hockey puck, plowing into and through a wooden retaining wall and hitting a cameraman.

The bike flipped. Evel was thrown onto the concrete below.

We all ran to him. The concrete was so cold. Evel was

unconscious. Huck slapped his face, and Evel woke up and tried talking, but all that came out was gibberish.

"Fuck," said Huck.

"There goes the CBS special," said Sideburns Tommy.

I couldn't believe how badly Evel was hurt. He needed to go to the hospital. "Did someone call an ambulance?"

"You done fucked up," Beer Gut Tommy said. I realized he was talking to me.

"If you were smart, you'd have got chomped by them sharks," Huck said. "Would've been less painful than what Evel's gonna do to you."

CHAPTER FOUR

LUCY

Washington, DC

June 1977

THE PHONE WOKE me up from a horrible dream about Jeannie McBean. It was Mom.

"You're on the front page!" she gushed.

I sat up, tried to gather my wits. "What's that?"

"I had no idea you wrote a story for the *Sentinel*," she said. "And you're on the front page. I'm looking right at it, sweetie! Your name! It's right here!"

"Oh my God!" I leaped out of bed, nearly yanking the phone cord out of the wall. But I didn't have a copy waiting for me at my doorstep. I had only been hired yesterday—I wasn't a subscriber yet.

I needed to see that paper! *The front page!*

Then I thought, *Why?* An uneasy feeling settled over me. Why on earth was my story—a missing woman found dead—on the wood of the tabloid, the all-important cover with its ENOR-MOUS BOLD-FONT HEADLINES designed to grab commuters in the split second it had their attention? Jeannie McBean had been murdered, strangled—which was terrible—but her death wasn't Watergate or a moon landing.[1] "What does it say, Mom?"

---

1   Approximately two hundred people in Washington, DC, had been killed the previous year in our city of seven hundred thousand, and I didn't recall

"Let's see. 'DC Serial Murderer'—"

"Serial *what?*" I shrieked.

"Oh, wait. There's a question mark. 'DC Serial Murderer?' And then in smaller writing: 'Manassas Mom Latest Victim.' And your name! 'Lucy Marder Scoops,' it says. Honey, I didn't know we had a serial murderer! What a terrifying assignment. Do be careful!"

I hadn't known we had one either. "You and Dad subscribe to the *Sentinel*? It's not exactly your read."

"Oh, but you are, honey!" she said. "You should have told me you'd started reporting for them! I was walking Chester[2] when Nancy Murphy from across the street ran out waving her copy at me. I'm so proud of you, sweetheart! I'll sign up today!"

After we hung up, I got dressed and headed out the door. On my walk to the corner café, I retraced the previous night's work. I had learned as much as I could from Officer Spanjian, discreetly gathered a handful of small details from other officers, and, from a pay phone in Mount Pleasant, I phoned the McBean family home in Manassas, Virginia, again and again. They never answered. After calling in what I had to the editor, I drove to the McBean town house. No one answered the door, so I knocked on some neighbors' doors and got other details—like the fact that she had two children—then called back into the office for

---

any other victims making a front page. Of course, I should note that most of the two hundred were killed by firearms, most victims were black, most were male. Only five white women had been killed. So Jeannie McBean was aberrant in that crude analysis. And the racial, even racist, component of that today seems all too obvious. And maybe it did to me back then too, if I'm being honest.

2   Chester was Mom and Dad's beagle, named after Admiral Chester Nimitz. All their dogs were named after World War II Allied commanders—before Chester, we had Omar and Montgomery. Dwight, aka Ike, was named after supreme Allied commander General Eisenhower; I'm named after suffragist and abolitionist Lucy Stone.

a notebook dump. Nothing told me that Jeannie McBean might have been one in a series of victims.

A customer held the café door open for me. I went straight to the newspaper stand. There was the *Sentinel* and its headline—"DC Serial Murderer?"—in bold type. And there was my name in red and white graphics—"Lucy Marder Scoops"—as if anyone knew my name, as if that phrase were a thing.

I studied the blown-up, fuzzy picture beneath the headline. A young and lovely Jeannie McBean, smiling in her wedding dress. Where had we gotten that photograph? When I called in the story, the editor didn't mention it. He must have sent someone, a stringer perhaps, out to the McBean residence. Except I had gone there, and no one answered the door.

Who else was working on my story?

I read the lede: "A source familiar with the investigation" told the *Sentinel* that law enforcement "had not ruled out" the possibility that the murder of Jeannie McBean was tied to a similar murder three weeks before. The source was not described, nor was there any suggestion of how this source might know. It didn't mention the name of the previous victim or the details of her "similar" murder or how these two murders might be tied to each other. It was a criminal theory I'd had no reason to contemplate, and it was attributed to me, as if I had written it.

I felt sick.

The next eight paragraphs were my reporting, what I had written word for word. After that, though, were five extraneous paragraphs about how serial murderers operated, complete with references to the Zodiac Killer of the late 1960s and the notorious Edmund Kemper,[3] who'd been sentenced to eight consecutive life sentences in 1973.

---

3 Trust me on this: When it comes to Kemper, the less you know, the better.

What the hell was this? What did the Zodiac Killer have to do with Jeannie McBean's death? It was outrageous to even suggest there was a serial murderer involved here, let alone invoke other completely unrelated murderers. I would never have written those words. Those words should never have been written.

What could I do? If this had happened to Ike, he would have approached Max Lyon with all the finesse of an Abrams tank and demanded to know how Lyon slept at night and what exactly gave him the right to *fuck up* his work—that would have been Ike's choice of words, not mine.

But I had long ago learned that women had no similar right to confrontation. Should I quit? Where would I go? If I left the *Sentinel* after less than twenty-four hours on the job, I would appear flighty to my next employer—if I could find another. And if I did, would the next job be any better? I was two for two on my stories being commandeered.

At least the *Sentinel* gave me the credit, I told myself. That was pretty important. *Okay, calm down. Let me get some information before I say anything.* I got in my VW, sped to the Georgetown office, took the elevator to the top floor, and went into the newsroom.

Everyone stood and began clapping.

I glanced over my shoulder. No one was behind me. I realized, with shock, they were applauding for me.

Don't get me wrong, I liked being recognized. But it was also very weird. Nothing like that ever happened at the *Star*. Not even to the male reporters whose scoops were their own.

Danielle hurried my way in her oh-so-high heels. Harry was right behind her. She pressed a *Sentinel* mug of coffee into my hand as though it were a trophy. "A clean kill," Danielle said. The metaphor made me wince. "No other paper had the details you had!"

"Actually, I'd like to talk to you about that," I said.

"Nice work, Scoop," Harry said with a slow smile.

My brain went blank, like it was having a power outage. Something about his smile, all that dark hair, and those bright blue eyes—what had I been mad about again?

I focused on Danielle. "Those details you think are so great? I didn't get them."

"I did," Harry said.

I blinked at him. "You?"

"Sure. Made a couple calls. Was that presumptuous? Did I overstep? First days are hard—I wanted to help you find your footing and all that."

My jaw dropped. "That was you?"

"We wanted to help." Harry appeared hurt. "You didn't want help? This is a collaborative place."

"No, of course...I appreciate..." Damn it, why was forming sentences so hard when I was around him? "It was kind. Only I do wish I'd known. Wish I'd been consulted. Or at least informed?"

"I'm so proud of you!" Danielle said, quickly moving on from the ethics issue I'd raised. She was proud of me. My mother had said the exact same thing less than an hour ago. Danielle's sentiment felt off, insincere; something was wrong, but I couldn't place it. She patted my shoulder. "Keep up the good work! See you after our meeting with Father."

She and Harry hurried off to the executive wing. I stood in the middle of the newsroom, utterly confused. The serial-murderer angle that Harry uncovered—did he have sources? He must be very good. Unless he was very wrong.

Was there a serial murderer?

All the other reporters were back at their desks, talking on the phone or pounding away on their typewriters. A voice called out: "You can put your Pulitzer over here."

I turned to find the source of the sass. A young woman patted the desk next to hers. She appeared slightly older than me and was very pretty. Stunning figure, like model-perfect. Something about her seemed familiar. I walked to her.

"Oh, I'm sorry, that's a coffee mug Danielle gave you, not a Pulitzer." She was smirking. My confusion was all great fun to her. She gestured to the desk next to hers again. "In any case, this is your desk now."

That's when I noticed what was on it: A lamp. A phone. A reporter's pad and a few pens and today's *Sentinel* in the inbox. Another copy of *Pride of Lyons: The British Family Reinventing the News,* in case I'd misplaced the one I'd been given. Underneath the newspaper sat the Jackie O. manuscript I'd pinched from Mom; I'd forgotten about it in the previous day's whirl. And in the middle of all that, an enormous boxy machine—a video display terminal, otherwise known as a VDT, or... "A *computer*?" I shrieked with delight. "Is it for me?"

My officemate laughed. "Of course it's for you."

"Oh my God! An actual computer!"

At the *Star,* computers were used for newspaper production, but in the newsroom, we still used typewriters. Even the *Post* and the *Times* were struggling to integrate this new technology into their newsrooms. But at the *Sentinel,* this was mine? I ran my hands over the big box of wonder, this gorgeous hunk of technology I had no idea how to use. I felt like a kid at Christmas.

"Well, Lucy Marder, you are as effervescent as everyone warned me you'd be." She held out her hand, and I thought, *What a knockout.* "I'm Ashley Mars, writer of your serial-murderer lede. And before you get indignant with me, just know, it was Heir-y's order."

"Airy?" That's what it sounded like. But no.

"The heir to the throne?" Ashley said. "The dreamboat who makes your face flush every time he walks by?" She lit a Marlboro, placed it in a small glass ashtray that read THE WATERGATE—real or novelty item, who knew—and turned back to her desk.

"Harry ordered you to do what, exactly?" I asked. Then, catching myself: "Just wondering how this place works."

She took a drag on her cigarette, then swiveled her chair to face me again. "You called in your copy, and Heir-y told me he had a tip on a similar murder. He gave me the details, such as they were, and told me to dress it up."

"Dress it up?"

"Dress it up like Sissy in Mom's Christmas outfit," she said. "That's when you take a solid but underwhelming story—"

"*Underwhelming?* A woman was murdered!"

"—and gussy it up to justify wood treatment," she continued. "In this case, that meant including an anonymous whoever speculating to Heir-y about some crazy predator out there." She gestured with her cigarette to a small black-and-white TV on her desk; there was no sound, but the reporter was presumably discussing the subject of the graphic, which read SENTINEL: SERIAL MURDERER IN DC. She smirked. "Now the local channels are chasing our lead."

I put my purse on my new desk, reached blindly for the chair, and lowered myself into it. "I'm so confused. If it's dressed up, does that mean it's untrue? There is no other victim?"

"I'm not saying *that*. Say what you want about Heir-y, but he's not a liar. I'm quite certain someone thinks whoever killed Jeannie McBean might possibly have killed another woman somewhere in DC or elsewhere, and that someone shared his or her speculation with Heir-y, who likes to run with things that are told to him, even stuff that's off the record. As do Ivan and Danielle and Max. Now, who this 'source familiar with the investigation' is and whether this person has direct knowledge or evidence to support these speculations? That's anybody's guess, including Heir-y's. I'm just saying, this paper has…different…standards than most American newspapers. It's all quite Bri'ish."

I didn't know what to make of any of this. Yesterday I'd quit the paper that had poached my story and screwed me out of a byline to take a job at a paper that augmented my reporting, perhaps irresponsibly, and—let's be honest—overhyped what I had. Maybe I should have stayed at the *Star*. Maybe their editors weren't holding me down but training me. Maybe they'd seen I wasn't ready to be on the front page.

"You've heard of the Forty-Four-Caliber Killer?" she asked me. She looked at me as if I should have.

My mind raced. I read all the important papers every morning—*New York Times*, *Washington Post*, and my old paper—before I had my first coffee. Nothing stirred.

"In New York?" she said. "In Queens?"

"Oh, wait, yes," I said. "Now I remember, I think. A few weeks ago Mayor Beame and the police commissioner asked for the public's help with finding a shooter. Three or four young women, all killed by the same gun? Was it a forty-four?" I hadn't paid much attention because it was New York, and I know this sounds bad, but in my mind, murders were just par for the course up there.

She looked up at me with astonishment. "That's all you know? Lucy, darling, I thought you were a newshound. You're missing the most exciting story in America."

"It's a local story, no? The *Times* reported people in Queens were afraid to go out."

"Good Lord, you're adorable," she said, frowning. "What if I told you the discos in Queens and the Bronx are *empty* because of the Forty-Four-Caliber Killer? That women are terrified to leave their homes?"

"I didn't know," I said.

"What if I told you the story was causing the *News* and the *Post* to be snatched off the stands, and the *Times* isn't even covering it?"

"I had no idea," I said. "Are you saying we have that kind of serial murderer in DC?"

"I'm saying *maybe*, in the same way we should *maybe* fear killer bees," Ashley said, alluding to a different story being hyped in a different part of the country by a different immigrant media magnate from the Commonwealth of Nations.[4] "Look, the *Sentinel* has different standards," Ashley said, "but it also allows us to report on stories the others won't touch. Like this story I'm working on."

She told me about the Whites, a family who had been denied permission by the FDA to use vitamin B_{17} to treat their cancer-stricken little boy, Caleb. This was the "cancer baby" story Max had barked about, the one that was headed for the wood until Jeannie Beanie's body turned up. "The parents say Caleb's not doing well on chemotherapy and they want to try vitamin B-seventeen, but bureaucrats won't let them," Ashley explained. "This story is Max's pet project. He swings by every

---

4   In the 1950s, a geneticist introduced an African species of honeybee to Brazil; they ended up spreading throughout South America. These bees weren't really deadlier than any other breed, but they were defensive and attacked (especially when provoked) in great numbers, so hundreds of South Americans were killed. In 1973, one of Max Lyon's rivals, Australian Rupert Murdoch, purchased the *San Antonio News* and its sister morning paper, the *Express*, and not long after, the paper was terrifying Texans with headlines like "Killer Bees Head North," though the threat to Americans was decades away and minimal. Circulation jumped. Bad journalism; great business. NBC followed his lead with an overhyped news special in 1975. Millions of people terrified just so Rupert could win a circ war in the fourteenth-largest city in America.

day for an update just about…" She glanced at her watch. "Now."

Max Lyon made his entrance from the executive hallway. Everyone in the newsroom stopped working, then resumed with performative intensity.

"The man himself," Ashley murmured as he came to stand over us. "Hello, sir. I was just telling Lucy about the miracle cure."

"Huge story, vitamin B-seventeen," Max said, pronouncing *vitamin* "viht-a-min." "Very promising results coming in from all over the world."

"Okay, I've heard of this," I said. It was in the newspapers—not the *Star*, but there'd been something in the *Post* maybe. "This is laetrile, right?"

Max nodded his approval. "Essentially."

"The FDA's been blocking folks from using it," Ashley said. "Congress and the states are pushing back, thank God; it's the only hope some of these folks have."

"Enter the Whites and their little boy, Caleb, at death's door," Max bellowed. "DC bureaucrats are actually threatening to take Caleb away from his mother and father if they give him B-seventeen and don't subject him to the regimen of poisons the medical establishment calls chemotherapy."

"Monstrous," Ashley said. "And can I just say, how is that even remotely in the entrepreneurial spirit of this country?"

Ashley's shameless obsequiousness seemed to please Max; he smiled at her. Dad always found such obvious attempts to ingratiate oneself annoying.

Max asked me, "Did you listen to our flaky president take questions from the common rabble? That CBS radio call-in show?"

I told him I had. (I hadn't.)

"Do you remember when that poor bereaved woman from North Carolina called in to beg for help from the government?"[5]

"Yes," I lied.

Max explained for everyone listening: "Her cancer-stricken father was dying. She wanted to know why rich folks were allowed to fly to Mexico to get treatments to save *their* lives but everyday Americans could not get the same treatments here. You know what that daft muppet said? He didn't want to make a *judgment* on the drug, but it might not do any good and people needed to be protected from it. What a flake."

"It's so elitist!" Ashley agreed. "God, that makes me angry." Then she smiled at Max. "I bet it'll make our readers angry too."

A smirk slid across Max's face. His grin reminded me of a nature film Mom made us watch where a copperhead slithered out of a hole in an adobe hut.

---

5   On a two-hour CBS radio broadcast in March, President Carter fielded calls from forty-two Americans, one of whom, a North Carolina woman named Opal DeHart, asked why her cancer-stricken father, Raymond Yarborough, was not allowed to use laetrile.
   "I feel that the people in this country should be permitted to use this treatment in this country," she said. "I realize that the AMA says it's not been proved safe, but for a terminal patient who is not going to live—and has a chance to live with it—I don't see how it could be dangerous. And hospital insurance does not cover treatment not authorized by the AMA. And most hardworking people in this country cannot afford treatments if not made under insurance benefits. And if a person has money available to leave the country for treatment in one of the seventeen countries where cancer specialists use this successfully, they have a chance of recovery. And a lot of people even from my area have done this. What I want to say is that we need your help, and the government's help, in checking this vitamin out so that it's made available to the American people."
   Carter said he would have someone from the Department of Health, Education, and Welfare reach out to her. The acting FDA commissioner called DeHart the next Monday and told her that many studies had been done but none found any evidence that laetrile worked, and there were no plans to lift the FDA ban.
   Her father, who had cancer in his neck and both lungs that had been treated with radiation therapy, died soon after.

"Why would the medical establishment want to stand in the way of it?"

"Profit," said Ashley. "Homeopathic healing kills pharmaceutical revenue streams."

"Quite," Max said, pleased. He gazed at Ashley as if she were his star pupil. Nobody had ever looked at me like that at my old newspaper. They'd never looked at me at all. There was also something else in the glint in his eye, I noted.

Here, everything was so different—I could talk to Max Lyon, British media magnate, Mighty Knight of Fleet Street, as if we were colleagues. Kind of. He was fearless and maybe a little fearsome, yet accessible. He had power he wielded effortlessly, and when you were around him, you felt a little powerful too. It was a kind of dark art, thrilling, seductive.

"It's pretty cool to be at a paper that goes where other newsrooms are afraid to go," I said, tripping over myself to match Ashley in sycophancy.

Max Lyon chuckled. "I need to run to a meeting with Jack Kent Cooke.[6] Good work today." He pointed to Ashley, then me. "Come to dinner at my house tonight. Both of you. We'll celebrate!"

It wasn't clear what we were celebrating other than our blessed existence, but that was okay. He walked off briskly, leaving Ashley and me to assume we'd satisfactorily sung for our suppers. "Think he bought our brownnosing?" she murmured, and I wondered if I'd found a friend.

---

6   Cooke, majority owner of the Washington Redskins, was, like Lyon, a rapacious immigrant from the Land of God Save the Queen, though in his case, the land was Toronto. Cooke owned the Los Angeles Lakers and the Los Angeles Kings, and there was talk of him moving to DC to take over the day-to-day operations of our local NFL team, the Redskins.

*   *   *

I was expected to write something new on the Jeannie McBean murder and what everyone was now referring to as the serial murderer—though I still wasn't certain there was one. Ollie told me Harry didn't have anything else from his so-called source, nothing about who this other victim might be, where that victim had been killed, whom I should call to follow up. I sat at the computer and started hunting through various newspaper databases for recent reports of women killed by strangulation and dumped in or around Washington, DC. It was arduous and the records were incomplete, and I found nothing.

I started delving into the records of a chain of newspapers from the surrounding suburbs in Northern Virginia, including one in the small town of Manassas, where Jeannie had lived. Previously I would have done all this by phone, calling around to small-town police departments and courts and local newspapers. But now all that information was blinking across a screen instantaneously, called forth by my keystrokes. I felt like Zeus, lightning shooting from my fingertips.

Then I found it. Or what I thought might be it. From a small Manassas, Virginia, newspaper called the *Journal Messenger,* the headline "Local Woman's Body Found Near National Battlefield Park." The dateline was three weeks ago.

My heart sped up.

The *Journal Messenger* reported the woman's body had been found in a wooded area along the periphery of the Manassas National Battlefield Park. She was identified as Janice Davenport, white woman, thirty-eight, married, a working mother, two kids. Strangled. No leads.

I called the Manassas police department and asked to speak to the detective investigating the Davenport homicide. Detective

Jim Sullivan sounded young and unaccustomed to questions from reporters, which was helpful. I asked about the coroner's findings, which were public, and Sullivan confirmed there had been marks around her neck that indicated strangulation with a rope or a cord. Then I asked about the accuracy of the paper's report that Davenport's body had been dumped in a park (though the article had said *found*). The detective confirmed that, yes, it had been dumped.

"So Davenport wasn't killed at that location?"

"Oh, I'm not going to confirm that."

"What about the theory that Janice Davenport was killed by the same person who killed Jeannie McBean?"

The line went quiet. Then: "Where did you hear that?"

"A source," I said, which was kind-of-sort-of in the neighborhood of almost true.

"I can't...I wish you wouldn't report..." He sounded flustered, unsure of how to handle the situation. I got that same thrumming feeling that I always got when I was ahead of the story, out there all alone. Dangerous, exciting, heady. It *was* a story. Maybe a *big* story.

"Detective, who are you talking to from the DC police department about this serial murderer? There's coordination in the investigation, right? Between you and the DC police?"

"His name was Hatfield, I think—" he said, then caught himself. "Wait, this is off the record, I never said—" His speech devolved into an argle-bargle, and then the line went dead. After a moment, I heard a dial tone.

I looked up at the clock. An hour until deadline. I had one last call before filing.

"Officer Spanjian," she said, when she finally came to the phone. After I told her it was me, she was curt. "I don't even know that

I can talk to you," she said. "DC serial murderer? Lucy Marder Scoops? What the hell, Lucy."

"We have a source—" I started.

"*Right,*" she said. "Do you know every reporter I talked to that day asked if Jeannie McBean was linked to any other cases? Every. Single. Reporter. And I said we didn't know, but we couldn't rule anything out. Your paper was the only one that put that question in the headline."

That was true.

"I know the *Sentinel* desperately wants DC to have its own Forty-Four-Caliber Killer. The DC police do not. Let me say this slowly so you can get it through the blond hair that shields your brain from journalistic standards: I know of *no* evidence indicating that another murder in this city or in the surrounding area is linked to Jeannie McBean's."

I'm sure you know of no evidence of plenty of things, I thought. But I said: "What about in Manassas?"

"Manassas, Virginia, is at least thirty miles from my jurisdiction. If you have a question about a crime committed thirty miles away, call the Manassas PD."

She knows I know. I could hear it in her voice. She was trying to figure out exactly what I knew without showing her hand.

"I have," I said. Then I climbed out on a limb. "I understand there's been coordination already between the two investigations, since Manassas has what might be the first body dumped."

"I don't know anything about Manassas or Janice Davenport or anything else," she said, her voice ice cold.

"I never said Janice Davenport's name, Mimi," I said.

Silence.

"But as long as we're on the same page here," I continued, "she and Jeannie McBean were both killed in the same way, strangulation, within weeks of each other."

"No comment," she said.

"Both dumped in a park."

"No comment."

"It'd be malpractice if someone at MPD[7] *isn't* considering the possibility that the murders are related, don't you think?"

"I didn't say we *weren't* considering it," she said, furious now.

"Right, of course you're considering it, thank you for that comment," I said. "Here's what I'm reporting: MPD is working with the Manassas police on the murders of McBean and Davenport. You're investigating whether this is the same killer, if Davenport was in fact the first victim, if there are others—"

"No comment," Spanjian said.

Then she slammed down the phone.

I was typing my exclusive into the computer system—I think I was getting the hang of it—when the switchboard buzzed. Mom was on the line.

"Mom, what's up? I'm crashing on a story."

"Do you have a minute, sweetie? It's about your father."

"What's wrong? Is he sick? Hurt?"

"No, no. I'm in the lobby. Can you come down?"

I glanced at the wall clock—the minute hand was marching steadily toward my deadline. "Of course. Give me five."

I finished up the story, hit Return, shouted to Ollie that I'd filed, and ran to the elevator.

In the sunlight slanting through the lobby windows, Mom looked as serene and lovely as ever. She put on a good face for strangers. In public, she rarely committed to any emotion

---

7   The Metropolitan Police Department, MPD, is what it's called, although seldom in movies or books, because it's confusing, I guess. Writers sometimes shorthand it to DCPD, which no one in DC ever says.

harsher than benign indifference. Within the sanctum of our family, though, nothing was off-limits. She led me outside and away from the entrance.

"Your dad's in a bad place, honey," she murmured as she turned to me, standing close. The frown lines deepened around her mouth. "He's really worried about Ike. And when he worries, he can't help himself—he drinks. He did it during a bad spell in the fifties, then when we were out in La-La Land with the Rat Pack. And now it's like he can't stop. Though he's trying to hide it from me. Poorly. He's so concerned about your brother."

"Ike's fine," I said. "He's always fine. Don't worry."

"Can you get him to call your father?"

"I told you, I don't have a number for him. I don't know where he is."

Mom tilted her head and gave me the Look. "I realize you're the daughter of a politician, and your skill at choosing words to avoid perjury might be in your DNA."

"*Mom,*" I whined as though I were a teenager again. "I swear to God, I do not know where he is. I wouldn't lie to you."

"Of course not, but you and your brother have a special relationship," she said. "Your childhood was unique, with your parents in the spotlight, and you feel protective of him. But you don't have to protect him from us." She put an envelope in my hand. It contained a plane ticket to Los Angeles for a flight leaving Saturday morning. Two days from now.

"LA?" I said, thinking that I might not know where Ike was, but I knew Los Angeles was where he wasn't.

"He's gone west. I can feel it. A mother knows. In the same way I know you can figure it out and trade in this ticket—the most expensive—for a ticket to wherever he really is. I bought it at Dupont Circle Travel, so have them send you wherever you need to go. Do this for me, sweetie. Dad is very worried about him, and I'm very worried about both of them."

Ashley and I were sitting in the back of the limousine that was taking us to the Lyons' estate for dinner when the cartoon light bulb came on above my head. "Ashley!" I said. "I finally remember where I know you from!"

She raised her eyebrows, used to this sort of thing by now.

"You were on that sitcom, the…what was it called? *Can You Dig It*!"

I didn't remember much about *Can You Dig It*, since I was in college and never watched it, but I knew the basics: The star was an adorable black cherub named Nathan Lance who played an eight-year-old, though in reality, the actor was twenty-three. Ashley played the eldest of his three sisters. The show was canceled due to some scandal—I forget what—involving Lance.

Ashley said, "Guilty," and didn't seem eager to discuss it, so I said, "Cool," and dropped the subject.

And on the limo went, speeding across the Northern Virginia highways that offered special, less congested lanes just for carpools. We didn't have the required four occupants, but the chauffeur used the lanes anyway. Eventually he got off the major thoroughfares and took us through the suburbs to the exurbs—what one of my professors called hinterlurbia—passing larger and larger mansions.

"Oh, look, a road named after good ol' Stonewall Jackson," Ashley remarked dryly. "How nice."

As sure a sign that you'd crossed the Potomac as the carpool lanes: every other road, drive, and avenue was named after a Confederate general, the historical figures Mom railed against as treasonous losers.

"My dad always notes we're the only country in the world that honors its traitors," I said.

"A lot of these 'honors' don't date back to 1865," Ashley said. "They're much more recent, and they seem focused on a different message than celebrating service."

We turned onto an old country road that wound through a forest. Around the last bend, I got my first glimpse of my new boss's magnificent residence. I was the daughter of a sitting U.S. senator; I'd grown up in Manhattan and Washington, DC, and summered on an old estate—a run-down one, admittedly, but an estate, nonetheless. I had lived a charmed life—but nothing in it prepared me for this.

The manicured property was enormous (later I would learn it covered forty acres) and sat on a bluff overlooking the Potomac River. We slowed as we went past a swimming pool, a tennis court, a greenhouse, hedges and water fountains and gardens, the most beautiful I'd ever seen. At the edge of the bluff stood a Colonial Revival manor house, all twenty-five rooms of it, and Danielle was waiting in its doorway.

Ashley went into the house while I took in the view. Beyond the Potomac River stood a proliferation of trees and wildflowers of such bright colors—orange and yellow and red threaded through all the green—it was like a van Gogh painting come to life.

"It's...breathtaking," I said.

"The McKee-Beshers Wildlife Management Area. Deer, wild turkey, more than two hundred kinds of songbirds," Danielle said. "There's an amazing sunflower bloom every July in that field. Thousands of giant orange flowers standing like sentries! Come, let's get a drink!"

The interior was equally stunning. Twelve-foot-high ceilings, heart-pine floors, intricate moldings, fireplaces with carved mantels. There was a majesty to it that resembled nothing so much as the White House, although the Lyons' estate had newer, more luxurious furniture and was better kept.

We walked into the living room, which looked like a set from *Masterpiece Theatre*, with Papa Lyon enthroned in a leather armchair in front of a fireplace. He was holding a glass of brandy. Ivan, the third of the Lyon children, sat at the end of a long sofa next to Harry; he was gangly and blond and gummy and exuded discomfort in his own bones. Harry stood when we came in.

"Lucy, hello," he said. Then he nodded to Ashley.

A maid in a full black-dress-and-white-apron uniform offered us a drink. Ashley eased down onto an eggshell love seat and motioned for me to sit next to her. Danielle stood near the window. The glow from the setting sun lit her face beautifully.

"You're quite mad," Max was telling Ivan.

We had obviously walked in on an argument. "What is it now?" Danielle asked with an eye-roll.

"Ivan believes it is the *Sentinel*'s responsibility to educate our American customers as to what brutes they are," Harry said, enunciating every syllable in his oh-so-posh accent. He winked at me as if I were in on the family joke. "What brutes *you* are," he said, gesturing to Ashley and me.

"Quite," said Max. "Tell them, Ivan."

"Well, it's just these—well, let me ask our guests. Are either of you aware of why the Oklahoma Panhandle exists?"

I knew—Mom and Dad had filled us in on the less What So Proudly We Hail aspects of our nation's history, the events that our schools didn't cover—but I instinctively shrugged. I had no idea where Ivan was going with this.

"See there?" Ivan said to his father. "Americans know so little about their own history. One would think it was purposeful."

"You're awfully pompous for someone who needed Daddy's help to get into the University of *Bath*," Danielle said archly.

Ivan shot his sister a dagger of a look, then continued. "This is more an observation about the overall narcolepsy in the American educational establishment. The Missouri Compromise said no slavery above the thirty-sixth and a half parallel, so when Texas, which had some territory above that boundary, was admitted to the union, it simply gave up that slice so that Texans could continue to brutalize Negroes. Eventually Oklahoma took the land."

"He isn't wrong," Ashley said. "We don't learn these things in school. We do use the term *black* or *Afro-American* now, though, Ivan."

"Oops, sorry," he said.

"One wonders how British colonization is taught in *your* schools," I said. "The Bengal famine, the Mau Mau uprising, your concentration camps during the Second Boer War—"[8]

"Well, that's bollocks, they needed to be civilized!" Max said. "You think those Hottentots—"

"Dad-*dy*!" Danielle interrupted, forcing the sun to set momentarily on that small corner of the British Empire. "Let Ashley and Lucy settle in and have a drink."

"Well, that's fine," her father said. "I need to make a phone call before we sup anyway." He stood and strode from the room.

Danielle turned to us. "You simply must try our new cocktail." She motioned to another woman sporting a maid's uniform. She was young and white with chestnut hair and violet eyes, and she brought our drinks in champagne glasses. Mine tasted of cucumber and grapefruit and a potent punch-you-in-the-face liquor—I think tequila, though I'm no expert on these things. After I took a sip, I found *les enfants* Lyon—Harry, Danielle, Ivan—waiting

---

8   Credit to my thesis adviser at Yale, Sterling Professor of History Gabriella Wright, author of *The Empire Has No Clothes: Dominion, Decolonization, and Death in the Post-Gandhi World.*

for my verdict. I was suddenly aware of being sweaty in my wrinkled work clothes, my hair a wreck from raking my fingers through it nervously during my phone fight with Mimi Spanjian. And the Lyons were sleek, not just in their looks but in how they moved, the way they sat together, like one of those photos of the royal family you'd see in *Life*.

Harry said, "Do you love it?" I almost said, *Yes, I love everything, this house and the gardens and, oh, that view of the river and the park across the river, and all of you,* but then I realized, *Oh, goodness, he means the drink in my hand.*

"I've never had anything so delicious," I said, though, truth be told, it was much stronger than I was used to.

"Bertie will be so pleased to hear it!" Danielle said. "It's his very own concoction. He made it up in honor of my trip next week to Mexico." She pronounced this "*Meh*-hee-koh." "You can get it nowhere else in the world except here!"

At my confused look, Ivan said, "Bertie is our little brother." His expression was difficult to decipher. He pursed his lips. A sudden tension filled the room.

"I didn't know you had a little brother," I said.

"*Half* brother," Danielle said, almost apologetically. "But we love him like a full one!"

"We don't talk about Bertie outside our home," Harry said. "We protect him from all that."

From all what, exactly?

A bell rang, and we all turned toward the dining room. A tall, lanky teenager in a double-breasted blue blazer and baggy khakis held the bell in his hand. He rang the bell a second time, and Harry put his fingertips to his temple, wincing. The boy smiled and rang again.

"Bertie, flirty, down and dirty!" exclaimed Ivan. "The boy who put the turd in *bastard*!"

Bertie's expression changed, became strange, flat, like he'd slid a mask over his face to hide the hurt. Danielle hugged him protectively, even though he was as tall as she was. He was in that awful, gawky part of adolescence when controlling one's arms and legs and basic impulses was an achievement in itself. Beyond that, he didn't really resemble his siblings; he had a round, pancake-like face. I assumed there was a story there, given that he had a different mother. Come to think of it, I didn't know anything about the mom of the other Lyon children either. Anyway, I felt bad for Bertie. Poor kid, stuck there among these perfectly coiffed and wardrobed siblings.

"Be kind to our sweet cherub," Danielle told Ivan as Harry playfully smacked Bertie on the rump. "He has to go take his insulin shot! Poor baby!" She kissed him on the cheek. Bertie tried to muster a grin, but it looked weird, like an alien creature wearing a human suit trying to smile for the first time.

I was seated between Bertie and Ivan. They were talking about Jodie Foster in *Freaky Friday*, which Ivan had taken Bertie to see the previous weekend. Ivan found Jodie Foster charming. Bertie called her a fox. It was good to hear young Bertie attempt conversation and succeed reasonably well; it made me happy. I thought about saying that I'd only seen Foster in *Taxi Driver*—she'd played Iris, a juvenile prostitute—but I decided to keep it to myself, since Bertie seemed too young for that movie and its twisted themes.

At the head of the table, Max was engaged in a tête-à-tête with Ashley. Harry and Danielle were chatting as though it weren't at all strange for their father to be talking so intimately at the table with a woman who worked for him. The maids in their uniforms kept filling our wineglasses, bringing out more dishes of food.

Ashley caught me staring. She gestured my way. "It's her story," she told Max. "Let's bring her in on it!"

"It's a ridiculous hypothetical," Max said.

"What is?" I asked.

"We were debating what would happen if your serial murderer or the Forty-Four-Caliber Killer up in New York was a woman," Ashley said with a drunken grin. "More broadly, what if women were responsible for ninety-nine percent of the murders in the U.S.? What if *we* were doing the murders, the rapes, the child molestations, the assaults?"

"National panic," I said. "Congressional hearings, a bipartisan White House blue-ribbon commission to get to the bottom of what is wrong with women."

"The WWW committee!" exclaimed Ashley.

"W-cubed!" suggested Danielle.

"There'd be NIH studies," I added. "Pentagon camps for feminist extremists."

"Ooh, I know," Danielle said. "Mandatory testosterone injections to counteract the biological evil."

Ashley nodded. "Absolutely."

"Curfews for women after dark," I went on. "Bans on women purchasing firearms; reeducation camps for girls and women, free self-defense classes for boys and men."

"This is a blarney conversation about chickens attacking fox houses," Max said dismissively.

Ashley inclined her head Max's way. "He brought up the prospect of the serial murderer being a woman. Now he wants to mock the obvious consequences of that angle."

"For love of the queen!" Max said. "It was just a dinner-table jaw, that's all."

Harry turned his bright blue eyes my way. "Newsstand sales already doubled thanks to 'Lucy Marder Scoops.' I can only imagine the jump if the killer was a woman."

"We wouldn't be able to fell forests for paper fast enough!" Danielle said.

I didn't know how to take any of this. Of course I was excited that this powerful family was gushing about me and that I was in their luxurious mansion. But I couldn't help imagining what Mom and Dad would think about all this jocularity and greed built on a foundation of murders. I smiled demurely and rode it out as I'd done hundreds of times at Yale when I didn't know the appropriate reaction.

"Did you see that pompous twit from the *Post* on *Washington Week in Review*?" asked Ivan.

Bertie leaned close to me. "What's he talking about?"

"Public television," I whispered. "Public-affairs show."

"What did that Washington plonker have to say?" Max asked.

"Same piffle we get from the snoots at the Beeb," said Ivan. "All the same rubbish, wankers who attack checkbook journalism or who believe the royals when they publicly deny the exclusives in our paper that they themselves are privately giving us. I mean, you know this better than I do, Father, how immensely full of it they are!" Ivan clearly had a desperate thirst for his father's approval, though his father seldom even looked at him.

"What did the guy say?" I asked him.

"Oh, bollocks, that we're alleging a serial murderer based on very little, sending the city into a panic."

Danielle's eyebrows lifted. "Surely not a *panic*?"

Ashley named the local universities that had requested police patrols, ticking them off on her fingers: Georgetown, George Washington, American, Catholic, George Mason. "Town meetings called throughout Northern Virginia. Especially in Manassas, where both vics lived. Local TV is going bananas."

Max was exultant. "Impact, my loves, impact! The presenters on the telly ought to be paying us!"

Impact, my loves, impact! Anxiety exploded inside me; the Furies in my brain raged. Had I made a terrible mistake? Or even a tiny mistake? It could just be a coincidence that two women from the same town had been killed the same way. It could even be that whoever killed Jeannie McBean knew the details of the Janice Davenport murder and copied it. I could be panicking the populace for no good reason.

From across the table, Harry was watching me with a gentle smile. "You're doing exactly what we want you to do," he murmured as if he'd heard my inner terror and wanted to alleviate it. "You're posing the right questions and reporting what we want reported the way we want it reported. And now everyone is reporting what you did first."

"Everyone except the *Post* and the *Star*," Max said with satisfaction. "What are they holding out for? A third victim? I cannot help wondering whether there is any other industry in this country that presumes so completely to give the customer what he does not want."

"Well," I said, "in their defense, those papers have different, more traditionally American, journalism standards."

"Standards that allow editors to steal a woman reporter's scoop and hand it to an older man?" Danielle said.

"Standards that mean they hesitate to report the most exciting stories, the ones people actually want to read?" Max said. "Standards that require them to bore their readers? To talk down to them? Fear and rage drives news consumers. Why pretend otherwise?"

Though I wasn't sober—that cocktail plus the waitstaff's

generous wine refills were doing their work—I was wise enough to hold my tongue. Hours before, I'd been praising him for taking on the FDA, for embracing advocacy journalism. It had landed me a spot at this table. I liked the table. But I hated what he was saying. I told myself to listen, to learn, to consider his words, as any good journalist would do. I was young; did I truly know what drove Ben Bradlee at the *Post*?

"We have to report the important news," Max said. "That's our basic responsibility. But we're not frightened to entertain as well. I'm rather sick of snobs who say the *Sentinel* is a bad paper, snobs who read the dullest papers. If they read them at all. Who are they to impose their rarefied taste on everybody else in the community? To hell with them."

After Max delivered this monologue, Harry raised his glass. "Hear, hear," he said. Ivan followed his lead. Bertie, ignoring his special meal, which looked rather unappetizing, glanced around the table, confused, trying to make sense of it all. Danielle beamed with pride, and Ashley, her eyes locked on Max's, appeared, frankly, aroused. Max gave her a knowing smile before he turned to me.

"What does your father think about your joining our merry band of pirates?" he asked. Which was funny, since one of my father's pet peeves was the degree to which folks romanticized pirates, who, by all historical accounts, were thieving, murderous rapists.

"He's wary of the news media in all its forms," I said, and it was true, Dad was. He despised most reporters, didn't trust a one of them except for me, though he was savvy enough to be kind to them.

"Smart man," Harry said.

Max settled back in his chair at the head of the table. "There is an anger in the country, one that I'm not certain any American politician, or British or Australian ones, for that matter, entirely comprehends," Max said. "An anger that needs channeling, a rage that needs to be sated. With enemies. They *need* enemies. They *have* enemies! America just lost another war, for God's sake! The Arabs are screwing the white world into an energy crisis. There are junkies and race riots in the streets and radical bra-burning feminists who quite literally want to destroy the very concept of family. And what is the feckless peanut farmer doing? Pushing people to carpool! Handing over the Panama Canal! Weak! Weak! Weak!"

"And don't forget that poor family Ashley writes about so brilliantly," added thirsty Ivan. "Maybe they don't know it in Washington, but out there in the rest of the country, people know something is wrong when the government won't let you give your babies the medicine you want to give them." Ashley was nodding, eager for her share of praise.

Max thumped his fist on the table. The glasses rattled. "Perfect example. We should be pushing that story harder. Everyone in the country should know their story and this magical cure the government is keeping from them!"

"I have a tip," Ashley said, "that DC Social Services is considering seizing custody of Caleb because his parents are refusing to let him have chemotherapy. Could be huge."

At first, I hadn't seen anything in Ashley's reporting that changed my impression of laetrile, or vitamin B_{17}, as a cancer treatment—it always seemed pure quackery. But Ashley's and Max's passion for the story now had me reconsidering. I was a daughter of American institutions, so maybe I was too trusting of the government and authority. Watergate, the Warren Commission report, the Gulf of Tonkin, the *Pentagon Papers*...how much more evidence did I need that the establishment, even the medical establishment, wasn't inherently trustworthy?

"DC Social Services is a monstrosity!" Max said, his fist thumping the table again. "And this serial murderer running around loose that our girl here *will identify and expose*—it's all a part of the same story." *Thump, thump.* "The government's *failure to protect its people.*"

"Hear, hear!" exclaimed Ivan.

"This is going to be so great," Danielle said. "And before you know it, the *really* big story will start—the race for the White House!"

"Exactly!" said Max, smiling and pointing at his favorite child. "Yesssss!"

"I hear Kennedy's going to challenge Carter, but the real race will be on the Republican side," Harry said. "They're going to win, whoever it is."

"Well, I'm sure she knows all of them, no?" said Ivan, pointing at me. "Connally, Ford, Bush, Reagan—"

"Lucy's political connections will definitely come in handy when she hits the campaign trail," Danielle said.

I did have those connections—at least, I had met most of the potential candidates—but it was weird how Danielle and Ivan talked about me as if I weren't in the room.

"We should bring Lucy with us to that weekend Bill Brock just invited us to," Harry said, referring to the newly elected chair of the Republican National Committee. "What's the place called?"

"Trinity Island," said Danielle.

She meant Pitchfork Island, which was what most Americans called it. There'd been a recent push to rebrand the resort locale, which was shaped like an *E* tilted to the left and had been called Pitchfork Island since the Civil War. A group of born-again evangelicals petitioned the Georgia legislature and the governor at the time, Jimmy Carter, for a less satanic sobriquet. They'd reached back and come up with one from the 1700s, and the Democratic presidential aspirant was only too happy to oblige and show off his Christian bona fides.

"What's that?" asked Bertie. "Trinity Island?"

"An island off the coast of Georgia. All the leaders of the Republican Party are gathering there to talk about the future of the party," Danielle told him. "We're going in August. There will be lots of fun things for us to do."

"And a plum assignment for any young political reporter!" said Ivan, drawing side-eyes from every adult at the table. Bertie seemed focused on trying to consume his stewed spinach.

"Absolutely." Max reached over and patted Ashley's hand reassuringly. "Ashley and Lucy are our bright new stars!"

His hand lingered over Ashley's a moment too long. Ashley gazed into his eyes and gave him a slow smile as if she were agreeing to something, a look I really didn't want to acknowledge. Max Lyon was too powerful, too old for her, too much her boss. There was also the fact that he was married, although the details on that were fuzzy. The *Wall Street Journal* had made a vague reference to Mrs. Elizabeth Lyon "recuperating" back in the UK, but there was no further explanation, and no one in the office had mentioned her. I figured it was best not to bring her up, as it might open a door that would release demons.

I wondered when I could leave and how I was going to get home. The limousine that had brought us here—would it ferry me back if Ashley wanted to stay? Should I try to keep Ashley from staying? And was there a graceful way to excuse myself? My eyes darted away from Max and over to the others. I was hoping I might see signs of exhaustion or boredom on their faces, but when I looked at Harry, he was watching me with smoldering eyes. I thought, *What kind of world have I gotten myself into here?*

CHAPTER FIVE

IKE

Butte, Montana

April 1977

Big boss man, can't you hear me when I call?...
You know you ain't so big; you're just tall, that's all

—Elvis Presley, "Big Boss Man"

I SAT IN the corner of the Dead Canary playing the drinking game Cheers to the Governor, and I was playing it with a governor.

Former governor Lucious "Lucky" Strong, to be specific, the boisterous, charismatic, populist onetime leader of neighboring Idaho. Lucky was even taller than me, with shoulders as broad as the Bitterroot Range, and he was wearing his trademark shin-length suede coat, which hid much of his middle-aged spread. He was an imposing figure. A cattle rancher who'd inherited half the private land in his state, Lucky was a lover of ladies and drink and tall tales. He'd served two terms as governor, had somehow tripled his net worth while in office, and was always looking for action. He was good company whenever he came by.

It was late on a Saturday in the spring, and Evel had healed from the injuries he'd gotten from the shark-jump attempt—a broken forearm and collarbone and a concussion. After being discharged from the hospital in Chicago, he returned to his home at the Butte Country Club, and he'd been generally taking it easy, riding-wise. Other than Huckleberry, no one on the pit crew had spoken to him. No one I knew of, anyway. We were all just waiting to hear what was next. Evel had other stuff going on; he'd flown down to Tampa to do some commentary with Frank Gifford for the Chitwood Auto Thrill Show at Golden Gate Speedway, and he'd taped a guest appearance on *The Bionic Woman*. He was treading water at *Battle of the Network Stars*–level celebrity, getting by, survivin', not thrivin'. The great unspoken topic was *Viva Knievel!*, which Hollywood insiders were rumored to be saying was going to be a pretty big turkey.

I'd met Lucky Strong through Evel; the former politician was one of his biggest local boosters. Lucky had invited Evel to jump the Snake River in Idaho a few years before (after it became clear that Evel's plan to jump the Grand Canyon was suicidal), and he'd given him a few hefty checks to return to the scene of that fiasco for various private events with fat cats who had businesses in the area—mining and tourism and real estate and the like. Donor maintenance, Lucky called it. His term-limited gubernatorial reign had recently ended, and now he seemed a bit restless and downright hungry for relevance.

Anyhow, that night Lucky explained to me and three of his aides that he'd learned Cheers to the Governor from British soldiers during World War II. The game was partly what inspired him to run for governor—that's what he claimed, anyway. With Lucky, you never knew.

The rules: Everyone is given a full beer, and we proceed around a circle counting to twenty-one, except seven and fourteen are swapped. The person who ends up being twenty-one is appointed governor and says, "Cheers to the governor," and everyone drinks. Then the governor makes up a new rule, like "All even numbers will be replaced by the words *dog crap*," or whatever. If you mess up at any time in the counting process, you drink. If this sounds to you like a game that prompts confusion and inebriation, you're correct.

Twenty-one landed on me, so I was the first governor. I ruled: "For any multiple of five, instead of the number, you say, 'I'm mad as hell and I'm not going to take this anymore.'"

Lucky winked. "Loved that movie."

"Wait, what?" asked Daisy. She was one of the governor's former aides. Three of them often played cards with us, and since Lucky was no longer in office, I assumed he paid them out of his own pocket—maybe just to keep him company. They were all young, all lovely. Daisy sat beneath a mounted white-tailed deer sporting a creepy shocked expression.

"It's a line from *Network*," said Elena, Lucky's former scheduler. She wore the Farrah Fawcett Majors hairstyle that everyone was wearing that summer, and a hank of feathered blond locks kept falling over one eye.

"So, one, two, three, four, 'I'm-mad-as-hell-and-I'm-not-going-to-take-this-anymore,' six, seven, eight," I said.

"You mean 'six, fourteen, eight,'" corrected Elena. "Don't forget, seven and fourteen are swapped."

I pointed at her—*Exactly right*—and took a big swig of Budweiser.

"Good man," said Lucky.

An hour into the game, we were all soused, which was the point of it all. Cheers to the Governor has no natural conclusion; you keep adding rules and playing until everyone wanders off or dies of alcohol poisoning.

Soon enough, Lucky was talking about a UFO sighting near Soda Springs.

"Two different police officers, fifteen miles apart, independently confirmed it," he said. "Officers Abrams and Christianson. Good men."

For whatever reason, the U.S. had seen an explosion in UFO sightings, and not just in the supermarket tabloids—everywhere. I'll be honest, I still didn't know what to make of all the folks who saw these things. They were *all* lying? *All* doing it to get attention—even though the attention was largely negative? Wasn't it more likely that they'd seen something and we all were just not being told the truth?

I mean, to state the obvious, governments lie. They lie about matters big and small, about events trifling and seismic. They lie about war; they lie about peace. They lie about death; they lie about taxes. They lie to insulate the public from ugly truths; they lie to shelter themselves from consequences; they lie to make sure they can still get good tables at restaurants. So why wouldn't they lie about things flying around that they couldn't identify, whether those things came from the Soviet Union or Alpha Centauri? I downed the beer and poured another, contemplated switching to something harder.

"What did it look like?" I asked. "The UFO?"

"Welllll," Lucky drawled. "I think they said it was shaped like an oval and maybe was as big as three or four police cars."

"Green and white, wasn't it?" Daisy said.

"And it made a whistling sound," Elena reminded her.

"They said it hovered at treetop level for three minutes, then zoomed north," Lucky said.

The third aide, Jess, spoke up for the first time. "That's why all the Yo-Yos are currently parked around Sheep Mountain." Her voice was low and clear, and you had to lean in to hear her. She had long, thick black hair and heavily lined eyes and a dark vibe in general, which I liked.

"Yo-Yos?" I asked.

It was the name of the local UFO cult, Lucky explained. "Thirty years ago, a pilot outta Bozeman flying a Lockheed Lightning claimed he saw a UFO shaped like a yo-yo. Got caught in his propwash over the mountains of western Montana, he said, and the damn thing came apart like a clamshell."

"Wait a sec," I said. "There's a UFO cult camped near here?"

"Sure," said Lucky. "Between Idaho and Montana and Wyoming, there's gotta be like fifty camps or some such."

"Fifty UFO cults?" I asked.

"No, not just UFOs," he said.

"We got everything in these mountains," dark-vibe Jess said. "Vietnam veterans. Survivalists. A self-declared messiah or two—"

"The Reverend Russell!" announced Daisy. "The Russell cult keeps getting bigger and bigger. I see 'em in town sometimes. Freaks. Zealots. Russell thinks *cancer* is an alien species."

"Don't forget the Bigfoot seekers!" Lucky boomed. "Hunting for a goblin-beast, half human, half devil, stalking fishermen on the Salmon River."

I set my Budweiser down and searched their faces, sure they were pulling my leg. But it looked to me like they weren't. "Where do these stories come from?" I asked incredulously.

"The goblin-beast came from Teddy Roosevelt," Elena said. "In one of his books."

I felt embarrassed. I had thought so little of my drinking companions, even the mention of TR was a surprise. I was a snob. Raised as such, I guess. I worked to hide it, but every now and again, it reared its head. When it did, I felt ashamed.

Elena caught my abashed expression. "What?" she said.

I lifted my glass to her. "Thank you for telling me the Roosevelt story is all."

I got lost in drunkenness, and before I knew it the three aides were talking about a tavern outside Wolf Creek: Black Jack's, a freight car taken off its wheels and set on one side of the bridge crossing the Little Prickly Pear. A fly-fishing legend from Missoula, a reporter with some bad gambling debts, had been beaten to death there, or so lore had it. Elena claimed that he'd actually been killed in Chicago. The mention of journalism and Elena's insistence on correcting the record made me think of Lucy. I smiled. Briefly.

Lucky leaned close and whispered, "Is Bob still mad at you?"

No one who knew Knievel back in the day called him Evel. Years before, then petty thief Bob Knievel spent a night in the Butte pokey in a cell adjacent to William "Awful" Knofel, a vicious repeat offender. A cop quipped, "Look at this, we've got an Awful Knofel and now we've got an Evil Knievel." Bob liked it. He'd tweaked the spelling, and he was off and running with his showbiz name. But to old friends like Lucky, he was still Bob.

So *was* Bob/Evel still mad at me? The question sometimes woke me up in the middle of the night. I loved being out here, working for this circus. Needed his approval, I guess because I'd idolized him so much when I was a kid.

"Unclear," I told Lucky. "Haven't seen the boss since the crash."

"I heard he was bitter about Chicago," Lucky said.

I'm sure. And by now we'd heard that the ratings were disappointing and that a critic for the *Washington Post* had called *Evel Knievel's Death Defiers* the worst TV program ever. Like, *ever.*

At a bedside press conference, Knievel had explained that he'd known he was going to crash but had to test the jump anyway in a sort of act of martyrdom. "I worried when I saw it all squeezed together that it wasn't going to work," he told reporters. "When we put it all together, the tank, the ramp, and the ski slope, it was too cramped." He blamed the accident on the hasty construction of the set. "I felt someone would have been killed. I figured there was going to be an accident, and the show couldn't be canceled, so I decided to take what was coming to me. I didn't want to see anyone else hurt. I made the practice run before an empty house so no parents or children would be hurt."

It was complete bullshit. Why would he say such a thing? It didn't make any sense. And what did it mean that he made up this nonsense and was so nonchalant about spreading it? "I really don't want him mad at me," I told Lucky.

"Know what you got to do?" Lucky said with a drunken grin. "This is going to sound wild, but you have to trust me."

"What is it?" I asked.

He leaned toward me dramatically. *"Tell him. He should run. For president."*

I just stared at Lucky for a long moment. I couldn't tell if he was fucking with me or not.

"Evel?" I said. "For *president?*" I reminded myself that Lucky and Evel were tight, that I shouldn't be too dismissive.

Lucky leaned back in his chair with his hands rested on top of his belly. That shit-eating grin was still on his face. "Sure, why not?" he asked. "This country needs a patriotic, shitkicking truth-teller!"

"But Evel..." What were the words? I couldn't even find the words to argue this. "As president...of the United States?" *Easy now, boy. Lucky thinks this is an actual idea.*

"Shit, I know it sounds nuts," Lucky said. "But we trotted it out as a stunt in '72, with buttons and everything. Set up a campaign HQ in downtown Butte. People loved it! Bob loved it. It was a good time. Now, did anybody think Bob had a chance in hell of making it to the Oval Office? Hell no. Did Bob want to be president? Too much work for his liking would be my guess. But people saying he *should* be president, the notion—well, it made people happy. Including Bob." He pointed his finger at me. "Bob might pretend he doesn't care about what anyone thinks, but in fact, that's all he cares about. That *Rolling Stone* story sunk him into a depression that lasted at least six months. And between the *Death Defiers* special failing and that turkey of a movie he shot about to bomb, he needs a pick-me-up. A presidential campaign could be just the thing. And the idea coming from you, a senator's son?" He let that speak for itself and resumed drinking.

I sat with my thoughts. Thing was, Evel had celebrity, wealth, and a big mouth, and all of that could probably get you to the White House. One of Dad's favorite movies was *A Face in the Crowd*, starring Andy Griffith as a folksy demagogue talking his way into the pinnacle of power. More recently, *The Candidate* featured Robert Redford as an inexperienced but charming senator's son who figures out the con too. Politics, man. I hated it.

Of course, as Dad often opined, the United States had devised a campaign system that required White House hopefuls to demonstrate abilities that had little relation to the job itself. Perhaps even the opposite. One needs to be tough to win the presidency and to be president, sure, but being president necessitates a moral compass that campaigns tend to demagnetize. I rubbed my temple. Evel as president? It was too awful to contemplate.

Still, it wouldn't be real. Just a con to get him some ego-stroking from the public and get me back in his favor.

"So, what, then?" I asked. "How do I even bring it up?"

"Tell him you'll help him!" Lucky said.

"You really want him to do this?"

"I think it would be a fucking gas," Lucky said. "Listen, son. You remind him you got that daddy back in Washington. Tell him you were talking to me and you think Bob has the makings to be the greatest president these United States have ever seen, or however you want to put it. I'm not saying you fund a campaign—just lift his spirits. Make him feel like a god again, and he will love you like the prodigal son come home."

"Don't you think that would be kind of...manipulative?" I asked.

"It's real-world strategy, son. I'm teaching you how to succeed with Bob."

It was deranged nonsense. Fucking bullshit. All of it. I now had to concoct a fucking-bullshit ridiculous way to distract Evel Knievel from seeking revenge against me—which was itself fucking bullshit—for an offense that was also my original sin of fucking bullshit. A matryoshka doll of fucking bullshit.

Lucky started regaling me with a wandering tale about a Republican event the previous year. An old buddy of his, Michigan governor George Romney, had invited him to a high-dollar fundraiser for the Detroit Institute of Arts, which had recently acquired a sixteenth-century masterpiece—donated by the state's powerful Ford family, descendants of the automaker. The painting was *Martha and Mary Magdalene* by Michelangelo Caravaggio. "A brilliant artist. Father of modern painting, they called him," Lucky said. "He told the story of Christ in a way folks could access it. Like, street-level."

I nodded. Wasn't sure where this train was headed. Rachel approached the table to see if we needed more drinks. She wore tight blue jeans frayed at the hems and cowboy boots that made a man a little crazy. No one wore boots like Rachel. I lifted my glass, suddenly thirsty, but she seemed interested in Lucky's story.

"Caravaggio was a brute," she said. I looked up. Second time tonight my snob alert had misread someone.

"Totally," Lucky agreed. "Insane. Brawling, attacking, throwing things at anyone who looked at him cross-eyed. In and out of prison. Killed a man. Fled town. A lot of his later paintings contained images of severed heads. Seriously disturbing. Masterpieces, though."

An amused smile crossed Rachel's face. "Lucky wants you to understand the need to separate the art from the artist," she explained to me, the dunce at the dance. She returned her attention to Lucky. "Does that apply to Henry Ford too, Governor? He had some curious allegiances to the guys you fought in France."

Lucky had been one of the 101st Airborne Screaming Eagles that helped recapture Carentan after D-Day.

"I mean, correct me if I'm wrong, sir," Rachel said, "but that Ford pickup in the lot is yours, right?"

Lucky scowled. "American jobs are more important than punishing a man who's been in a crypt for thirty years. My larger point—"

"Your larger point is that the work should stand apart from the man, whether the man is a homicidal painter like Caravaggio or a Nazi-loving industrialist like Ford," Rachel finished.

Lucky raised his glass. "Clever girl," he said.

They smiled at each other.

All around us were the sounds of a Montana dive-bar symphony—glasses clanking, darts thudding into their targets, pool balls clacking against each other. The former governor's aides were gossiping about whether Burt Reynolds was really dating his *Smokey and the Bandit* costar Sally Field. Nitty Gritty Dirt Band was blasting from the jukebox.

Finally, a thought cut through my Budweiser haze: "Wait, you were really serious about Evel, weren't you?"

Lucky smiled. "My point, Marine Sergeant Marder, is that

when it comes to great men—or, if you prefer, men who achieve great things—one must make allowances for their special brains. Genius and madness are often Siamese twins in the soul." He sang: "*This I tell you, brother, you can't have one without the other.*" He had a surprisingly lovely voice.

"Never heard Evel Knievel compared to Caravaggio," I said, turning to Rachel.

"White people around here love him," Rachel said as she replaced our empty pitcher with a full one. "They seem to see him as one of their own. And sure, he uses the system to get what he wants, but he's up-front about it. As up-front as a con artist can be."

It made sense. It was also how I'd viewed Evel before he turned on me. Maybe great men were all similar in that way. Dad said Nixon had sashayed into the White House with decades of respectability under his belt but turned out to be a garden-variety hoodlum with a shakedown artist as a vice president and a bunch of thieves and dirty tricksters chasing down every one of his paranoid fantasies. Evel might have hyped up the danger he faced, but that was showmanship, and that was also who he was—he didn't pretend to be anything different.

Rachel waited until Daisy and Elena got Lucky's attention then put her hand on my shoulder and whispered, "There's been an Evel sighting at Muzz and Stan's."

This was news. I didn't know Evel felt well enough to leave his house, let alone saunter into Muzz and Stan's Freeway Tavern.

"Word is, he's still obsessing about his Chicago crash," she said. "He can't talk about anything else. You know how he is about his failures."

My stomach sank. Evel was so unpredictable. He could have forgotten my name or he could be plotting his revenge against me. Maybe he'd grab a posse and beat the shit out of me. Or, worse, call a press conference and tell my secret to the world. "Was my name mentioned?"

"He was cursing you to Muzz," Rachel said. "He said he wants blood. Don't know if he's just talking or what—you know Evel. But you should be careful, Ike. You need to fix this."

CHAPTER SIX

LUCY

McLean, Virginia

June 1977

THE MORNING AFTER the dinner party at Chez Lyon, I woke up alone in a guest room on the family estate, my mouth as dry as Arizona. I had a vicious hangover, and now someone was cruelly pounding on the door. "Lucy, you in there?" came Ashley's voice.

I put the pillow over my head and groaned. "I'm not here."

Ashley came in anyway. She pulled the shades up, filling the room with harsh sunlight. She leaned over me and threw off the covers. She smelled like sex.[1]

"The car's ready to take us back to the city," she said. "We leave in five."

"What time is it?"

"Six oh six, which means you're down to four minutes."

I sat up and looked around for my skirt. It was folded on a wooden chair, a *Thank Jesus* reminder I'd been sober enough to end my night the way I should have—alone. "Give me a minute to dress. I'll be right out."

I stood, reeling a bit from the booze. Put on my clothes from the

---

1   I inherited my father's acute sense of smell, which, as he notes, is more accurately described as a curse.

previous night and slowly opened my door. Bertie was standing right there, wearing pajamas and carrying a bucket of toiletries. He mumbled a few indecipherable words and scrambled away like a crab.

The limousine was waiting in the same spot it had left us in, as if it'd never moved. Last night's chauffeur got out to open the door for me. He was clean-shaven and wearing a fresh shirt, which only made me yearn for a shower. I slid into the back seat next to Ashley. She was reading the *Sentinel* and only barely glanced up at me.

The chauffeur started the limo. "Mind if we listen to news?" he asked. It was a funny question, given that Ashley and I were journalists, but who knows what kind of women he was used to driving home in the early mornings from the Lyon manse.

I told him I loved listening to the news. What I didn't say: Maybe the news din would drown out any possibility of conversation with Ashley about Max Lyon or where she'd slept—or done whatever the hell she'd done—last night.

The chauffeur turned on the radio, and a news anchor's voice filled the car: "In Miami–Dade County, Florida, a crowd of roughly two thousand homosexual activists protested Anita Bryant and the instrumental role the singer played in overturning an ordinance protecting homosexuals from employment and housing discrimination. Eight of the protesters were taken into custody. A spokesman for Anita Bryant said that long before she became active in the—"

I stopped listening. I'd met Anita Bryant at Super Bowl V in 1971, where she'd sung "The Battle Hymn of the Republic," and again at LBJ's funeral a couple years later, where she sang it again. She seemed nice enough, but I couldn't understand why anyone cared what she thought about, well, anything, especially matters of the heart. I'd never really understood why anyone thought musical or athletic or acting gifts conferred some wisdom when it came to politics. Public service required a particular skill set, and the ability to hit a high C was not among them.

I slumped back on the Corinthian leather. Outside the window, a doe stood wide-eyed among the birch trees lining the edge of the Lyon property. The limo drove slowly along the dirt path that turned into a country road. When the car picked up speed, my thoughts drifted to Harry.

Last night, after everyone went to bed, he'd asked if I wanted to take a moonlit tour of the property. It was country-dark, the kind I was unused to, having grown up in the glow of two cities. We followed fireflies down to the dock, where we listened to the Potomac coursing beneath us. He reached over and held my hand. When I thought I couldn't stand it any longer, he leaned down and kissed me as if it were a dare. The kiss was soft and sweet and made me want more. But he pulled away and said, "It's getting late. Let me walk you back to the house." He left me at the guest room's door, confused. We were both single. Harry wasn't even my boss. My direct supervisor was Ollie, the managing editor, and Max was everyone's boss. I didn't know exactly what Harry wanted from me, but I loved the way I felt when I was with him, and I hadn't wanted the night to end. It was a very different feeling from being with Skylar, who always seemed to be looking past me for people who were better connected and more powerful and thus more deserving of his attention.

And yet I knew it might be odd at work. How would that play out? Ashley and I needed to be discreet.

"Can we stop for some coffee?" Ashley asked the driver. "Please?"

"Absolutely," he said.

Outside the car window, vistas of forests and mansions had

given way to strip malls and gas stations. The driver swerved into a shopping center with a Chinese restaurant, a framing store, a dry cleaner. We parked in front of a café called the Daily Grind. The driver turned in his seat. "How do you want your coffee?" he asked. "It will be my pleasure to get it."

"Black," I said. Every reporter I ever knew took his or her coffee black, a sign you were as tough as your stories. I drank my whiskey neat and my coffee black; no girlie drinks for me, thank you.

"Me too. Biggest cup they've got," Ashley added.

The chauffeur went into the café. The news on the radio blared on, something about gas and oil producers lobbying against President Carter's energy proposal. I was distracted by well-dressed workers in business attire gathering in a parking lot next to a giant Sears. Cars pulled up near the workers and idled. The workers shouted at drivers, and some climbed into the passenger seats of these cars, which then drove off.

"What are they doing?" I said.

Ashley glanced up from her newspaper. "The slugs?"

"Umm, *what*?"

She laughed at the expression on my face. "Not garden slugs, gross. *Slugs* like the fake coins you use to fool a tollbooth. That's the name for commuters who link up with drivers looking for three more people to meet the carpool-lane requirement."

"I've never heard of them."

She waved it off like it was old news. Years ago, she said, when she worked for the *Post* Metro section she'd written about slugs. "After Nixon signed legislation to fund ridesharing—when was that? In '73, '74?—they allowed carpools of four or more to use the special designated lanes that actually moved while everyone else was stuck in bumper-to-bumper."

It sounded complicated. And annoying. I couldn't imagine

beginning every workday by bumming a ride from someone. "But how do they meet the right driver going to the right place?"

Ashley leaned over the seat and turned off the radio. "Roll down your window and listen."

From the crowd, we could hear drivers shouting different destinations: "Pentagon!" "State!" Then a woman about my age, dressed in a pantsuit, held up her hand and yelled, "I'm going to the Hill!" She climbed into the back seat of a brown sedan. A man was in the driver's seat, another in the front passenger. They sped off.

"That woman just got in that car with guys she doesn't know?"

Ashley lifted a shoulder lazily. "What's there to know? She'll get to work quicker. Everyone out here does it."

Less than an hour later, I was at my desk, feeling well caffeinated, though my mind couldn't settle. Was it the oddity of the whole night? Ashley and Max, me and Harry? Way too many libations, a night away from home? The long commute into the city?

I was lucky to live so close to the office. My daily commute from my apartment on the Hill to the office was, depending on traffic, fifteen minutes tops (sometimes it was faster to cross into Virginia and zoom to Georgetown that way). I couldn't imagine living out in the hinterlands where that Hill staffer got into the strange men's car. The freewheelin' hitchhikin' sixties notwithstanding, my whole life I'd been warned not to talk to strangers, much less get in their cars. But I knew myself too well; if I had a long commute every day, I'd inevitably be late unless I got into that carpool lane. After all, what's the worst that could happ—

Aha. That was what had been bothering me.

Quickly, I pulled up my notes on the *Journal Messenger*'s story about Janice Davenport's murder. Wife and *working* mother of two children. But where did she work? I turned on my computer and did another search of the *Journal Messenger* for her obituary. It said Janice Davenport was a beloved wife and mother mourned by her family, her friends, and her colleagues *at the Pentagon*, where she worked as a civilian administrator.

That was a long commute, from Manassas to the Pentagon. Had she been a slug? What about Jeannie McBean? The searches I did on her proved less productive. The family had made no statements to the press. The police were equally tight-lipped. The body hadn't been released for the funeral yet, so there wasn't even an obit.

I searched for Ashley's *Post* story on the slug phenomenon, but the newspaper archives were incomplete. I picked up my phone and called the research desk. "Can you get me everything that's been published about Janice Davenport and Jeannie McBean? I'm looking for biographical information too. Like previous addresses, car registrations, what they did for a living."

"Sure, Lucy," the researcher said. "No prob."

"Also, a map for slug stations. How far do they go into Northern Virginia? Is there a Pentagon stop?"

"I'm sorry, slug what?"

I explained the commuter-carpool lots. "I'm looking for a lot in Manassas and a drop-off point at the Pentagon."

"Okay, well, um, boy. I don't even know where to look."

Of course, I could have asked Ashley—after all, she'd written the *Post* story. But I hesitated. I didn't think she'd scoop me—would she? I considered us friends, not competitors, but I'd known her for only a few days. My gut told me to keep it to myself until I confirmed.

"I'll be right down," I told the researcher. "What floor are you again?"

In the research library, I pulled up a white-on-black microfiche copy of the *Post*'s slug station map that had been published alongside Ashley's story three years ago. It was smaller than its original size. The format was tough to read. Thankfully, the *Post*'s graphics wizards kept it simple. The eleven-mile stretch of Interstate 95 that ran concurrently with the Capital Beltway surrounding Washington, DC, contained the carpool lanes. There were no slug routes where the women had lived in Manassas, but there were seven in nearby Woodbridge and another four in Springfield. In DC, there was a drop-off at L'Enfant Plaza, several across the Fourteenth Street Bridge, and one at...*bingo*, the Pentagon.

I paged through my notebook for Janice Davenport's home number. The phone rang three times before her husband, William, answered. I told him who I was and said how sorry I was about what had happened to Janice. Out of all the things I'd done so far in my short career, intruding on a person's grief was the hardest. I told William I was working on a story; I wanted to find out who'd killed Janice and wondered if I could ask him a few questions.

"Well, I'm glad someone is trying," he said. "It's been three weeks, and I call Detective Sullivan every day. He says he'll call when he has something. Why doesn't he have anything? Now there's this other woman killed. Do you think police forgot about Janice?"

"I don't know, but I won't forget her," I said. "Sir, did your wife know Jeannie McBean?"

"Not that I'm aware of."

"So they never commuted together?"

"Goodness, no. I don't think so. Janice had to get up so early. It would have been so much safer for her to have a private carpool with neighbors. I always worried about that. But Janice didn't know anyone around here who had to leave as early as she did."

My hands shook from the adrenaline. "She carpooled to her job at the Pentagon, right?"

"Well, first she had to drive to the pickup location."

"Which lot was that, sir? The one in Woodbridge?"

"Oh, no, she went to the big one that everyone uses," he said. "We agreed more people at a busier location was safer, so she went to the Springfield pickup. The lot on Old Keene Mill Road."

I thanked him and promised I would call him back as soon as I had more information. After we hung up, I went over what I knew: Both victims were Manassas women, white, blond, thin, married. The main difference? The locations where their bodies were found—Rock Creek Park in DC for Jeannie McBean, the outskirts of Manassas National Battlefield Park for Janice Davenport. Neither area was close to a slug station.

Still, Janice had been a slug who'd made the long commute to the Pentagon. Did Jeannie even work? Was she a slug? If so, where was her drop-off?

The researcher brought out the press clippings I'd requested. There was nothing in these stories that I didn't already have. I glanced up at the clock. I had time to drive way the hell out to Virginia and hit the bricks in Jeannie's neighborhood, hoping someone might give me answers, and still make deadline—maybe.

Or I could bluff my hunch.

I picked up the phone and dialed Mimi Spanjian at MPD. As soon as she answered, I said, "Hello, Mimi. When were you going to start warning Virginia ridesharers that one of the drivers was a serial murderer?"

"*Motherfucker!*" she yelled, and I knew my hunch was right.

Spanjian asked if we could go off the record.

"Yeah, I'm not sure I need to do that," I said.

"Look, I don't know who's leaking to you, but if you overstate this, you could do real damage. This is not the Forty-Four-Caliber Killer! So stop!" She was attempting to appeal to what she thought were my better angels. But I was a journalist, not an angel. My job was to find out as much as I could about Janice's and Jeannie's killer or killers and share that with the public. I didn't automatically assume that whatever the police department wanted—usually to hide information from those they had sworn to serve and protect—was the right course of action.

"I'm not overstating anything," I said. "This is simply what I have. Both victims lived in the same far-flung small town in Virginia. Both worked in DC and commuted. And both were slugs. As John Adams said—possibly apocryphally—facts are stubborn things."

She exhaled dramatically. "Lucy, you could cause a panic," she said.

"Is that a yes?"

"Lucy—"

"Tell me this," I went on. "These women left their cars behind at slug stations, right? William Davenport says when Janice didn't come home, he worried she'd had a breakdown or something at the slug station on Old Keene Mill Road. That's where he found her car abandoned. Where did Jeannie leave her car?"

"The slug angle is just one of many being investigated. If you report that slugs are definitely being targeted by this killer, you will be reporting an assertion no one in law enforcement has established as fact."

"I've never written a word for publication that wasn't one hundred percent accurate," I said, which was true; I didn't count what had been written by the boss's son and inserted under my name. When she didn't answer, I asked again: "Which station for Jeannie's car?"

"Please convey to your bosses the panic you're about to cause," she said, understanding my meaning. "You know what? I'm going to have my boss call yours."

Oh, you silly, silly, woman, I thought.

MPD chief Maurice Cullinane did in fact call Max Lyon, Mighty Knight of Fleet Street, and, thinking Max had better angels, or any angels, or at least some acquaintance with seraphim (he didn't), the chief begged him not to run the story.

I'd gone to Max's office to give him a heads-up about the call when it arrived, right on cue. Max laughed at Chief Cullinane's request. "Thanks for the confirmation, mate," he said and hung up. To the newsroom he shouted, "Can you imagine the temerity of this bobby, thinking he can ask us to do him a favor as if we work for the powerful and not for the people?"

The newsroom erupted in applause. This time I didn't leave my copy to chance. I sat at my terminal and watched, aghast, as the white-on-black-screen words were edited and rewritten. Some editor was trying to sex it up, turning possibilities into assertions, speculations into facts. My reasonable lede: "Law enforcement is investigating the possibility that recent murders of two Virginia women were related to their participation in local rideshare efforts, two police sources tell the *Sentinel*."

The rewrite: "The serial killer murdering Virginia women may be finding his prey in the sketchy strip-mall parking lots where so-called slugs, often vulnerable women, hitch rides into the city, a repercussion of Jimmy Carter's energy crisis."

I stormed over to Ollie's messy desk, where Harry sat at his computer. Sensing me, he held up one long and elegant finger, and I remembered his hand in mine and then on me last night. He was staring at the screen, and I was momentarily relieved. I hadn't figured out how to deal with the two of us at work yet. Maybe he hadn't either.

Ollie did his normal thing around women, which was to look down, stand up, and back away. Weirdo.

"Lucy, hello. What's up?" Harry asked, talking into his keyboard.

"You're writing things that aren't true."

A faint smile lifted the corner of his mouth. "I said *may*."

"That *may* is doing a lot of work."

He stopped typing and swiveled his chair toward me. He looked right at me with those deep blue eyes. There was an emotion in them I couldn't quite read. I wondered if he too was struggling a little.

"Lucy," he said. "*Darling*. Your copy is as bland as the bangers and mash they fed us at Eton. If people want boring, they have the *Post* and the *Star*. We offer excitement."

Darling. My face got hot. "Excitement is good." Then I caught myself. "But it can't be *wrong*. If we declare this as a definite thing and not just something they're looking into, we could cause a panic!"

"You sound like the police chief," Harry said with a soft smile. "Are you not certain of your scoop?"

"I'm sure that the police are looking into it just as they're looking into a hundred other possible leads. I'm not sure that the victims were picked because they were slugs. I have more investigating to do."

"Well, the police chief bolloxed that up by calling Dad! He wants it to be tomorrow's wood."

"I need to make it accurate if that's going to happen," I told him.

He stood up and offered me the chair. "So rewrite it. But don't just retype what you had before."

I sat down and started typing: *An ongoing police investigation into the deaths of two Virginia women is now exploring whether the women's participation in ridesharing is relevant, law enforcement sources tell the* Sentinel.

Harry stood over my shoulder, laughing. "That's almost exactly what you wrote before."

"Because what I wrote was correct! It was good!"

"Fine, Lucy." He said this in the same tone he'd used on the moonlit dock. "I can live with it. As long as you put the word *slug* in the lede so we can blast it on the wood. The slug angle is compelling. It's sexy. It will sell papers."

"Okay," I said. "Where is this term *serial killer* coming from?"

"Ah! Glad you asked." He called for an assistant to bring him a file from his desk, which he then handed to me. Inside was a small research packet about FBI profiler Robert Ressler, who was using the term *serial homicides*, about an author who had used the term *serial murderer,* and a 1967 *Washington Star* review of a book using the term *serial killer.*

"*Serial killer,*" Harry said, tasting the word. "It sings. It's almost the start of a haiku. And you can't say I didn't do my research!"

"No," I said softly. "No, I can't."

We traded places. I continued watching his edits, eyeing every peck of the keyboard, this time standing over his shoulder and pushing back. I told Harry to remove his effort to tie the murder to President Carter's energy-conservation policies, and—like Woody Allen in *Annie Hall* pulling the real Marshall McLuhan out of nowhere to settle an argument about McLuhan's oeuvre—I called Ashley at her desk. Ashley confirmed that ridesharing was originally pushed by Nixon.

Harry suggested a compromise: He would add *Critics noted* to the beginning of the low-in-the-story sentence *Carter encourages policies for ridesharing, which in this case may have cost at least two women their lives.*

"It's irresponsible," I said.

"But factually accurate," said Ivan, who had joined us.

"What critics?" I asked.

"Harry and Dad and myself!" Ivan cried. "We're critics! And sure as eggs are eggs, we're noting it!"

"Take the win, darling," Harry said.

It didn't feel like much of a win when, an hour later, on my way out the door, I was handed a facsimile of tomorrow's paper. "Slug Killer," the wood blared. "Serial Killer Slaughters Carpooling Moms!" And "Lucy Marder Scoops!"

I would have killed Harry, but I had a promise to my mother to keep. I looked down at the plane ticket she'd put in my hand. Los Angeles was not the right destination. I had to figure out where the hell I was going.

After the mysterious incident in Lebanon that left Ike with a broken leg and two gunshot wounds in his back, he was airlifted to Germany. Final destination was Bethesda Naval Hospital in Maryland, where a medical team managed his longer-term recovery.

We visited him all the time, Mom and Dad and me, first all of us together, then later divvying up days so Ike wasn't alone at any moment from breakfast to when he dozed off around sunset. After about a month at Bethesda Naval, he asked us to take it down a notch. He was kind of crabby about his injuries and wouldn't answer questions about them. He soon designated one of the nurses to act as a go-between before allowing visits. After that, Mom would call the nurse every morning to find out if Ike would tolerate one of us popping by and, if so, when. We were all on pins and needles, worrying about his mental state more than his physical one.

I was thinking about those desperate days when something in the clutter of my inbox caught my eye. It was the manuscript I'd swiped from Mom that day at the Senate Dining Room, the one I thought Ike would like because it was about one of his childhood heroes, motorcycle daredevil Evel Knievel. It was written by one of Evel's former public relations guys, Sheldon "Shelly" Saltman, who handled the press for Evel's Snake Canyon jump. The manuscript, which had been submitted in January, according to the date on the first page, was called *Evel Knievel on Tour* and painted an ugly picture of the superstar using verbatim remarks documented in real time via a tape recorder Saltman had openly brandished while they prepped for what turned out to be the Snake River fiasco.

This was more than just rapscallion stuff. Saltman depicted an anti-Semitic Evel popping pills, abusing his wife, and more—"the most amazing, contradictory, hateful-likable, Jekyll-Hyde character of modern times." Saltman described his former client as "the most difficult man in the world to be around," someone who alienated sponsors and allies and who had "a girl in every port" because of deep insecurity, not machismo—"he doesn't want to be alone in a hotel room." Evel was quoted mocking the story of Christ: "I don't think that a guy could walk across the water; He probably had trouble swimming. And I don't believe a man and a jackass with a beautiful woman on it were in the desert for months and he never touched her."

The brute of Butte. My brother's childhood idol looked just awful.

And then my brain started to go *clickity-clack*.

You get to know nurses, doctors, and staff when you have a

loved one in the hospital. One of the nurses, Candy O'Leary, had once hinted that Ike had VIP visitors. When I asked her who, she pretended she had misspoken. She was especially loyal to him. Ike has a way of making people want to look out for him. After he disappeared, I pressured Candy to tell me the names of those so-called VIPs for Ike's sake. She confessed that it was actually just one: Mike Mansfield, the Senate majority leader, a Democrat and a Montanan who was close friends with Dad. Dad and Mansfield were from different parties, but they'd bonded over their leeriness about the war in Vietnam. Mansfield was a navy veteran who at fourteen had lied about his age to fight in World War I. Dad and Ike had visited Mansfield several times, purportedly so they could learn how to fly-fish—though the real reason was another attempt by Dad to bond with his son.

I'd held off on calling Mansfield directly, figuring he'd avoid me; I suspected Ike didn't want to be found. Mansfield wasn't easy to reach anyway. He'd retired from the Senate in 1976, and a few months ago he'd been confirmed as President Carter's ambassador to Japan; he was currently living in Tokyo. I glanced down at the ticket my mother had given me, then I put in a call to Tokyo. The secretary took down my number and told me to stay by the phone. About an hour later Ambassador Mansfield called me back.

Mansfield hadn't known Ike had gone AWOL, but he helped me sleuth. Yes, he had visited Ike in the hospital often, and Ike told him some of what had happened in Lebanon, though the ambassador wouldn't tell me. He said Ike had confided that he longed to escape the Beltway, and Mansfield, who thought the fresh air and big skies might do Ike some good, gave Ike the phone number of a fellow Montana Democrat, a former state representative from Butte, who was related to Knievel. Apparently, Knievel had seen Ike on *60 Minutes* and was impressed with his motorcycle heroics.

Ike had joked he would break his other leg for a chance to work with the daredevil.

Mansfield soon got wrapped up in the 1976 elections and the Carter transition, then his own confirmation hearings, so he'd had no idea Ike had vanished without telling anyone. He hadn't heard that my parents were distraught. Seemingly worried himself now, he quickly gave me the phone number of Pat Williams, who had run for the House in 1974 but lost in the Democratic primary. Williams was Evel's cousin. I sensed Mansfield wasn't telling me everything, but I felt like I'd made progress.

Of course, extracting this information was more complicated than I'm making it seem. Being a journalist is about convincing people to share facts with you that you desperately need but that they're reluctant to freely offer or may not even realize they have. Often that means being as friendly as a maître d', setting a table of understanding, acting as if you already know much of what they're about to tell you. Quite a bit of investigating can be bluffing—not lying, but pretending you know more than you do.

When I reached Williams in Butte, he acknowledged putting Ike in touch with his famous cousin. When had he last seen Ike? Just a few days before, Williams said. At a bar called the Dead Canary. He suspected Ike had a thing for the bartender. "Couldn't have been the bar he was attracted to. The place is a dump."

On Saturday night, I strolled into my brother's alleged hangout, a run-down, loud, dirty biker tavern in Butte. The glossy eyes of dead animals stared at me from their mounts to the wall. Behind the bar was a beautiful dark-haired bartender, maybe Native American? In any case, exactly the kind of woman Ike had a weakness for, and I knew I was in the right place. Three Native

American guys were joking with a broad, bearded white guy who looked like a bigger, hairier version of my brother. The man had a drink in his hand and another on the bar behind it. Then the man turned toward me and I saw it *was* Ike.

I'm not sure who moved first, but we crashed midway, him crushing the life out of me. He lifted me off my feet and spun me until I was dizzy. He had booze on his breath and a beard I'd never seen him wear. I tugged at it and smiled. "What's all *this* about?"

But he looked good, sun-kissed and strong with muscles on top of muscles. He was wearing his old devil-may-care expression I hadn't realized I'd missed. He staggered a bit on the way to a table. I told myself I wouldn't nag him about the drinking. He was a grown man. It was a Saturday night. When in Butte and all that.

We talked and talked. I told him about hopping to the *Sentinel*, about my hopes for going to Pitchfork Island for the GOP retreat to meet the candidates (he wondered whether Mom and Dad would be there, which was a good question), about how I was no longer dating Skylar, about Mom dragging Dad to see *The Tempest* at the Folger.

He saw through every leading question I lobbed his way and turned my questions into questions of his own. I had forgotten how cagey he could be. As children of a famous dad (and a mom well known by the right people), we had grown up steeped in discretion and distraction. If Ike didn't want you to know a thing, you would never know it. When he was a boy, he had hidden a motorcycle he'd discovered in the trash heap we referred to as our summer estate *for years*. Ike was an expert. I reminded myself that so was I.

When my questions got too tough, he ran to the restroom. I could wait him out. He had to face me eventually. I sipped my beer and listened to the band play AC/DC. I wasn't leaving until I figured out what the hell he was hiding.

A biker sidled up to me and leered drunkenly, as if I were a plump woodchuck and he a bird of prey. It was hardly the first time I'd been annoyed by a drunk guy—the men in New Haven and Georgetown bars were as persistently awful as they were awfully persistent—but this was my first drunken biker thug.

"My watch says your skirt is off."

"Beg pardon?" I asked.

"Oh, sorry." He tapped his gas-station Timex. "My watch must be twenty minutes fast."

I grimaced. "Better check it again, I think it's still on daylight scumbag time."

He put his foot on the wooden chair and his hand on my shoulder. It was sweaty and gross. I shrugged it away, and suddenly there was Ike, pulling the chair out from under his leg. The guy staggered back, fell, and smiled a crazy thug smile on his way back up. This was what he really wanted—a fight. I looked at my brother. He wore the same expression.

"I was handling this," I said calmly.

"I thought you were with the redskin slut." The thug sneered at Ike. "Or is *this* your slut?" Ike punched him in the face, and then everything started happening very fast. The two men lunged at each other clumsily. The rest of the bar patrons had gathered around, pushing closer. I stepped into the fray to stop Ike, but one of the guys from the bar pushed me back.

"Ike, stop," I screamed. "Someone, please stop this!"

Nobody listened, least of all Ike. He was blind and deaf to everything except his fight. His expression was so cold, almost removed. This wasn't about protecting me. This wasn't my brother anymore. I didn't know who the hell this stranger was. *That* was terrifying. "Please—someone!"

I saw the bartender pick up a pump-action shotgun, but everyone kept pushing closer to the fight. The jackass thug pulled out a rusty knife. Ike came away with blood on his shirt. This only made him madder. Somehow they were on the floor, and then Ike was on top. *Pummeling* him. The boys from the bar yanked him off the now-unconscious thug.

Ike was breathing heavily. He kept blinking as if to clear his vision. Then the pretty bartender—Ike called her Rachel—told us the unconscious guy that Ike had nearly killed was an Idaho Nazi. Look at his SS prison tattoos, she said. He was in cahoots with a crooked local sheriff, and we'd better flee before the both of us got locked up—or killed.

I paused before jumping onto the back of Ike's motorcycle.

"Can't do sidesaddle," he told me, gesturing at my skirt.

"I was worried about how much you had to drink."

"The fight sobered me up plenty," he said. "More sobering, a bunch of Idaho Nazis are going to show up any minute. I'll apologize later, but right now I need to get you out of here."

"You mean *us*." He was the one who almost killed the guy. He was the one Rachel was trying to help.

"What? Yes, *us*. I'll get *us* out of here. Hurry up, get on."

He revved the engine. I hiked up my skirt and climbed on the bike. We took off with the urgency one might expect from two Yankee prep-school kids fleeing armed Aryan Nation psychopaths from Idaho. I held my breath, but his driving was good, steady, despite his drinking, which was oddly not surprising; Marder men were functional alcoholics.

"Where are we going?" I shouted after about ten minutes, but I don't think he heard me.

He veered off the highway and onto a local road, paved, thankfully, pitch-dark except for a billboard advertising Fairmont Hot

Springs Resort, Gregson, a few miles straight west. Before we could hit the resort, however, Ike made a hard left onto another country road. I read the sign—GERMAN GULCH ROAD—in that fleeting second when his headlight provided a bit of illumination. (I recalled a quote from *Zen and the Art of Motorcycle Maintenance*: "County-road-sign makers seldom tell you twice. If you miss that sign in the weeds that's your problem, not theirs.") I had no idea of how Ike was negotiating any of this.

The route was winding and steep, cutting through a forest. There was no light except the beam from the motorcycle's headlight and the star-filled sky above us like a beaded tapestry. After the road's first sharp turn, I asked Ike to slow down. At the next turn, I glanced over the edge of a precipice and saw only blackness. My heart thrummed with terror. We sped up the mountain into a dark void, maybe death itself. I hugged Ike tighter.

Soon Ike slowed the bike and turned right onto a small, rocky driveway, then he turned off the engine and glided us onto a grassy patch. A small wooden building came into view.

"Where are we?" I asked.

"Northern Fleecer mountain cabin," he said. "A fishing camp. Not a ton of people know about it." He held the bike steady while I got off. "There's an outhouse over there," he said, motioning to the far side of the cabin. He got off his bike and steered it between two huge bushes. "We can get water from the creek beyond it."

"The Nazis don't know this place?"

"Nazis don't do a lot of fishing," he said. "They're not rugged live-off-the-land types—they're eat-cold-beans-from-a-dented-can dirtbags."

He walked into the cabin and, with the World War II Zippo Dad had given him for his sixteenth, lit the candles in each corner of the main room, which held a wood stove and a small square table with two metal folding chairs. Two other chairs hung from the wall near the door, as did a pot, two frying pans, and a spatula. I followed Ike into the bedroom. Moonlight poured through its windows, revealing two sets of bunk beds on which lay bare and scrawny mattresses covered with spiderwebs and dust.

Yikes. "We're sleeping here?"

"The Ritz is booked."

"Ha-ha. I mean, is it safe?"

"We'll be fine for the night. Rachel will meet us here as soon as she can." He eased his massive frame onto one of the bottom bunks, which squeaked. I stood in the center of the room.

"What are we going to do when the sun comes up?" I asked.

"We need to figure that out," he said. "Rachel will come help us tomorrow. She'll give us options."

"How do you know she's going to come?" I asked.

"She said so," he said.

I stood there a minute and tried to process it all. Then I sat down on the other bottom bunk.

"I read this crazy book about your boss, about Evel," I told him.

"Oh yeah?" he said sleepily, barely feigning interest. "A book? That's weird. Evel is obsessed with his coverage. I feel like I would've heard about a new book."

"It hasn't been published yet—it was a manuscript, to be precise," I acknowledged. "Mom got it from Jackie O. And I kinda borrowed it."

He yawned audibly. "What's it say?"

"Horrible stuff," I said. "That he's a pill popper and beats his wife and lies and is a jerk and insecure and a flimflam man and a drunk and an anti-Semite."

Ike yawned again. Finally he said, "I've never seen him beat his wife."

And within a minute or so, he was snoring.

I lay down on the bunk, but I didn't sleep a wink. I was less worried about the Nazis and more about that horrible fight and Ike's nonchalance about the jerk for whom he worked.

Ike had changed. It was like a switch had flipped. One moment, I was laughing with my sweet, devil-may-care brother, and the next I had no idea who that violent guy was or how to get him back to my Ike. I didn't even know what had made Ike that way.

He started twitching in his sleep. A bad dream, maybe. He said something that sounded like "Schmitty." Didn't make any sense. Then he said, "Hang tight." I called his name and he went quiet.

What was wrong with him? Was it Lebanon? Was it being out here for so long in the middle of nowhere with bikers and miscreants and God knew who else? Was it the drinking? I only hoped that this latest twist meant I could get him to leave Butte. Soon, maybe, we would be going home.

The next morning, in that sleepless haze of dawn—when birds and insects were waking up and slowly beginning to chirp—came the sound of a car engine rattling several miles away, echoing off the mountains. The chugging grew louder as the car came closer to the cabin, then it was replaced by a high-pitched squeak of brakes. Ike jumped up like a jack-in-the-box.

"Someone's here," I whispered.

He looked out the window. "It's Rachel."

He walked out to meet her. I started to follow, then hesitated. They were talking intimately, it seemed to me. They stood so close, they might have been touching. She looked up into his face, trying to read it. What I saw was clear: This woman cared for my brother. I didn't know what it meant, but I was glad we had someone we could trust. I stepped outside.

She turned and smiled at me. The two of them walked my way, and Rachel said, "I'm so glad Ike got you here in one piece."

"Rachel thinks the best thing for us is to take her Jeep to an airport," Ike said. "It's the last place they'll think to look."

"Idaho Falls," Rachel said. "Maybe three hours? You think you could get a plane out?"

Jesus, I thought. "You think the airport's safe?"

Rachel gave me a grim smile. "It's a good question. Your brother sent an Idaho Nazi to the emergency room last night. There are maybe twenty folks in his gang and easily another hundred in allied gangs. Aryan Nation moved its HQ to Idaho in '74. They've got a compound north of Hayden and chapters all over the state. They're going to want your brother dead. His only options are to join a rival gang or get the hell out of here."

A thought occurred to me. "You must have a bunch of private airports out here, I would think."

Rachel drove me to a pay phone at a gas station outside Butte, where I called Danielle Lyon. She was on her way out of town—to "*Meh*-hee-koh"—but understood the panic in my voice. I explained my dire straits. I had gone out to Montana to bring my brother home and we found ourselves on the run. She told me she was sending their plane, the one she was about to fly to Mexico in, to retrieve us. "You and your brother need to stay hidden until it gets there," she said. She would delay her trip.

Early that afternoon, Rachel drove us to the airfield. A medium-size hangar and a teeny control tower were the only indications that it was an airport. That and the swanky new private jet, property of the Lyons, waiting there.

A pilot greeted us. "Montana sure is pretty," he said as I got on the plane. I turned around for a last look, squinting through the sun's strong rays. And then I realized Ike wasn't behind me. He was on the tarmac talking to Rachel, who was in her Jeep. I went back down the steps and met him on the asphalt.

"Come on, Ike," I said. "The pilot's anxious to take off."

"Listen, Luce, I'm not going with you," he said.

"What?" I was stunned.

"I can't go back. Not now."

"What about what Rachel said? That you won't be safe here. That the only place for you to go is away from here!"

"That's not exactly what she said."

I was near tears. Only my brother got me this angry. "You need to get out of here!" My voice was rising. "You need to come home. Mom and Dad and me, we'll keep you safe! We'll get you the help you need!"

"Luce?"

"*What?*" I said angrily.

"Don't cry." He wiped a lone stupid tear escaping down my cheek. "Save your energy for the important stuff. Crack the case of that serial killer. Be the next Woodward. Get on that plane."

I heard the stubbornness in his voice. I knew there was nothing I could do to get him to board. It was the worst kind of failure. I hadn't been able to save my brother. "What will I tell Mom?"

"Tell her you saw me, and I'm good." His voice had the same cool sincerity that Dad had whenever he tried to assure us that we would emerge not only unscathed but stronger from whatever the latest family crisis was—a mixture of patronizingly confident male ego and putting on a good face. "Tell her I love her, and I'll come home as soon as I can. Maybe by Labor Day. Tell them both that. Tell them whatever you want, whatever you need to."

"Why can't you just do what I tell you? You know I'm always right."

"Big sisters," he said, shaking his head with a smile. "I love you to pieces, but unless you have chloroform, you're not getting me on that plane."

He walked back to Rachel. After a long moment, I climbed aboard the plane. As it taxied down the airstrip, I watched him from the window until he was so small I couldn't see him anymore.

CHAPTER SEVEN

IKE

South of West Yellowstone, Montana

June 1977

You're the devil in disguise
Oh, yes, you are, devil in disguise

—Elvis Presley, "Devil in Disguise"

YOU COULDN'T FIND Clem's Bait and Tackle on any map. It was as hidden in those woods as the survivalist encampments you also couldn't find, all of them somewhere in the unmarked no-man's-land of the abutment of Montana, Wyoming, and Idaho. Fishermen and drifters, the Yo-Yos and Russell's religious freaks and Vietnam vets and other clans, all depended on Clem's for supplies and sustenance, and they held close the secret of its location. If you ran into someone in these backwoods, *maybe* he'd tell you where to find it. Just as likely, he'd stick you with a knife.

I'd only heard tales of Clem's, so I was shocked when Rachel said that was where she was taking me. She hooked a right off the Island Park Dam onto a dirt road I never would have noticed. Her Jeep rumbled through a maze of paths and clearings until we were bumping along a gravel path. We pulled up to a rocky stream. She turned off the car. "This is your stop."

I looked out the window. There was the stream and trees and more trees. No sign of human habitation anywhere. "You want me to get out here?"

"Follow the creek a little over two miles. There'll be dots of green paint to mark your way. You'll come to a snag of dead trees and, in the middle of it, a huge fallen pine. That's where you climb the bank that'll take you to the store's entrance. Look for the guy in the store holding a tin of Spam. That's the Colonel."

"Are you fucking with me?"

Her hands were still on the wheel. Her eyes were straight ahead. "I would never joke about Spam," she said. "When you see him, give him two thumbs-up."

"What if there's more than one guy with Spam?"

"Well, then, it would be your lucky day."

I wanted her to look at me. Was this goodbye for now or forever? Would I see her again? I didn't know.

"Listen to me, Rachel—you saved my ass," I said. "It was crazy and reckless and brave, and I'll never forget it." I steeled myself: "Or you."

She turned and looked at me then. Something in her expression softened. "You better get going."

Getting out of that Jeep was the emotional equivalent of an exercise I'd done in boot camp, jumping out of a moving vehicle. But I did it. Hopped out, shut the door.

"I'll see you," she shouted out the window, then shifted into reverse. The wheels spun and kicked up dirt as she sped back to civilization.

I stood there, gulping dust, listening to the rumble of her Jeep driving away until I couldn't hear it anymore. *I'll never forget you,* I'd told her. What a fucking idiot. Why hadn't I played it cool? There was a good chance I'd never see her again, and every part of me wanted to shout: *You're the most amazing person I've ever met and watching you driving away from me will crush my heart.* That would have been worse, of course. The perfect thing to say—I never had it. The thing that might've made her stay or, if she couldn't stay, come looking for me again. I had no clue about women. None. What a fucking moron.

No wonder she drove off.

I let out a sigh and headed off in search of Clem's. It was a good forty-minute hike and was as easy to find as Rachel had promised when you knew to look for certain rocks and trees marked with painted green dots every fifty yards or so. It might've been a nice hike if I weren't so goddamned heartbroken and worried about Nazis and if the damn path weren't so buggy and muggy and if there were nothing dangerous about it.

A bunch of times in Lebanon, I'd been forced to consider how folks cut off from society by geography and lack of roads survived. How did they get food? Medicine? Fuel? Caravans of traders and traveling merchants found success by targeting various crossroads, oases, and souks for regular visits. But I'd grown up pampered in DC and Manhattan, so American versions of such situations never really occurred to me. Eisenhower had created the interstate highway system. Given that achievement by my namesake, I grew up knowing that whatever I needed, I could hop on my motorcycle and get it. So many folks didn't have that luxury.

I finally found myself at a run-down shack that had to have been a century old if it was a day. It was nestled by a dried-up creek and surrounded by various dirt paths that led into the dense woods. DON'T TREAD ON ME warned a wooden sign with a crudely rendered Gadsden snake hammered to the front door.

The floorboards of the porch stairs creaked under my feet. A bell jingled as I opened the door. I had expected to see some wizened old man running the place, but the shopkeeper was a skinny guy about my age, washed-out-looking. He wore a beige shirt and khaki pants the color of his hair.

The shop itself was three aisles with two white refrigerators at the far end, each of which had a sign painted in black letters on cardboard and taped to its door. One read MILK, the other BOOZE. Choice was not a hallmark of the establishment. Cheerios or oatmeal; locally bagged and tagged elk jerky or Generic potato chips—that was the brand, Generic. There was exactly one beer option in these mountains: Coors. No pretense.

Standing in the far aisle, a white guy in his thirties was giving me the once-over. He had long hair and a thick brown beard. Something about him screamed *veteran*, the kind who'd let himself go after being discharged. I went into his aisle, and, yes, he wore dog tags. He was holding a single can of Spam.

This had to be the Colonel. I gave him two thumbs-up, Fonzie-style, just as Rachel had directed me. The Colonel nodded and put the Spam tin back on the shelf. I followed him to the counter, where two boxes and two backpacks full of goods were waiting. "Grab what you can," he said.

The Colonel led me down the other side of the mountain to a valley stream. We used a fallen tree to cross the creek at a riffle, then continued downstream. I waited for him to say something, but he didn't. About twenty minutes into the walk, I could no longer contain my curiosity. "So how long have you lived out here?"

"Not long enough," he replied, and that was it. We listened to the birdsong and buzz of bugs. The rapids were loud in our ears. Finally, he broke the silence: "Came to Jackson Hole for a job. Discharged in '69."

"Marine?" I asked. He just seemed like one. Difficult to explain.

"Yep," he said.

"Khe Sanh?"

"Yep," he said again.

The seventy-seven-day bloody conflict of Khe Sanh in 1968 was one of the most controversial U.S. battles of the war, and no Marine I knew felt good about it. It began when three divisions of the North Vietnamese army attacked two regiments of Marines stationed in an isolated base near the Laotian border just south of the DMZ. Fearing Khe Sanh would be his Waterloo, LBJ told General Westmoreland to hold the land no matter what. So the Marines dug in, as is our wont. And the North Vietnamese were beaten back. And the Pentagon presented the battle as a U.S. victory. "Only" two hundred and seventy-four Americans were KIA, while thousands of North Vietnamese died, which made General Westmoreland super-proud. The Pentagon thumped its chest in triumph and abandoned the base, and the North Vietnamese immediately moved in and declared victory.

All those Marines dead and wounded for a territory we didn't even care about. If the Colonel had lived through that U.S. government goatfuck, it was no wonder he ended up in the wilds of Montana. I thought about Beirut, thought about Gonzo and Schmitty, and felt my own disgust with the tragic misuse of the loyal sons who serve in the U.S. military.

The Colonel stopped and took a tin of dip from his pocket, pinched a chew, deposited it between his gum and lip. Then we started walking again. We passed a cascade, and the Colonel turned at a tributary that led to a quiet pool of water.

"Here we are," the Colonel said. Through the leaves of sagging cottonwood branches, I could see a tent.

The Colonel pressed his tongue against the roof of his mouth and made a sound mimicking the squeak of a goldfinch. The signal brought out of the brush two men dressed in fatigues. Then more men emerged. We crossed the pool, sloshing knee-deep, and pushed aside leafy branches to walk into a well-shaded campground with dozens of guys, all looking at me warily. Someone shouted, "Boys, the kid's here." Many seemed to me veterans in various phases of disarray. Some were still wearing their camo, some were in tie-dyed hippie nonsense, others were sporting whatever thrift-store irregulars they could grab. I looked around. They lived in shanties, tents, lean-tos. An entire village that went deep into the woods, who knew how far back. Was this still Montana? Had we crossed into Idaho? Wyoming?

"How many people live here?" I asked the Colonel.

"However many need to," he said. "They come and go, somewhere between fifty and a hundred. Maybe around seventy-five now? We had to ask about a dozen fellas to leave a couple weeks ago. They were getting violent."

A vague unease ran down my spine. Were these men here because of what had been done to them or because of what they'd done to others?

After Lebanon, I realized that the officials who sent soldiers into horrible places where they committed unspeakable acts were the ones responsible for those crimes, even if tribunals didn't see it that way. Two of the Marines in my ill-fated platoon had since been dishonorably discharged for drugs; another three got in serious trouble for their part in a bar fight where a local was blinded. War isn't an isolated hell. The aftermath pours like lava into the souls of its participants and victims and smolders in perpetuity.

Were these men trying to escape that?

I followed the Colonel to a shelter made of thick branches tied together like a gabled roof. Dozens of curious faces turned my way. They all had the age and look of Vietnam veterans, late twenties to mid-thirties. Some chatted around a fire, grilling several fish. Others behind them baited hooks on poles; a circle of six looked up from a game of cards. There were men lying deep in the shadows of the woods. These last seemed to me sick or injured, although some were probably just asleep.

When I was a kid, in my *Boys' Life* phase, before girls or motorcycles entered the picture, this all would have seemed pretty cool. But now it seemed sad. Recluses. Father Damien and the leper colony.

A guy with an eye patch and a mess of tattoos approached me. "I'm Dante," he said, throwing me a handshake. "Heard about your dustup with the Nazi. You're safe here." He gestured toward the fire. "But I can't say you're going to like the chow."

"Can't be worse than Lejeune." I shrugged.

"Don't bet on it, kid." Dante's hair was black as india ink, as were his eyes. He had sunken cheeks and thick eyebrows. I tried to figure out his tattoos, but they were blurry and amateur, as if they'd been made with a ballpoint pen and a shiv in prison.

"Where do I sleep?" I asked. "Are there extra tarps or whatever? I mean, I don't need much."

Dante motioned toward the far side of the camp. "There are a few spaces in the back that will be fine until it rains, which I don't think we're due for soon. You'll have time to build something. Right now, why don't you join me in finding food."

He reached into a duffel bag and withdrew a rifle, a bow, a quiver full of arrows, and two knives, one of which he handed to me. As an afterthought, he grabbed a miniature pillow from the duffel and threw it at me.

We headed for the deep woods, away from the river. It got darker and colder with every step. "We're not fishing?" I said, following him.

"We can't catch enough fish to feed all those men. Not sure

you know much about this kind of living, but that's okay, enough of us do."

I'd thought I was tough enough and had been through enough with the Marines that it wouldn't be a problem. But he was right, I knew next to nothing about living off the land long term. "I spent some time in the Middle East surviving on grubs and grass, which was nothing like these cushy forests."

Dante chuckled. "You can eat the entire cast of *Watership Down* and still die of starvation. The meat's too lean."

"So what should I be looking for?"

"Deer or pronghorn, which come out about now, though, if we get desperate, possum. Porcupines, even. I'll eat frogs and grasshoppers before I'll starve."

"Okay, I'm on it," I said.

"Also vegetation. Know what to look for?"

"Mushrooms?"

"No. God, no. I'm talking wild hyacinth, sweetroot, acorns, pink monkey flowers. Any flowers you see, let me know. You'll figure it out soon enough. But we'll need more than a sack of leaves to keep the men from grumbling. If we're lucky, we'll hear hooves."

Dante was chattier than the Colonel. He told me he was born Anthony Alighieri, nicknamed Dante by a smarty-pants lieutenant who knew more about thirteenth-century Italian poets than about how to avoid Vietcong trip wires. Dante had come to the camp two years before with his brother, Johnny, who suffered from a mysterious cancer the VA refused to treat. Johnny was seeking an experimental new drug. He'd heard the Colonel could get it for him.

"Is the drug working?"

"Seems to be," Dante said. "He's stronger than before."

Dante had been a navy pilot with Carrier Air Wing 17, assigned to the USS *Forrestal*. In June 1967, his squadron left Norfolk; they arrived in the Gulf of Tonkin at the end of July. "We flew about a hundred and fifty sorties against the north in four days," he told me matter-of-factly as we hiked down the mountain. "We thought we were going to be the most decorated unit in the war. Before the fire."

We all knew about the fire. There were a hundred theories as to what went wrong, but, bottom line: a parked Phantom bomber accidentally fired a rocket into the fuel tank of a Skyhawk, prompting a chain reaction of explosions as jet fuel flooded the flight deck.

"It was like the tide rolling in from the Styx," Dante said. "A hundred and thirty-four KIA, a hundred and sixty-one WIA. Some of them are still in VAs."

"Is that how Johnny got cancer? From the *Forrestal* fire?"

"No," Dante said. "Johnny was air force. Flew C-123s."

We were following a small stream down the mountain. Suddenly we found ourselves in a field that gave me a strong sense of déjà vu. I remembered a similar scene when I was little, on vacation in Idaho one summer, walking from the Snake River to a cabin with my dad and Senator Mike Mansfield, who like Dad was a former history professor.

This memory was so clear: It was a bright, cool morning, and my dad wore a brown corduroy jacket. The Marine shrink they'd sent me to at Bethesda Naval might suggest that I was trying to find the father I'd been missing, a replacement dad, in the Montana backwoods. But that would be horseshit. I had come to the camp to escape danger. I was asked to help forage with this man. He wasn't a father figure. Any similarities were just happenstance. I told myself all these things. Yet weirdly—and strongly—it hit me that maybe I was foraging for more than a meal.

The sun hid behind a mountain. I checked my watch—it was almost five. In the distance, I could hear the *chicka-dee-dee* call of birds, a cry of alarm. Dante surveyed the valley with his binoculars. I scanned the meadow between the stream and the deeper forest. There was nothing to see. Then the wind kicked up, and my nostrils twitched. A musky scent of animal traveled upwind.

"Something's coming," I said.

Dante took a knee, put his gun sack on the ground, and began loading the shotgun. I asked for his binoculars, and he handed them over without looking up. It took me a minute to focus, and then I saw it: a buck pronghorn, young and strong and alone. Without its herd. Through the binocs I watched it turn its head my way, as if it could see me. Or as if it had caught my scent. It was a beautiful creature, and I felt an odd kinship. Then Dante said, "Cover your ears," and fired.

A second crack—I thought an echo of Dante's shot—followed.

I watched the pronghorn fall, and a wave of sorrow came over me. It was a great shot by Dante, especially considering that he had only one eye. I guess he'd figured out how to correct for it. I didn't dare bring it up.

"Fuck," Dante said. "The other guy must've got him." Through the binocs I saw a man with a rifle emerge from the distant brush. "Come on, kid," Dante said, rubbing his chin. "Let's see what's what."

"Who's he?"

We began walking toward the carcass and the other hunter, me trailing behind Dante. "There're a bunch of groups around here," Dante said. "UFO weirdos called Yo-Yos, survivalists, Reverend Russell and his Jesus freaks."

"Could be any of 'em?"

He shrugged. "All of 'em eat."

"There are certain folks I don't want to see me."

"No, this isn't one of the Nazis," he assured me. "Those motherfuckers don't leave the roads. And I think I know this guy. A Yo-Yo."

"How can you tell?"

"Couldn't you see through the binocs? Junior's like a hundred feet tall. Used to play for the Lakers."

Junior the ex-Laker was waiting for us. He was an old dude, seven feet tall if he was an inch, long and wiry, with a Rip van Winkle beard and a wrinkled face the color of a catcher's mitt. The buck lay bloody at his feet. "Dante," he said. It was delivered as a greeting but with half a cup of *Fuck off*.

"Junior," Dante said.

"This is my buckshot in there," Junior said. "My kill."

"Yep," Dante said, shaking his head down at it. "I see that."

Junior seemed confused. He eyed Dante, trying to make sense of sportsmanship.

"Tough news about the Lakers," Dante said. They'd been swept in the playoffs by the Portland Trail Blazers. "Kareem's fifth foul in the third was the final nail." He'd told me he listened to games at night on his transistor radio if the winds allowed him to hear.

"Fuck you, Dante," Junior said.

"I guess you don't want our help with the buck?" Dante asked.

I looked again at the dead pronghorn with the blood on its neck. That was odd. Then I noticed the entry wound. "Wait a sec," I said, pointing at the neck. "Look at the wound."

Dante took a knee and inspected it. "Does look like my bullet hit first." He looked up at his adversary. "How you want to handle this?"

"That's a lie!" Junior snarled. "You fired and it was still standing, then I shot it!"

Dante got to his feet. "Junior, we don't want no trouble," he said kindly. "But the facts are what they are. There were two shots and mine was in the throat, yours in the rump. That's an entry wound in the neck, the kid's right. Let's be logical here."

Junior tightened his grip on his shotgun. Dante raised his eyebrows ever so slightly. Would Junior shoot *us* over this buck? My heart began pounding. I calculated the odds of my tackling him before he got off a shot.

Not good.

"How 'bout this, my friend," Dante said. "I'll gut him right here. You get what you shot—rump, hind legs, hind shanks. I'll take what I hit—neck, shoulders, front shanks. And the rest of it—loin, tenderloin, ribs, flank—we'll chop up and divvy down the middle. Everyone goes home, everyone gets fed. And you get first pick on the middles, of course."

Junior's sneer faded slightly.

"Steaks, burgers, chops, kebabs, soup, jerky," Dante said.

"All right, fine," Junior said. "But fuck you again, Dante."

I let out the breath I hadn't known I was holding. I lowered my backpack. "I'm going to take out the knives and show you where to start," Dante said to me. He taught me how to field-dress that buck. We gutted and skinned it and took the liver and kidneys with the meat but left the rest of the organs in a pile by some rocks.

On our walk back to camp, carrying the bloody meat in old potato sacks Dante had brought, I asked him whether Junior would think he was weak for compromising rather than fighting over the meat. True, the Vietnam veterans *and* the Yo-Yos would go to bed with full bellies that night. But didn't Dante worry there was danger in being seen as a coward?

"Nope," he said. "I got nothing against him. He never did

nothing to me or my guys. We were just two cavemen squaring off over a carcass."

Every impulse in my body had told me to fight right away, before there was time for a conversation. Even though I knew that would probably lead to at least one of us not making it back to camp with a heartbeat, I couldn't comprehend what Dante had done, didn't understand the notion of backing off.

"And that buck was too much for us to carry three miles, Ike," he said. "C'mon, boy."

I grinned. Dad had often used that phrase. *Don't make your poor mom clean it up,* he'd said after one of the dogs left a bloodied bunny on the porch. *C'mon, boy.*

The men at the camp were pleased with our haul. We made a big fire and ate half the meat that night and cut the rest into strips and smoked it. The next day we went out again, and soon foraging for food with Dante became my daily gig. There were forty-seven of us total—clearly the Colonel was shitty at roll call—all Vietnam veterans except for me. Thirteen were sick with the mysterious cancer, in various stages of bodily collapse.

Dante's brother, Johnny, seemed the sickest, his eyes sunken and his skin tinged with a greenish hue. He mostly got up only to use the latrine, a tent over a wooden platform with a hole in it about a hundred yards from camp. Dante or one of the others usually had to help him there.

I asked why we didn't move Johnny closer. It was such an ordeal to get him from the edge of the encampment to that tent. But Dante gestured at their humble abode: beds of Navajo rugs under sloped tarps tied between redwoods where they could sleep alongside the river. It was peaceful there, and the air was sweet. "Johnny likes the sound of the water," Dante said.

"I do," Johnny agreed. "Soothing."

The guys with the beer came around distributing warm cans. Dante took one for him and another for Johnny. I cracked mine open. You get used to warm beer pretty quick when it's the only option.

A few tents over, someone was strumming a guitar. The guy, a Creole from New Orleans, had spent the previous three years at the camp teaching himself to play. Dante said the first year, he'd been so god-awful, they made him hike out of earshot to practice. Now he was pretty good.

"Some folks are born made to wave the flag," a few of them sang. *"Ooh, they're red, white, and blue..."*

"His song selection always feels like the soundtrack of whatever movie this is we're living," I said. "'Fortunate Son' is a little on the nose."

The Alighieri brothers chuckled. "I'll drink to that," Johnny said.

"But isn't it chicken or egg?" Dante asked. "Do we listen to Simon and Garfunkel because of *The Graduate*? Or did *The Graduate* hire Simon and Garfunkel because we were listening to them already?"

"Yes," Johnny said. He gulped the dregs of his warm Coors and tried to crush the can. It was a sad struggle.

"What did you do on those C-123s, anyway?" I asked.

"Defoliation." Johnny looked around at our green surroundings. "A shame, really."

The Colonel came through the brush with a manila envelope in his hand. It held the pills for Johnny's cancer. "You ready?" he said.

"Yes, sir," Johnny said.

Dante jumped up to take the pills the Colonel offered. He handed them to his brother, along with his beer to wash it down.

Johnny swallowed the pills with a wince. He gulped the rest of the beer.

"Taste bad?" I asked.

"Bitter," Johnny said. "Not too bad."

"It is cyanide, after all," Dante said.

"You just swallowed *cyanide*?" I said, stunned.

"To be precise," Dante said, "it's a substance found in fruit pits, like apricots, that your body converts to cyanide. Kills cancer cells."

"Or so the theory goes," Johnny said.

"But doesn't it also harm you? I mean, *cyanide*?" I couldn't get over it. Poor Johnny poisoning himself to get rid of his cancer.

"What do you think chemotherapy is?" Johnny asked.

"That shit's poison too," Dante pointed out. "The hope is you get enough to kill the cancer but not kill you."

"Right," I said.

"But this shit's natural," Dante said.

"Natural-ish," said Johnny.

"What do you think cancer patients die of?" Dante asked. "Let me tell you, brother: It ain't always the cancer."

I didn't know anything about it, so I didn't say a word.

That night, after a couple minutes of missing Rachel, I chased away the self-pity with Johnny's pain. Here were two patriots truly suffering, abandoned by their country and the VA. I was just a punk kid, a little over twenty, with an unrequited crush. I told myself that, and it helped a little, but I still missed Rachel a lot. Ain't nothing wrong with a functioning heart, I told myself.

Johnny smoked grass every day. Early on, I figured out that in the camp, you didn't ask where things came from, so where he got his weed I never knew, but it was clear that what Johnny needed, his brother found a way to get. Johnny said it was for the pain, but Dante joined him quite often. Johnny would smoke until he passed out, whereupon Dante would rise and tend to whatever needed tending to.

"How much did joes smoke in the jungle?" I asked them once.

Dante grinned. "We smoked a lot in the jungle." Then his smile went away. "Until fucking Steinbeck."

"That's right," Johnny said. His eyes were closed, and he was smiling, enjoying the buzz. His brother took the joint from him.

"*Grapes of Wrath* Steinbeck?" I asked.

"His son," Dante said. "He wrote an article painting every one of us in-country as potheads. Set the news media's hair on fire, per usual."

"Oh, boy," said Johnny.

"Army Joe-Fridayed it from there," Dante said, "busting a thousand dogfaces every week for possession, adding the defoliation of Vietnamese marijuana crops to its list of objectives."

"To *my* list," Johnny added.

"So of course, troops switched to heroin," Dante said.

"Not all," said Johnny.

"No, maybe a quarter," Dante said. "Some jackass senator even blamed heroin for My Lai."

"Nuts," said Johnny.

"You never heard of Operation Golden Flow?" Dante asked me. I hadn't.

"Get this," Dante said. "Nixon literally required a piss test for anyone heading home. Before you stepped onto the bird. If you failed, you had to stay until you were clean."

"Jesus," I said.

"Jack Ford was sparking doobies the whole time," Dante said, referring to the former president's son. "Eighth circle, brother."

I waited for an explanation, but none was forthcoming. Johnny let out a soft snore, prompting Dante to stand and offer me a hand up. I followed him away.

"What's *eighth circle*?" I asked when we were out of earshot.

"I did read the *Divine Comedy* after I got the nickname. Much later. You ever?"

"Um, yeah." In truth it'd been an *X-Men* version—*Nightcrawler's Inferno*—and I didn't remember much of it.

"The eighth circle of hell is for frauds," he said. "Read it again. A special kind of torture for each type of charlatan. Bullshitters are buried in shit, fortune-tellers have their heads twisted backward, and so on. I wonder what punishment awaits those bastards who knew we were fighting a losing war and kept sending in kids to be cannon fodder."

He had fought as I had fought. I could feel his frustration because it was mine.

"*Those* motherfuckers," he went on with an intensity I'd never seen in him before. He must have reflected on this a million times over the past few years, and yet I could see his eyes were hot with anger, and I could feel that anger, searing and purifying.

"They got Johnny sick but won't admit it," he said. "They know he's suffering but won't help him. We held up our end of the bargain. We put our lives on the line for our country. We did everything those motherfuckers told us to do. What did we get in return? Look at us, Ike. Do you see?" He held out his arms, a gesture taking in the river where we bathed, the trees we used to hide from the sun, and the forest that might or might not provide the food we needed to survive another day. I turned and took in the ravages of his brother, his sunken eyes and green-tinged skin, how thin he was, that awful cancer-thin, and there were a dozen other men just like him.

"What did we do to deserve this?"

"Nothing."

"And yet this…" His arms were still out. "*This* is what we got."

"It's a goddamned betrayal." My voice was low and furious and did not sound like my voice at all. "All of you deserved a fuck-ton better."

"I tell you, Ike, there will be a reckoning."

He meant it. A reckoning was coming. I could see it, and, to be honest, I wanted in.

CHAPTER EIGHT

LUCY

Washington, DC

July 1977

"AT THE RISK of cliché," Max Lyon said, "stop the presses."

We had just returned to the office, the Lyons and I, after spending the evening at a black-tie fundraiser for some city revitalization effort with an acronym that, five seconds after hearing it, I'd already forgotten. Max had been off glad-handing the bigwigs while the rest of us drank all night from the fire-hose of free booze the waiters kept bringing to our table. The city's elites were all around us. On the dais, the mayor, Walter Washington, droned on.

But for me, it was only Harry in the room.

He was gorgeous in his tux. As Harry's plus-one, I'd glammed up in my mother's diamonds and a backless gown. After the speeches ended and we were being served dessert, Harry had leaned over to me and asked, in a whisper, if I was happy; he'd called me *darling* in that posh British accent that made my toes curl.

"This is the best night ever," I'd admitted. "Maybe after we get out of here, you can come over?"

A slow smile spread across his face. "I thought you'd never ask. Let's go." Then he glance-scanned the room and groaned. "Oh no."

He'd seen Max storming back to our table. "I just got a major tip," Max said. "We need to blow up the wood!"

On the other side of our table, Ivan looked stunned. (Danielle was still in Mexico on that mysterious business trip. No one would tell me what it was.) Harry lifted his champagne glass. "Right, Dad. Hilarious." But Max was pink-faced with excitement. His disheveled hair suggested he was more than a tad pickled.

"I'm quite serious, Harold. No more talk until we're back at the office," Max said. "Too many damn spies around. Come on, let's go."

We rushed back. It was just after eight when we arrived at the newsroom; the rest of the staff had returned to work in their jeans and T-shirts or collared shirts with the sleeves rolled up. A strange contrast to our party's formal wear—my oh-so-high heels, my back exposed. Whispers buzzed from every corner of the newsroom. Everyone wanted to know what Max was up to.

It was Ollie who broke the silence. "How was the dinner, boss?"

"Full of Hebrews, homos, and Hottentots," Max announced. That was when he risked cliché and told Ollie to stop the presses. "Get on the phone and alert the printer."

Ollie's eyebrows were up near his receding hairline. Blowing up the wood was a very big deal, financially as well as logistically. Another press run cost money. Starting all over again took a while, and you had to make the scheduled delivery time. You blew up the wood only if you had to do it, if a huge story forced you to.

"The Whites got their baby back and have vanished," Ollie reminded him. "Ashley's scoop, that's our wood."

"I know what the wood is, you kumquat, I said blow it up!"

Max waited for Ollie to call the newspaper printing plant in the blighted, industrial section of Northeast DC. Ollie did. "Done, boss," he told him.

"We have a new lede," Max announced. "Police are looking at a colored boy in the slug murders."

Gasps went up in the room. Everybody started whispering at once. "A what?" I said to Harry. "Police are looking at a black child?" That made no sense.

Max cut his eyes my way. "Not a child," he said. "A young colored man is law enforcement's so-called person of interest. My source tells me he was seen leaving the area where Janice Davenport's body was dumped. Police want to interview him. No one else has this. Big scoop, and that's how we'll play it."

I was stunned. For more than a month, I'd been reporting on the story. I'd interviewed family and friends and coworkers, gone to the site where both women were last seen—the busy slug stop on Old Keane Mill Road in Virginia—and talked to commuters there. I had off-the-record chats with the first U.S. Park Police officers on the scene and the homicide detectives for both jurisdictions. They'd had no witnesses; no one had mentioned seeing anyone near the bodies' dump sites, certainly not a young black man.

It didn't feel right. You got an instinct for a story when you'd worked on it as long and as single-mindedly as I had on this one, when you dreamed about it and woke up thinking about it. This felt wrong. Had someone who'd seen this person come forward? Or was this police-speak for "A young black man is a suspect"? I wanted to ask the police myself.

"Who's the source?" I asked. "MPD or Park Police or—"

Max ignored my question. He was barking orders at Ollie, asking about the placement of the story I'd written before the tip.

Ollie double-checked his notebook. "Page seven."

"Let's rework the existing story," Max said. "Put the new dish in the lede. Get some bobby response—'No comment,' or whatever they belch. Show it to her"—he gestured to me as though I were an annoying fly to shoo away. He turned. "You"—meaning me, the insect—"bang this out with Ollie," he said. "For the wood!"

My chardonnay haze was lifting, and worry set in. Max's scoop was incendiary if it wasn't handled properly. Did Max understand the racial tensions in this country, in DC? Did he know from ghettos and centuries of discrimination, slavery and Jim Crow, and "Burn, baby, burn"? Some readers might hear *person of interest* and assume it was code for "suspect" or even "criminal" because the man was black. I thought, *Oh, boy, we need more clarity in what exactly the man was doing near the site. Because if I write it wrong . . .*

And I thought of the long, terrible history of white mobs taking the law into their own hands, of lynchings and the Waco Horror and Mary Turner. I thought of Emmett Till's tortured body in the glass-topped coffin and his mother saying, "Let the people see what they did to my boy." I thought of a night sky I saw when I was a young girl that was so bright it seemed like dawn and my father telling me people were burning city blocks in protest because a white man had murdered Dr. King. Did Max know about any of this—and, more to the point, would educating him about it make him care?

Max was going over notes with Ollie and Harry. Ivan was handing out assignments. "Sir, a little clarity here," I said, trying again. Everyone stopped and looked at me. A bored, almost feline expression crossed Max's face. Harry made a sweeping gesture across his neck: *Cut it out.*

I ignored him. This was my story. I was being told to bang out a lede I hadn't confirmed myself, and it better damn well be accurate. "Sir, when your source said the man was seen leaving the area, what did he mean exactly? Do we want to use the word *leaving*? It sounds like it means 'fleeing,' which suggests criminality, as you know. Maybe just—"

"It's *leaving*. He said *leaving*," Max told me angrily.

"Maybe a second source can clarify?"

Harry hurried to my side. "Lucy, not now," he said in a low warning tone.

"Or amplify," I told Max. "To be sure—"

Harry gingerly grabbed my wrist and gently pulled me into the kitchenette, where stale pastries cluttered the counter and a massive coffeepot gurgled. My face was hot with embarrassment— he had dragged me from the newsroom discussion about *my* story. But I was my mother's daughter; I wouldn't rip him a new one unless we were alone.

And now we were. "How dare you! What the hell do you think you're doing? Treating me like—"

He put his fingertips over my mouth. I was so shocked, I shut up.

"Give me one second," he whispered, taking his hand away.

"We're talking about my story out there."

"You were pissing him off. He's in his cups. Not the time to challenge him."

"Challenge him? I was just asking basic questions. He's adding information to *my* story."

"*His* story. They're all his stories, Lucy, because this is his paper, Lucy," Harry said. "You would do well to remember that."

"But—"

His fingers went over my mouth again. "Now, listen: I have information you need to know. After you have it, you can react. Okay? This is a reasonable proposition."

There he went again, appealing to reason and logic. I nodded.

"My father would disinherit me if he knew I was telling you this," he muttered. "Can I trust you? Can you keep this secret?"

"Of course I can. But you'd better tell me."

He looked nervous. He brushed his thick bangs back from his face. He took a deep breath and said: "What if I told you Dad was talking to the DC police chief tonight at the event?"

"Chief Cullinane?" I'd wondered if Max had talked to someone with direct knowledge of the investigation. MPD chief Maurice Cullinane would know everything. He could order his homicide detectives into his office for an update; he had full access to investigative files. He could get on the phone with the Manassas police and find out anything on a moment's notice. Such was a city police chief's power.

Chief Cullinane was also a trusted person. He had a good reputation in a racially divided city as a progressive and a reformer; a photo of him as a beat patrolman bending over to talk to a little Asian boy during a Chinese New Year parade had won the Pulitzer Prize twenty years before.

If Cullinane had leaked the existence of a witness near the Manassas National Battlefield site where Janice Davenport's body was found to help find this killer, any newspaper would be thrilled to publish it. No wonder Max had been so excited—and so annoyed with me.

"Dad has a way with police officials," Harry said. "They love to talk to him, don't ask me why. Maybe because he started out as a crime reporter at the *Mirror*, and he learned long ago how to talk to them, I don't know. And remember, his last tip was right. There *was* another body."

"You said that was your tip!"

Harry had the grace to wince. "Dad wanted it that way, and I...I wanted to impress you."

"Oh."

"And...and I don't want you to get mad..."

"Yes?"

"But I feel like you're being unfair to my father," he said. "Now that you know Chief Cullinane said they'd like to talk to a black man who might have seen the suspect, you accept the tip. But why wouldn't you trust Dad? He has let you have the glory. He gave you the original scoop, and he's sold you to readers as if you're Woodward and Bernstein combined and reincarnated."

I glared at him.

"Don't hate me, but it's true," he said. "Those were all good things. Dad's been good to you. In my opinion, he deserves your faith and trust. He's earned it."

I woke up Mimi to collect her "No comment" and plunged into the copy. Per Max's exclusive source, whom I pretended not to know was the chief, one eyewitness saw a black man leaving the edge of Manassas National Battlefield Park where Janice Davenport's body had later been found. That was it. That was the whole thing. I asked Max if there was anything more.

"Well, there aren't a whole lot of bloody coloreds sashaying around Manassas Park, are there?" he said.

I told myself to remember everything he had done for me. I glanced over at Harry, who was giving me a kind of pleading look. "Did your police sources tell you that, sir?" I asked.

Max glared at Harry, then turned to me with a smile. "Absolutely," he said, and so I added that to my copy. Within five minutes I had a new lede and an official "No comment" from the police spokesperson. I added a bit about how most serial killers were white.

"Where did that come from?" Max said when it was his turn to sit at my desk and read the copy.

"It says right there, from Ressler, the FBI profiler I spoke to that Harry told me about. Most are white men, between the ages of twenty and forty, and loners."

Typing with his index fingers, he read out loud what he added: "'Though...the study...of serial killers...is relatively new....so no one...should be...ruled...out.'" He looked at me. "Okay, boss?"

I nodded. It wasn't wrong.

"All right," he said. "Let's do this."

I was hit with a wave of exhaustion, as if all the adrenaline and alcohol had suddenly evaporated. It wasn't until the next morning that I realized I'd forgotten to see how they planned to present my story on the wood.

"Slug Killer Probe: Cops Seek Black Man," blared the headline.

Nausea.

Gasping for air.

The paper was on my doormat. I looked up, then down again. Nope, still there.

I stared at it as though it might bite me. "Cops Seek Black Man." Not "Witness Sought" or "Police Searching for Person of Interest" or anything less sensationalized. *Sensationalized* wasn't really the right word for it, given that there was nothing sensational about it. *Crudded up*, more like. *Leprosized*. Oh God.

I picked up the paper and carried it inside and locked my door. I wondered if Mom and Dad had seen it; I feared that they had. Oh Lord, everyone was going to see it. A wave of revulsion went through me. What would Mom and Dad think? Maybe I could visit and ask for their counsel. This was bad, but they always made things better.

Then I remembered: I'd been avoiding them since I'd phoned and told them about seeing Ike in Montana. There was no way to dress it up—I had lied to them. By omission and otherwise. I told them Ike was fine, he was working for Evel Knievel, he seemed healthy and happy, and he would return home in the fall. Nothing to worry about; he would try to call but he was so busy and didn't have easy access to a phone, all good. Dad was so happy and Mom so relieved that I hung up before my conscience could get the better of me.

Good Lord. Had Harry known what the wood would be? I wasn't ready to talk to him about this, not until I knew what I wanted to say. I needed to speak to someone. In a momentary lapse of judgment, I called the only person not in my family or at my job with whom I'd relatively recently had a serious conversation: Skylar.

I phoned him at his office in the White House. "Hello, Lucy," he said icily. "To what do I owe the pleasure?"

"Hi there," I said. "Do you have a minute? I wondered if you could help me think through a quandary."

"Does this quandary involve helping the Lyon family overturn the FCC's cross-ownership rule?"

"The what, now?"

"Oh, come on, Lucy. Don't play dumb. Everyone's been talking about the hot-and-heavy between you and the young prince."

"Harry?"

"Of all people," he said. "Harry Fucking Lyon. The dark prince himself. You know what you can pillow-talk to him about tonight? Tell him your friend at the White House said good fucking luck trying to buy a TV station in a city where you already own a newspaper. Tell him I said there's a reason the FCC doesn't let fucknuts like the Lyons own every goddamned megaphone to spread their mulch. I don't give a damn how much money his daddy throws at it, that law will not be overturned. They will not corrupt *American* brains. I mean, Lucy, how could you? Harry Lyon. I can't believe he's why you stopped calling me."

"I didn't stop calling, Skylar," I said, taken aback at his

anger. "You were the one who said everything was moving too fast for you. *You* stopped calling *me*! I just had to *assume* we'd broken up!"

"Well, we're pretty busy here trying to help POTUS heal a broken nation," he said. "Energy-conservation plan, fifty-dollar tax rebate for every American, nuke treaty with the Russkies, not to mention addressing the simmering racial tensions that some irresponsible assholes in the press continue to inflame with bullshit headlines." *Yes, yes, yes,* I thought, *you're ever so important.* He raised his voice: "I mean, Christ on a Popsicle stick, Lucy, who the fuck *are* you anymore?"

"I'm the same person I always was," I said. "Read the story, Skylar. I wrote the story, not the damn headline!"

He laughed bitterly. "What does the story matter when the headline screams 'Cops Are Looking for a Black Guy!'"

Then he slammed down the phone. It hurt because I knew he was right.

I quickly got ready for work, jumped in my car, and turned on the radio. Max's scoop under my byline led the local radio news station, WTOP. I parked my VW (no valet for employees) and went up to the newsroom. Every television was turned to one of the three morning news shows—*Good Morning America,* the *Today Show, CBS Morning News*—and all were reporting my story along with the latest horrific handiwork of New York's Forty-Four-Caliber Killer. A nation terrified of serial killers, and while I should have been thrilled to be the main reporter covering one of them, I felt unmoored.

The TV reporters focused on the news that police investigators were searching for a possible witness seen in the area where Janice Davenport's body had been found, each citing his race but not until the third or fourth sentence of the presentation.

That was how I would have written it. I gazed down at the front page of my own paper and once again cringed.

Ashley appeared unsettled when she eased into the desk beside mine. She pursed her lips, glanced at me, then looked down.

I rolled my chair to hers so we could talk more privately. "You okay?" I asked. "Sorry the boss bumped your big scoop on the Whites. I didn't want him to."

"I mean…" she said, her voice trailing off. "I just hope this doesn't—" She stopped.

"You can tell me anything," I said, staring into her eyes. I wanted to console her but I knew I was part of the problem.

"I just worry about my little brothers," she said. "You know?"

I did.

And I knew in the movie version of this tale, I was a villain.

Then Mimi called and chewed me out for irresponsible speculation that fed into preexisting racial tensions. "Your paper's insinuation," she told me, "that a black male serial killer is hunting white female commuters is wrong."

"That's not what the story says."

"In my experience as an actual police officer, men tend to commit violence against women of their own race and ethnicity and class."

"This article does not debate that. My words are clear. *Person of interest. A possible witness.*"

"That's not what the headline suggests! It's not what people are saying!"

"Then tell them to read my words." But it was too late. She had already slammed the phone down loudly in my ear.

I left messages for the detectives in DC and Manassas and with the Park Police. I got nothing from a source at the DC crime lab. Mom phoned in the morning, Dad shortly after noon, but I didn't take either call. I knew what they were going to say, and I

160

didn't want to hear from Mr. and Mrs. Jiminy Cricket. Mostly I fielded calls from black clergy and activists and city councilmen who were upset by the front page. All of them were angry, and with reason.

"I didn't do the front page, I just wrote the story," I said over and over. "I understand your objections and will pass them on to my editor."

"Just turn the ringer off," Ashley barked.

I put my forehead on my desk. I was struggling not to cry.

Ollie stopped by to see if I had anything new.

"The wood really burned me, Ollie. I don't know that any of my sources will ever talk to me again."

"Does that mean you're not filing tonight?" Ollie always focused on what was next.

"Tough to file if no one takes my calls."

"Cheer up—they're doing a 'sermon on the mount' today." Ollie put his sweaty palm on my shoulder. "So that'll likely be the wood. If there's ever a day to crap out, it's today."

When he walked off, I asked Ashley what that meant.

"Sometimes if they don't have any big breaking news to distinguish themselves from the *Post* and the *Star*, they just come up with a particularly strong 'take' on the old news via a house editorial," she said.

"Any idea what this one is about?"

"No, but I'm sure neither of us will be consulted and neither of us will care for it."

I put my head in my hands. "Great."

"Yep," she said. "Maybe we should just start drowning our sorrows right now."

At three p.m. or so, I asked the switchboard to screen my calls and take messages from anyone providing feedback, but the operators didn't honor my request. The calls kept coming. I suspected I knew why that was happening but I kept it to my-self. This was my penance. I took my phone off the hook, went down to the lobby, and bought myself a pack of Virginia Slims and a Bic lighter. I went for a walk around the block and smoked two of them, slurping in the nicotine.

"Since when do you smoke?" asked Harry, walking out as I was walking in.

"I'm trying to learn," I said.

"You okay?"

All my anger toward him had dissipated. I was too beat up for another fight. "Feels like we crossed a line on the wood," I said, shrugging. "Now people think I'm a racist."

He seemed incredulous. "What people?"

"Well, police officers, various sources I rely on, and of course black leaders in the community."

"Who?"

"Councilmen Barry, Moore, Hardy, Winter...um, Reverend Fauntroy—"

"Who?"

"Our congressman," I said.

"I thought DC didn't have a congressman," Harry said. "Lotta whining about that."

"He can't vote on the floor of the House, so fat lot of good it does us, although he can vote in committee, so I guess that is something." I gazed at him. Harry was really very beautiful, and he was kind to me, but goodness. "Have you really never heard of Congressman Fauntroy?"

"No, Luce. I've been globe-trotting for years, and the local government officials blur together, whether it's in Sydney or Auckland or Dublin. I'm not the one in my family in charge of cozying up to those folks. That's Danielle's gig." He cocked his head. "Is she still in Mexico?" he wondered. Then he resumed looking at me, studying my face. He cupped my cheek in his hand. "Poor girl. Sounds like you're having a tough day. I'm sorry about that."

The expression of concern was nice to hear. He was watching me closely and, I thought, tenderly, and I wondered what he saw. I had a sudden yearning to rest my head on his shoulder and cry about this crappy day. It was nuts that I was so attracted to him; he was not my type in theory, but I was drawn to him like a ship to shore. But we were on a busy Georgetown street in front of the office. And I certainly wasn't going to make the first move.

"Don't be sad," he said. "The issue sold off the stands. Best day the *Sentinel* has had by far. And that's really all that matters. Dad's celebrating by taking us all to Studio Fifty-Four tonight."

"Studio Fifty-Four?" I said excitedly. "In New York?"

"Why don't you go home early and have a little rest before the car comes? Get gussied up. Wear your best dress. Let's have a good time. You're entitled to some joy."

We climbed aboard Max's business jet, a swanky new Cessna Citation II, the most gorgeous aircraft I'd ever laid eyes on and a long way from coach on Continental. We were dressed to the nines. I wore a gold lamé dress, and Danielle, who had finally returned from Mexico, wore a black satin Halston. Stunning. Ashley joined us, looking as if she'd walked off the cover of *Cosmo*. Then Harry came aboard, late but effortlessly cool in a dark blue suit straight out of *The Spy Who Loved Me*, and he was all I saw. The flight was boozy and fun, and we landed in Teterboro, a private airport across the Hudson River from Manhattan, and climbed into limos. There was one set aside for only Harry and me.

On our way, Harry looked at me after pouring his third glass of champagne and my second. Impish. Bad-boy scamp. Rakish. I wished the Connecticut snoots at Yale, the gals who didn't understand why I worked so hard at school, could see me now. I would have loved to take a photograph of Harry—or, better yet, some Super 8 film!—and send it to the reunion committee.

"What are you thinking, my love?"

I lifted my champagne glass. "To all the mean girls. I wish they could see me now."

"Oh, no, darling," he said, low and seductive. "This is a private party of two. You and me. Don't admit any goblins."

We drank. Harry boldly talked about *joie de vivre* and *carpe diem*; I told him these were great tenth-grade conversation topics but what was he driving at, and then a small glass container with white powder and a tiny spoon appeared. "Oh, I don't know, Harry."

"You've never done this? But you're the American princess."

"Hardly, Harry."

"Trust me," he said, so I did.

Music in the car turned up, Rolling Stones "Shattered"— *Shmatta, shmatta, shmatta, I can't give it away on Seventh Avenue!* Then we got to the actual Eighth Avenue, and at Fifty-Fourth Street, Harry helped me out of the limo, and there stood Max and Ashley and Danielle and Ivan, and everything around us was bright and wild, moving fast, oh so fast; fashionable crowds spilled off the sidewalk, super-skinny girls I'd seen modeling in *Vogue* and sweaty faces of all ages surged forward to the entrance, the sounds around me of French, German, and Arabic. I met the kind and ingratiating owners, Steve and Ian, Jewish guys with Brooklyn accents who came right over to the door and greeted each of the Lyons by name. I introduced myself, but they assumed I was just some piece of ass Harry had brought with him.

"Oh, you know them?" I asked Harry when they left.

"No, never met them before."

And a tall, lean doorman with feathered blond hair lifted the theater rope, and . . .

"Remember, polyester melts under the lights," Steve or Ian reminded a hulking bouncer. He meant the couple at the door in cheap clothes, shoes, and jewelry. To him, they were trash, the bridge-and-tunnel crowd. I caught the sad expression on the woman's face; she was crestfallen. *Polyester melts under the lights.* What a jerk. Harry tugged my hand: *Come on.*

Through the black doors and we were slammed by a ten-megaton blast of disco music, "Got to Give It Up" by Marvin Gaye: *Move your body, ooh, baby, you dance all night!* A Hiroshima explosion of sensory experiences, flashing lights and lasers and a fog of marijuana hit like a World War I chemical weapon, then — *Holy shit, there's Liza Minnelli and Paul Newman and Farrah Fawcett Majors and Richard Pryor* and *Did you see Cher and Woody Allen and Warren Beatty and Diana Ross?* I'd never before (nor have I since) been in a room with so many celebrities. *Holy fuck, it's Elton John, and is that Halston?* Andy Warhol and Barbra Streisand and Henry Winkler and Bianca Jagger and Truman Capote — *Is that Liz Taylor? Jesus* — and Peter Frampton and Sylvester Stallone and Carrie Fisher and Iman and the Bee Gees and Divine, and I didn't know which celebrities were really there and which ones were just people who looked like them. *I'm trying to keep my bearings but the walls are cabernet, mirrors like a haunted house.*

And Harry was wild, the way he moved on the rainbow floor squares. He didn't care what anyone thought, and where was his dad, anyway? Or Danielle or Ivan or Ashley? Then Harry grabbed me as the beat blended seamlessly into the Trammps' "Disco

Inferno," *Satisfaction came in a chain reaction!*, and he pulled me closer and we were grinding, and then he was kissing me, and I couldn't get enough. His hands were all over me, tugging at the waist of my dress, and he said, "Is this dress made out of gold? You're made out of gold, aren't you?" We were so high, and I was so happy. I had never been this wildly happy or free. But then, I'd never dated 007 or flown in a Cessna into a private airport or danced my ass off at Studio 54, and the music, the music, which was not exactly what I listened to on the radio, this four-on-the-floor *thumpa-thumpa-thumpa-thumpa*, was primal and decadent, deep in its syncopated bassline, strings and horns like Harry's kisses on my neck, chicken-scratch guitars and synthesizers, the latest hottest hit whipping the crowd into madness—

> *Dogs in heat (Whoo! Whoo!)*
> *Sweaty beasts, give the dog some bones*
> *Dog wants meat (Whoo! Whoo!)*
> *Fetch and beg and make 'er moan*

Harry and I were joined at the hips now, grinding like a pepper mill, and he was whispering, "I want you so bad, do you feel it, tell me you feel it too," and it was a heady thing, this beautiful man wanting me, and I threw my head back and laughed and then I glanced around the room at the lights and the crowd and the celebrities and...*Jesus.*

There was Max, standing with Ashley and a Twiggy-esque model whose skimpy tank top and short shorts left zero to the imagination, and next to her was...Roy Cohn.

Roy Cohn.

Roy. Fucking. Cohn.

Holy crap.

Roy Cohn, my dad's onetime enemy, Senator Joe McCarthy's

former chief counsel, a major instigator of the deranged Red Scare: *Are you now or have you ever been a Communist?* Mom and Dad hated him. An unscrupulous demagogue who had suffered no consequences from his reign of terror, his destruction of countless lives. What had Mom said? *At least McCarthy had the courtesy to drink himself to death.*[1] And here was Cohn, his wide-collared shirt unbuttoned to his navel, drinking with my boss while the disco version of the *Star Wars* theme blasted and R2-D2 bleeped and blooped.

Why was Max with Cohn? Why was that thug Roy Cohn even at a place like Studio 54? Then either Steve or Ian gave Cohn a backslap and a light kick in the rear followed by a tousle of Cohn's thinning hair, all in one sleazy disco *battement fondu.* Cohn looked turned on and somehow also annoyed, and I figured the owners had hired Cohn; he was a New York lawyer, after all, he could help grease some palms on permits and liquor licenses...

The music changed, and Harry took a step back. "Stop thinking," he said. "You don't think at a place like this. It's a rule."

"Okay."

He smiled down at me, his eyes strange, like an animal's at night. "Tell you what. We'll go back to the limo, drink champagne, do another line, and make love."

My mouth opened. Nothing came out. People danced in a frenzy all around us.

Harry laughed with surprise. "You've never made love in a limo?"

"No."

A slow predatory smile crossed his face. "Oh, princess,

---

1 McCarthy was censured by the U.S. Senate in 1954 and died of a liver ailment in 1957.

another first for you. How lucky for me." He grabbed my hand, and the crowds parted for Harry as we made our way off the dance floor.

Suddenly everything went black.

Complete darkness. All the lights went out. The music stopped. I heard cries of "What is it, what's happening?" People started flicking on their lighters, which threw an eerie glow across their faces but was otherwise not much help. All around us, there were more and more flames from lighters, like stars in the sky. My teeth were chattering so hard, I thought they would break.

Then there was shouting, and a woman cried: "I can't see!" Another woman was weeping. It was so hot with everyone pressed together. Harry pulled me closer and said, "Let's get out of here."

Someone pushed me. I stumbled, but Harry yanked me up. Then we were scrambling to the door—or where we thought the door was—Harry shielding me with his body, gripping my wrist so hard it hurt. He said, "Look there," and I saw the flashlight's beam. Maybe a cop?

"Come this way, slowly!" the man with the flashlight bellowed. "Be careful. Don't push. Here's the exit."

Then we were out on the street. And it was chaos; police sirens from every direction, glass breaking, hoots of jubilation and shrieks of terror, men running down the middle of Eighth Avenue. A cacophony of car horns of every pitch and octave. We spotted Danielle on the street. She had her hands over her ears, a pose that made her look like a frightened child, horrified, victimized, Munch and Keane and the Napalmed little Vietnamese girl all in one. Ivan and Ashley stood behind her. Max was shouting orders.

"Took your bloody time, didn't you, Harry!" Max yelled when

he saw us. "Did you stop for a bite?" Then, to someone else, he barked: "Where the hell is that driver!"

"Rocco'll be here in a minute, Mr. Lyon," came a voice from behind me. I turned and saw two tall, muscular men, darker shapes against a dark sky. Bodyguards, I figured. Not even Dad, a sitting senator, had that sort of security. There had been men on the plane too, but I hadn't paid them much attention. Jesus, was I becoming one of those people who didn't even notice the staff around them? Was it privilege or discomfort? I wasn't sure. All I knew was that those bodyguards had moved us a block away from the huge crowd pouring out of Studio 54. The coke was fading. Danielle was still freaking out.

"What the fuck is going on?" she demanded, panicked. "Get us out of here! Get us fucking out of here now! What is happening? *What is happening?*"

"The car will be here in a second," the bodyguard said soothingly.

"No, I mean what is actually happening?" she shrieked.

"Blackout, who knows why," said Harry. "Energy crisis. Carter. You know. Is this our car?"

A limo was honking its way through the crowd in the street. People were beating on the window, asking to be let in. The limo swerved to the corner where we stood. The musclemen opened the doors and shoved us inside.

Max, in the seat behind the lowered divider window, leaned forward and barked orders at the chauffeur, Rocco. "Just go fast, and the rabble will leap out of our way," Max said.

In the passenger seat, the bodyguard watched the windows impassively. He had a gun on his lap. It was terrifying. Max kept shouting: "Put on the high beams! Honk your horn! Don't worry, if you run something over, I'll pay for your lawyer. Just go!"

As the limo moved forward, we watched people shatter store

windows with bricks and trash cans, then run off with whatever they could grab—televisions, record players, stacks of clothing. It felt like it had taken only minutes for the city to erupt. Someone tried to open the locked car door I was leaning against. Danielle screamed, "No!" The bodyguard lifted his gun, tapped the car window, and smiled at the man trying to get in. He saw the gun and ran.

"Lean on the horn!" Max yelled. "Hot-rod it!"

Over the course of one block, we saw two bonfires flaring in the streets. Something banged on the trunk of the car, and we all turned our heads. Then someone slapped on the window to my left.

"Listen to me!" Max shouted at Rocco. "Get. Us. The. Fuck. Out. Of. Here. Or I'll throw you out in that madness and drive us myself!"

"Yes, sir," Rocco said, speeding up into the crowd, causing folks to run onto the sidewalks. We came perilously close to barreling over pedestrians. Soon we were heading north, the only light coming from the headlights of other fleeing cars. Up ahead was Columbus Circle.

The crowds there were more jubilant but the streets were also more congested, prompting the limo to stop and start, stop and start, stop and start, causing another Max Lyon snarl. *"Move this fucking car and get us to the fucking bridge right fucking now, you fucking cunt!"* he yelled, and before any of us knew what was happening, Rocco pulled hard on the wheel and the limo was slicing through the crowd, and I heard screams and saw a man go over the front bumper and tumble off into the dark, and then we were up on the curb, ramming through a kiosk, wood splintering and spraying, and pushing through Central Park, and in my head all I could hear was *No, no, no, no, no,* but no words came out.

"What fresh hell—" Ashley said under her breath. I grabbed

her hand in disbelief. The Lyon children were impassive, as if it were completely appropriate for Max to demand that his driver plow through crowds, and of course the driver would do it. This was simply what one did if one was a Lyon caught in a blackout in Manhattan.

The limo tires made a terrible grinding sound as they ruthlessly chewed up park paths, and we bumped along past landmarks I'd loved since my childhood: Tavern on the Green, the lake, the reservoir, the Great Hill.

What the hell had I been thinking coming here? What kind of people were the Lyons?

"Just ride with me and I'll get you there, mates!" Max said, turning to us and smiling like a goddamned maniac.

Then we were out of the park and onto Central Park North and soon enough we were crossing the George Washington Bridge. The lights were on in New Jersey and at Teterboro Airport. We all let out a huge sigh of relief when we heard air traffic control was functioning fine. We were let in through the fence by guards and driven right to our plane. We ran onto the Cessna, everyone laughing and, soon after, drinking and applauding Max's audacity. Ashley was being wooed by our fearless leader and seemed distracted by that and she looked about three, four, or five sheets to the wind, and everyone celebrated King Max. What good fortune to have Max as the captain of our pirate ship, everyone said.

Everyone, that is, except me. I stared resolutely out the jet window, watching the lights of East Coast cities slide beneath us. Harry had gotten me out of that dark tinderbox called Studio 54, and yes, I was thankful for that. But what if our limo had hurt or even killed someone in those crowds? We had no idea and probably we'd never know, given the chaos. Max had kept us safe, I supposed, but he'd also demanded the driver run people over to get us to safety. I had never been a part of anything like that in my life.

I was ashamed.

We landed at National Airport, where cars waited for us. Harry ran his finger along my cheek and said we had unfinished business. He asked if he could come home with me. I told him I was tired, and I was driven back alone.

When I arrived bleary-eyed and exhausted at my apartment, the *Sentinel* was being delivered. The wood read: "Sacrificing Slugs: Do Carter's Wacko Energy Policies Endanger White Women? Our Editorial Inside." My disgust had to wait until I got some sleep. Little did I know how badly I would need it the next day, when everything got even crazier.

CHAPTER NINE

IKE

South of West Yellowstone, Montana

August 1977

I've got those hup, two, three, four, Occupation
G.I. Blues
From my G.I. hair to the heels of my G.I. shoes

—Elvis Presley, "G.I. Blues"

THE WHOMP-WHOMP-WHOMP of a nearby helicopter jarred me awake. Dante was already hoisting himself up, rubbing the sleep from his eyes. Johnny, in a sluggish, marijuana-induced haze, could barely lift himself off the rugs that made his bed. The chopper kept buzzing the camp, getting louder and louder.

"What's going on?" I asked Dante, scrambling to get dressed.

"Lucky Strong," Dante said. "Once or twice a year, the guvnor buzzes the camps to bring us news, like when Nixon resigned or if there's a blizzard coming. We all meet out in the field."

There was no way to survive these camps in winter's arctic temperatures. Dante had told me weeks before that some camps had winter lodging, which in our case was a low-rent fishing lodge roughly seven miles away whose owner was a veteran and let people crash until snow melted in the early spring. The Yo-Yo

UFO weirdos would move into an abandoned cannery. The survivalists stuck it out in a burned-out cabin with a wood-burning fireplace. Dante said that each winter, a few men died of exposure.

The Colonel came up from the river, apparently having just cleaned his face and teeth. "You all heard the rotor, right?"

"Sure did, Colonel," Dante said.

"Well, then, come along." Behind the Colonel came the campers who were healthy enough for the trek, including the guy who'd lost part of his left foot during the Battle of Dak To. Dante and I fell in behind our CO, as it were.

At the meadow, other groups poured in from different directions. Junior led the group of UFO cultists, all of them sporting raggedy clothes and long beards.

The helicopter whirring got louder. Then the bird appeared over the mountaintop, looped around the field, and started its descent. Leaves and thin branches flew off trees.

As a Marine, I'd flown on dozens of helos, and in Lebanon I'd seen guys knocked on their asses from the rotor wash and heard stories of service members chopped up by tail rotors. Given the flashbacks I'd been having since Lebanon, I girded myself for one now, but it never came. I watched the propeller slow to a stop as an image came into my mind of the blade lopping off my head. I can't really explain why, since I wasn't suicidal. Then again, I wasn't really enjoying being alive. The thought of Johnny and the others dying of cancer in that dark forest punched into my consciousness, reminding me how lucky I was to be alive. *C'mon, boy, stop the self-pity.*

Other groups trickled from the woods, losers and drifters and has-beens and never-weres, fringe freaks who sought refuge in the wild. The pilot shut down the engine, and in the sudden silence I wondered again how the hell I'd gotten here. Then wondered where there was left to run.

I thought about home. Before I dropped out of high school and joined the Marines, my best friend, Tony Trabucco, and I had gone to an end-of-the-school-year party with girls from Holton Arms, a local prep school. I bumped into an ex, Katie, who'd dumped me after her Nixon-donor father called my dad a traitor for coming out against the president during Watergate. I told Katie I missed her. It hurt to see her again, and we talked for a bit. I felt happier than I had in a while.

Then Tony approached us and said they had a friend in common, some lifeguard at the camp where she worked. He began flirting with Katie right in front of me. She didn't seem put off by it. I wanted to punch him in the face. Instead, I asked him when his girlfriend was getting back from her family trip to fancy-pants Pitchfork Island. Wasn't that just off the coast of Georgia? Katie soon left the conversation. Tony said, "Why the fuck would you say that? You guys aren't together anymore!"

But we got another beer. We acted as though it had never happened.

Until.

A few months later, toward the end of the summer, when Tony and I were about to return to Georgetown Prep with plans to rule the school, Mom and Dad went out of town for one of their capers, and Lucy was in New Haven, so of course I threw a kegger. It was a perfect end-of-summer night, a haze of grass and Everclear, cherry-red Jell-O shots and music blasting:

Billy, don't be a hero, don't be a fool with your life / Billy, don't be a hero, come back and make me your wife . . .

No, woman, no, woman, no, woman, no cry / No, woman, no cry, one more time I've got to say . . .

Now Watergate does not bother me / Does your conscience bother you? . . .

About midnight, we were standing on my porch and Tony

said, "Hey, man. Remember that night a few months ago when you told Katie I had a girlfriend?"

"Sure."

"Well, like two weeks later, when my folks were out of town, I picked her up and we went out and got hammered at the Tombs and I fucked her brains out." A shit-eating grin spread across his face.

I joined the Marines three days later.

Maybe that doesn't make any sense to you. But my universe already felt false, treacherous. I wanted out of the phoniness and cruelty of the Washington world our family had gotten trapped in. The president was a corrupt goon, and my best friend was a slimy asshole. I was seventeen, and nothing was real, no one was on the up-and-up. Mom and Dad were loving, but they didn't get me at all, and with Lucy off at college, I was utterly alone. I couldn't take it anymore, so I got out, which, looking back, was kind of crazy, since it tossed me into a world of Lebanese guerillas firing Kalashnikovs at my ass and me running for my life.

Three years later, here I was, looking for an escape from the escape from the escape. Maybe the locations weren't the problem.

Lucky Strong—big, burly, wearing his trademark long suede coat and ten-gallon hat—emerged from the helicopter. He waved when he saw me coming down the hill. He was shouting something I couldn't hear. The mystery vanished when a lanky man wearing a white jumpsuit and giant sunglasses popped out: Evel Knievel.

Evel strode through the waving grass with the confidence if not the buoyancy of Jesus on the Sea of Galilee. He raised his arms when he saw me, embraced me like a lost son. He smelled of bourbon and Lucky Strikes. "Ike, my main man, how you doing?" he said as if there'd never been any bad blood between us. "Lucky told me where you were and that you were safe. You're a sight for sore eyes."

I let the love wash over me, speechless, as he mussed my hair. The helicopter was still making quite a racket.

"Great to see you," I said, and then, not knowing what else to say: "These vets are amazing."

"Don't I know it!" He gave Dante a bone-crushing hand-shake, gave Johnny a gentler one. I'll say this: Evel, when he wanted to, could read people, and he knew how to work a crowd. I stood there and watched him do his magic. Evel looked back at me. "This campaign is going to be a hoot, jarhead! I'm so glad you're on board. We're going to shake shit up!" He turned to the Colonel.

Campaign?

Lucky pulled me close and shouted right in my ear: "I told him that you want him to run for president for real, that this is your idea! There's a whole plan." No one except me could hear him over the chopper engine. "I told him that you offered to hook him up with your dad and his advisers! All is forgiven!"

"But," I protested, "but—"

"Don't worry about details, tomorrow is a year away!" he shouted. He patted me on the back and pointed to the men coming to meet Evel.

It was like something out of ancient lore: different tribes walking in hierarchical choreography toward a central figure, though in our case not a warlord or patriarch or god-made-man but a middle-aged hustler in a white leather jumpsuit tight enough to show every muscle and a bit of middle-aged girth.

The survivalists, maybe seventy-five of them, were gritty and wiry and intense but benign enough. The Yo-Yos, though, were a whole other kettle of catfish. They seemed quite annoyed that they'd been brought out here. Their leader, a guy in overalls and flip-flops, sported a mohawk. His followers seemed high or insane or both; many of them wore dirty tunics or ratty bathrobes with not a scrap of clothing beneath.

As if reading my mind, Lucky turned to me and said, "Only a few still have any real sense of place and time. But we feel a degree of responsibility for all of them."

"Where are the people from the other camps?" I asked. "Reverend Russell's zealots and the rest."

"Different valleys," he said. "We'll hit them after."

The different groups gathered near the chopper. "All right, ladies," Lucky shouted through a bullhorn. "Thank you for coming, thank you!" The crowd cheered. "Thank you!"

"Where's your bike?" yelled some idiot Yo-Yo.

"The bike's waiting for me off the interstate," Evel shouted back, some anger in his voice, or maybe tension; it was tough to read. "And that's part of why we're here. Tell 'em, Lucky."

"Thank you, Evel, my friend," Lucky said, the bullhorn echoing across the field. "And everyone here—the honorable veterans, the inquisitive alienists, the resourceful survivalists—let's give it up for Evel and his advocacy for the privacy of these forests."

Big applause. I'd never heard anything about Evel championing these groups or their freedoms in any way, and I was skeptical of the claim. If Evel even let you use the pinball machine before he did, he'd alert Oslo about the Nobel he felt he deserved.

After the cheers subsided, Evel took the bullhorn. "I have some very, very sad news," he said, and—snap of the fingers—the mood of the crowd changed; they grew fidgety, anxious. "It's not news I ever wanted to have to deliver about someone so young."

He'd already had our attention, but a still silence came over the meadow.

"Elvis," he said. "Elvis Presley has died."

Ugh. What a kick in the gut.

"No!" shouted some people in the crowd. "No!"

I could relate.

"Can't be!"

"What are you talking about!"

"How?"

Fuck.

"The news is just coming in, so there are a lot of unknowns," Evel continued, "but the sad reality is the King had a heart attack—he was only forty-two—and died at home, at Graceland. He's now with his beloved sainted mother, Gladys, who only made it to forty-six..." He choked up, took a moment to collect himself. "Only made it to forty-six herself," he finished.

Evel had bragged plenty of times that he and Elvis were friends. How much of that was rooted in reality? I didn't know. But to watch him before this crowd, the way he kept tearing up, you'd believe theirs had been a true brotherhood. Maybe it was.

And, man, I got it. There was nobody I loved more than Elvis. It was hard to explain if you didn't already worship at the altar of the King—as they say, fifty million Elvis fans can't be wrong. I always felt like I had a special bond with him; I was born in 1956, the year he burst onto the scene with his single "Heartbreak Hotel," which rose to the top of the charts in pop *and* country and western *and* rhythm and blues. That was followed by his first album, which became the very first rock and roll record to hit number one on the *Billboard* charts. He was history, a rock and roll phenomenon who almost single-handedly dragged the United States out of the repressed Puritanism of the 1950s and into the wild 1960s. But beyond that, he was just fucking cool, and, for the first decade-plus of his career, he seemed pretty down-to-earth. He was drafted into the army and served honorably. He loved God and his mama, not necessarily in that order. Sure, his films—thirty-one of them!—varied in quality, but *King Creole, Loving You,* and *Jailhouse Rock* were all legitimately great, and I defy you to name a better hour of live TV than his 1968 NBC comeback special.

Then, of course, the songs. Even the late-era ones.

"In the Ghetto": *People, don't you understand? | The child needs a helping hand…*

"Kentucky Rain": *Seven lonely days and a dozen towns ago | I reached out one night and you were gone…*

"Suspicious Minds": *We're caught in a trap—I can't walk out…*

The man did more than just titillate teenyboppers in ways that would rightly concern any local town council. He spoke to a generation of men; he was the last musical icon of that 1950s and 1960s era to care about traditional values like honesty and country and Main Street. My dad was born in 1920 and Elvis came a full fifteen years later, but they were of a type, both men of that era, strong and kind, providers, protectors.

And now he was gone.

Just like that.

"Now, now, I know this is tough," Evel said to the masses, surveying the crowd, seeing everyone so distraught by the news. "I know how this cuts." He put his hand on his chest. "It cuts deep."

As Evel continued praising the King and sharing personal stories—the first time he'd met Elvis, the first time they'd gotten drunk together, the first time they'd gambled in Vegas together—some folks, mainly the Yo-Yos, wandered back in the direction they'd come from. By the end of his monologue, half the crowd was gone.

"And that's why I'm organizing buses and bikes and we're

going to convoy to Graceland!" he said, and I snapped back to attention. "We're going to pay our respects and have a good time doing it."

People cheered wildly.

"And *then*," he continued, "*then* we're going to go to Washington, DC, to tell Jimmy Carter and the Congress just what we think of the job they're doing! The refusal to acknowledge the cancer our soldiers are suffering from! The refusal to allow people to exercise freedom when choosing their medicines!"

I turned to Dante and Johnny, who looked—well, *pleased* wasn't the word, really, but they looked relieved, or maybe acknowledged, or heard. Seen.

Evel turned to the remaining Yo-Yos. "The secret files about extraterrestrial life that they refuse to share with us! Tell us the truth about Area Forty-One!"

"*Fifty*-One!" a guy in a bathrobe corrected.

"Fifty-One, I mean!" Evel said.

The veterans and the Yo-Yos were cheering, but I noticed confusion on the faces of the survivalists.

Lucky grabbed the bullhorn. "And we'll serve them notice on any other issue you have!" he said, pointing to the hairy bunch.

"Inflation!" one of them yelled.

"Arabs!" shouted a second.

"Welfare!" said a third.

"All of that!" Lucky thundered, and the cheers grew louder, exultant, angry. "All of it! They're going to hear from all of us!"

An hour later I grabbed the clothes and gear that had been loaned to me, handed them to the Colonel, saluted him, and said goodbye to the camp. Lucky and I flew with Evel back to the giant stone mansion Evel had personally designed. It sprawled across eight acres of towering cottonwoods and bright green ponderosa pine, the Butte Country Club abutting one side of his property, the jagged mountain range to the east. It was astonishingly beautiful land.

Evel offered me a bed to rest up in before our adventure began. His kind and lovely wife, Linda, and their kids treated me much better than Evel's crew ever had. Evel himself was hospitable enough, but his family was so warm and sweet, it made me long for mine—and wonder why this wasn't enough for him. After I showered and changed, Linda told me I could find Evel and Lucky out on the property, near the sixteenth green.

As I approached, I could hear Lucky and Evel discussing *Viva Knievel!*, which had been released to disappointing box office and, unsurprisingly, vicious critical reviews.

"So what does it mean?" Lucky asked.

"It means"—Evel looked down—"they're not gonna make any more Evel Knievel movies."

Lucky put his hand on Evel's back and said: "Disappointment's just a moment in time, friend. Who knows what doors will open after you burst into America's living rooms as a presidential candidate!"

Lucky looked around and noticed me standing a few feet away. "Hey, Ike, Evel was telling me earlier about Bob O'Bill," he said, deftly changing the subject. "You know Bob?"

"The electrician, right?" I'd met him at the Dead Canary once or twice. He'd done work there after a fuse-box mishap.

"Anaconda Electric Company," Evel said. "You know his wife, Joyce, had cancer?"

"I didn't," I said.

Evel took a pack of Lucky Strikes out of his jean jacket pocket, offered me one, lit both, and handed me mine. "He prayed and prayed and prayed for God to save his beloved Joyce.

Nothing. Cancer only got worse. Then one day, he changed his prayer. Had a vision, he said."

"No kidding?"

"A vision of the statue of the Virgin Mary. Right up there on the Continental Divide. Looking out over all of Butte." He took a long drag from his cigarette. "He said to God: If You cure the mother of my kids, I will build a statue to *Your* mother."

"Huh."

"Her cancer went away," Evel said. "Bob's a welder, so he made a five-foot-tall statue of the Virgin Mary, but now he's convinced it's not enough. He wanted to make a hundred-twenty-foot statue, but the FAA told him no go. That'd be so tall, it'd require blinking lights on Mary's head to keep the planes from crashing into it. So he's making it ninety feet. It'll go right there." He pointed at a mountain beyond his land. "Leroy Lee is designing it, and Bob's got a collection going, and the mayor and city council are all on board."

"Our Lady of the Rockies," Lucky said.

I didn't know what to make of any of this. Faith is a funny thing. On the one hand, I knew from near-death experiences, and I understood why Bob might want to express his appreciation. There wasn't anything I wouldn't do to protect my savior, Lucy, which was how I'd ended up camping in the woods to begin with. On the other hand, I could all but hear Mom arguing that the God I had been raised to believe in would prefer good works to a giant statue.

Evel squinted at the mountain. "I don't know how I feel about the Virgin Mary staring at my house. Lucky was saying a ninety-foot statue would be visible from here. What d'you think, jarhead?"

I glanced over at the mountain, then at Evel. "Lucky's right."

"I'm worried," Evel said. "I've made love to every woman in

Butte, married or single, and this statue is definitely going to be a boner-buster."

"Think of it as a sacrifice before the Lord," Lucky said, laughing. "'If a man will let himself be lost for My sake, he will find his true self.'"

Evel exhaled deeply, releasing not just the cigarette smoke but all concerns about the pending giant Virgin Mary. "I don't want to think about it anymore. Listen, jarhead, Lucky give you any details about the trip yet?"

The governor explained: Seventeen hundred miles to Graceland. Lucky planned for us to average seventy miles an hour and calculated we could be in Graceland in a few days. And after that, another long hard day or so of riding—depending on the weather—the nine hundred miles to DC, to the Capitol. To rally and protest and make a stand.

"You're making sure reporters cover this," Evel said.

"Absolutely," Lucky said. "Me and the girls talked to a bunch of national reporters, people from *Newsweek*, *Time*, the *Chicago Tribune*—"

"How did you know who to reach out to?" Evel asked. "Did you call that guy from Chicago?"

"Marty Pasetta? No," Lucky said. "Remember the PR guy we had for the Snake River jump? What was his name?"

"Shelly Saltman," recalled Evel.

"Shelly Saltman," Lucky said. "Back in '74, one of my girls copied his list of press contacts, all the names and numbers. We never had much use for it—until now. So me and the girls called a lot of them today. Told them about our trip to pay homage to the King. A bunch of folks from papers and local TV stations, the AP wire, they'll record us at stops along the way. After we get some notice," he added, turning to me, "you call your sister and get us coverage in Washington!"

"Lucky, that's a real light bulb you got going off there," Evel said, laughing.

I wasn't surprised they knew about Lucy's work. Lucky always knew much more than he revealed. "So the plan is head to Graceland, get attention along the way, and then what?" I asked. "Talk to the local press about Evel running for office?"

"Not just any office—president," Lucky said.

Evel peered at me. He must have discerned some skepticism. "You don't think I can be elected president?" he asked.

"Of course you can," I said. "Why *not* you?"

"Exactly," Evel said. "I mean, they almost nominated goddamn Bonzo last time."

"And Reagan's mission is to end Medicare," Lucky said. "Yours will be a bit more friendly to voters. *Giving* them things instead of threatening to take stuff away!"

Did Evel need a platform? What a bizarre topic to have to ponder. I hated this politics shit, but I knew you had to have an agenda, so you might as well have a good one that sought to help people. "That's smart," I said. "Think about those poor guys out in the camps. The guys in our convoy. You'll demand better treatment for our veterans, of course."

"Definitely," Evel said, latching onto my idea. "And that Vietnam cancer, we need to get to the bottom of that."

"And not just veterans—every citizen should have access to vitamin B-seventeen," Lucky added.

Those seemed like legitimate issues. Didn't know much about the vitamin. What else? I thought of Dad and everything he stood for, everything that made him good at what he did and good, too, for the country. You had to have vision, you had to stand for things, you had to have plans to make people's lives better. "And what then, Evel? Demand that the government tell the truth about JFK, about Martin Luther King, about aliens?"

I asked. "Demand that they stop sending our boys to die in foreign countries?"

Evel slapped me on the back. "You're real good at this stuff."

"Point is, Evel's gonna tap into that anger," Lucky said. "Doesn't even matter what our convoy is angry about, just that everyone's angry. We use that. We ride it to sixteen hundred Pennsylvania Avenue."

The next day, I was on my Harley with the wind in my hair and sun on my face. In RVs and on bikes, we all zoomed east on I-90 through Bozeman and Billings, then veered onto 212 near the Crow Rez. Made me think of Rachel—not that I needed any reminders. I had no idea if I could ever safely step foot in the Dead Canary again. Was there any way our paths could cross? Would I even be able to visit Butte? Would I ever see her again?

I didn't even know if she still worked at the bar. I remembered she'd told me that she was tending bar to help out a friend and she had no intention of sticking around that dump past Labor Day. What friend had she been helping? Who knows. Why Labor Day? She refused to explain. Like so many of Rachel's stories, there were gaps you could drive a convoy of Mack trucks through. I had never been able to figure out if her mystery made me want her more or less. Sometimes her opaqueness was truly annoying.

Evel rode at the front of the pack on a chopped Bonneville 750 and wore his trademark white jumpsuit. Lucky rode beside him, a little unsteady on an Electra Glide with gaudy after-market pipes, his suede coat flapping in the wind. Dante rode a Honda CB450 that Evel had set up with a stylish Steib sidecar; Johnny sat alongside him looking a bit like a World War I flying ace in an open-cockpit Fokker. Behind them were a few guys from the camp and a handful of others I didn't know. Five giant RVs followed closely behind us.

We rode for a full day, stopping only for gas, lunch, a bathroom break, and to fill our canteens with water. At some point, Evel swapped his good-looking but backbreaking hardtail chopper for a Glide with decent suspension and a proper seat. The 212 brought us into South Dakota—Spearfish—then back onto I-90, then Deadwood, Sturgis, and Rapid City, where Evel held a press conference.

"Our country is in serious trouble," he said. "We don't have victories anymore. We used to have victories, but we don't have them now." He kept it vague, and people nodded along like dippy birds. "Our enemies are getting stronger and stronger, and we as a country are getting weaker." Applause, applause. No proposed solutions, just lots of bad guys: Carter, the IRS, the Pentagon, reporters, Arabs. Lots of telling-it-like-it-is, even if the telling was actually just airing grievances. People loved it. Unpolished. Frank. Wild. Unpredictable. He was swarmed by newspaper photographers and TV reporters begging for his attention. He signed autographs for locals, and women screamed as he drove off. Kids ran after us waving flags. Everybody loved Evel, so he was happy.

We parked for the night near Mount Rushmore—Lucky knew Governor Kneip, who'd instructed the park folks to treat Evel in a manner befitting an American icon. Evel joined us in the field we'd transformed into our own campground. A big bonfire raged in the pits. The guys were all in high spirits. Evel grabbed a sixer from the fridge in one of the RVs and joined me and Dante and Johnny on our side of the fire.

"Good to be back on the road," Evel said, dragging a lawn chair over next to mine. He stretched his legs as the sun slid behind the enormous head of Teddy Roosevelt.

I knew exactly what he meant. My anxieties had vanished the moment we hit I-90. The unbridled speed under my complete control, the wind full force in my face, my jeans and boots my only protection from becoming road pizza—pure adrenaline, no speed limit. I loved it.

"The best," I said. "A nice dry sunny day too."

"Not much rain around here till spring," Evel said. He looked at Johnny, whose face was sunken and pale. "How do you like riding in that sidehack?" he asked.

Johnny rasped: "Would rather be riding"—he broke off for a moment, coughing—"but feeling the wind on my face in the sidecar is a close second."

Evel watched him. "You have access to those pills, right?"

Dante responded by shaking an orange bottle of the stuff.

"It's working?" Evel asked.

Johnny thought about it. "Not sure," he said. "It seemed to and then it seemed not to."

The fire crackled, and some tourists attempted to approach us. A pit-crew gang held them at bay; they'd set up a security perimeter around our circle. I took another gulp of my Coors.

"I read in the paper," Dante said, "that without Elvis, we'd all still be in crew cuts and saddle shoes. Without him, no Beatles, no Rolling Stones."

"No Evel Knievel," Evel added. "He was a daddy to me in a bigger, um, a *spiritual* sense, you know?"

"The longest-running show on Broadway is *Grease*," Lucky said. "And now they're making a movie version. Two of the top TV shows are set in the fifties, *Happy Days* and *Laverne and Shirley*. Fonz *is* Elvis. We're all his children in some ways."

"Is there any more beer?" asked an odd-looking fellow I'd never noticed before. I say *odd* because he wore a relatively clean white button-down shirt and khaki pants despite presumably living in a tent like the rest of us and shitting in a hole in the ground. He was with two other guys who looked and dressed the same.

"I can get some." I stood up. "Ike," I said and shook his hand.

"I'm Justice," he said. "That's Prudence and Fortitude."

"Are those *your* names or the names of your horses?" Evel asked.

"We were given new names by the reverend," he said.

"Ah, right," said Evel, nodding. "Reverend Russell."

"Yes, sir," said Justice. "Have you met him?"

Evel wore a flat smile I couldn't quite read. "Can't say I've had the pleasure."

"The question is whether Russell has met Evel!" Dante chuckled.

"Oh, no, sir," said Prudence. Or Fortitude; I wasn't sure. "You shouldn't even joke about that. The reverend is a righteous man who communicates with our Lord every day."

Evel snorted and downed his beer. "Yeah, okay," he said.

"Be right back," I said, heading to the RVs. I couldn't take that piety here any more than I could in DC. I'd never met Russell, but I assumed his followers were harmless Jesus freaks dedicated to worship and good works.

That said: *Shut up, man.*

I wondered when Reverend Russell's flock had joined us, and why. Elvis had recorded a lot of gospel; maybe that was the reason.

Five RVs were lined up nose to tail in the parking lot across the road. Only one had its lights on. I rapped my knuckles on the thin metal screen door and opened it before anyone could respond.

When I walked in, there sat Rachel.

CHAPTER TEN

LUCY

Washington, DC

August 1977

POLICE FIND THIRD SUSPECTED VICTIM OF SLUG SERIAL KILLER

By Lucy Marder

WASHINGTON, DC—The woman's body was found by a late-night jogger in the meadow with her arms splayed out and legs crossed, as if impaled on a crucifix. Police believe she may be the third victim of the Slug Killer. But that wasn't even the most frightening thing about this crime scene, according to investigators, who agreed to speak with me only on background. No, what most alarmed police was that this latest victim—whose identity is being withheld until her next of kin can be notified—was found in Lady Bird Johnson Park, a very public strip of federal land on the west side of the Potomac River, just off the George Washington Memorial Parkway in the line of sight of Abraham Lincoln sitting solemnly in his memorial chair. Out in the open. Easily discoverable. Meaning the killer may be growing bolder.

*　　*　　*

The tip had come to my home phone. A garbled voice my sleep-fuzzy brain couldn't identify said, "We got a call for a woman's body found in Lady Bird Johnson Park. The Slug Killer has another victim. Homicide en route."

"Who is this?" I asked, but the line went dead.

I glanced at the clock. It was almost three in the morning. I got up and dressed in a black sweatshirt and slacks and laced up my hiking boots with slightly trembling hands. Well, so what if I was afraid to go out to that murder scene alone in the middle of the night? Where the Slug Killer might still be? Jesus, I was only twenty-three! Whenever I was frightened, I told myself Ike would do it. And anything Ike could do, I could do better—*and* in cuter boots. Right? Right. I grabbed my stuff. Camera, check; press pass, check; car keys, check; purse in which I had re-porter's notebook and pen (I looked in quickly to make sure), check, check, and check. Three minutes after the call, I was out the door.

I knew Lady Bird Johnson Park well. When I was a teenager, as soon as I got my license, my friends and I would hang out in the park, drinking, gossiping; sometimes I'd go alone with a boy. We'd lie on the lawn and watch the jets coming in from the south to land at National Airport. There was a marina nearby, and sometimes boats would race past. It was the best view of the city, a beautiful place.

After crossing the Memorial Bridge, I sped down the GW Parkway. I thought I'd park at the marina like we did when we were kids, but the police had closed off the lot entrance. I had no choice but to leave my VW on the side of the highway—"Sorry, baby," I said, patting her warm hood—and I hoofed it from there. The police had closed off the marina, so they'd stop me from getting near the crime scene, but I remembered all the little paths from my girlhood.

Through the brush, I could see headlights in the distance. The sound of men's voices carried in the night. I followed the river, sheltered by the trees along it, then pushed through the foliage, and that's when I saw her.

That first glimpse stopped me in my tracks. I didn't believe I was seeing what was in front of me. That is, the body didn't seem real. I took a deep breath. *Details*, I told myself. *Look at the details*. I had to describe this if we were ever going to stop this guy.

I lifted my camera to get a better view.

A woman's body, illuminated by various electric lights. She was a redhead with curly hair, her body matronly, curvy. Fair-skinned. Her arms were splayed out, legs crossed. My mind reeled. *Okay, don't panic. If you panic, you can't think*. What were these details telling me? Was there a message sent in the way the woman was displayed? A warning? To whom?

No, it was about the woman, I thought. I detected anger at positioning her like this out in the meadow. I remembered Dad saying that for the Romans, crucifixion was the most brutal and cruel punishment. It was a warning, yes, but also a spectacle. And a great shame for the victim. I felt her shame in being left like that.

Her corpse was like macabre religious artwork. Art was owned. Her body had been used as a piece of property, not belonging to her but to the one who killed her.

I had no idea where those thoughts came from or why that image of the woman displayed like that said those things to me. Even as I stared at her, I thought, *I must be wrong. And how can I know? Stick to the facts*. I adjusted the camera's telephoto lens to see the face of the victim—once a beauty, she reminded me of a slightly aged figure in a Caravaggio I'd seen at the National

Gallery of Art. I took a single snap, but then a police official in a white shirt appeared a few yards in front of my lens, blocking the shot.

He did a double take when he saw me in the bushes. He came my way, waving his hands. "I'm sorry, Miss Marder, this is a crime scene," he said, surprising me by knowing my name. "No pictures. You got to go."

"I'm the press." I held up my press pass for him.

"I know who you are," he said.

"Who is she?"

"We don't know."

"Is she a victim of the Slug Killer?"

"Jesus, you people. That's only a theory. Who tells you this stuff?"

He ordered an officer to walk me back to my car. The sight of what the Slug Killer had done to that woman—let's just say I wouldn't be forgetting it, not for a long time.

"Your prose is more Bernstein than Breslin," Harry said. We were in his corner office with astonishing views of the Potomac and Roosevelt Island and, farther off, the Virginia skyline. He was reading the piece I'd just filed.

"Thank you."

"It's not a compliment," he said. "We're tabloid. *We're* Breslin."

"I don't follow," I said.

"Are you aware that the Forty-Four Caliber Killer wrote a letter to Breslin? The paper just published it."

I got chills. "The killer wrote to Jimmy Breslin?" I whispered, in awe of the legendary *Daily News* columnist's get. Or maybe it was envy. Sometimes it was hard to know the difference.

Harry's bright eyes glowed with excitement. "He called himself 'Son of Sam,' and those letters, that reporting, is sending the

Daily News circulation, especially newsstand sales, as high as the Empire State Building. Wait, let me show you."

He got up from behind his desk and grabbed a newspaper from his sofa. I loved the way he moved and the timbre of his posh British accent when he got excited like this. From the beginning, he had been my most stalwart supporter in the newsroom. I loved the way he made me feel in the office—and, on that Manhattan dance floor though not replicated since, outside of it.

But the night of the blackout still bothered me. His dad telling the driver, *Move this fucking car, you fucking cunt!* and the horror of Rocco knocking over pedestrians, driving through the kiosk, barreling across the grounds of Central Park. *I'll get you there, mates!* Max grinning like a maniac as Danielle and Ivan and, oh God, even Harry toasted him later. Max, the captain of our pirate ship.

Harry handed me a *New York Daily News*. I unfolded the paper to see the wood: "Breslin to .44 Killer: GIVE UP! IT'S ONLY WAY OUT!" On page three, Breslin in gripping detail recounted receiving the letter and responding in kind.

"Isn't it amazing?" Harry said.

I read it, and it *was* exciting, and also terrifying. I wondered what the letter the killer sent to the cops had said and thought how relieved the *Daily News* writers must've been to have the story going in new and gripping directions, leading into the unknown.

"People are terrified," Harry said. "The madman is stalking young women and shooting them for no reason. And while your precious *Times* has written, what, two stories about this? The *Daily News* and the *Post* are eating the *Times*' lunch!"

"I mean, they're eating hot dogs from a street vendor," I said. "That's not what the *Times* is eating for lunch."

Harry gave me a slow, knowing smile. "The sweaty masses

are lining up for those hot dogs. *Daily News* circulation is up fifty percent and the *Post*'s is up twenty-five percent since the killings started."

I knew what he was saying. Son of Sam's letter to Jimmy Breslin was mesmerizing, but it wasn't the sort of thing that had gotten me into this work. "Well, it's your dad's menu," I said. "Hot dogs—fear and anger."

"Oh, he didn't invent the menu, darling," Harry said. "Consumers did. And I know you want to be William Safire, but you could be so much bigger. You could be Breslin. But young. And ravishing. A woman at the beginning of a stratospheric career. That's what I want for you. *Stardom*."

It was heady. Who wouldn't want to be powerful? Ravishing? A *star?* I could really get into being a star. But the way Harry was setting it before me, like a gift, or a seduction—I felt like there had to be a catch. What was the catch? Then I realized what he was driving at. "Your dad wants a Son of Sam of his own, doesn't he? That's what you're saying?"

Harry's bright eyes sparkled with barely contained excitement. "No, darling, I'm saying we already have one."

The next morning, I was determined to do another story on the third victim, who she was, why she might have been targeted, why the killer might've altered the scene for this latest killing, why he changed the way the body was staged.

The image of her corpse haunted me. Fair-skinned, with long curly red hair, not blond hair like the other victims, and heavier, or at least not as athletic and lean as the first two women killed.

The differences in body type and staging weren't all that bothered me, though. There was something more. It felt different—nightmarish, an escalation, somehow angrier, if that makes any sense. I couldn't quite put my finger on why. I needed someone close to the investigation to talk to me.

I left messages for the same police sources who hadn't returned my calls from the day before. I banged away at the keyboard of my swanky computer, searching through the database, scanning other newspapers for any reporting about this third victim, but I came up empty. The police still hadn't released the victim's name, although they had to know who she was. After notifying family members, they always put out a statement to the press. Why the delay? Out of desperation, I called my nemesis, MPD spokesperson Mimi Spanjian. "There's been a holdup with ID'ing the victim," she said.

"What kind of holdup?"

"I can't say."

"Please, Mimi. Throw me a bone."

Mimi laughed. It was the first time I'd heard a joyous sound from her in years, although I knew it was intended as a criticism. Even back in high school, when she laughed, it was often at my expense. "My boss would prefer me not to chat with you," she said, smug as hell.

"Your boss? Who?"

"Who do you think? The chief. You made us look like we're leaking racist shit. Do you have any idea how that plays in DC? With a white police chief? Also, if I can point out, none of our people know *who the hell your alleged person of interest is.* Our detectives don't have a person of interest. Maybe he's a figment of your racist imagination."

Except that their chief had told Max. But Harry had made me promise not to say a word, so I had to sit there and take it.

While I was on the phone, a flunky from Photo handed me a manila interoffice envelope. Ah! They'd developed the one shot I got of the corpse! I opened it. The developers had zoomed in on parts of her body, so I could see the bruises on her neck. I also saw that the vic had subconjunctival hemorrhages—bloody red eyes. Another sign of a strangling death. "Look, Mimi, you've got to give me the name of this victim. It's public record."

"Not yet it's not," she said happily. "And when we release that info, guess who gets the very last call?"

I studied the photo. Something had stuck in the back of my brain that night, a matter unsettled, an aspect of the crime scene I'd seen from a distance and fleetingly and that this photo now resolved for me.

"You can take that position, of course," I said. "Or you can tell me about the hypodermic needle in the vic's arm."

"*Motherfucker!*" she said. She liked that word.

Then, after a pause: "Okay, please don't report that. Please. It will impede the investigation. Please, Lucy. I'm requesting this on behalf of MPD."

"And?" I said.

"You'll be my first call when the ID comes in. Not last. First."

After I graduated from Yale, Dad took me to lunch at Martin's Tavern in Georgetown, where Jack had proposed to Jackie and where Mom and Dad had had a night drunkenly reciting poems with the two of them and Bobby and Ethel. *The world is more transactional than anything you've ever experienced up to now*, he'd said. *Find out what people want and provide it.* I'd never better understood what he meant.

Not long after, Otto stopped by my desk and told me Max wanted to see me, so I went to his office. "You wanted to see me, sir?"

Max was behind his desk, feet up, *Washington Post* spread wide. A copy of the morning *Sentinel* lay on his desk: "Slug Killer Slays Third Vic," with an artist's rendering of the as-yet-unidentified victim crucified on the grass with the Lincoln Memorial behind her, and "Lucy Marder Scoops!" in white letters on a red oval. Beside the *Sentinel* was a steaming mug of the rich-smelling South African coffee imported for the top editors.

"PR's going to get you on local TV news," he said. With the paper pumping me up as some sort of star reporter and others unable to match our scoops, local TV stations had been clamoring for an interview. If you can't beat 'em, interview 'em.

"Sir, I appreciate it, but I already told Harry and Ollie *and* PR that I'd prefer to lie low until this storm with my sources blows over a bit."

He lifted the mug of coffee, watching me over the rim. "We're trying to get face time for our scribes, especially the ones we're going to be putting out on the campaign trail," he told me, ignoring what I'd said. "Has anyone talked to you about the trip to that Georgia island? The GOP retreat?"

Ah, there it was. The dream dangled again. The Pitchfork Island event itself was off the record with no journos formally invited, but Dad had been going to the confab since the 1950s, and I could go and keep him company (he'd brought Mom a few times, but she'd hated it and spent the whole time bird-watching). Once the site of a Confederate outpost, Pitchfork Island now boasted a posh hotel and a beach community accessible only by boat, an exclusive locale that made Sea Island look like Atlantic City. I could make contacts, get in with the candidates and campaigns, get a leg up on the competition for Campaign 1980.

I felt like Pavlov's dog running out of drool.

All the most ambitious reporters in America were jockeying for a chance to pack up for Campaign 1980. Many Republicans seemed to think Carter's narrow victory the year before was a fluke, the last lingering Nixon hangover. Ford was contemplating another run, though a Gallup poll had former California governor Ronald Reagan favored by a full one-third of GOP voters. But it was early, and dozens of senators and governors and former FBI and CIA heads were contemplating campaigns. Moreover, another Gallup poll showed Democrats preferring Senator Ted Kennedy to President Carter, and California governor Jerry Brown was making rumblings about possibly running as well, so a Democratic primary fight could happen too.

Reporters like me ate it up. We read everything by Woodward and Bernstein, Hunter S. Thompson's *Fear and Loathing: On the Campaign Trail '72*, and Timothy Crouse's *The Boys on the Bus*. We wanted on that bus so badly. We had the fever. The presidential campaign was *the* plum assignment. I wanted it, and the *Sentinel* wanted me; a major reason for my hire, Danielle had said, was my deep connection to all those Republican luminaries I'd grown up around.

But if I wanted that dream, I had to do what Max said: Go on TV and defend our newspaper. Problem was, the editorial Max was telling me to defend—"Sacrificing Slugs: Do Carter's Wacko Energy Policies Endanger White Women?"—was indefensible. It did what my journalism professor taught us was the worst thing reporters could do: make ourselves the story. Mayor Washington, the DC City Council, the *Post*, the *Star*, and seemingly all local news outlets condemned us and our tabloid journalism. A few hours after that hit the newsstands, Carter's press secretary Jody Powell said at a press conference that the *Sentinel* wasn't worthy of lining Misty Malarky Ying Yang's litter box. I suppose there were worse things to be compared to than the paper on which Amy Carter's pet relieved itself, but the entire White House press corps laughed. At us.

"Sir, I'm worried about going on TV and exacerbating an already difficult situation."

"What in heaven's name are you going on about?" Max thundered.

"Our coverage is making it so no one will talk to me about the story anymore. My information well has dried up."

Max pursed his lips. "Because of the blacks?"

I winced. Boy, the Lyons were clunky on matters of race. "Because everyone from the mayor's office down to the beat cops on Fourteenth Street think I'm a reckless, scaremongering racist."

"Oh, that. Well, they'll get over it after we become the number-one paper in the region," Max said confidently. He set his mug down with a smirk. "Trust me. And then after that, we'll be the number-one local news on TV!"

"You can't own both a paper and a TV station in the same city," I said. "Not in the United States. You know that, right?"

"Not yet," he said mysteriously. "But we will be able to. An era of freedom is coming to this country, and when it comes, we'll be ready. There is a segment of the public who want us, who need us. Badly."

"Either way, it doesn't make sense to alienate the black population in a majority-black city."

"Well, I'm not talking about them, and in any case, *alienate*? Says who?" He looked bemused. "You have data for that? Or are you just going by a bunch of bloviating politicians?"

"We've been pushing this black person of interest, something no other news organizations have reported, and the wood headline? 'Endanger White Women'?"

"We didn't say the perp was black," Max said. "We just noted the two—now three—victims have been white."

He couldn't possibly be this thick, could he? "But, sir, why even bring race into it?"

"We didn't—the murderer did," he said. "If the victims were

all Chinese girls, you don't think we'd note that? You don't think black readers care about white women being killed?"

"I think they don't like racism," I said, wincing on the last word, sure he would blow up. He was my boss, everybody's boss, he was *Max Lyon*, and I really needed to stop arguing and get back to working the story. Except I couldn't stop. I was right, damn it. This would be such a good job, if only he could see...

"You Americans are so bollixed on this stuff," he said. "If a black man kills a black man, is it news? What about if a black man kills a white man? Or if a black man kills a white woman? I can't keep track. You're all over the bloody map."

I thought about Dad sitting me down to tell me about Dr. King, about the city burning, not even ten years ago. Could I say I was afraid we were running in the wrong direction in our nation's hideous four-hundred-year history of racism and charging right back into telling one group of people to be terrified of another? That I knew how violence generally followed that fear? That I couldn't be responsible for someone being hurt?

Would he even hear me?

Max was still puffed up and ranting. "Our newsstand sales were up thirty-five percent in white suburbs. Thirty-five percent." He smashed his fist on the desk. "And our circ, including newsstand sales? That didn't change in black neighborhoods, not by half a percent. Not with *this* edition. If these blacks are so offended, why are they still buying? Why would you assume every black thinks exactly like whatever pompous knob you're talking to? You know what else I think?"

"I'm afraid I don't, sir."

"I think our black readers care very much about a serial killer who preys on women, including white women. And I'm alarmed you suspect otherwise."

"I didn't—" I began.

He interrupted me, thankfully. "Perhaps Harry's wrong about you. Perhaps you're too young and naive to understand that condemnation by public figures is not reflective of public sentiment. That it's a big show for their loudest, whiniest constituents. If you can't understand *that*, how in the hell can we assign you to our presidential campaign coverage?"

"I'm not naive." I straightened my back. I made myself sound more forceful. "I can handle the campaign."

His eyes were so cold. "Prove it."

The next day, I dressed in my favorite man-tailored pantsuit, a knockoff of an Yves Saint Laurent outfit I'd seen Cheryl Tiegs wear on the cover of *Glamour*. The suit made me feel pretty but also confident. I needed confidence. I was terrified of going on television in general—I had never been on TV before—and wondered if PR had purposely set me up with Channel 4's Jim Vance and Sue Simmons, the first black coanchors of any local TV newscast in any major market in the U.S. Surely they'd ask me about the racial subtext—or text, really—of too many of the *Sentinel*'s headlines and covers. It wasn't fair of Max to throw me out there to defend his worldview, one I didn't share and even found frightening.

I took a cab to WRC-TV headquarters on Nebraska Avenue NW. A production assistant shuttled me over to the anchor desk as Sue Simmons was finishing a report on the arrest of suspected Son of Sam serial killer David Berkowitz, a postal employee.

The lights were hot and I began to sweat. I looked down at my hands, which were shaking, and pressed them flat against the anchor desk, then folded them again, telling myself to be calm. Jim Vance, who was even more charming in person, gave me a reassuring smile as I exhaled and tried not to completely embarrass myself.

"Sadly, New York is not the only major metropolitan region dealing with serial killers," Simmons told viewers. "As you heard earlier, DC's own Slug Killer has struck again. Jim?"

"That's right, Sue," Vance said to the camera. "This victim, the third, has yet to be identified, but we wanted to take a moment to review what we know about the killer with a journalist who has been breaking more stories on this than perhaps anyone else, Lucy Marder of the *Washington Sentinel*. Lucy, thanks so much for joining us. Are police sure this third victim is related to the other two?"

Phew. "Thanks for having me, Jim and Sue, it's an honor to be here," I said, giving Jim a wobbly smile. "Right now, investigators are operating under the assumption that it's likely the same killer because the victims are all white women, and the method of death, strangulation, is the same. But they are not yet one hundred percent there."

"So no physical evidence tying the three together, though?" Vance said. "Fingerprints, hair follicles? Forensics?"

"Not that we've been told," I said. "Obviously, there are details being withheld for investigatory reasons. But you mentioned Son of Sam, who, we should note, was caught for a few reasons. Most important, a woman saw a guy acting weird in the neighborhood where the killer had murdered Stacy Moskowitz, and she remembered seeing a cop giving out parking tickets on that street. Cops checked out all the cars ticketed in the area that night and began to suspect Berkowitz. They staked out his building and questioned him when he got in his car, and he confessed. The Slug Killer has never been spotted, so there are no leads, no tickets, no police sketches—though I should note that even those sketches of Son of Sam were apparently way off, based on the pictures we've seen of Berkowitz. Eyewitness testimony is hardly definitive. It's actually pretty suspect, in my opinion."

"It's interesting you raise the question of the credibility of witness testimony," Vance said, "because the *Sentinel* has been criticized by many public officials for reporting that a black man was seen near one of the crime scenes, with nothing more than that. Have you learned anything more about that alleged person of interest? And what is your response to the criticism that the reporting and the cover suggesting the killer is targeting white women and that somehow President Carter is to blame is the worst kind of tabloid journalism?"

Whoa. Okay, I thought. *Composure.* Also: *Remember, he's, you know, right.*

"A lot to address there, and I appreciate your asking," I said. "First, the man who's a person of interest is *not* a suspect. He's a person of interest. The police wonder if he saw anything. That was all explained very clearly in the story."

"Maybe not as clearly in the headline," Vance said.

I nodded, then pretended he hadn't said that and continued. "I haven't heard of police receiving any reliable information about who that man might be. If anyone watching this show does have information, I would be thrilled to talk to them. Please call me at the *Sentinel.* But as of now, we have nothing new."

Vance reached under his anchor desk and brought out a copy of the notorious edition I loathed. "And this paper? You stand by it?"

"I stand by my reporting, of course," I said.

"But not the paper itself?"

"What you're referring to there is an editorial written by the opinion folks, which is separate from the news. I knew nothing about that editorial or the plans to put it on the cover. Which is similar, I suspect, to NBC's news division airing that preposterous special on killer bees in prime time without your knowledge or say-so."

Vance grinned, seemingly amused by my verbal jousting. "I thought that special was silly," he said. "What did you think of that cover?"

I considered this. "I think my job as a journalist is to educate and enlighten, and the job of an editorial writer is to provoke."

"I suspect that you would argue that you're not saying a black killer is out there murdering white women."

"We're not," I said. "We're reporting that police are seeking a possible witness, a person of interest, who is black, and separately we're reporting that all the victims so far have been white women. These are facts. Experts say serial killers tend to be white men. I don't know anything about the killer, but I'm working my tail off to make sure the public knows all the facts about him so he can be caught and stopped. And I'm sure, Jim and Sue, that you feel the same way. The connection to the carpool lanes that the Nixon administration started and the current energy crisis that President Carter is trying to deal with—that's editorial, that's opinion, that's not my lane. Pardon the pun."

"Well, if I may," Sue said as the director and cameramen scrambled to include her in the conversation, "you are, it is well known, the daughter of a prominent Republican senator." I nodded. "And your boss, the publisher of the *Sentinel*, is Max Lyon, a conservative, proudly so. I mean, he's a member of the British Conservative Party."

"Yes?" I said.

"A critic might say that conservatives in this country tend to suggest negative things about the black community, tend to emphasize our community only in terms of those who live off the public dole or who are perpetrators of crime," she said. "We hear it in every message from party leaders. Do you not think your reporting is possibly being twisted to achieve those ends, those messages?"

In my gut, I agreed with Sue about the twisting. But oh, my father was being drawn into this. And oh, how I hoped he wasn't watching.

"My father is a major supporter of civil rights, and you know that if you look at his record, and anyone with knowledge of LBJ's push for the Civil Rights Act knows that, percentage-wise, more Republicans supported those bills than Democrats did," I said. "Now, that said, that's my dad, not me. I am a journalist invited here to discuss my factual reporting about a killer I hope the police will catch before another woman is murdered, which seems to me of more interest to your viewers than who my father is. All the rest of it, the debate over an opinion piece, how to get people to pay attention to news, whether those methods create impressions in readers and viewers that are unintended or careless—it's a debate, for sure, but it's not part of my job, and frankly I'm focused on something else: the killer and the risk to women's lives."

Vance said, "If I may—" but I interrupted, thinking of what Harry had told me about the Son of Sam letter to Jimmy Breslin and that New York might have caught their Son of Sam, but we still had ours.

"Just one more thing, Mr. Vance, and please forgive me," I said. "The Slug Killer remains at large, and he is very, very dangerous, and we know nothing about him. Not his race or his motivations, not where he lives or where he might strike next. And I know you at WRC and we at the *Sentinel* will keep working on this story until he's no longer a danger to our community. Whenever that is. We've got to find him. And if anyone out there has any information that might help, please call the police or call me at the *Sentinel* or call Jim and Sue here at WRC. He must be stopped. I've seen his handiwork and he must be stopped."

I'd filibustered, which I'd seen others do on live TV. That

hadn't been my intention, but Vance gave me a look that said, *Nicely done, kid*—though I wasn't sure if he meant it as a compliment—and turned to the camera. "And with that, we'll be right back."

One thing I'd learned from Dad was that the zeitgeist was often malleable and depended on what experts told the public to think. Were the Kennedy years Camelot? Only after Jackie, blood still on her pillbox hat, decided that was the word that should go forth to historians and journalists. Was Howard Baker a hero? Maybe not really, but Fred Thompson figured out a way to fix it in post. As I cabbed from Tenleytown to Georgetown, I didn't know how it had gone. Jim and Sue had worn their professional masks. The producers and crew were polite and thanked me for my time, but they were focused on what was coming after the commercial and on makeup, scripts, the teleprompter, the control room in their ears. Print and broadcast news differed in many ways, but that one fact was the same; it was always *Okay, what's next?*

I tried to game it out in the taxi once I left, but I had trouble remembering it all, and I wasn't great at assessing how I came across to others. Sometimes when I thought I was being witty, my comments were interpreted as snobby. Or bitchy. When I thought I seemed like a doofus, some found me endearing. I imagined Max would think I hadn't defended the paper forcefully enough, and Harry would argue that I'd performed more than adequately. Who knew where Danielle would come down. Wherever her father landed, I supposed. While she had originally wooed me to join the Lyon brood, she'd not spent as much time as I'd thought she would in the newsroom; she was always off on unexplained missions. I'd figured we'd be closer friends by now.

Oh, how I wished Ike were here. God, I missed him. Only

Ike ever gave it to me straight, the good and the bad, like the wonderful little brother he was.

It was a swampy DC summer night. The cab had no AC—or the driver had no desire to burn the extra fuel for its Freon—so I rolled down the window and breathed in the humid air. The bus exhaust punched me in the throat. What I wanted was to go home and have a glass of wine and a nice cool bath. Where I actually went? The *Sentinel* offices on the Georgetown waterfront.

The newsroom was busy putting the paper to bed; deadline was coming at them like a train. No one said anything about the Channel 4 interview. Max and Harry were nowhere to be found. I sidled up to my desk. Next to it, Ashley was typing furiously. Had she seen the interview? Did she think I did okay?

"I feel you looking at me, sister," she said. "And I got a lot of thoughts. Many, many, many thoughts. But I'm crashing on a front-pager on the Whites and B-seventeen. Social Services teamed up with MPD, found the White family, and seized Caleb. Ripped him from his parents. So I can't."

As she typed away, I looked through the mail on my desk, using the letter opener Dad had given me for graduation (among other gifts; Dad's a spoiler), then reached into my inbox.

The first letter was from an angry city councilman. The second was already opened; it was an irate note from the proprietor of a black-owned furniture store in Northeast DC to the *Sentinel* business department canceling advertisements for a pending Labor Day sale, which had been ever so helpfully forwarded to me. Another dozen were angry letters from readers. They were raw and vitriolic, suffused with grievances both recent and centuries-old, some profane and some decorous, and all of them completely on point.

"Can't wait for the p.m. batch of hate mail, right?" I said to Ashley.

"Still crashing," she said, head bent over her keyboard. "If I had the time, though, I'd write one of those letters myself."

I sighed. I would have too.

Across the newsroom, next to Max's enormous desk, Ollie yelled: "Get the hell out of here!" He was arguing with Dick Flug, our slim, slick, chain-smoking Capitol Hill reporter. I wandered over.

"This is a great story, Ollie!" said Flug, who thought every one of his stories should be the wood, and if you had a free hour, he'd be happy to explain why.

Ollie took off his glasses and rubbed his weary eyes. "The very mention of the words *Senate hearing* has me falling asleep, Flug. Ashley has a huge story on the White family's kid being seized by Social Services, and the boss has a house edit calling for Secretary Califano to resign or be impeached over his refusal to support families that want laetrile. *Those* are good stories."

"But this is too," Flug protested. "Senate's holding an antitrust investigation, very hush-hush, and a witness went missing."

"Jesus, you managed to get the word *antitrust* in there too?" Ollie said. "Work in *reconciliation* and *markup* and you win Boring Bingo!"

Flug was indefatigable, though. "This laetrile thing is pure quackery," he said, bemused, not angry, as he walked by my desk. To me he said: "Ironic that my story's being shit on for that nonsense."

"That's not what *ironic* means,"[1] I said.

But he couldn't have cared less. Over his shoulder, he warned: "I'll come back tomorrow with more in my quiver."

---

1 People: *Irony* is when a phrase is used to express the exact opposite of its literal meaning. It's not a synonym for *coincidental* or *funny* or *annoying*. Please stop misusing this incredible word or by next century it will have lost all meaning.

You couldn't rain on Flug's parade.

I checked something on my computer, then walked to Ollie's desk. "You should have someone reach out to a woman named Opal DeHart," I told him. "Back in March, President Carter was a guest on a CBS radio show, and she called in and asked the president why the government wouldn't allow her cancer-stricken dad to try laetrile. He was terminal, what could it hurt? She was compelling. I think she was from North Carolina?"

He looked at me and his eyes lit up. "You're good," he said. "You wanna do it? Nah, too small for you. I'll find someone."

Harry came into the newsroom. I watched him swagger through the desks, smiling at me proudly. "You were amazing on TV," he said. Then, in a low voice: "Beautiful, smart. I want to take you to dinner tonight, a very late, very intimate dinner."

I looked up into his oh-so-blue eyes. And I did something he wasn't accustomed to: I hesitated.

He took a step back. He stared at me, confused. "What's wrong? What happened?"

I didn't know how to explain what I'd been feeling—the blackout, the limo running *over people* on the way to the private jet, the god-awful headline that still smarted, the fact that his father was the opposite of what I thought a journalist should be—none of it was Harry's fault, but still. These were feelings, not words; intuition, not a decision arrived at. But the newsroom was the last place to have any kind of personal discussion with Harry.

A staffer from the mailroom came toward us, waving an envelope. "Late-day delivery for Lucy Marder Scoops," he said with a grin. "You want me to drop it on your desk?"

"I'll take it," I said, thankful for the interruption. "Thanks, Bobby."

Bobby gave me the envelope. It was typed, with no return address, and postmarked Manassas, Virginia.

Inside:

I AM NOT A KILLER OF SLUGS, I AM A KILLER OF DEMONS. IF YOU CONTINUE TO CALL ME THE SLUG KILLER YOU WILL FIND THAT BERTIE LYON WILL BE NEXT! DO NOT TEMPT ME. PLEASE UNDERSTAND I AM ONLY DOING WHAT THE LORD INSTRUCTS. LUKE 11:15

CHAPTER ELEVEN

IKE

Keystone, South Dakota

August 1977

For the same God that made you made him too
These men with broken hearts

—Elvis Presley, "Men with Broken Hearts"

SEEING RACHEL AT the camp near Mount Rushmore screwed with my head for the first few hundred miles I was on the road the next day. As we went from Sioux Falls through Sioux City and Omaha, I replayed that scene over and over. I'd walked into the RV, and she was sitting there with the Yellowmountain boys.

"Oh, look, it's Gomer Pyle," Paul Yellowmountain had said.

"What are you doing here?" I asked Rachel. She looked down at her beer bottle, refusing to make eye contact with me or even acknowledge my presence.

"She's headed east and getting paid for it, I-Don't-Like-Ike," said Adam Yellowmountain.

"Hey, fellas," I said in the nicest tone I could manage. "Do you think you could give us a minute?"

Rachel nodded at the Yellowmountain boys. They obediently

left. It was odd; I would have expected some razzing and taunting, but they just marched out as if they'd been given orders.

"So, yeah, he's right, I'm headed east anyway, so when Lucky was looking to hire someone to drive the buses, made sense," she said.

I'd worried that I'd never see Rachel again, and I'd thought a lot about what I'd say to her if I were given this gift. Instead of spilling my guts, I sat on the couch and told her what I thought she wanted me to say. I remembered Mom telling me about how you should meet people where they are and ignore your needs at that moment, how that was the best way to flip the script and convince someone to give you a second look. Be the relief, not the demand.

"I'm so glad I get this chance," I said, sitting down. "I was in a rough place when I got out west and you were a friend. You gave me not just free drinks, but companionship. And an escape route! I just want to thank you. Obviously, for whatever reason, you want to put some distance between us. That's your decision, and I respect it."

She looked surprised, as if she'd been expecting me to say something else.

"All I can say is, maybe someday back in civilization, I can return the favor and buy you a drink."

"Sure," she said.

I stood. That seemed to surprise her too, but I figured I'd take Dad's advice—always leave the audience wanting more. When I reached for the RV door, she called my name, and I turned around.

"It might be soon," she said. "That drink, I mean."

"Yeah?"

She gave me a mischievous smile. "Maybe sooner than you think."

I nodded, confused but happy—drinks with Rachel! Sooner

than I thought! What did that mean?—and, resisting every impulse in my brain, I walked out.

At first light, we took I-90 to Sioux Falls, South Dakota, then went south on I-29 along the Iowa/Nebraska line. Rachel was driving the third RV. It had a green stripe on the front, and I kept it in my mirrors for four hundred miles. All day long Elvis songs kept popping into my head, and I sang to keep myself company. No version of "A Little Less Conversation" can compare to the one you belt out at the top of your lungs on an FX Super Glide at eighty miles an hour: "*A little less fight and a little more spark, close your mouth and open your heart.*"

By the time the convoy stopped for the night in a meadow near a gas station outside Kansas City, my mind had cleared. What had Rachel been to me, really? She wasn't interested in anything beyond friendship, and she'd been chilly to me at the end there. I didn't understand it, but it wasn't for me to understand, maybe. I thought of Staff Sergeant Jesús "Gonzo" Gonzales, my platoon leader in Beirut, who always said, no matter what challenges came our way, "'Don't take life so serious, son. It ain't no how permanent.'" It was a quote from the comic strip *Pogo* and the wisdom was from a porcupine, but it made even more sense over there.

It was impossibly hot that night, so after we did some drinking at a local dive bar, Evel invited me to hit the hay in his air-conditioned RV. Lucky Strong got the bedroom in the back, of course, and Evel got the one up front above the driver's seat. Both men were joined by young ladies from the Reverend Russell congregation who had not, apparently, taken vows of sobriety or chastity. My head was spinning a bit as I wedged myself onto one of the sofas. Huckleberry and one of the Tommys were also on sofas, and the second Tommy grabbed the floor under the kitchenette table. There were giggles and grunts from the front and back, and the RV was a-rockin', but we were too happy to be in the AC to care.

"This is great," I said. I'd ridden a buzz perfectly, so I was just drifting off, no spins.

"Evel for president!" exclaimed Huckleberry from where he lay splayed out on the couch. He was jazzed up, having stood next to Evel while he took questions from the Kansas City news media about his pending trip to the capital. Evel was going to demand that lawmakers allow veterans with the mysterious Vietnam cancer to use vitamin B_{17}. I listened to him while we ate dinner around a bonfire, and he fluffed a number of the details—he called it *vitamin 16*, didn't understand a journalist's reference to laetrile, didn't know what HEW (the Department of Health, Education, and Welfare) was—but the reporters didn't seem to notice, or if they did, they didn't care.

"Evel 1980! Evel 1980!" Lucky Strong and Huck began chanting at the press conference, and soon some of the journalists joined in; they thought it was a gas, and a couple of them might even have meant it.

A few hours later, as we lay in the dark, Strong started the chant again from his bunk in the back, and the boys joined in: "Evel 1980! Evel 1980!"

"He'll open the FBI files on Watergate and show the world how the New York media fucked Dick Nixon!" Strong yelled.

Evel, in his bunk above the driver's seat, poked his head through the thin blue polyester curtains. His shirt was off and his hair was being mussed by a young lady's hand. "America is a wonderful country!" he exclaimed. "But we're headed for disaster."

"Amen, motherfucker!" yelled Lucky.

"It's a country that is now of the government, by the government, and for the government," Evel said. "Our system is failing us! We must change it for the better!"

The Tommys began whooping and cheering and applauding, swept up in the moment. Huckleberry and I joined in. I did it to surf on a wave of silly.

"Now shut up," Evel said with a demonic grin. "I got business to attend to." He tucked his head back behind the curtain and turned up the music so we couldn't hear anything over Elvis.

You have made my life complete | And I love you so…

"He gonna actually run this time?" asked skinny Sideburns Tommy from his couch.

"Think so," said Huckleberry. "I saw a couple boxes of 'Evel for president' T-shirts in one of the other RVs. Boxes addressed to Lucky, natch."

"I mean, it's not so crazy," said Beer Gut Tommy. "I'd much rather have a straight shooter like Evel than the Bible-thumping peanut farmer we got in there today."

"Or Tricky Dick!" I added.

"You know, this isn't even the first kinda political road trip Evel's done," Huckleberry recalled, slurring his words a bit. "Back in '61, he did something similar."

"In '61?" I asked. "How old was he?"

"'Bout your age," Huckleberry said. "Twenty or thereabouts."

"So what'd he do?" I asked.

"This was back when Evel was a hunting guide," Huckleberry said. "Every year, the park rangers in Yellowstone would get snipers to cull excess elk, and they'd give the meat to Indians and food banks. Evel was PO'ed that the park wouldn't let sportsmen come in and hunt them. I mean, he would still sneak customers into Yellowstone to poach, but he wanted to do it legally if he could."

"Didn't make no sense, those rules!" Evel yelled from behind the curtain. I heard his lady companion laughing.

"He wanted the rangers to open up the federal lands to

hunters, but they said no. So the kid grabbed a pair of antlers and hitchhiked all the way to the White House."

"What?" I asked, amazed I'd never heard the story.

"Yep!" said Huckleberry. "He got to DC, and Senator Mansfield helped him get a meeting at the White House."

"Met with JFK hissel!!" Evel shouted.

I assumed Evel was, per usual, exaggerating. Nothing that happened in reality was ever good enough for his storytelling. A lanky fellow had to be seven feet; every fish landed was the size of an alligator; every conquest a *Playboy* centerfold. If he had truly met with the sainted JFK, he would have told us the story a hundred times by now.

"Anyway," Huckleberry said, "he had a meeting at the White House and I'll be goddamned if he didn't convince the secretary of the interior to relocate thousands of elk to states where they *could* be hunted."

"He met with the fucking secretary of the interior?" I asked.

"Yeah," Huckleberry said. "I forget his name."

"Udall," I said. Stewart Udall was secretary of the interior for both JFK and LBJ. Mansfield had brought him over to our house a few times, and he'd told us stories about his fifty missions as a gunner on a B-24 Liberator in World War II.

Huckleberry shrugged. "Anyway, Udall called off the elk shoot and had the excess moved out of the park and to other states where they could be legally hunted."

"This is a true story?" I asked.

"True as my pecker's hard!" Evel yelled. His companion giggled.

It was a wild story, and, assuming it had actually happened, it kind of changed my view of Evel. For the better. Not that I was going along with the idea of him running for president or believed that he had the temperament and discipline for such a job, but there was maybe something there, a kind of political acumen, that wasn't completely hot air.

The boys chatted. Songs from Evel's Elvis eight-tracks wafted from his bunk. Thoughts of Rachel crossed my sleepy brain. I smiled into my pillow. She was so pretty. The most beautiful woman in Montana, and tonight she'd said she'd let me buy her a drink. Soon.

Sooner than you think. What did that mean?

My eyes grew heavy. As I drifted off, a whiff of diesel tickled my nose. Then I was sleeping hard, and then I was back in Lebanon.

That anyone at the Pentagon thought it a good idea to send a platoon of U.S. Marines straight into the Lebanese civil war was proof that the morons who got so many of us killed in 'Nam were still running the show.

The Best and the Brightest, David Halberstam called them in 1972, the most ironic book title in history. And even though that phrase had been serially misused and co-opted by folks too dumb to understand that Halberstam couldn't sell a book titled *Shitheads on Parade,* to those of us still subject to their whims, it stung.

The civil war in Lebanon began in 1975 and at any given moment it was difficult to understand just who was fighting who. As I recall, there were like half a million Palestinians in refugee camps there—they'd been ejected from Jordan—and along with them came the PLO and Fatah and a bunch of Leftists from Algeria and Libya, which was one of the reasons Jordan kicked them out. The extremist Muslim groups joined with the Communist Arab groups, forming common cause in wanting to take down the Christian leaders of their new home in Lebanon.

Christians pushed back, forming their own militias, variously armed by West Germany, Belgium, Romania, Bulgaria, and even

Israel. There were secular militias too, such as the Communist Action Organization and the Lebanese Communist Party, plus the Syrian Social Nationalist Party, which wanted Syria to subsume Lebanon into one greater Syria. There were Sunni and Shiite and Armenians and Druze.

And the best and the brightest thought it would be smart to send our rifle platoon of forty-three U.S. Marines, average age nineteen, into this powder keg.

We were First Battalion, Bravo Company. Captain Benedict Jones, a vile-looking toad of a man, was our company commander. He'd once read Sun Tzu's *The Art of War,* which led him to mistakenly conclude that he was brilliant. Our platoon commander was First Lieutenant Brandon Hardcastle, an admiral's son who seemed haunted and tentative; he might as well have been a mannequin that someone occasionally placed in our general vicinity. Gonzales was our platoon sergeant, young and hungry and demanding and deeply concerned about the rest of us, which was annoying during furloughs but reassuring otherwise. We all loved Gonzo, even though he was exacting.

We'd flown from Camp Lejeune, North Carolina, stopping briefly at Ramstein Air Force Base in Germany, to Ashdod, Israel, then boarded a ship under the command of a MAU—a marine amphibious unit—that had been stationed in Spain and came across the Mediterranean to meet us. On the ship, we were briefed by a guy we assumed was CIA—Hawaiian shirt, khakis, Wayfarers, baseball cap—who explained that the Syrians were about to roll west across the Bekaa Valley in their Soviet tanks. The Syrians had initially backed the Marxist Muslims but now for whatever reason they were with the Christian nationalists. (It's okay if you're having a tough time understanding all these warring factions; so did we.)

"More shifting winds than a *khamsin,*" the CIA guy said, his lower lip packed with chaw. "The Syrians claim they just want to stop the bloodshed." He paused for comic effect, spat his tobacco juice on the ground. "I got an oil field near the Qarah Shuk to sell ya if you believe that. We all have lotsa theories as to what they're really planning and why. In any case, Uncle Sam's supporting them and we have our orders."

At oh-dark-hundred we heloed off the deck of the ship and headed northwest to an area outside Beirut (the CIA guy called it "the Root," which kind of stuck). The pilots opened the back of the CH-46 Phrog and we splashed off the coast of the Root and swam to a sludgy, isolated, industrial shore. The city might have been at war, but it was also at that moment asleep.

Half of our platoon had splashed before us, and Hardcastle was leading them to an abandoned refinery. Our nineteen followed Gonzo up the beach and down an empty pier to a warehouse we'd been told was empty. Inside, it was dark and dank, suffused with the stink of dead fish.

Sergeant Lars "Schmitty" Schmidt reached into his ruck, pulled out some papers, and spread them out into a map. Me, Gonzo, Schmitty, Sergeant David Kimmel, and Sergeant Nathan Edison knelt down. Using a mini-flashlight, Gonzo indicated specific locations. "We're here," he said, his forefinger pressing into a spot on the map. "We're supposed to seek cover here," he said, pointing to a bombed-out hotel. "When we hear Hardcastle and them are in position to give us cover, we head here," he said, his finger sliding down the tiny markings of an alleyway through the middle of the Root. We would take that alley three blocks to a popular restaurant, in the basement of which intel said an American professor, an asset, had been hiding for three weeks.

"How good is this intel?" I asked.

"That's a great question," Gonzo said. "I don't know. It comes from the Hawaiian shirts."

"We got this far," observed Schmitty.

"True," said Gonzo.

It wasn't a horrible point, I remember thinking. We'd gotten inside the Root during a war, seemingly undetected. But the CIA guys reminded me of the preppy DC douchebags Lucy liked.

"Send out a scout," Gonzo told me. I shuffled to a dark corner of the pier where Marines were huddling and tapped Private Fred Bartels and Private Steve Suo and told them to make sure we were safe to head to the hotel. Each was carrying on his back an AN/PRC-77 portable transceiver radio and handset—a short-range, two-way radiotelephone nicknamed "the Prick." Bartels would go out and inform Suo and whoever was pulling similar duty for Hardcastle and his team that we were good to go.

Ten minutes after Bartels darted out into the night, we heard his voice from the Prick. He was on a roof, he said, and had a clear view.

"All's quiet on the Middle Eastern front," he whispered. He was wry like that; didn't say much for days on end, then delivered a quip with perfect timing.

Gonzo had us line up at the front door, then we ran out, following him from the waterfront into the town. It was so quiet that the shuffles of the men on the gravel and *click-clack*s of their M16s against their uniforms seemed shockingly loud, but that was likely just my fear. I'd never been in a hostile territory before, never been anywhere someone might shoot me at any moment, where in fact that would be a normal event.

Napalm Napalm sticks like glue / sticks to women and children too—we ran orderly, as in drills, and as quietly as we could to the hotel, which had been hit by a missile and was now a pile of rocks and rubble. Gonzo found the entrance and ordered us all into the basement. There wasn't much room because so much of the building had collapsed in on itself. Inside, it was dry and oppressively hot.

"It's approaching oh-two-thirty," Gonzo whispered to me, Schmitty, and a couple others whose faces I couldn't make out in the dark; the only light came from Schmitty's lighter as he brought the flame to his cigarette, illuminating his profile.

"Hardcastle and platoon on way," Suo said quietly, standing closer to the entrance. "Will alert when in position to provide cover." Hardcastle's team was headed to an elevated point near the restaurant where they'd be able to provide us with cover.

We waited, catching our breath, hearts pounding, all of us full of dread but also eager to get it over with. It was suffocating in that basement, and there was no way out other than how we'd come in. The anticipation of what we had to do next—sprint through alleys in the Root in the dead of night, come to a restaurant we hoped was closed, escort an American asset back to shore—was utterly terrifying. Would we be able to accomplish such a feat? The underlying, unspoken fear: No one had much confidence in our officers. And even less in the brass above them.

Gonzo stood two feet from me, partially visible from a streetlamp casting light through cracks in the rubble. He seemed the same as always, determined and serious. He glanced at his glow-in-the-dark wristwatch and shook his head. Then he walked to Suo.

I had never been more frightened in my life. And yet, I said to myself, was this not why I had enlisted? Was it not to serve bravely in moments like this, to help people, to deliver justice? Was that not why I had raised my hand? I had watched Mom and Dad in their efforts to bring balance to this wicked planet, struggling to help blacks, Hispanics, Native Americans, women, the poor, trying to provide them with some semblance of a fighting chance, and it all took so long, it was all so slow, sclerotic, and the successes were measured in individual starfish returned to the ocean, not the doomed thousands washed ashore. Politics, hearings, legislation, petitions, elections, rallies, speeches, activism, spending so much energy and effort to convince those in power to help even as the boulder inevitably rolled back down the hill at the end of the day.

"What?" Gonzo whispered, an unmistakable edge in his voice. I walked over to figure out what was going on.

"It's not working, sir," Suo said, meaning the radio.

"Can't you fucking fix it?" Gonzo asked.

Suo pressed the Prick-77 but no sound came from his pack. He clicked it again. Nothing. "Something's fucked," he said. "Something's fucked with the Prick."

"Okay," Gonzo said. "Okay." He took a second and rubbed his forehead as if the act would bestow wisdom.

Suo kept trying. "Fuck," he finally said. "Fucking Prick."

"All right," Gonzo said. He turned to me. "Ready the men to follow me to the target. We discussed a contingency in case this happened, and we're gonna be outside the target at oh-two-forty either way." He looked again at his watch; I looked at mine.

"So—now?" I said.

"Copy," he said, and the other eighteen Marines, who were all paying attention, readied themselves.

He looked out the exit, then turned back to us. "Schmitty and Edison, you follow me. Kimmel and Marder, you bring up the rear."

We poured out, Schmitty and the others tearing down the alley while I stood to the side, counting down to the last Marine and then bringing up the rear. *F-18 flyin' high / Drop the Napalm watch 'em fry.* Moving as fast as we could in our gear, knowing that we needed the element of surprise and that the cloak of night would soon be removed.

The restaurant was three blocks away, but I'd made it

down only one of those blocks before I heard the explosion of machine-gun fire. I kept running. Toward it.

Bullets pinged around me. Some of the guys took cover in doorways. The machine-gun fire didn't seem particularly targeted; more just a spray around us, a firehose.

I took cover in a doorway a few yards from the end of the alley, where a streetlamp revealed six Marines lifeless on the ground in the midst of a whole mess of assorted garbage including a tire that had been shredded. Gonzo was bloodied but alive, tucked behind a trash dumpster, firing his M14 at the restaurant from a narrow slit between the dumpster and the wall. He looked bad, though. He'd clearly been hit in his shoulder and torso, and the spreading stain on his uniform suggested he was bleeding heavily.

Schmitty and Edison returned fire from behind the dumpster. I knelt down in the doorway and took off my helmet. Slowly, holding it in my hand, I poked the helmet out close to the ground to see if it would draw any fire.

It didn't.

I put the helmet back on my head and looked to see if I could determine where the machine-gun fire was coming from.

The enemy gunner had apparently set up shop in the restaurant and was firing from the first floor toward us from a window that was maybe in the kitchen or a back office. I aimed my M16 at the window and fired, but all that did was draw his attention and bullets. I retreated behind the door.

Gonzo looked back at me. He pointed to the nearby dead body of Private Evans, or, more specifically, to Evans's M79 single-shot, shoulder-fired grenade launcher. Then he pointed back toward where we'd come from and started whirling his finger, conveying that he thought I should go around the block, approach from a different angle, maybe even from the wall where

Hardcastle was supposed to be. I nodded. He grimaced, lifted himself, and began more aggressively firing at the restaurant. When the enemy machine gun returned to peppering the trash dumpster, I ran back down the alley, away from the restaurant.

I passed the dark silhouettes of other Marines on my way out of the alley. Some were trying to advance, a couple were wounded; some maybe had just taken cover. I didn't know what to tell them—the whole thing was so fucked up. I yelled for them to follow me but I wasn't sure what they could hear above the din of gunfire and their own terror. Lights began turning on inside Beirut apartments. I could see some folks closing their windows and others looking out, rifles in hand.

An M79 grenade launcher sat on the ground in my path and I grabbed it.

After a block, I turned right. Headlights came my way and I began testing doors to see if any of these homes or shops had been left open. One knob I tried turned, and I opened the door and slipped in. My flashlight revealed an empty garage. The machine-gun fire continued outside, and I heard a car drive by while I looked around.

A dingy gray tarp covered a familiar-looking object. I peeled back the canvas, and, holy shit, it was an FL Harley, a Panhead from the early 1950s. I took a closer look; it was banged up and the tires were cracked but, miraculously, the key was in it. I rocked it and heard fuel slosh in the tank.

If the engine turned over, this thing could give us an edge.

As quietly as I could, I wheeled her out to the sidewalk and climbed on. Panheads are difficult bikes to start. I remembered trying to learn how to ride one at fourteen, at the gas station near Dupont Circle; it was like cracking a code. The Linkert carb liked to be flooded, so I turned on the fuel, gave it full choke, and kicked it over a couple of times. What next? I tried to recall. Key on, then...give it a half choke? I stomped on the bicycle-pedal kick-starter and—

Nothing.

Then I remembered: *I have to retard the timing a little. That's right, that's right.* I reached down and gave the mag a few degrees of twist. *Okay, try it again now...*

Ba-BANG—it came to life!

It sounded like thunder from rain clouds over a parched land.

My heart cracked wide open with hope.

That rumble again. What a sound.

I positioned the strap of the M79 grenade launcher around my head and arm and held the weapon with my right hand at my abdomen, pointed to the left.

I sped down the block, took a right, and headed toward the machine gun. The Lebanese gunman must've stopped to reload, or maybe he'd released the trigger to try to see where the sound of the motorcycle was coming from. I blew past the front window of the restaurant, slowed just a touch, and felt the import of the moment; I fired a grenade through the plate glass and took off like a bat.

As I sped past the trash dumpster that Gonzo and the others were hiding behind, I heard the explosion. Rubble and burning wood and other shrapnel flew everywhere.

After a beat, I U-turned to get the guys.

The restaurant was aflame and half gone, the machine gunner blasted out of existence. But I heard sporadic gunfire in the distance; we had to get out of there.

I steered the bike around the dumpster. Gonzo was barely breathing, his eyelids heavy; he was struggling to keep them open. Schmitty was next to him, shot in the arm and leg, and seemed out of it. Others lay motionless, some facedown, several twisted into impossible positions.

The gunfire grew louder and drew closer, though I couldn't be sure where it was coming from. "Schmitty," I yelled. "Can you walk?"

He looked up at me, dazed.

With our comms out, we had no support. This was all on me.

I could fit only one of them on the bike.

I was nineteen years old.

How was I supposed to make this decision?

"Listen to me," I told Schmitty. "Gonzo's bleeding out. I'll get him help, then come right back for you. Okay?"

Schmitty made a vague gesture with his hand. I said it again. "I'm coming back for you, Schmitty. Okay? Do you hear me? I promise."

I pivoted that long kickstand, lifted Gonzo, and tried to drag him up onto the bike. It was tougher than I'd thought it would be, and the gunfire—fuck, it was too damn close. I bent and tried hauling Gonzo up onto the FL like he was a heavy duffel; that worked, and he slumped over. Bullets pinged off the wall behind me. I shoved Gonzo up in front of me, wrapped my arm around his waist, hoisted the bike off the stand, and, with another "Be right back" to Schmitty, took off.

The street was dark, but I had a general notion which way was west. Gonzo's size and weight and unconsciousness made balancing the bike difficult, and I couldn't go as fast as I wanted, but for the first block or two I had hope. I wanted to save Gonzo's life, and where the fuck was Hardcastle? Why the fuck had everything gone so FUBAR? Whose stupid fucking idea was this? How many of my brothers were now KIA?

Where was command? Where were my idiot fucking officers?

A bullet hit the speedometer, and it exploded. Fuck. I didn't know if it was from a sniper or just a lucky shot. I twisted the throttle to the stop. I had to get to the beach, get Gonzo to the evac, then haul ass back to Schmitty and the rest of the guys. Time and distance were distorted. That old FL still produced a good shove of torque with each upshift, but it was taking too fucking long.

How much goddamned farther to the beach? We kept buzzing along, bullets flying around us...

Then there it was, just below me, the main drag parallel to the shore.

I pushed Gonzo over the handlebars and leaned hard left as I turned right, wondering where the evac was. More gunfire, but there was the exfil point, the dock right there...I just hoped to fucking hell they had a boat and a corpsman or medic. I needed to go back for Schmitty and tell Hardcastle's men where to go but then—

Fuck.

A pickup truck full of unfriendlies waited at the intersection by the pier.

To further make the point that we were not welcome, they began firing at us.

I slowed and skidded, turned around, and saw a little narrow staircase to the beach, almost hidden. I flew down it, hoping there'd be a short drop to the sand at the bottom.

Gunfire pinged parts of the bike.

A bullet struck Gonzo.

I revved the engine. My front tire hit the beach far harder than the FL's ancient suspension could handle, and the bike bounced and we zoomed up onto a concrete slab, a dock of sorts perhaps.

And then we were flying—a jump from the land into the sea.

And that was the last thing I remember before I woke up in Germany.

And learned that we'd lost eleven Marines, including Schmitty.

And that Gonzo was a vegetable.

And that I'd been put in for a medal. Along with Hardcastle.

Later, at Bethesda Naval Hospital, I learned the Hawaiian-shirt CIA dipshits had been given bad info. *(Gee, you think, fuckwits?)*

And the asset we'd risked our lives to save? He'd escaped to a safe house in Jordan two weeks before, a fact that somehow got lost in the mail.

I woke up early and angry in Evel's air-conditioned RV in a parking lot on the outskirts of Kansas City. A year had passed since that night in the Root, but it might as well have been yesterday. I was still that hot.

The sun shot beams like lasers through the bare RV window.

Lucky and Evel were snoring in stereo.

My mouth was parched. I staggered to stand. The hangover didn't cause my foul mood, though. Disillusionment was what was polluting my body.

I thought back to the American hospital in Germany, where Sergeant Kimmel—suffering from bullet wounds to his face and back—filled me in on what happened to the other half of the platoon after they'd splashed into the Mediterranean: Command had never left their first position after running from the beach to a bombed-out Lebanese bus depot. Hardcastle froze and refused to proceed. The comms hadn't gone out; he'd ripped out the radio so they could only hear, not transmit. It was the craziest thing Kimmel had ever seen.

"You made it to the sea with Gonzo," Kimmel told me. "Couple Marines in a rubber duck waded ashore and picked y'all up."

I was on morphine, drifting in and out. Later, I was shipped stateside. I recovered and then—the medals. Hardcastle had put me and Gonzo and others in for them. And the lieutenant colonel put Hardcastle in for one. The ceremony was at Bethesda

Naval, me stuck in my bed, Gonzo a vegetable down the hall, Hardcastle there but avoiding eye contact with me.

He should have been court-martialed. Anything else was sickening.

I tried to tell folks, including Dad's friend Senator Mansfield, a navy man who visited me a few times, what had actually happened, but everyone told me to keep quiet.

"People are desperate for heroes," Mansfield said. Left unspoken: *The military punishes truth-tellers.*

A Pentagon PIO ordered me to share an "approved" version of my story with a CBS News crew and commanded me to discuss only what I'd seen firsthand; I was not to mention Hardcastle or my reservations about all of it. No one in the news seemed to understand that the entire mission had been a giant goatfuck. It wasn't their fault; the Pentagon was sharing only certain details and classifying anything bad. My actions had been the result of a terrible plan, flawed intel, and Hardcastle's cowardice. None of it made sense. And the generals sold it all to the American people as heroism and valor. CBS helped sell it as a feel-good adventure story, and I lay in recovery day after day until finally I couldn't take it anymore. Mansfield understood my despair and said he'd heard that Evel wanted me to look him up if I ever made it to Butte. He also gave me the phone number of a colleague of his who happened to be Evel's cousin.

So one night I put on my civilian clothes, slipped out of the hospital, hitched a ride to Georgetown, emptied my bank account, got on the red, white, and blue Super Glide I'd bought the year before, and headed west.

CHAPTER TWELVE

LUCY

Washington, DC

August 1977

A NORMAL FAMILY would have alerted the police about a letter from a serial killer threatening its youngest child. A normal family would have tried to keep the matter private because the killer explicitly named that child. But there was nothing normal about the Lyons. I don't mean that in a disparaging way, necessarily. They had become quite powerful, wealthy beyond imagination, by casting off society's traditions. So the decision—unanimously agreed to by Max, Harry, Ivan, and Danielle—to make the next day's wood about the letter and to publish *a copy of the letter itself* did not surprise me. A serial killer threatening the publisher's son would obviously be of interest, plus it put the Lyons family in a category of which no one in Washington, DC, had previously regarded them: victims.

I'd spent the morning talking to psychologists and law enforcement experts in serial murder, and I was typing away at my desk, comparing our Slug Killer to Son of Sam, when Max popped by.

"Take as many inches as you want," he said. "Let Ollie know as soon as you can, sweetheart."

Sweetheart? I looked up.

Ye gods. His eyes were red, his pupils enormous. He was as drunk as a boiled owl, and it was only eleven a.m.

"Cullinane called me, you know," he said, referring to the DC police chief. "He said, 'Don't publish the letter.' Police always want to hide everything. We have the exact opposite business model." He smiled in a sleepy way.

I was careful about what I said next. When Max was legless, as Harry called it, he could lash out, he was intemperate; you never knew what might happen. "My source says if we keep some info private, the lack of details will keep the so-called freaks from falsely claiming they're the Slug Killer," I said, thinking of the hypodermic needle detail I had yet to reveal and that Mimi said would hurt the investigation if I reported it.

"That's their problem, not ours," Max said.

"But doesn't the chief think publishing the letter puts Bertie at risk?" My source sure did.

Max scoffed. "Yes, yes, all that," he said. "But nothing is going to happen to any of us. We have security. You were with us in Manhattan when the lights went out! You saw!"

I kept my mouth shut.

A bead of sweat popped on his temple. His color looked odd. Whatever he'd been drinking must have made him sick.

"Max," I said, "are you okay?"

"Fine, yes," he said, brushing off my concern. "Just fine. And we shall protect Bertie."

I nodded. "Max, why do you think the killer would threaten Bertie? The experts I talked to, Robert Ressler and others, say it's unusual. In lots of ways, it's a big change for the killer. For one thing, Bertie's a boy, and he's far out of the limelight. If the killer wanted attention, why not threaten you? Or Harry, even? Why not Danielle? She's a woman, not exactly his type but closer to it. Or why not threaten me? Why—"

"Why should this maniac do anything?" Max interrupted. "Kill three women, toss them out like yesterday's rubbish? Not exactly batting on the full wicket, that one."

Okay, that was a good point. "You can tell Ollie I'll be done in thirty anyway," I said.

He winked at me. "The retreat at Trinity Island is coming up," he said.

I'd always called it Pitchfork Island, but I knew what he meant.

"Your parents will be there this year?" he asked.

"I believe they will."

"You'll come and meet everyone! It's off the record, so you can befriend Reagan and Connally and Baker and all the scribes and smarties and capitalists who will put the White House back in competent hands! Expect some downtime too. Make sure to pack a swimsuit!"

I was delighted to go, whatever the island's name.

A few days later, I went to my parents' house in Georgetown for dinner. While Dad made a salad and Mom pulled a chicken out of the oven, I stared through the window at the sidewalk where I'd learned to hula-hoop and jump rope. This was the Dent Place NW town house they moved into when Dad joined the House in the 1950s. When Ike and I were younger, our folks frequently reminded us that as a senator, John F. Kennedy had lived across the street with his new bride, Jackie. Lots of tears since then, of course. Jackie was now widowed twice over; her second husband, Greek shipping magnate Aristotle Onassis, twenty-three years her senior, had died of a heart attack a couple years ago. Mom still talked to Jackie, though Dad had washed his hands of the brood after Attorney General Bobby Kennedy essentially blackmailed him into doing his dirty work for him out in Hollywood. But that's another story.

I turned away from the window to see Dad placing a pitcher of water on the dining-room table. Mom followed him, carrying her wedding china serving bowl filled to the brim with gazpacho.

"Ike must be sad about Elvis," she said.

Dad considered this. "Maybe," he said, taking his seat at the table. He turned to me. "Do they not yet know the identity of the killer's third victim?"

I lifted my hands, frustrated. "If they do, they're withholding her name. None of my sources will say why."

"You mentioned they had to notify next of kin," Dad said.

"Your dad reads everything you write," Mom pointed out.

Their love warmed me. "But why take so long?" I moaned. I noticed my parents were looking at me with obvious worry—the fragility that I thought I'd hidden was crystal clear to these people who had watched me my entire life. At my mother's concerned expression, I said, "I'm sorry, Mom. Breaking news about this psycho has almost become an obsession."

"Well, you come by that one-track mind quite naturally," she said with a soothing smile. "I've been able to think of nothing but Elvis since the poor man died, I guess because Ike worshipped him so much as a kid. Did I tell you that one of the manuscripts Jackie O. asked me to review was about Elvis? Goodness, when was that? Almost a year ago, I think."

"What?" I said. "No, you didn't tell me."

She frowned with distaste. "I still have it here somewhere. Jackie passed on it. It was too tabloid. Too disgusting, frankly. Last month it was published by a different house. Just *before* Elvis died."

She described it as a hideous tell-all based on interviews with three of the singer's most trusted bodyguards, all of whom Elvis's father had fired the year before. Written by a tabloid hit man who now worked for the *New York Post*, the book seemed to Mom to be an act of vengeance; it focused on all sorts of allegations about prescription drug abuse.

Mom went to her study and returned with the manuscript, titled *Elvis: What Happened?* "'He takes drugs to go to sleep,'" Mom read, quoting former bodyguard Red West. "'He takes pills to get up. He takes pills to go to the john, and he takes pills to stop him from going to the john. There have been times when he was so hyper on uppers that he has had trouble breathing, and on one occasion he thought he was going to die. He is a walking pharmaceutical shop.'"

Mom stopped reading. "We'd been hoping to get Elvis's autobiography," she said. "He was trying to get ahead of this, furiously talking into a tape recorder for his own book." Scuttlebutt in the publishing world was that he was alternating between rage and despair about his private life being exposed to the world. And right before he died, Elvis learned that this tabloid tell-all had stories about not only his addiction to drugs but also his violent outbursts, including with women. One of the guards claimed Elvis had told him to put out a hit on the karate instructor with whom his wife, Priscilla, had run off.

"The book came out literally just a few days before he died," Mom said. "It had to have played a role in his death…" I waited for Mom to finish her thought. "The sources were bodyguards who'd betrayed him. It must have broken his poor heart. Do you think a book about his drug abuse drove him to abuse those drugs to the point that they killed him?"

I wondered if Mom was suggesting that the author of the book was no longer a mere journalistic observer, chronicling a situation, but a player. I had no reason to doubt the allegations, but if reports ended up shaping events, not just describing them, did that transform those reports from journalism into something else? Activism? Woodward and Bernstein had certainly played a part in Nixon's resignation—was that different? Mom seemed to be asking whether, ultimately, the author's fingerprints were on the murder weapon.

Did she wonder this about me as well?

Ten days later, with Mom and Dad, I flew from National Airport to Savannah Municipal, where we rented a car. I could've traveled with Harry, who had offered me a seat in the Lyon private jet, but I decided against it. However weird it might sound to say this, I felt more independent as a member of the Marder family than as a friend of the Lyon family.

There were no cars allowed on Trinity Island, so we cabbed to the pier, grabbed our suitcases, and hopped aboard the ferry. The trip would be short; the island was less than a mile from shore. We sat on wooden benches on the deck of the ferry. The sea air was invigorating, and the ocean vista reminded me of the larger world outside myself. Mom and Dad were cute and flirty in a way that didn't gross me out, and the weather was sunny and pleasant—though dark clouds hovered in the distance.

Mom's hair blew around her face. "I have a special love for barrier islands," she said, her cheeks flushed. "They have such unique ecosystems. They take the brunt of storms so that the mainland can go unharmed. Imagine being a tiny island taking on the force of a hurricane. But they hold firm, don't they? So that mainland coastal life can survive. It's so generous of these dear sweet islands."

Dad laughed. He loved it when Mom talked like this, as though a landmass had emotions. She pointed to the high rocky cliffs jutting out above the pier. "That's unusual, though."

"It is?" I asked, intrigued.

"Sure. I know this from my dissertation a hundred years ago. About the wild ponies of Nanticoke and Susquehannock Islands?

So—barrier islands in the Atlantic are fortified by the sand and sediment deposited by waves. But to my untrained eye, that rocky cliff looks as though it might have been augmented by man. Look at its height, how jagged and deadly it is. And the flat rocks below it to hold the cliff intact? It's possible those rocks were shipped in to build that promontory up higher."

"Maybe the merchants who ran the slave trade did it? To fend off pirates?" Dad posited. "For defensive reasons, there's a fort and a cannon on the cliff. Pitchfork was a stop for slave ships, you know. Those cliffs and those cannons, all to protect the slave trade. They gloss over a lot of this, you'll see, Cindy-Lou, in the way the South alternates between being proud of its history of murderous slave owners and not acknowledging it." He was in a chipper mood, which was good to see. I guess my lies about how great Ike was doing had done the trick.

Was Ike okay? After returning to DC, I'd called the Dead Canary. Rachel said he was fine but wouldn't offer any details. I'd left my number and asked her to stay in touch, but she hadn't, and my subsequent phone calls to the bar went unanswered. Ike had said he'd be home soon, that I just had to trust him. In any case, there was no point in telling Mom and Dad he was in the woods hiding from Idaho Nazis.

Exhale. Take in the sea air.

"I thought you hated this retreat, Mom," I said.

"I do," she said, tucking her hair behind her ear. It was windy. "But I don't often get an opportunity to spend a weekend with both of you."

Dad looked out at the ocean, then at clouds gathering behind us in the west. "Hope the weather holds."

"Beatrice just left Mexico," Mom said.

"Who?" Dad asked.

"Hurricane Beatrice," she said. "Well, it's a tropical storm now, but it could strengthen again and make its way to us in the next couple of days. Storm front could be here before that. Hopefully not."

Two men came up the stairs from belowdecks and walked to the railing catty-corner from us. Dad nodded toward them. "Reagan's here," he said. The former California governor, tall and handsome, turned when he heard his name. He raised his eyebrows at Dad and walked over to us.

"Charlie, so good to see you again!" Reagan said. "It's been a long, long time, as Sammy Cahn might say!"

Dad extended his hand, gave him what looked like a vise-grip shake. Men.

"Long time, Governor," he said. "This is my wife, Margaret, and my daughter, Lucy."

"Yes!" Reagan exulted. "The zoologist and the journalist! Wonderful to meet you!" He beamed at us. "Lucy, are you visiting Trinity Island as a daughter or as a member of the fourth estate?"

"Well, sir, I know all the events are off the record," I said. "But I'm excited for the opportunity to meet the candidates. Such as you! Very excited to cover the 1980 campaign. So I guess I'm here as a journalist incognito."

"Three years away, still," Reagan said, "but these things have a way of creeping up on you. Perhaps the third time will be the charm for me."[1]

"Perhaps!" Dad said.

---

1 Reagan had previously run for president twice, in 1968 and 1976. In '68, the more moderate Nixon handily beat Reagan, his main rival and the hero of the conservative movement, in ten primary contests. Reagan beat Nixon only in California, where Reagan's was the sole name on the ballot. Nationally Reagan won the plurality of the popular vote—1,696,632 votes to Nixon's 1,679,443—but the delegates at the Republican National Convention in Miami selected Nixon as their nominee on the first ballot. In 1976, Reagan challenged incumbent president Gerald Ford; he won twenty-four contests to Ford's twenty-seven and ultimately lost both the popular vote and the delegates.

"You don't want to follow your father into a life of public service?" Reagan asked me.

"No, sir," I said.

"Ah, then," he said. "The road not taken."

"That's not what that poem means," I said, and I felt Mom softly kick me.

"Pardon me?" said Reagan.

"You're hardly alone in misinterpreting 'The Road Not Taken,' sir," I said. "And I don't mean to be rude."

"Lucy," Dad cautioned.

"No, no, it's all right, Charlie!" Reagan said, smiling. "This young generation is the smartest we've ever had! Go on, sweetheart."

Sweetheart. "If you reread the poem, you'll see that Frost's narrator actually sees the two paths as interchangeable. He says in the future, because of the lies we tell ourselves in nostalgia, he'll ascribe all sorts of meaning to one path versus the other, but he knows it's all hokum."

Reagan just looked at me, not sure how to respond.

"Well, Ron, let's definitely try to grab a bite together," Dad said.

"Absolutely," said the former governor. "See you on Trinity Island!" He walked back to his companion.

When he was out of earshot, Mom started giggling. "You picked a hell of a guy to talk to about the hokum of nostalgia!" she said.

"Honestly, Cindy-Lou," Dad said. "Do you have to correct every mistake you see or hear?"

"Look at all the Coast Guard cutters," I said, trying to change the subject. At least four of the boats were buzzing around the bay.

"Yeah, more of a Coast Guard presence this year," Dad said. "My guess is it's because of Squeaky."[2]

---

2 Charles Manson cultist Lynette "Squeaky" Fromme tried to assassinate

"Did you hear the way he called it *Trinity* Island?" Mom was still fuming. "We don't just let the South rewrite what happened in the Civil War."

Oh, well, since we were going *there*. "We don't?" I asked. "Of course we do. How many Robert E. Lee High Schools do we have just in Northern Virginia?"

"Those are Southern Democrats doing the rewriting," Dad said.

"True, but Dad, why is your party running away from the civil rights platforms you helped create?" I asked. "I'm hearing whispers that y'all aren't going to include the ERA or voting rights for DC in your platform in '80 either."

"I don't know," Dad said. "I don't understand it. Politics is about addition. And our party is about freedom! And civil rights! Jackie Robinson endorsed Nixon!"

"In 1960," I said. "Not in '68 or '72."

"I think you do actually understand what's happening, sweetheart," Mom said to him. "You just don't want to admit it."

As we disembarked from the ferry, a large wooden sign greeted us: DON'T TOUCH HISTORICAL ARTIFACTS. This was the same warning the ferry conductor had given us, that we should be careful around the displays scattered throughout the island, as some of the weapons might actually still contain gunpowder and be dangerous. The ship had slowed so we could admire the Civil War–era cannons along the battery. The conductor had pointed out a long shack of a building, not much more than a cattle barn, and told us it had once contained slave-trade stocks and whipping posts, remnants of the barbaric legacy.

Ford in Sacramento, California, on September 5, 1975, though she hadn't chambered a round in her pistol. She was protesting his inaction in curbing pollution. Seventeen days later in San Francisco, Sara Jane Moore fired two shots at Ford but missed. Moore wanted to foment revolution.

Beyond the dock, our valet was waiting for us in a golf cart. We hopped in and he drove us past bicyclists and other golf carts, the only vehicles on the island other than a few mopeds used by the resort staff. It was the kind of carefully manicured environment that didn't occur in nature but that the truly wealthy demanded.

We passed a shop that the valet said offered local artwork and high-end knickknacks ("For ungodly sums," my mother whispered in my ear); another shop that sold sundresses and purses and beach hats ("Even more overpriced," Mom said); a wine store that featured the finest vintages from France and Italy ("There's a 1929 Château Mouton Rothschild behind the counter, and I'm afraid to even ask how much it costs," she murmured). Off to one side was a small museum that, in a previous life, the valet said proudly, had been Confederate army headquarters. Mom pressed her lips together, and Dad laughed.

At the end of Main Street, the valet turned onto a well-tended path and drove us up a grassy hill to an antebellum mansion with a wide lawn and white pillars; it was honest to God like something out of *Gone with the Wind*. As we got out of the cart, Dad told us that the ritziest of the VIPs stayed there—Reagan, Ford, Baker, Senator Bob Dole, major donors such as the Scaifes and the Mellons and the Firestones, influential others like the Buckleys and Lyons.

"But folks like us?" Dad said with a wink as he headed inside. "This is just where we pick up our keys."

I laughed. Dad liked to make fun of himself, but the truth was, although I might not be a Lyon, being a Marder was a pretty good life.

Dad came out of the mansion alongside CIA director George Bush, his wife, and one of the Bush sons. Dad lifted the key and jangled it. "I've got directions to our villa," Dad said.

"Ohhhh, sounds fancy," I told him.

"We stayed in a villa last time I was here," Mom said. "A one-bedroom little house on the periphery of the glen. Not nearly as plush but a touch more private than the mansion."

"Better to bird-watch, right, sweetie?" Dad said to Mom.

As the valet gunned the little golf cart, I saw a larger version of our cart driving up. In it were the Lyons—Max, Harry, Ivan, Danielle, Bertie—and Ashley. Harry shouted, "Hello, Lucy! Senator Marder! Mrs. Marder!" I tried to make eye contact with Ashley but she stared straight ahead.

Dad gave them a grin and a wave and turned to me. His smile faded. "Is that the fellow you've been running with? Maybe I'll have a little chat with him."

"Charlie, behave," Mom said, slapping his shoulder. She turned to me in the back seat and mouthed: *So handsome, honey.* I knew she hated the Lyons and was just trying to be supportive.

"Their youngest looks like the kid from *The Omen*," Dad said.

"Charlie!" said Mom, slapping him lightly again. Poor Bertie.

The valet brought us to our villa. Like everything else on the island, it had been restored after the resort leased the island from the state of Georgia. It had air-conditioning and modern plumbing and amenities, all of it faux historical, new but made to look old, like something by Disney.

In our villa were two king beds and one large desk on which had been placed six gift baskets. The attached cards indicated top-shelf booze from the Distilled Spirits Council of the United States; cigars, cigarettes, and dips from RJR Tobacco Company; chocolates and candies from IBM; dried apricots and jams and that stupid *Pride of Lyons* book about their family from my boss, and so on. William F. Buckley Jr.'s publisher had provided copies of *Four Reforms: A Program for the Seventies*, and Pat Buchanan's had supplied us with *The New Majority: President Nixon at*

Mid-Passage. Also included was an advance copy of George F. Will's *The Pursuit of Happiness and Other Sobering Thoughts*, which would come out next year.

"Can't believe Big Oil didn't send a barrel of crude," Mom said. She sighed dramatically. "I'm glad I brought my birder binocs; these people are going to be insufferable."

"Avoid looking at the right wings," Dad joked. "When you're out there taking a *gander*, I mean."

I groaned, but Mom said: "Toucan play at that game, Mr. Marder."

"Can I just stop you both right now before this gets out of control?" I asked.

"You're crying fowl?" Dad asked.

I threw a pillow at his head. "Why do you even come to this thing, Dad?" I asked.

"You know why," he said. "Because I care about the party! We need a thriving GOP to offset the incompetence and insanity of the Democrats. And I want to show support for the practical governing wing, the Rockefellers and the Schweikers. I've told you this a thousand times." He moved his shoulders as though he felt constricted. "The gifts I could do without."

He began unpacking, and Mom sat in a corner armchair and studied a weathered copy of *Georgia Birds* by Thomas Burleigh. I turned on the radio to see what news I could find. When you work in journalism, you develop a hunger for what's new, what's latest, what's happening right this second. It's a jones for the info coming over the ticker via the Associated Press or UPI or Reuters, from TV or radio, from reporters running in with the latest from their notebooks. You grab used newspapers and folded magazines when traveling; you find yourself constantly on patrol.

It was from said local news report that I learned Tropical

Storm Beatrice was now making its way to us, and Mom would almost certainly not get a chance to look at birds this weekend. It was how I learned that Caleb White had died in Mexico at a laetrile treatment facility and the Carter administration had declared that it would push back against any political pressure to allow cancer patients to take laetrile until the science fully supported it—which assuredly would never happen. And it was how I learned that in Manassas, Virginia, the previous night, an angry white mob, terrified of the Slug Killer, chased an innocent black man onto Virginia State Route 234, where he was struck by a speeding car and killed.

CHAPTER THIRTEEN

IKE

Memphis, Tennessee

August 1977

I'll be so lonely,
I could die

—Elvis Presley, "Heartbreak Hotel"

THE SUN WAS rising and we were rolling down the highway, and after a while we stopped for gas and coffee and candy bars, and then we were crossing into Arkansas and we knew pretty soon we'd hit Graceland. We'd gotten up with the roosters to avoid the crowds, but five miles outside the Presley manse, it became clear that was an idiot's errand; folks had been waiting for days to stand in front of the King's house and pay their respects to their Rock Lord and Savior, Saint Elvis Aaron of Tupelo, who'd crooned for our worship and died for our whims.

Evel didn't even think twice about turning around. From the seat of his Harley, he instructed Huckleberry to tell the buses and RVs to meet us at the first rest stop east of town. Then he said, "Come on, boys," and those of us on motorcycles followed him and buzzed past the bumper-to-bumper traffic on I-55, whizzing by the patient faithful who had been sleeping in their cars, weary yet determined, pilgrims on their way to Mecca. Off the exit, we sped onto Elvis Presley Boulevard, where police were lining the streets. I felt a little weird cutting the line so brazenly, but the officers presumably recognized Evel—he was wearing a white shirt with fringes and red, white, and blue stripes around the collar and wrists—and afforded him VIP treatment.

In 1977, Graceland was just Elvis's home. And though his ex-wife, Priscilla, and their daughter, Lisa Marie, had moved to California, it was reportedly seldom empty. His dad, Vernon, and his second wife lived next door. His buddies in the so-called Memphis Mafia would crash there. Groupies and bandmates and business associates were often on hand. But those of us who knew and loved the King were well aware that the kitschy two-story Colonial Revival mansion at the top of a hill was truly a monument to his isolation and estrangement from the world, from life, from joy.

The closer we got, the thicker the crowds of mourners became and the heavier my mood grew. We rode up to the gates and peered up the hill from the street, where a long line of onlookers slowly shuffled by, many leaving flowers and letters at the gates.

This was, for me, unspeakably sad. There were four men I had idolized in my life: My paternal grandfather, who was gone. My dad, whom I'd run away from. Evel, who, the more time I spent with him, the less I cared for him. And Elvis.

I wondered what Dad felt about the King being gone. Did he care? He knew I liked Elvis, so he'd taken me to a bunch of his movies as a kid, all of them pretty good—*Kid Galahad, Flaming Star, Blue Hawaii, Viva Las Vegas, The Trouble with Girls.* The sudden urge to hear Dad's voice was nearly overwhelming. I could have called him, but what would I have said? *Do you know the King is gone?* Of course he knew it. Could I tell Dad that so much of what I'd once admired in the King I also admired about him, that in my mind, they were associated? That despite how hard I tried, I wasn't sure I could ever become the kind of man my dad was?

Maybe I wouldn't have to talk at all. Or maybe I could call and tell him what I was feeling at that moment: *Dad, I'm still struggling to find the words for Lebanon and going AWOL and the psycho Nazi I nearly killed and the running and the drinking and how I've failed at everything I've tried so hard to do, and what I want right now, standing at the gates of Graceland, is to hear the steady rise and fall of your voice, strong, rational, good. Because the sound of your voice is the sound of home, and if I hear it, maybe I won't feel so lost.*

It was dumb, I guess, to feel overwhelming personal grief at the death of a celebrity I'd never met. But I had to admit something I'd avoided thinking about over the past few years: Although nobody could match the King for cool, it had been clear to anyone watching that he was deteriorating. Like so many things in America.

I had a full flask of Jack Daniel's in my back pocket. I started drinking from it.

A chubby woman with a giant brown beehive hairdo had apparently been granted a special dispensation to stand solo by the gate holding a PA device hooked up to a transistor radio tuned to a local AM station that played only Elvis songs, like "Crying in the Chapel": *You'll search and you'll search, but you'll never find no way on earth to gain peace of mind...*

Evel pulled up and the assembled mourners and tourists quickly recognized him and began approaching, seeking his autograph or a photograph or even just an encounter. He was in so many ways the stuntman version of the rock icon they'd come to praise, and Evel seemed to enjoy the attention, even if it was in the shadow of the King.

But after a few minutes, his mood seemed to change. He began scowling at the park across the street, where merchants had set up tables and booths and were hawking T-shirts, baseball caps, sweatshirts, photographs, paintings, lamps, lighters, balloons, patches—every possible Elvis Aaron Presley 1935–1977 memorial you could think of.

It was a humid late-summer morning, scarcely seven o'clock, and yet more and more salesmen arrived and set up stands to sell newspapers memorializing Presley's death, quickie paperbacks, including one called *Elvis: What Happened?*, posters, sculptures, key chains, records, eight-tracks, songbooks, cookbooks, picture books, kids' books, bookmarks, VHS and Betamax and 32 mm film prints of every movie from *Blue Hawaii* to *Viva Las Vegas*, stuffed animals, towels, bedding, toy replicas of his cars and motorcycles, pictures of Elvis as a kid, Elvis with his mama, Elvis with Nixon, Elvis in his black belt, skinny Elvis, fat Elvis, rock-and-roller Elvis, Hawaiian Elvis, army Elvis, black-leather Elvis, comeback-special Elvis. I'd never seen anything like it, even at an Elvis concert, where there was always merchandise aplenty.

Sprinkled throughout this Tennessee souk were images from the funeral. Elvis had left the proverbial building on August 16 and—away from any source of news, since Evel and Lucky told us what had happened—most of us weren't aware that he'd been buried just two days later. Photos were for sale of various funeral attendees: George Hamilton, who'd played Evel in the biopic, Ann-Margret, James Brown, Caroline Kennedy, Burt Reynolds, John Wayne. One artist had made a collage of Lisa Marie Presley and John-John Kennedy. Kind of creepy.

"Gross," spat Evel, which surprised me, given that this was a man who loved merchandise himself, who signed off on all sorts of Evel Knievel items, including Ideal Toys' bestselling

Evel Knievel Stunt Cycle, one of which I had in my room at my parents' house. Yes, Evel was out to make money, but he understood some places were sacred. And some moments, like the King's death, were sacred. You do not make coin off the death of a king. Evel was, at least for this moment, the good Evel.

"Crass profiteers," he said.

"Never seen anything like it," agreed Huck.

It was crass, no question. But it also wasn't a surprise to me. Selling towels with images of the King's grave seemed a logical manifestation of how everything in our culture became commercialized. Every visitor at Mount Rushmore was wearing a T-shirt bearing the faces of not Washington, Jefferson, Lincoln, and TR but R2-D2 and C-3PO and Farrah Fawcett Majors and the freaks from KISS.

I set my bike on the kickstand, took another deep swig from my flask, and walked through the market. It looked like a hillbilly Morocco, with fans by the dozens wandering through, browsing, purchasing, ogling. Closer, I saw that truly anything from Elvis's life that could be turned into a product had been; there were eight-inch pewter Elvis statuettes, authentic Elvis Hawaiian shirts, silver TCB—"taking care of business"—necklaces, key chains with lightning bolts, giant gold replica sunglasses, signature scarves, snow globes, faux-stained-glass Graceland peacock portraits, teddy bears, Elvis Presley Boulevard street signs, guitar picks, mini-guitars, real guitars, Christmas ornaments depicting the mansion, Vernon's barbecue sauce, and Elvis's images on perfume, playing cards, mugs, wrapping paper, earrings, hats, dolls, coasters, socks, underwear, flip-flops, purses, wristlets, handbags, coin purses, pens, pencils, charms.

"This all new?" I asked a cop. Thin, mustachioed, bored expression on his face.

"Most of it," he said. "When he went to the hospital in April, bunch of vendors showed up, and I think that's when they started manufacturing all the stuff outta Taiwan. Then he went out on the road again and they mostly disappeared, but when he passed, they all rushed back. Like locusts. And they had all the cheap junk ready because of the April false alarm."

I walked back to Evel and the crew. A bunch of others from the RVs and buses, including Justice and the other members of Reverend Russell's church, had congregated around them.

"Thought the plan was to meet you at a rest stop outta town," I told Justice. I was slurring my speech a bit from the whiskey.

"Plan changed," he said. "Reverend Russell managed to convince law enforcement to escort us here."

"That's right," bellowed a deep baritone, and I turned and realized the Reverend Russell was among us. He had pock-marked pale skin, dyed-dark shaggy hair, and thick black Roy Orbison sunglasses. He was short but broad, with a potbelly and lit cigarette suggesting appetites. There was definitely a charisma that surrounded him like a strong cologne. "What's your name? I'm Samuel Russell." He extended a fat palm to me for shaking. Before I could meet his hand with mine, however, Evel began shouting behind me. I turned and he was standing on a milk crate. He was something to see, Evel working himself up in the defense of Graceland.

"This is BS!" Evel yelled. "BS!"

The crowd began to circle around Evel quietly. A couple of the cops shot each other looks that conveyed: *What's this? On alert, boys.*

The woman with the beehive turned off her radio and handed the PA mic to Evel, who eagerly accepted it.

"This is heresy!" he yelled. "This is an abomination!" He

extended his arm toward the market. "They're desecrating your King, our King!"

Reverend Russell stepped toward Evel; he held up the PA mic for the reverend to speak into.

"John, chapter two, verse fourteen," Russell intoned in that stylized way preachers do. "And Jesus found in the temple those that sold oxen and sheep and doves. The *merchants*. And He drove the merchants out of the temple! And Jesus poured out the merchants' money, and He overthrew their tables, and He told the merchants: 'Remove these items! Stop making My Father's house a marketplace!'"

Evel took the mic back, prompting a momentary squeak of feedback. "Exactly right, Reverend," he said. "Stop. Making. My Father's house. A. Marketplace!"

I looked at the merchants, many of whom seemed scared, though some looked angry.

"Stop making the King's house a marketplace!"

The crowd, however, didn't seem to be with Evel at all. They liked their souvenirs; they didn't want to leave Graceland empty-handed, because if they had no proof of their experience, no evidence that they'd been there, no hat or key chain or T-shirt, had it even happened? They wanted to show everyone, just as believers wear the cross.

"This isn't what the King would have wanted," Evel declared, demoralized a tad, the air leaking from his balloon. "He was about soul and love, not commerce, not cheap chintzy souvenirs."

I wondered if Evel was jealous; he wanted people to worship him to this degree, and because all their love and grief and attention was aimed beyond the gates of Graceland and *not at him*, he was trying to insult it. To this day, it's the best theory I have. Evel looked confused; the crowd began to murmur, unsure of what to do. They were willing to listen, prepared to be swept off their feet. But he was failing. I looked around the crowd. Everyone from our crew was there: Huckleberry, the UFO freaks, Reverend Russell's faithful, the vets I'd camped with; Johnny and Dante were leaning against a tree. Governor Lucky Strong approached Evel, whispered in his ear, then patted him on his back. Evel hesitated, then brought the mic up to his mouth.

"But that's not what I'm here to talk about with you good people," he said. "I'm here to talk to you about a nation adrift. A government disconnected from its people. This here's Governor Lucky Strong of Idaho."

Strong eagerly took the mic. "We're leading a march on Washington and we want to tell you why."

The crowd took an interest in this and, as luck would have it, two different TV crews exited white vans that had been permitted access to the gate. As Strong began speaking, they eased through the crowd and set up their cameras on tripods. A photographer put his camera lens right in Strong's face.

"Evel and I are here today—along with a group of patriots from Idaho and Montana and Wyoming—because our hearts are broken," he said. "Just as your hearts are broken."

Strong looked around, seeking expressions of agreement. From what I saw, he got them.

Crowds are weird things. Being a politician's son, I've seen my share. They are not the sum of their individual parts; they are a whole. They can be angry or joyous or mournful. They can be incited or energized; a speaker who holds the crowd's attention, as my dad sometimes did and as Strong was doing now, can reach and sway the crowd, can touch the better angels of its nature, or lead them into someplace dark and ugly.

"Your hearts are broken because Elvis is no longer on this earth, here with us," Strong said. "But in another way, you know that the Elvis we all loved has not been here with us for a long time. Any of us who've seen him in concert or followed his career in recent years—we all know we've been losing him for a while."

Lots of nods, some tears even. Those of us who loved the King knew his struggles were real because they'd played out in front of us. He slurred his words, he gained weight, he stumbled. His jumpsuits split. He forgot lyrics, he cursed, he was cruel, he was pitiful.

"We've been watching this great man fall apart in front of us, just as we've been watching this great country fall apart in front of us," Strong said. "And while we were not able to save our beloved Elvis, we can still do something about saving the United States of America!"

Folks started looking at one another with confused expressions. I took another gulp of whiskey.

"He began a social revolution—he changed everything. *Everything*," Strong said. "He combined white country with black rhythm and blues but tried to remain apolitical. He used his hips to free us from Puritan repression. At the time he was born, our biggest export was agriculture. Now it's entertainment. Every single thing we are—good and bad—is in his image.

"What took down Elvis? Think about the decisions he made. RCA over Sun Records—why? More money. Thirty or so movies, but you and I know very few of them were good, few let Elvis try to become the next James Dean as he wanted. Like *King Creole*. Or maybe *Wild in the Country*. But most of them weren't that, most of them were just popcorn. Why? More money. Never got to tour the world, though he wanted to do so, because Vegas came calling—offering what?"

Strong paused.

"I said, *offering what?*"

"More money," chanted about a quarter of the crowd.

"That's right. The system would not let him be who he wanted to be because the serpent slithered over. And this was a patriot! Lest we forget, when the draft board came callin' in '57, Elvis put on his uniform and reported for duty! And how did Uncle Sam repay Sergeant Presley? With appreciation? With gratitude?"

"No!" shouted people in the crowd, though I had no idea what the government had ever done to Elvis, to be honest.

"Corporations wanted a piece of him and forced him into a grueling schedule to support his family, the way big business does to all of us!" Strong said, his voice rising, the crowd growing excited with him. "And let's be honest here: We don't know what happened at this house, but no forty-two-year-old just has a heart attack. The drug companies! What they call in Washington, DC, 'the pharmaceutical industry,' they plied him with pills! They know all that stuff isn't safe! They bribe doctors to prescribe these pills so they can make millions!"

"That's right!" yelled Evel. "It's a dirty business!"

Strong looked over at Evel and offered him the mic. Evel gladly accepted.

"My friend Governor Strong is right on," Evel said. "And I'm going to tell you this. We are traveling to Washington right now to stand up to those drug companies! Companies that have such a stranglehold on Washington, they can actually prevent you from getting medical treatments that can save your lives! You've heard of it, maybe—vitamin B-seventeen, they call it. In DC, they just stole a baby from his own family because the parents wanted to use that vitamin to save their baby's life! I ask you, is that the United States of America that you and I know? Does that sound like any country you'd want to live in?"

"No!" came the cries from men and women alike.

"We're gonna fight for our veterans, the men that so many hippies spat on when they came back from the jungles of Vietnam where they'd bravely served—unlike the draft dodgers Carter pardoned on his first day in office! These men, you can see some of them in the back there near the trees"—he pointed to Johnny and Dante and others—"they have a cancer they picked up in Vietnam, and the VA won't pay to treat it! And now the government won't even let them try vitamin B-seventeen!"

More boos and hisses from the crowd, especially from men wearing hats or shirts from local VFWs.

"The whole country has lost its way," Evel said. "Elvis knew it, and he died for our sins."

Strong put his head near the mic and barked, "Come with us and this great man, Robert 'Evel' Knievel! We're driving to Washington. Less than nine hundred miles—we should be there before midnight. We're going to make sure they know how unhappy we are with the fools running this country!"

Evel grabbed the mic again. "We the people," he said, "are *pissed*!"

The crowd cheered enthusiastically and some—maybe a hundred?—left the line and the crowd, presumably to get in their cars and follow our convoy. "Give 'em hell, Evel!" one shouted as our group proceeded on foot and on bikes to the RVs and buses, surrounded by eager new recruits.

After we'd put about three hours' worth of Interstate 40 behind us, we pulled into one of those giant truck stops with fast food, hot showers, and, if you knew where to look, prostitutes. I felt a bit sick from the drinking. We needed gas, Evel wanted to take a break from riding and put his Electra Glide on the trailer one of the RVs was dragging behind it, and frankly, I was game for a break too.

After Graceland, about a hundred new cars had joined our caravan. When we pulled into the truck stop, I realized more than half of those cars had broken away. It wasn't tough to picture wives asking their husbands just what in the hell kind of vacation marching on the Capitol was. Why follow some has-been daredevil to the White House? A few hours of watching Tennessee recede in the rearview mirror might cause a man to wonder if he'd been swept up in some chicanery, and if so, maybe the next exit was a good option?

Everyone from our motley crew of caravanners went to TCB, as the King would have said—take care of business. Bathrooms, food, stretching their legs, getting pills (aspirin or speed) or water or beer or bourbon. Whatever one needed. Whoever ran this place—and honestly, you had to assume it was organized crime just because of how efficient it was—knew what they were doing. The illicit stuff was hidden from view unless you were looking for it, in which case it was right there.

I'd satisfied a few needs—toilet, aspirin, cheeseburger, coffee—and was contemplating purchasing soap and availing myself of one of the showers when I stumbled on Evel in the middle of a tirade. Ranting to Huckleberry, he stood near the magazines and paperbacks in the large convenience store, incensed. Furious. He wore a baseball cap so no one would recognize him, but he couldn't control himself and lashed out in all his narcissistic, charismatic glory.

I walked over and patted Evel on the back, unsure of what he was mad about, curious if I could help. He was gripping a white paperback with his picture on the cover. I grabbed another copy from the shelf.

THE INSIDE STUFF ON THE HIGH-LIVING
DAREDEVIL HERO NO PG-RATED MOVIE COULD
EVER SHOW!

EVEL KNIEVEL ON TOUR

BY SHELDON SALTMAN
WITH MAURY GREEN

WITH PHOTOS OF EVEL IN ACTION

The first page of the book was headed "X-Rated Evel" and had quotes of his about his prowess, boasts I'd heard him make before, close to verbatim.

On the back: A photo of Evel in his rocket, set to jump the Snake in Idaho. The copy:

They say it takes a hustler to know one, and Saltman got to know Evel Knievel very well. On a breakneck nationwide tour to promote the Snake River Canyon jump, Shelly got a good, honest look at the man behind the myth. Here's everything that goes on behind the scenes—big money, big wheeling and dealing, big hoaxes, parties, booze and broads—AS AMERICA'S SUPER-STUNTMAN WAGS HIS TONGUE AND SHAKES HIS FIST AT DEATH FOR THE SHEER, CRAZY, MONEY-MAKING HELL OF IT!

As Huckleberry tried to calm Evel down, I did a quick browse: "A tale of fear, greed, duplicity, bigotry and lust"; "Jekyll-Hyde character"; "'Hell, I never knew a broad who wasn't a pushover'"; "The roar of the mob was constant, punctuated by occasional crashes, gunshots, and the screams of girls being raped"—that last bit a description of the insanity at his Snake River fiasco. The book suggested that he mistreated his wife and didn't care for his own mother.

And now I understood what Evel's problem was: the truth. Evel was being confronted with it—with facts about who he was and what he was about. Something closer to reality than the propaganda Evel fed the world. And it devastated him. Not because it was false—because it was true.

"This piece of shit depicts me as an alcoholic and a pill popper," Evel said. "It makes me out to be immoral and anti-Semitic. It insults my goddamned mother!"

"Now, now, Evel, it can't be that bad," Huck said.

"The fuck it can't!" he said. "I just spent the last twenty minutes reading this garbage!"

He seemed ready to hit someone or something. Huckleberry apparently sensed that and tried to gently push him out of the store so he didn't destroy anything. Evel looked insane. There was spittle on his lips; he was literally frothing at the mouth. The two Tommys rushed over, and all three men tried their best to calm Evel down, but he was pacing crazily, like a psychotic you'd see on the street. The men were able to get him out of the store and into the atrium of the truck stop, and I headed away from them to get more coffee, but I could still hear bits and pieces of their conversation.

"I'm going to fly to fucking LA and take a fucking bat to that fucking shyster is what I'm going to do!" Evel yelled. "I'm going to break his fucking arms and pummel his fat fucking face! That two-faced rat!"

After the crew muscled Evel out of the store, I went to the window and pressed my hot forehead against the cool glass. It was starting to rain. Folks were tying down bikes on long trailers hitched to the RVs. The caravan was now maybe seventy-five vehicles. The pit crew moved quickly in the downpour. The rain provided a pleasant, lulling sound after all Evel's hollering. I refilled my coffee cup and went to pay at the register.

"Raining like hell, innit?" said the cashier.

I agreed. "Today I am thankful for RVs and bike trailers."

"That'll be thirty-nine cents for the coffee," the cashier said. Then: "Least we're not getting that big-ass storm heading up the coast."

"What storm?" I said, handing him a dollar.

"Was a hurricane. Think it's been downgraded, but still. Forecasters said it was gonna head out to sea. They were wrong. Took a last-minute turn and now it's coming up the coast."

I loved riding, but not in dangerous conditions. "Do you know the storm track?" Thinking, *Please don't let it be DC.*

"Last I heard, the Florida Keys to Baltimore were all in the warning zone."

That was very bad news. "Say, do you have change for a dollar? I need to call home."

I called, but no one answered. It's not like I expected my parents to be waiting by the phone, but Dad not picking up made me unaccountably nervous. There was something about the storm that unsettled me; I couldn't explain it. I needed to talk to him, I wanted to check on him and Mom and Lucy.

I called Dad's Senate office through the switchboard, but when no one picked up there, I remembered it was August recess. Of course nobody was in the office. I called information and got Lucy's number, but she wasn't home either. I was worried I might run out of dimes. I tried the *Sentinel* newsroom in DC, but they put me on hold. The operator eventually returned and said

Lucy wasn't at her desk. She wouldn't tell me anything more. "How do I know you're really her brother?" the operator asked me, and it was a fair question.

My next call was a total shot in the dark, but at least I remembered the number of the White House switchboard from random times I'd called Dad there over the years: (202) 456-1111. Pretty easy. I got patched right through to the person I asked for.

"Skylar Allen" was how he answered the phone, as if he were stating an impressive fact.

"Hey there, Skylar, it's Ike—Lucy's brother." I didn't want to talk to him—I couldn't imagine *anyone* wanting to talk to that guy—but I figured he'd know what was going on.

There was a pause. Finally, dryly: "Hello, Ike. To what do I owe the pleasure?"

"I'm trying to get hold of Lucy," I said. "You know where I can find her?"

"Your sister and I lost touch after she started seeing Harry Lyon," he said coldly.

"Who?"

"Harry Lyon," he repeated. "The right-wing heir apparent to the Lyons' ill-gotten fortune? I imagine they bought their way onto the Pitchfork Island retreat this weekend. You could check with them there."

I'd never been all that interested in politics, but I vaguely remembered Dad dragging Mom to the island retreat in years past. Usually he promised her time for bird-watching. "Is the retreat this weekend?"

"Indeed."

"Skylar, this hurricane? Is the island in its path?"

"It's been downgraded to a tropical storm, but yes, it seems to have turned toward the Georgia coast," Skylar said. "What a shame."

"Okay, thanks, Skylar," I said. "And, uh, good luck with your personality."

I hung up and headed to Evel's RV. Rachel was in the driver's seat. She mouthed the word *Hey* with a kind look on her face, which was confusing.

"Hi," I said. I stood there awkwardly. The rain started to fall so hard it hammered the RV's rooftop as if we were under attack. I was anxious and the rain wasn't helping and I had to get going but I just stared at her face. I missed being able to do that. We looked at each other for a bit, then she seemed to think better of it and she jerked her chin toward the rear of the RV. "Go on, now. Evel's in the back."

I headed to a corner seat while Evel continued to rant about Shelly Saltman. He'd stolen a copy of the book and was poring through it. "Not true," he said, over and over. "That's a lie," he said. "That would be adultery," he said, as if he hadn't been bragging to everyone about his conquests for years.

Lucky got up and headed for the bedroom. After a couple minutes, I followed him. He was sprawled out on the bed with his head propped in the basket of his hands.

"Hey, Lucky, can I ask your advice?" I said.

"Shoot."

"So Graceland got me thinking a lot about my dad, and he's down at Pitchfork Island, which isn't any farther from here than DC is."

Lucky lifted his head and gazed at me curiously. "What's Senator Marder doing at Pitchfork Island?"

"A retreat with the leaders of his party," I told him. "Bunch of bigwigs, who cares. I mean, *they* care, it's like the brain and money trust of the whole party, which is about to retake control of Washington."

"Oh, *right*," Lucky said. "I remember hearing about that. Back when I was governor. I was never invited to it—never really invited to be a member of the establishment, per se; I reckon I'm a little rough around the edges—but I remember that thing. I thought Trinity Island was its name, though."

"Right, Trinity," I said. "Point is, I've been thinking about breaking away at the next stop and heading out to catch up with my dad."

"What?" Lucky asked, some anger in his voice.

I needed to make things square with my dad. I didn't really know how. Maybe an idea would come to me on the road. All I knew was, I had to try. "He's stuck on this island with a storm coming, and I just feel sort of weird about it. Being so close, and maybe them needing me, I need to make sure he and Mom are okay. I'll just check on 'em, say hi, and meet you in DC."

"Huh," Strong said.

"You understand, don't you, Lucky?" I hated to desert them, but it wasn't like I could roll up on my parents with a ranting, insane, out-for-vengeance Evel and the rest of the crazy caravan. The more I thought about it, the clearer it became. I could do this on my own.

Lucky told me he understood. It was like the story of the prodigal son; I had to go home. He quoted scripture: "'There's a time to plant and a time to harvest, a time to kill and a time to heal.' This, son, is your time to heal." Then he put his hand on my shoulder and told me to get some sleep. He would wake me at the next rest stop.

I woke up four hours later, and Lucky was gone. The RV's weathered brakes squealed as we slowed and pulled into a gas station. Everyone exited, presumably headed to the restroom or to buy some smokes. It felt like evening, though the pouring rain made the time difficult to determine. I wasn't sure where we were or even what time zone we were in anymore. Through crowds of folks exiting their vehicles, I saw Damon Yellowmountain gassing up the RV.

"Four hours east of Nashville, we should be…where? Somewhere outside of Knoxville?" I asked him. The rain was relentless.

"We would have been," he said. "But Evel changed our plans."

"What?"

"He demanded we drop him at the Atlanta airport," he said.

"Atlanta?" Atlanta was actually good. It was closer to Pitchfork Island. "Why Atlanta?"

"Wants to catch a flight to California. He said he has business in LA and he'll meet us in DC."

"What business? Oh, that fucking book? Shelly Saltman?"

"That'd be my guess," he said. "About an hour back, we drove past a drive-in theater showing *Viva Knievel!* and it was completely empty. That made him even madder."

What a fucking lunatic. He was actually going to fly to LA and beat up some PR flack because of a quickie paperback that sounded pretty goddamned accurate to me. Had he always been this nuts and I'd just never seen it before?

A gas-station attendant scurried to fuel a car at the full-serve lane. On closer look, I realized he was wearing a Stone Mountain Park T-shirt and a Confederate flag baseball cap. I knew what Stone Mountain Park was because Mom and Dad had made such a ruckus about it when it was finished a few years ago. The biggest tourist attraction in Georgia, it was the largest bas-relief in the world, and it depicted three leaders of the Confederacy: Stonewall Jackson, Robert E. Lee, and Jefferson Davis. So—wow, Evel had done me a favor without knowing it. From here, I could make Pitchfork Island in maybe four hours.

I went looking for my bike. I wasn't sure which trailer it was on or how easy it would be to unload, but I was happy. I was breaking from the guys, but I didn't have to feel guilty. Evel was canceling the march—or at least postponing it—for some insane vendetta in LA, so I wasn't abandoning Johnny and Dante and the other veterans. I didn't have to feel that crushing guilt.

I heard footsteps come up behind me—a crew member, I figured—and as I turned to ask about my bike, I felt a devastating blow to my head and everything went black.

CHAPTER FOURTEEN

LUCY

Pitchfork Island, Georgia

August 1977

I TOOK THE news of the Virginia mob essentially lynching that innocent black man about as well as you'd expect—which is to say, very badly. I immediately thought about the Elvis tell-all and my mom's theory that the book had driven the King to his death.

"It's not your fault, sweetheart." Mom knelt before me as I sat, slumped on the bed, my palm over my mouth, staring blankly into the void, horrified.

"I specifically said *person of interest*," I said through my fingers. "A *possible witness*. Damn it all to hell, I wrote that he might have *seen* the killer, that he was the best hope of describing the killer! Not that he *was* the killer. And it wasn't even my reporting—it came from Max!"

Mom and Dad flinched at this but quickly suppressed their reactions. I chose to as well.

If I sat still one more second, I might explode. I got up from the bed and paced, waving my arms wildly. "This is exactly what they warned me about. The city councilmen and the mayor and all the people who wrote letters." I turned to my parents. "Did I do this? Am I responsible for what happened to that innocent man?"

Mom came and hugged me like I was a child again. "You didn't tell that white mob to chase down the next black man they saw."

Dad was conspicuously silent.

"Dad?"

"Do you want me to respond as a loving father or as an honest public servant?" he asked.

"Charlie, she's in pain," Mom warned.

"I want to hear it, Dad."

He sighed. "You're not responsible for the actions of a mob of ignorant adults hundreds of miles away, of course not."

I waited for the other shoe to drop. "But?" I said.

"But the news media covers certain stories certain ways and sometimes those ways are designed to provoke emotions. Rage. Or fear. Sometimes that's great—witness the coverage of the civil rights struggles, which created outrage and made change happen. But even though your stories were written factually, did you not have any misgivings about how they were packaged?"

"I did," I admitted, "of course I did."

"Right," he said. "So, no, I don't think you're responsible for this horror. Not at all. But do I think your newspaper's publisher may own some of the blame here? Yes, I do. I mean, remember the *Maine*."

Dad's Spanish-American War reference wasn't as out of place as it might seem. The year before, 1976, Dad's friend Admiral Hyman Rickover released a report that essentially absolved the Spanish for the explosion that sank the U.S. battleship *Maine* off the port of Havana. The 1898 incident—and specifically the jingoistic war-drum-beating newspaper coverage of the sinking—drove up the circulation of William Randolph Hearst's and Joseph Pulitzer's newspapers and, arguably, helped further sell to the public the U.S. war against Spain. "How Do You

266

Like the Journal's War?" the front page of Hearst's paper asked readers early in the conflict, boasting.

"You're being a bit tough on Lucy, darling," Mom said. "Honey, you know the disdain Dad has for many practitioners of your craft." She cut him a disapproving look. "Too much judgment and seldom at the right time."

She went to the bathroom to check her hair. That was Mom's gentle way of telling Dad he'd made his point, now drop it. I watched her through the open door as she pulled out a tube of lipstick and applied it. Her hair was perfect; her social graces so fine. My hero stylistically as well as intellectually. As she slipped a diamond stud in one ear, the lights flickered, and she said, "Oh," with a little laugh. Then everything went dark.

We didn't move. A deep rumble of thunder growled over the island, like a dog about to bite. Sheets of rain began slapping the cabin.

"I'll open the curtains, get some light in here," Dad said and he stumbled into the desk on the way to the window. When he pushed the drapes open, a strange pale light filled the room. Mom found her purse on the desk, pulled out a lighter, and lit the candles around the room.

"I thought you quit, Mom."

"I'm down to one a day," she admitted. She pawed through the gift baskets, looking for more candles. From the basket gifted by the Lyons, she grabbed a plastic bag of apricots and that book I knew all too well. "Did you see this?" she said with a wry smile. "*Pride of Lyons: The British Family Reinventing the News.*"

"Every employee gets a copy," I said and laughed. "No one reads it. Though I did look at the pictures!"

The wind picked up, shook the villa's windows and clunked branches across the rooftop. Outside, trees began bending sideways. Mom plopped down at the desk and chewed apricots and paged through the book, using the candle to read, though her squinting suggested it was easier said than done. Dad handed her the flashlight he'd brought, a heavy one, the kind I'd seen police officers carry, his old standby for escorting her to early-morning bird-watching positions or for taking Ike camping. "Here, darling," he said. "If you're going to read, do it by flashlight or you'll harm your eyes." She stuck out her tongue at him, well aware of the aging he was acknowledging.

The knock at the door surprised us. I opened it to find a soaking-wet Ashley looking like something the surf had churned up. Her umbrella was bent, broken from the wind. Her expression was less pathetic than furious. I wondered if she was upset about Caleb White dying in Mexico, but she was focused on another story. "Did you hear what happened in Virginia?" she demanded.

"It's awful. I have no words for how sorry I am."

"How sorry *you* are?" Ashley said archly. "What about them?" She motioned toward the mansion, where the Lyons were staying. "*They* should be sorry. *They* did this. We've got to stop them. I've been trying to warn Max for weeks, but he just dismisses me because—y'know."

"Because?"

"Because I'm a former actress."

"Really?"

"No, not really," she said, irritated. "Because I'm black, Lucy."

"Ah, yes," I said. "That."

Dad came up behind me. "Cindy-Lou, invite your friend in out of the rain," he said.

Dad brought Ashley a towel to dry herself. Mom offered her a bottle of water, and when Ashley refused that, a glass of wine. Then a bag of apricots.

"From the Lyons?" Ashley said, sitting in a desk chair. "No, thank you."

Dad chuckled. "I thought it was from the Laetrile Association of America."

I didn't know what he meant. Which the silence underlined.

"Laetrile," Dad explained, "is made from apricot pits."

"The pits of apricots from *Mexico*," Ashley seethed. She was the resident expert on vitamin B_{17}. She would also not throw down a detail she didn't want me to pick up.

I looked at the book in Mom's hand, the apricot bag that came along with it. "Mexico?"

"Oh, yes," Ashley said, her eyes daring me to think—what, exactly?

"All those trips Danielle makes to Mexico," I said, realizing. "*Meh*-hee-koh. All that pidgin Spanish she throws around, *dios mio, ay-yay-yay*."

"The night we flew to New York, I happened to look at the flight manifests," Ashley continued. "Never been on a private jet before, wondered where else it had flown. The book was sitting right there. There were a whole lot of stops at an airfield near Tijuana, *la plantación de albaricoques*."

"Don't tell me," Mom said, "let me guess."

"The apricot plantation." Dad had picked up some Spanish on the campaign trail.

"You wrote about a laetrile lab in Tijuana," I recalled.

Ashley nodded slowly. "Yep."

"You know what happened to Caleb White," I said.

"Poor kid," she said. "But let me tell you, the more I learn about this, the angrier I get."

"Why?" Dad asked.

"We've been part of the campaign to sell this snake oil to the most vulnerable people in society," Ashley said. "I mean that literally. We're literally selling this snake oil."

"Holy smokes," Dad said, the light bulb going on. "You mean

to tell me that Max has you pushing this quackery while he simultaneously *manufactures* it?"

"Yes," said Ashley. "And now I think he's building a laetrile hospital in Mexico specifically to cater to rich cancer patients."

"Well, when you think about it, Charlie," Mom said after we'd all paused to reflect on this, "is it really any different from the TV networks pushing us into wars while running ads for General Dynamics?"

Ashley got up from the desk chair. She looked stronger now. "I've never told you details about that time when I was an actress," she said. "But there was a lot of bad stuff going on, and no one said anything, and then it kept getting worse and worse until we were all out of a job and our reputations were in the trash heap."

"Like boiling a frog," Dad said. Mom sent him a sour look harkening back to a previous conversation about how the analogy was ridiculous, of course frogs jumped out of the pot when the water got too hot, but this wasn't the time or place to discuss it—so much conveyed in one stink eye. I loved them.

"I'm not going to let that happen again," Ashley continued, "I'm going back to my room to change into dry clothes. That first meeting in the dining room will begin soon. I need to talk to Max before it starts."

"Talk to him about laetrile or about the incident in Virginia?" I asked.

"Virginia," she said. "Nothing we can do about Mexico—they're all in on that one. But maybe we can convince them to stop throwing gasoline on the race war they're pushing."

"Could you use me for backup?" I said. "I can meet you in the lobby."

She nodded. "We can corner Max and Heir-y. If you get Heir-y to see how bad all this race-baiting is, Max will listen. Honestly,

Heir-y is the only one Max listens to." She gave me a grim smile. "One way or another, this bullshit has to stop. All of it. It's getting people killed."

The storm's effect on the resort's shaky electrical grid delayed proceedings at the mansion a tad (and the pouring rain gave Mom a very good excuse to stay at the villa), but within the hour, most of the top GOP presidential hopefuls, movers and shakers, donors, intellects, and influencers in the United States had assembled in the grand dining room of the main mansion. Dozens of thick white candles stood like totems along the centers of ten long oak tables, illuminating the room in an almost romantic fashion. We were warm and the liquor was flowing, and outside, the sky crackled and wind rattled the shutters.

I moved between the lobby where I was supposed to meet Ashley and the dining room. Dad was at a table in the back, catching up with George Bush, a fellow moderate and decorated World War II veteran. Reagan, Baker, and Connally were swapping tales. Max Lyon rubbed shoulders with the fellow media magnates, international captains of industry, and conservative journalists such as William F. Buckley. I felt very much like a child sneaking downstairs to a raucous adult New Year's Eve party.

I crept over to Max's table, thinking he might know where Ashley was. But he didn't acknowledge me. I wasn't even sure he saw me. He was off his trolley, as Harry liked to say, arguing with the men at his table.

"The problem we Republicans have is our incapacity to articulate a principled alternative to the passion of the Democrats," Buckley said in his elite-to-the-point-of-parody affect. "They have a lust to find central and statist solutions for social problems. So we have an incoherence, an ambivalence, concerning

Democratic programs. We as conservatives always depend upon principle rather than particulars."

"Like thou shalt not kill?" jousted Max.

"Quite," Buckley said. "Thou shalt not kill is good conservative doctrine even though it fails to specify what you should do while *not* killing. We have not succeeded as a negative political force and probably cannot succeed as an affirmative one."

"Come on, now," said Patrick Buchanan, a brawling Nixon White House aide I recognized from TV. "So conservatism can't survive?"

"It was thought that the party's exorcism could be effected by the deposition of Nixon. And it is now thought by some that it will not be enough, that nothing less than the party's formal immolation will do. Whence the talk of changing the party's name."

"You're just bitter your brother lost to a Democrat," Buchanan said. "If your brother had just called a spade a spade, maybe he would have won! But he was mealymouthed about the problems of New York City, a city packed with welfare mamas like the ones we saw the night of the blackout, ripping off jewelry, clothing, and liquor stores, lumbering about like overfed heifers. The black communities of New York contain a disproportionately high percentage of animals without civilizing potential. And we can't be afraid to say so."

His racist rant was delivered with a smile, and no one at the table batted an eye. It was otherworldly. *Welfare mamas. Animals. Without civilizing potential.* I thought of the innocent man lynched by the angry white mob, the complex pathologies dating back to slavery and Jim Crow that the table ignorantly blamed on racial inferiority. Why were they all just sitting there? Why was this hideous man part of this club? Was *my* journalism part of this filth in its way?

After all, Max sat there smiling as Buchanan disparaged women who looked like Ashley as welfare mamas—Ashley, with whom he'd been sleeping for months; Ashley, for whom he should have stood up. Instead, he was sinking further into his cups.

I headed for the lobby to try to find her. Maybe tonight wasn't the time to confront Max. We could wait until morning, when he was sober and away from the Buchanans of the world. As I walked by my dad's table, he waved at me, so I stopped to say hello.

They were a sweet but sorry bunch, the Republican moderates: Dad, Baker, Bush, Nelson Rockefeller, Senators Charles Mathias of Maryland and Ed Brooke of Massachusetts (the only non-Caucasian in the room). They were all smiley and friendly enough but the mood was funereal compared to Reagan's lively gang across the room, where there was raucous laughter and literal backslapping. The last time Dad and these men had been at this event, they'd still had hope their moderate hero President Ford would win in November.

"It makes no sense," said one of them, a guy I didn't recognize. He had a shock of white hair and thick white eyebrows.

"The Southern strategy makes perfect sense," Dad said, "if morality isn't part of the equation."

"What bothers me more are the zealots Reagan is cozying up to," said a different guy, a beefy guy with a Midwestern twang. "Why do they care so much about everyone else's privates? They're obsessed. Homos, birth control, gynecologist stuff. I can't understand it. *That's* big government."

"They're growing in strength," said another man. "Anita Bryant raging against homosexuals in Florida with that TV evangelist Falwell."

"God forbid the religious loons wrest control of the party from us," said White Eyebrows.

"You know what's really activated them," said Dad. "It's not these 'moral' issues or prayer in school or obscenity laws or abortion. It was the IRS going after the private Christian schools that refused to desegregate. That's what got them involved in politics. They say that themselves."

I patted Dad on the back then resumed making my way to the lobby. As I struggled to peer through the shadows, the lights in the mansion came back on. Everyone cheered. "Thank God for private industry and backup generators!" one of the bigwigs said.

But I couldn't cheer. In the bright light, I saw the lobby was empty. Ashley wasn't there.

The person behind the reception desk was a slender well-groomed man in his early thirties. I asked if I could call up to Ashley Mars's room, and he checked the registration book and dialed the number for me. The phone rang and rang.

"No one's picking up," he said. "Would you care to leave her a message?"

If she wasn't in our villa and she wasn't in the dining room or the lobby, where could she be? "Could you please tell me her room number?"

He looked at me sideways. "I'm not supposed to share that information. But I suppose this is the same 'work emergency' Miss Mars pleaded about to get your villa number?"

"Exactly," I said, grinning.

I hurried up the stairs and found the Benning Suite, which was in the back corner of the second floor. The first odd thing was that Ashley hadn't closed her room door firmly. The lock hadn't caught. I walked right in.

Clearly, she hadn't been robbed. Her jewelry was strewn across the bureau from the lamp to the room phone. Next to that phone was her reporter's notebook, opened to a page where she had jotted down a number with a DC area code. I ripped off the page, folded it up, and held it in my palm. I don't know why I did it, but I did. I felt myself shifting into protector mode the way I used to with Ike when he was a little boy.

An evening dress was laid across a made bed. A pair of her favorite shoes, Chanel slingbacks, were on the floor, placed neatly beside the nightstand.

The bathroom was empty with fresh, unused towels. I looked around and saw a door to an adjoining room that was slightly open. I was moving toward it when a man's voice called from the hall: "Hey, Luce! What are you doing here?"

It was Harry.

"You startled me," I said.

Harry came into Ashley's room with his easy smile. "I've been looking for you everywhere," he said. "Let's go down to dinner. Can I meet your parents?"

"Have you seen Ashley?"

He gave me a look I couldn't read. "Not recently, no," he said slowly. He went over, closed the door that led to someone else's room, and rested his back against it.

"Why are you closing that door?" I asked.

He frowned. "Why can't we just go downstairs and have fun? Why do things like this always get in the way?"

"Things like what?"

He waved his hand around. "Like looking for your friend."

"She asked me to meet her downstairs and she never showed," I said. "She was upset about that mob, Harry. In Virginia. You heard about it, right? We did that, Harry. We did that." My voice broke but I didn't want him to see me crying, so I turned away.

He came over and tried to hold me. I resisted but ultimately fell into his embrace. "Shhh, darling. Shhh," he said, rubbing my back. "It's the storm. Everyone's on edge."

"It's not the storm."

He pulled back and smiled at me in a placating way. "Let's do this: We'll leave a note for Ashley at the front desk, hmm? Tell her we're in the dining room enjoying a fine meal and even better drinks and she should meet us there. I hate to see you all wound up like this."

He was pushing me out of her room and into the hall. "That door you closed—whose room is that? Is Ashley in there?"

He stared at me. His eyes had gone cool. "What? No, that's my father's room."

"Is she in there?"

"What are you talking about?" he asked. "You're acting odd. This isn't an Agatha Christie mystery, and you're not Miss Marple."

"I want you to open that door. I want to see for myself that she's not in there." And when he didn't move, I said it a little louder, too loud for how close he was to me. "Open the door, Harry."

He held up his hands, went to the door, banged on it, and said, "Anyone in there? Hello?"

A deep sense of dread stirred in my gut.

"Voilà," he said, flinging the door open wide, showing the room was empty. I caught a flicker of relief on his face, gone quickly, and then he was giving me the lovely smile that used to make me lose my mind. "See? I told you she's not here."

I carried Ashley's scrap of paper through the dark night and the lashing rain with the winds sandblasting me. The farther I got from the only building with electricity, the darker it got. When I lost my footing, I slowed. Soon the villa was in sight. Through the windows I could see Mom reading by flashlight, and then

I was on the porch and stumbling through the door, tracking in mud and wet sand and water. I pushed the door closed.

"My God," Mom said, reaching out to me. "Lucy. What on earth—"

"Is the phone working?"

"Why aren't you at the dinner? Shouldn't you be there meeting the candidates, impressing your boss?"

I just stared at her. Her inquiries seemed a remnant from an earlier, easier time.

"Is your father being rude or something?" she asked. "I know he doesn't approve of Mr. Lyon. The laetrile business *is* rather disgusting, you have to give him that."

It was, but that wasn't where my mind was, although I didn't know how to explain it.

"Honestly, that man," Mom was saying. "I have half a mind to march right up to his dinner table and tell him what I think of his media critiques. As if this entire trip weren't already a complete nightmare!"

"Maybe you should."

She stopped ranting. "What?"

A thought had struck me: She might be safer there. It was just a feeling—nowhere on this island felt safe, but she'd be safest with Dad, and he would be safest with her.

"You should go to the mansion," I said carefully, not wanting her to know what I was really worried about: That I had no idea where Ashley was, if she was okay, and that I was afraid that she might be out in the storm, frightened, lost, who knew what. Mom would think I was being paranoid, and she might be right. I *felt* paranoid. But I fixed what I hoped looked like an easy smile on my face. "Go check on Dad. See how he's doing."

She narrowed her eyes at me. "What are you up to?"

"Nothing." I held out my hands, all innocence. "I heard they were serving chocolate mousse for dessert. Better than those stupid apricots."

She held my gaze a moment longer; she didn't believe me. She always was the harder parent to fool. Then she said, "No, I'm quite fine here, thank you. Did you catch up with Ashley?"

"No, I couldn't find her," I said casually. "I need to make a call, though, if that's okay." I smoothed out the paper scrap with Ashley's handwriting and dialed the number on it. After four rings, a familiar voice answered. "Dick Flug here."

Dick Flug? Why was Ashley calling our congressional reporter?

"Is this your home phone, Dick?"

"Who is this?" he demanded. Then: "Ashley?"

I glanced over at my mom, who was plainly eavesdropping. "No, uh, actually, this is Lucy." I cleared my throat, then told the whopper: "Calling for Ashley."

He made a weird sound like a cat purring. Gross.

"Tell me what you got for us," I said as if I were in on whatever Ashley was up to.

"Good news is I confirmed everything," he said. "Bad news is no way we can report it."

My pulse sped up. "All right. Well. Shoot."

Here's what Dick and Ashley had uncovered: A person with knowledge of Max's business practices had been invited to testify before the Senate Commerce Committee in a closed-door antitrust investigation into the FCC's cross-ownership rule—something everyone on the Hill and at the White House knew Max Lyon and some other business barons were trying to circumvent. This was the missing witness Dick had wanted to report on before I left for Pitchfork Island, a story that got shot down in the newsroom as boring, stupid, not worthy of the *Sentinel*.

"So your missing witness was going to testify against the Lyons?"

"Well, uh, yeah. Against Max. But the witness was a no-show at the last minute. I'm also hearing—and look, again, there's no way we can report this." I heard him take a long drag of his cigarette. I waited. "So a Senate staffer told me this particular witness has inside knowledge of all the family's business practices in the UK and elsewhere and is alleging that Max uses his paper to settle scores, smear rivals, blackmail and bribe people, boost some stocks, tank others, promote shady international deals with known members of organized crime. Umberto Eco: 'Today a country belongs to the person who controls communications.'"

"Promote shady deals like the laetrile thing? Ashley already knows about that."

"Right, she told me," Dick agreed. "But according to my guy on the committee, that's just the tip of the iceberg. This witness hinted at all kinds of extracurriculars, corruption and fraud and illegal payoffs to politicians all over the world like you wouldn't believe. Then before she could testify—*poof*. Gone like Saigon."

"She? A woman?" I said, surprised. Don't ask me why. Cultural bias? Doubting Max would ever let a woman not related to him in on his business practices? "Did you get her name?"

"I *know* her. It's Max's former executive assistant. I worked with her when the paper started, before she went back to the UK. Her name is Penelope Watters."

I hung up, dazed. Before I turned around, I fixed another smile on my face, gave my body a minute to catch up to my racing thoughts. "May I borrow that book for a moment?"

Mom was looking down at it. "The photos are self-aggrandizing, the content is worse," she muttered. "I wanted to learn about the company you work for. The only thing I learned? The Lyons might be the only ones at their offices in England to have ever seen a dentist."

"Mom!"

She glanced up. "Honey, what's wrong?"

"Nothing, Mom. Please give me the book."

"Sweetie, tell me. You look...you look awful."

"Mom, *I need the book*," I said sharply. She handed it to me. "I'm sorry. And the flashlight. May I borrow that too?"

I carried the flashlight and the book to the desk, where I sat alone staring at the cover. *Pride of Lyons: The British Family Reinventing the News*.

When I first started at the *Sentinel*, I was given the book, yes, and I'd made all the same disdainful statements that every reporter had privately made, true, but when I went home, I skipped to the parts about Harry. I wanted to know about him. How to impress him, what to ask him about his life before I met him. I wanted to seem interesting to him. I had been like a fangirl, flipping past anything that wasn't Harry Lyon.

Was Penelope Watters in these pages? The name wasn't entirely unfamiliar. The memory was hazy, but I thought it was from this book. There was no index, of course. I leafed through the sections on the newspapers in the UK, on the various expansions into Ireland, France, Germany, Australia, New Zealand. The one page at the end about plans for expansion into the U.S. But it was all Max, Max, Max, Harry and Danielle, Max, Max, a dollop of poor Ivan, Max, Max, Max...nothing. Lots of wood, lots of splashy photos of royals and football (soccer) stars and celebrities. No mention of any executive assistants. Of course not.

The camera loved the Lyon family, and it was a requited love, so there were lots of pics. I looked at every one, scanning the captions, starting with the most recent photos toward the end. Nothing. Then the front of the book. Nothing. Then the middle. Jesus, there was—

I gasped.

Harry was arm in arm with a woman in a crowd shot in the office of the *Evening Standard*. The caption identified her as Penelope Watters.

That long curly red hair, that fair skin. I recognized her. I'd seen her before.

In Lady Bird Park with her arms splayed out and her legs crossed, the Slug Killer's most recent victim.

CHAPTER FIFTEEN

IKE

Pitchfork Island, Georgia

August 1977

Tomorrow will be too late
It's now or never

—Elvis Presley, "It's Now or Never"

I CAME BACK to consciousness, confused. My head throbbed as if it had been stampeded over at Altamont, and then I remembered: *Oh, yeah, somebody sucker-clubbed me from behind.* I felt nauseated and had no idea where I was.

I tried to get up from the floor. "Easy," warned a familiar voice. Rachel hurried across the RV and sat beside me, looking down with concern, studying my face. "Welcome back."

Her dark beautiful eyes made me sigh wistfully but I shook it off. She handed me some aspirin and a glass of water. "You've been out for a few hours," she said. I sat up and she went to the fridge, put some ice in a towel, came back, and placed the ice pack on my head. I was woozy, and it took me a bit to put all the pieces together.

We were in the back of Lucky's RV, I realized, remembering where I'd been conscious last. I noticed duct tape on my wrists.

I'd been bound, but someone had cut it and freed me. I ripped off what was left of the tape. "Where's Evel?" My mouth was dry and tasted of old blood.

"On his way to LA to beat the shit out of the guy who wrote that book," she said.

What a thing. He was flying to Hollywood to physically hurt the former PR guy who'd written truths about him that he didn't like being shared. I mean, I understood the rage to a degree, but what an effort.

"There goes his presidential campaign," I said. I lifted myself to a chair, poked through the venetian blinds, and was surprised to see it was night. And pouring rain. Streetlights revealed folks milling about a parking lot, beyond which lay the ocean, the waves frothing with whitecaps. We were at a run-down marina with several small motorboats. At the end of a dock, a small white passenger ferry bobbed up and down like a cork. I scratched away the duct-tape glue from my beat-up Timex. It was 8:10 p.m.

"Evel's a nitwit," she said under her breath. I laughed. "Do you want to know who hit you on the head?" she asked. "Lucky. Or one of his goons."

"The governor?" He had just been praising me for deciding to talk to Dad. He'd called me the prodigal son. "Why would he do that?"

"Because he didn't trust you," she said.

"Trust me? Why wouldn't he trust me? And why are we here? And where is here?"

Rachel ignored my questions, seemingly eager to get something off her chest. "We've been tracking him for a while, Governor Strong."

"What do you mean, you've been *tracking* him? You're a bartender."

Thunder cracked outside the RV. "I'm not who you think I

am. My name isn't Rachel Two Bears, Ike. I'm sorry I couldn't tell you before now."

My head throbbed and I wondered if maybe my brain was having trouble catching up. Rachel—or whatever her name was—reached over and touched my shoulder, but I still couldn't fully comprehend what the hell she was saying.

"You're not Rachel Two Bears?" I said, so confused. "Then who are you?"

She put her right hand out to shake mine. "I'm Field Agent Rachel Esposito, FBI," she said. I shook it, feeling queasy. "I work in domestic terrorism, mostly in Indian country, but our office covers Wyoming, Idaho, and Montana."

"So, you're Rachel...but not Two Bears?"

"No, although my mom is Crow. My dad's Mexican. I've been undercover for a year, following these extremist groups, biker gangs, Reverend Russell's cult, and those Idaho Nazis you took a shine to back in Butte. You have no idea what's going on out in the Northwest with these Nazis and assorted white-supremacist freaks. Strong has been wink-winking with the lot of them. He funds them. Nasty stuff."

"So that's how you ended up in Butte?"

"Yeah," she said, peeking out the venetian blinds, "it was a decent perch to keep an eye out. But right now we're in Georgia, at the ferry to Pitchfork Island. The island is the new target."

"Island?" I got up, moved closer to the window, peered out again. The crowd had grown to maybe seventy-five or a hundred people. Lucky's crew. The folks from the caravan. The Yo-Yos. The Reverend Russell's zealots. All those angry people with grievances, *they were all here*. Someone started passing around poles of some sort and then someone else lit the end of one of them, then another, then another. They were torches. Holy hell.

"Pitchfork Island," Rachel said. "Republican retreat."

"Jesus fucking Christ, my parents are there. What are these fuckwits planning to do?"

"They want to storm the retreat—I'm not sure they even have a plan beyond causing mayhem. But they don't have a boat to cross the sound to the island. So maybe a protest on this side? To get attention? We're on standby, in case it gets violent. Or if they steal—" Whatever else she was going to tell me was interrupted by crackling static. She lifted a two-way radio to her lips. "Copy. I'm with Ike in RV four," she said.

"Backup is thirty minutes out," the voice on the other end said.

"We can't stop a hundred maniacs by ourselves," Rachel said. "They have torches."

The walkie-talkie crackled again. "Do you have eyes on them? Are there any weapons beyond torches?" It was a voice I knew from somewhere.

"Copy that. A few rifles, half a dozen sidearms. And some bats and clubs and pipes and stuff."

"Wait a sec, is that Damon? Are the Yellowmountain boys FBI too?" She shushed me.

I pushed back the blinds and pressed my nose to the window and saw that at the edge of the parking lot, close to the ocean, Governor Strong was yelling something, but it was difficult to make out the words over the thunder and downpour. But Lucky looked angry. Furious. And the men who had assembled—the group seemed to have been whittled down to the hardest core—were equally mad, some with torches that cast demonic shadows on their faces. "So much anger," I said. "What would they do if they were able to get to the island?" I asked Rachel.

"Our intel on that is pretty spotty," she said. "They're angry about... I'm not exactly sure what, injustice and theft and cancer and aliens."

"The snooty elites taking away their freedoms?" Those snooty elites, I knew, included my parents. They would consider my parents elites. My adrenaline kicked up at the thought.

"Could be," Rachel said.

"It doesn't always matter what the specific injustice is, I guess," I said. I thought about the Alighieri brothers. Sometimes people just felt like life wasn't fair, and they wanted to make sure someone was paying attention. I tried to stay calm. Dad, my own personal Atticus Finch, always told me to walk in another person's shoes. But what did you do when those shoes were marching toward your parents to kick them in the face?

So long as there was a large body of water between that anger and my parents, I could stay calm. But if they touched one hair on Mom's head...or Lucy's...

Rachel's walkie-talkie crackled. "They're just outside the RV," she told Damon over the radio. Then to me: "It's tough to determine the motivations of a mob. Some of them are mad Evel abandoned them, some of them are mad about the book by Shelly Saltman—and a lot of anti-Semitic stuff gets channeled into that, Hollywood, publishing, the normal crazy—but frankly, some of those guys were halfway to the Sudetenland already. The alien stuff can manifest itself in an unhealthy distrust of government; the laetrile stuff is pharmaceutical companies putting profits over lives. There's Vietnam-vet-cancer stuff, aliens-causing-cancer stuff. Don't get me wrong, there's legit reasons to hate the government. Some of the anger is valid, some is not, and all of it can be channeled in dangerous ways."

"So the causes don't compete," I said. "They coagulate."

Outside, someone had lit a fire in an oil drum, and the flames broke through the downpour and reached into the sky. There must have been actual oil in the drum. Some of the torches had fizzled. I saw that giant freak from the Yo-Yos, Junior, clutching his shotgun. I saw some of Reverend Russell's weirdos—Justice, Fortitude, Prudence—holding small crucifixes. Then the group started chanting. This we could understand: "Burn, baby, burn! Burn, baby, burn!"

I don't know if the mob had learned that cry from the Watts rioters in the 1960s or from the disco song by the Trammps, but it sounded menacing. They sounded like they meant it. Then they began walking to the dock.

"You're sure they don't have a boat, right?" I said. "Maybe we should go out there."

"Negative, Mr. Concussion, you sit there." Rachel grabbed the walkie-talkie. "They're heading to the ferry."

"Are there other boats visible?" Damon asked.

"Only the ferry that's out of service," she said. "Where's the Coast Guard?"

"Commanded to dock because of the big storm."

"Did you get through to Atlanta?"

"Affirmative, but the storm grounded the choppers and they can't get comms to the island."

One of the Yo-Yos scaled the fence easily and unlocked the gate from inside, and the horde surged ahead and started boarding the ferry. "Rachel, are you seeing this?"

"Copy, over," she said on the radio, ignoring me. "Subjects boarding the ferry. We have to assume—"

We could hear the rumble of the ferry engine turning over. "Rachel, someone just started the engine," I said, panicking now. "I'm going out there."

"Our orders are to sit tight until backup arrives." Then, into the radio: "Someone just started the engine on that ferry. I assume they're commandeering it." She looked out the window, shaking her head. The rain pounded on the roof of the RV. Finally, she turned to me. "We're fucked," she said.

"My family's fucked," I said. "My parents are on that island. Maybe my sister too. I can't sit here and watch this." I lurched to my feet. "Are you coming?"

"I've been given explicit and direct orders to stand down and wait for backup," she said. "And I've been told to instruct you to stay with me and wait for backup. Two of us can't do anything on our own." She paused. "Though of course, technically, you're not under arrest, and though the FBI would never officially tell you this, you are an American and you're free to do whatever you want."

I looked at her, trying to process what she'd said. "You won't try to stop me?"

She gave me a sad smile. "No."

"Can I have your gun?" I asked.

"Ike, what do you think?"

I went out the door and down the stairs. The rain pelted down. My head throbbed.

I walked briskly away from the pier and toward the beach, trying not to draw anyone's attention. In military training, they call it "becoming the gray man"—you fade into the background, hands in pockets, gait neither too fast nor too slow, nothing to see here. I reached the sand and walked right into the rollicking surf; it was August and the water was warm and the waves whipped up by the storm were powerful, unpredictable.

A few dinghies and small motorboats were anchored in the shallows, and I trudged through the surf to the closest one, which also happened to be the shittiest: dented, dirty, with patches in its hull. I hoisted myself up, soaking wet, and pulled the anchor. Thankfully the key remained in the ignition; presumably no one would ever be desperate enough to steal this bucket of bolts.

I started the two-stroke outboard engine and steered away from the ferry, which had departed heading east, and prayed that the rain and dim light hid me from their line of sight. There was no plan except getting to the island before the ferry, finding my family, and—that's as far ahead as I'd thought.

At Camp Geiger, they would send us into the surf during thunderstorms just to stress-test us, but these waves were worse, the roughest I'd ever experienced, the sea churning, whirlwinds wrestling for control of my boat. I knelt and held the gunnels; the sky was filled with billowy purplish-black clouds, lightning popping and strobing the sea before me. The bottom of the boat already held a couple inches of water. One well-timed swell could knock me into the tempest and sink this rust bucket.

A gust of wind slapped a wave across my face; it stung. The chop was high and I sucked in seawater. It was a nasty brine, a witches' brew of sand and seafoam and silt and salt.

And I loved every minute of it.

Yes, I was terrified, and yes, I was worried about my family, but I also reveled in the purity of the moment and the mission. I saw trees on the horizon, and as the water got choppier, there were rocks I hadn't expected that laid treacherous traps.

The vessel banged and dragged across boulders along the shore, and I hit the embankment and hauled the boat up onto the rocks, sure that it would be gone if I ever actually made it back here.

I staggered through the brush, needing to find Mom and Dad—and Lucy, if she was on the island—and warn them and everyone else that an armed mob was on its way. I couldn't find a path off the rocky beachhead but there was a glow in the distance, presumably lights from the buildings. Following the glow, I wrestled my way through dense scrub until, stumbling, I emerged onto a manicured lawn at the edge of the resort.

In the distance, I saw the source of the glow—a huge mansion, all lit up. Around it were smaller buildings, dark shadows against the night. I went to the closest of these buildings and pounded on the door. No one answered, but the doorknob turned when I tried it, and I went in. I hit the light switch, but nothing happened. I realized the power must be out on parts of the island. I fumbled in the darkness for a flashlight, matches, candles, anything. I found a phone, but there was no dial tone.

I went back outside, and the wind drove sheets of rain into my face as I raced past cabin after cabin toward the giant mansion aglow on the hill. I took the last fifty yards at a furious sprint and burst through the doors, carrying with me wind and rain, startling the clerk behind the desk.

"I'm looking for Senator or Mrs. Marder," I said, panting from the run. "Or their daughter, Lucy. Is Lucy here?"

The clerk took in my state, muddy and soaking wet, my overgrown beard flat against my chin, my hair dripping in my eyes, my all-around desperation. "You're looking for the senator?" he said as if he were thinking about calling security, and honestly, I wished he would.

"I'm Ike Marder, Senator Marder's son."

"They're not here," he said, obviously not sure if he should believe me. I didn't blame him. I could hear a din off to my right but couldn't see anything from the lobby.

"Any idea where they are?" I asked.

He just stared. Then, dumbass that I was, I finally remembered my ID. I fished my sodden wallet out of my wet pants and stuck my ID under the clerk's nose. "See: Dwight David Marder. Nickname's Ike."

The man looked at the ID, then at my face, then back at the ID and smiled. "Thank you, Mr. Marder," he said. "Welcome to Trinity Island. Your sister ran out some time ago, and your father went looking for her."

Jesus.

"Their lodging is, let me see here," he said, inspecting his ledger, "cabin sixteen. But I don't know where they might be." He showed me a map of the three-pronged shape of the island. "A lot of our shops are in this area, but I believe everything's been shuttered because of the storm. I'm sorry, sir, I truly have no idea."

"Is there law enforcement on the island?" I asked. "Do you have some sort of sheriff or something?"

"No, but there's Secret Service in the office," he said, motioning with his chin toward a door slightly ajar up the short staircase. "Plus, of course, more agents at the dock. There's a Coast Guard cutter out there in the harbor. May I ask why?"

"Please ask the guests to stay within the confines of the mansion, okay? At least until they hear otherwise from the Secret Service. Can you tell me where I can find the agent in charge? Is he in the office?"

I took the stairs two at a time to the office and found three men in suits sitting comfortably, their sports jackets off. "You're Secret Service?" I asked. They sat upright, perhaps wondering if I constituted some sort of threat. I extended my hand to one of them.

"Marine Sergeant Ike Marder, son of Senator Charlie Marder, sir," I said. Most of these Secret Service guys were ex-GIs. "There's a boat of hostiles making their way to the island."

"Who are they?" the man asked.

"The FBI's been tracking them—angry, armed, uninformed extremists."

He picked up his walkie-talkie. "Pier, this is Red Six, do you see any boat traffic?"

"Some lights in the distance, looks like the ferry," came the reply.

"How many are you at the pier?"

"Two of us."

"What about the Coast Guard?"

"The cutter's gone. They were forced to dock on the mainland when the storm swept in."

He turned to me. "We haven't heard anything from the Coast Guard or the Feds."

"Of course, comms are down," one of his agents reminded him.

"We have two dozen senators, nine governors, and something like thirty members of the House at this conference." He looked at the two other agents in the little office. "Jesus, there's five of us on the island to guard, like, a third of the government?"

"Six of us," I said.

He ignored that. "You said they're armed?" he asked. "And how do you know this?"

"It's a long story. I was—"

"Pier, the group coming in on the ferry is armed," he said into the walkie-talkie.

"Roger that. Senator Marder is down here looking for his wife and daughter. I'm going to send him back to you," the voice said.

"I'm heading down there," I told the agents.

"Hold up a sec," said Red Six. "Are they staging some kind of protest?"

"More like a rebellion."

"What are they rebelling against?"

"Whaddya got?" I said. "I need to get to my dad."

"Well, then," he said, and stood. "The golf carts are parked out back. Take the paved path down to the pier."

Behind the mansion, I found a garage holding gardening supplies, golf carts, and bags of fertilizer. Behind the golf carts I noticed that familiar shape under a tarp, and I knew right away what it was: a motorcycle, my ever-loyal steed. I hoped it was a Ducati, since my luck in finding motorcycles had always been excellent. But when I pulled back the dusty tarp, what I saw was a moped.

I'd never ridden one before. These fuel-efficient not-big-enough-to-be-motorcycles, too-motorized-to-be-bicycles motor-bikes had really caught on during the energy crisis a few years earlier, and I'd seen lots of kids zipping around on them.

This one was a Puch Maxi; it looked like a small motorcycle but still had auxiliary pedals. I hopped on it, found the fuel tap and choke lever, and turned the key that had been left in the ignition—it was nice being on an island where everyone trusted everyone else, I thought. Of course, the moped didn't just start. For that, I had to pedal it like a bicycle. It came to life, sounding like a very large and angry insect and filling the shed with a haze of two-stroke oil.

I rocked it forward off the stand with the throttle wide open, causing a squeal of protest as the spinning rear tire hit the garage floor. The little 50 cc motor was willing, but I had a hundred pounds on the average moped-riding kid, so I pedaled for all I was worth around the mansion and down the trail to the pier. I zipped through puddles and passed shallow ditches and gullies filling with water. The moped kept skidding—the island was flooding.

The two small blocks of stores I drove past were a blur, not because of the bike's speed but because of the darkness and the storm and the terror I felt inside. Didn't see Dad anywhere. Or anyone else. As I reached the pier, I saw the two Secret Service agents standing in the rain with twelve-gauge shotguns, looking out at the sea, at the approaching vessel. It had a beacon, and a man was up on the rail.

"That's the ferry!" I yelled over the storm's rumble, and they looked back at me and nodded. "Where's Senator Marder?" I asked.

"He left a couple minutes ago!" one of the agents yelled. They both stood there watching the approaching ship. "We told him to head back to the mansion, but he was looking for Mrs. Marder and your sister! We gave him directions to the Confederate fort and cannon. They're that way!"

A wooden sign behind them warned: DON'T TOUCH HISTOR-ICAL ARTIFACTS. CANNONS AND OTHER MUNITIONS FROM THE WAR BETWEEN THE STATES MAY STILL BE FUNCTIONAL AND SHOULD BE CONSIDERED DANGEROUS.

I got back on the moped and twisted the throttle. Even with the bike in first gear, I felt the revs dropping as I climbed the hill. I truly believed that the mob, fueled by righteous rage and the madness of crowds, might kill anyone they saw. It was up to me to save Mom and Dad and Lucy. I started pedaling as fast as I could.

CHAPTER SIXTEEN

LUCY

Pitchfork Island, Georgia

August 1977

I NEEDED TO find Ashley.

Standing at the door, armed only with Dad's flashlight, I didn't know where to even start. No one had seen Ashley at the mansion, and she hadn't been waiting for me at our villa. That meant she was out there somewhere, in the storm or at the dock or tucked in one of these dark villas taking shelter.

The resort grounds were black against the glow of the mansion on the hill. Last time I'd seen her, she was distraught, planning on confronting Max about that innocent man lynched by the Virginia mob. She also, unbeknownst to me until moments ago, was at least somewhat hip to Max's possible involvement in that witness's disappearance. But what did she know? Did she have any idea that the witness was Penelope Watters? Or that Ms. Watters had been murdered? What would happen to Ashley if Max found out she'd been poking around in all of that?

Would that put Ashley in danger?

I shivered, and not from the cold rain pelting the island.

Did *my* knowledge put *me* in danger?

And what about Mom? And Dad?

I looked at Mom. If she learned any of this information, she would feel compelled to act. That was my mom, strong and brave. But I didn't need her getting involved. I needed her safe.

"Mom, can you do me a favor?" I asked. "Can you please just go to the mansion and sit with Dad? I know it would mean a lot to him. He suggested as much."

"What?" she asked. "Why? Whatever for?"

"Mom, please just do this for me. It's miserable in here anyway, with no lights. You asked me to find Ike because you were worried about Dad, and I did, and now I'm asking you to go keep him company. Please?"

"You are acting very odd, Lucy," she said. "There's obviously quite a bit you're not telling me."

"Mom, I will tell you everything the next time I see you if you promise to just go sit with Dad at dinner."

She looked at me. "Everything?" she said.

"Promise," I said. "Just don't leave Dad's side."

Pitchfork Island's name came from the fact that it was shaped like a pitchfork with three tines, or like the letter E slightly tilted to the left. The top corner of the letter was closest to the mainland and where we docked. The stores and lodgings, then the mansion and cabins, were on the long base of the island. The middle prong was the highest part of the island, the spot where the celebrated Confederate fort and its cannons stood, facing the mainland. The third tine, entirely wooded, was the least traveled part of the island.

As I watched Mom walk up to the mansion, leaving a streak of footprints in the grass, I noticed another smear of footprints on the path, heading to or from the middle prong of the island, to my right. I followed the trail; it went down past some villas, then curved left up a hill. I brushed my wet bangs from my eyes and swept a wide arc with the flashlight beam. My shoes made wet sucking sounds as I went. The imprints were not the same as Mom's individual sloshy footprints. It was more like following the path of a sled.

The beam of my flashlight caught a rusted green sign at the trailhead, which read THIS HALLOWED SITE WE DEDICATE TO THE GLORY AND HONOR OF THE VALIANT SOLDIERS OF THE CONFEDERATE STATES OF AMERICA DURING THE WAR OF NORTHERN AGGRESSION FOR THEIR UNPARALLELED COURAGE AND GALLANTRY IN DEFENSE OF THEIR HOMELAND AND VALUES AND THE LOST CAUSE AND TO THEIR FAMILIES AND FRIENDS FOR THEIR SACRIFICES AND UNWAVERING LOVE AND SUPPORT.

The words flickered in the lightning. The beam from the flashlight was unsteady in my shaking hand. The words made me remember driving with Ashley on all those roads named after Confederate generals on the way to the Lyons' estate, her obvious disgust with how we covered the Slug Killer, her panic after the mob chased that innocent man into traffic. And then I thought there was no way Ashley would want to visit the Confederate fort. Wild horses couldn't drag her there.

And then it hit me. Oh, good Lord, was that what these weird marks were from? *Had* someone been dragged?

Had Ashley?

I ran the rest of the way up the hill as the rain let up. As I reached the crest of the promontory, the moon slid out from behind the clouds. The storm's first band of rain was passing, and the next band would come soon, but for now I saw the area was deserted. I was alone in the moonlight with the Confederate cannons to my left and the small fort to my right. The promontory ended in a cliff.

I went to the edge, steeling myself for the worst, and looked down. Giant waves crashed onto the rocks below, accompanied by a tempest of thunder and lightning, a malicious swirl of danger and death.

On the water between the island and the mainland, light bobbed faintly. Perhaps from the Coast Guard patrol boats? A gust of wind pushed me closer to the edge. A loose branch sped by me, missing my head by inches. I leaned into the wind and headed for the small fort. It was built of heavy logs; maybe Ashley had taken shelter in there? If not, at least it could be a place for me to catch my breath and figure out where to search next.

"Hello?" I said, ducking inside. The fort was empty, dark. It smelled dank and...of something else that made the hair on my nape stand up. I pointed the flashlight down to watch where I was going. Three steps led to a small room.

That's where I found Ashley. Spread out on the floor in that terrible pose, one shoe lost and her heel muddy, her eyes bloody and lifeless.

I don't remember crossing the stone floor to her. I don't remember kneeling by her side or grabbing her wrist. I kind of blacked out, I guess. I remember hearing someone wailing: "No, no, no, oh, please, no," and I thought, *What a terrible noise.* Then I realized that wailing belonged to me. And then I found myself on my hands and knees next to her, the flashlight lying on the ground and shining on her face.

She had no pulse. Her head was to the side, and her eyes were blood red, like Penelope Watters's eyes had been, as though she'd been strangled, like Penelope. And Jeannie McBean and Janice Davenport. And then I saw it. A syringe. Tangled in her hair.

The Slug Killer was *here*, on the island.

I felt ill.

I heard a branch crack outside the fort.

Someone was there.

I looked around the room. There was nowhere to hide in this abandoned fort. There were no weapons either. There was nothing.

I clicked the flashlight off and crouched low next to Ashley's body and held my breath.

From just outside the door, I heard "Hello?" in a harsh whisper, low and wary.

I gripped the flashlight, felt its weight. I could bash the Slug Killer in the head. No way was I going out without a fight.

A dark silhouette filled the doorway. *Don't crouch defensively,* I thought. *Assert yourself.* I clicked the flashlight back on and aimed the beam in his eyes. The man put his hands up to block the glare.

It was Harry.

I didn't know whether to feel relief or terror. I wanted to feel safe, but I didn't. "What are you doing here?" I asked. I was trying to sound brave but my voice trembled.

"Lucy, is that...is that Ashley?"

I didn't have time to react before he ran to her side, checked her pulse, put his face next to hers to see if he could discern a breath.

"Oh, bloody hell," he said, slumping.

He suddenly stood. Ran his hands through his hair, then rubbed them together.

"Who killed her, Harry?" I said. I aimed the flashlight at his face again, blinding him. He looked quite pale. There was something wrong with his reaction. His eyes seemed flat and cold.

He was not surprised.

"Who did this, Harry?" I said. "Was it you?"

"Lucy," he said dismissively, "you know I'm not capable of this."

"I don't know anything right now," I said meekly.

He tried to embrace me but I pulled away.

Lightning flashed outside.

"Lucy, listen to me," he said, trying to look me in the eye, though I resisted. "You need to go back to your villa right now. No one must know that you saw this."

"Saw this?" I said. "What do you mean? We have to call the police!"

"That won't happen," he said.

"What are you talking about?"

"This," he said, motioning toward Ashley, "was done by a very sick person, someone completely out of control. But this...this...will be taken care of. It'll all be cleaned up. By the time the police arrive on the island, this will be long gone."

I hated him. *This* was how he referred to Ashley. *This.* As a problem. Not a person. No sorrow or pity or anger, nothing. As if she weren't lying there as she was, hadn't suffered the way she had, *as if her life hadn't been ripped from her.*

"Why aren't you upset, Harry? Why is it you don't seem to care what's happened to Ashley?"

"What? Of course I care," he said, staring into my eyes with a pleading look I didn't understand. "But what is to be done?"

His hair plastered to his skull, his eyes red-rimmed, his clothes rough, not elegant—he didn't seem like the Harry I'd fallen for. Or had I not been paying attention? The Lyons had known Jeannie McBean was the victim of a serial killer. The Lyons had played up the black "person of interest." That terrible intuition I'd had earlier in Ashley's suite at the mansion—that I had been so close to falling in love with this beautiful man, and the terror, the realization that I utterly did not know him in any real way, that what I'd been looking at was a magician's distraction.

All along, Harry had been protecting someone. Was it himself? The flashlight was heavy in my palm.

"Are you the Slug Killer, Harry?"

"Good Lord, no, Lucy," he said. "You think I prey on women? That I'm capable of harming two women I worked closely with? No, scratch that. Two women I care about?" He dropped his hand from his hair. "Penelope and Ashley were my friends."

"I haven't mentioned Penelope, Harry," I said.

He thought about that, realized his mistake. "Well, it's not as if I'm oblivious to what's going on and who's behind it," he said. "Look, darling—" He started walked toward me again.

"Too close," I warned him, brandishing the flashlight. "Stop right there. I'm not messing around here."

He paused. "I'm going to assume that you are in shock. It is very shocking—trust me, I know. But you get over the discomfiture eventually."

"What does *that* mean?"

"You—you learn to fix things, to keep everything together, keep your sanity together, but first, I know, my darling, God how I know, how horrible, what a scare to the soul it must be."

He started to say something, then thought better of it. I watched all these thoughts storm across his expression the same way I'd seen the suave mask of the elegant heir to the Lyon fortune fall over his face.

"I'm not the killer, Lucy. But the person who is *will* get away with it. Because the killer is protected by my father. And you have no idea what my father is capable of."

"I know he uses his newspapers to manipulate markets and settle scores and encourage the worst in the public," I said. "And I know you're not much better, even though you tell yourself otherwise."

He smiled. He had the look of someone who knew the jig was up. "You came into the newsroom with your American hokum, myths fed to you in Saturday-morning cartoons, bumper-sticker philosophies about complicated ideas like facts and truth. As if there were such a thing as truth in this world." He exhaled and looked at me lovingly. "All we did was try to make you a star."

"Well, I have a hell of a scoop for tomorrow," I said.

Over the din of the storm, I heard a buzzing. A motor. High-pitched. Like a chain saw.

"Bollocks," Harry said. "We need to get out of here."

Before he could say another word, I ran.

I raced out of the fort door and into the clearing. There in the distance, through the sheets of rain that had started again, I saw a big, burly, bearded figure struggling up the hill toward me on an odd-looking little contraption—a moped? The man was hunched over its handlebars, the way I'd seen Ike a thousand times, and he was pedaling furiously, but I thought it couldn't be Ike. My eyes were playing tricks on me. All this insanity must have made me lose my mind.

Then I laughed and saw my eyes weren't playing tricks on me. It *was* Ike. Of course it was. We would always come to each other's rescue. The bond between us, among all the Marders, transcended everything.

He pulled up. "Hey, sis," he said. "I'm so glad to see you."

"'Hey, *sis*'?" I laughed. "Like I didn't wish for you and *poof,* here you are." I hugged him. "We need to get out of here." I looked behind me, but Harry wasn't there.

"Out of here, like off the island?" Ike asked. "Have they hit shore yet?"

"What?" I asked, glancing down now at what he had been hunched over. It was a large bag of commercial fertilizer on the seat in front of him. "Is that *cow shit*?"

"Commercial fertilizer, which contains ammonium nitrate," he said. "Where are Mom and Dad? There are a bunch of psychos on the way to the island."

"There's at least one psycho here already," I said.

He looked at me with a confused expression, hopped off the moped, and ran with his fertilizer past the old Confederate cannon to the edge of the cliff. I followed. He pointed to the ferry a few dozen yards away from the dock. I could see the front deck packed with men, and on the winds of the storm, I could hear some sort of angry chant.

"Unfriendlies at the perimeter," he said. "They came here for all of you. And because of the storm, the Coast Guard cutter is back on the mainland and there are only five Secret Service agents on this whole island."

Lightning flashed again and I saw movement a few hundred yards to the left, on the westernmost headland below. "Someone's down there," I said. Ike had turned his back to me and was stuffing something down into the open end of the cannon.

I turned the flashlight on and aimed the beam where I'd seen movement, but whatever it was, it was gone now.

"Step away, sis!" he yelled. He was standing behind the cannon. His hands were filthy. "I jammed a bunch of fertilizer and a big rock in there!" he said.

"What? That's crazy!" I yelled.

"Stand back!"

I ran away from the edge of the cliff and out of the trajectory, throwing myself onto the grass just in case. Ike shielded his lighter, then pushed his hand into the ignition chamber.

"The thing is a hundred years old," I yelled. "It will never—"

I was interrupted by a giant *boom*. Smoke began pouring out of both the barrel and the chamber of the cannon.

"Holy fuck, it worked!" Ike yelled, jumping up in the air like a kid. He ran to the edge of the cliff. We both saw the splash where the rock had landed, missing the boat by several yards.

"I missed," he said. "But not by a lot! Help me aim!"

We ran back to the cannon, and Ike started rocking it, throwing all his weight against it. "Help me push it a foot to the right!"

There was a powerful stink of manure in the air. I joined him on the far side of the heavy cannon as we rocked it together. It started to give, and we pushed it into position.

"Check my aim," he said. He lifted two chunks of rock that had been holding the cannon in place and pushed them down into the cannon, followed by more fertilizer from the bag.

I ran to the cliff and tried to line up the shot. It looked fine to me. "Good to go!" I yelled.

Ike shielded his lighter again, then jammed his hand into the back of the cannon. The fertilizer caught fire and he screamed, "Fuck!" But he kept the lighter down in the firing chamber and the cannon again went *boom*.

We ran to the edge of the cliff. Lightning flashed again, illuminating the scene below—the ocean, the beach, the ferry. There was a direct hit from the cannon to the bow. The ferry appeared to be taking on water and foundering near the pier. Black smoke rose from the cockpit, from a big hole in the side of the ship, and then we saw flames. The ferry had caught fire.

"They're abandoning ship!" Ike yelled, laughing maniacally. "Holy shit, I can't believe it worked!"

The lightning was on top of us, almost nonstop, like a power line had gone down. I caught that movement on the rocks below the cliff again, across the water, on the other promontory. "Look!" I yelled.

It was Mom. She was lying on a giant rock, unmoving. The strobe of the lightning created a weird effect; it looked like we were watching an old-time movie.

"Mom!" he yelled.

I cupped my hands around my mouth and screamed, *"Mom,"*

hoping she'd hear me and wake up. Waves were whipping up around her.

"Who the fuck is that?" Ike asked. He pointed to the low trees and scrub behind Mom; shadows wrestled, shaking branches and leaves. Three men came crashing out of the forest and onto the shore. One of them glanced up, and we saw his face clearly.

"Dad!" Ike yelled. "What the fuck?"

The other shadows soon came into focus: Little Bertie Lyon. His older half brother Ivan. They were pummeling Dad. I shrieked.

Bertie looked around and then up to me, above him on the cliff.

"We see you, Bertie! Give it up!" I yelled. We had to get down there to help. I turned, looking for Ike, so I could grab his hand and show him the way.

That was when I heard the moped again, and Ike yelled for me to get out of the way.

CHAPTER SEVENTEEN

IKE

Pitchfork Island, Georgia

August 1977

Stoke that pedal down to the floor
As much as you give, crowd wants more

—Elvis Presley, "Speedway"

I STUCK THAT MOTHERFUCKER.

I mean, it was simultaneously the bravest and the stupidest thing I'd ever done. The Root included.

But there wasn't even a question in my mind.

Mom was in trouble. Dad was taking a beating. I needed to get down there five minutes ago. I looked at the sad little moped. It had carried me this far. But could it make a jump of that magnitude? Over the cliff and onto the rocks? The terrain might play to my advantage; there was a good few yards of a downhill run to a sort of lip that would serve as a launch ramp. The key is to have enough forward propulsion in the vector to cover the distance before gravity inevitably kicks in.

The other key? Knowing you could do it. I had stuck landings before—over a tank full of sharks, over creeks in upstate New York.

The last consideration? Knowing I had to do it. But that wasn't always enough. In the Root, I had failed.

I revved the engine and crouched over the handlebars, and then I hesitated. Mom was on the goddamned rocks in the middle of a hurricane, and Dad was getting destroyed by a couple young maniacs and all I could think was *I can't fuck this up.*

I had fucked up a jump before, and Gonzo was now a vegetable, and I hadn't been able to go back for Schmitty. What if I let Mom and Dad down, like I'd let Schmitty down—but then I thought, *Fuck that. No.* That wasn't my fault, that was Hardcastle and the generals, I was Ike Marder and I was a better biker than Evel Knievel and I was going to go save Mom and Dad, and fuck anyone and anything telling me otherwise.

The one second was over. I revved the engine hard, pushed it off the stand again, and was pedaling hard before the spinning rear tire even touched the ground, blowing past Lucy, who was waving her arms wildly, screaming something, but I kept going, thinking, *I can do this. I can stick the landing, I can save Mom and Dad.*

Then I was curling over the handlebars, pedaling as if I were in the Tour de France as I shifted gears to accelerate down the slope toward the lip, the little moped giving her all. Suddenly, I was airborne, off the edge of the cliff, flying over every past mistake—the Root, Bethesda Naval, Chicago, Butte, everything now in the rearview. The moped soared, defying gravity, and when she buckled, I muscled the front tire up, knowing I could stick the landing here as I'd done in Chicago, as I'd tried to do in the Root...

...and I was sailing over the rock where Mom lay, and Dad was jumping away as if I were an incoming grenade. The other two, that little shit Lucy called Bertie and the bigger shit, who I later learned was Ivan Lyon, froze in shock and amazement, horrified as they realized I was airborne, yes, but falling fast, headed toward them, and whatever they had hoped to get away with was done, over, there was no place left to run.

Thankfully we came in rubber-side down, though in terms of control, the bike—and me on it—might as well have been flung by a medieval siege engine. Both wheels completely buckled, and I could have sworn I distinctly heard the engine cases hit the deck, but momentum carried me and the bike into Ivan, and we skidded together.

I heard his head smack against a rock. A terrible sound, like a machete opening a coconut.

Bertie was on his ass being manhandled by Dad. I tried to get up to help but something was wrong with my arm. Or my ribs. Or both.

"Get your mother!" Dad yelled.

I stood up and made it to her. She was unconscious, perilously close to the edge of the rock. I grabbed her with my good arm and saw a hypodermic syringe dangling from her wrist. I pulled it out and was tempted to throw it into the ocean but stopped myself. Evidence.

Lucy had run down to the beach and was yelling to Dad, but I couldn't hear her above the tidal roar. As I held on to Mom, I felt woozy, and when I looked up, I thought I was dreaming. A big ship in the cove turned its lights on us. A Coast Guard cutter with dinghies already deployed was coming toward us. A little while later—it felt like forever—a Secret Service agent reached us. It was all kind of a blur.

A medic leaned over Mom. Someone put me on a stretcher. I saw Bertie in handcuffs, and Ivan lay motionless on the ground. They put us in a dinghy and took us to a bigger boat, and it was great because Dad and Lucy were already there, the four of us safe and sound in the same boat together.

From the ship, I watched Coast Guardsmen corralling those maniacs who'd been on the ferry I destroyed; they'd waded off it as it burned and stumbled to shore. I saw Junior and Lucky Strong and the Reverend Russell and Justice, Fortitude, and Prudence, all of them with their hands behind their backs, all of them chastened and demoralized, staring at the deck of the boat.

As I lay there in the stretcher, Dad approached me, and I tried to sit up. He put a gentle hand on my shoulder. "Stay down, buddy," he said. "Try not to move."

"I'm so sorry, Dad."

"Sorry?" he said. "You saved our lives, son. Your mother's and mine. Possibly Lucy's too. And who knows how many others you saved by stopping that ferry full of goons. I mean, imagine what they would have done had they reached the power brokers in the mansion."

"I went AWOL, though. Disgraced the family."

Dad gave me a sad smile. "I couldn't be prouder of you, Dwight."

He looked out at the sun that was beginning to rise. The storm had blown out to sea, and the sky was clearing.

Behind us, Mom was getting fidgety, lying on her gurney, wrapped in a blanket, being tended to by the medic. She was outraged by what had happened to her. "I was outside the mansion when I heard footsteps behind me, and that sick little boy ran up and jabbed me," Mom said. "What a cowardly thing! He stuck me with this needle, and it knocked me out!"

"I think that's his insulin," Lucy said. "He's diabetic."

"Insulin can cause a hypoglycemic coma," said the medic. "It can be reversed, as we're doing now with the glucagon, but without medical intervention, it can kill you."

"I'm so glad we got to you in time," Lucy told Mom.

Dad leaned against the interior hull of the boat, his face covered with bruises and cuts. "I was running around the island looking for you two," he said. "I saw the older one, Ivan, heading away from the resort, and my gut said to follow him. He went down to the rocks and that's where the kid, Bertie, was dragging your mother. So I tackled him."

Mom put her hand over her mouth. "So he was the serial killer? Bertie?" she said. "Those other women, the first two? The commuters? Did he kill them also?"

"I think so, Mom. And also the third woman, Penelope Watters, who was about to testify against them."

"I don't get it," Dad said. "So they killed two women who got in their way, Ashley and Penelope. But what did those two commuters have to do with the Lyons? Why kill them?"

"Hmm," Mom said. "Maybe this is like the ABC killer, Lucy."

"The what?" asked Dad.

"Agatha Christie novel, dear," Mom said. "Man kills two randoms to create the illusion of a serial killer so as to murder a third guy and throw Poirot off the scent."

"Doesn't feel quite right to me, Mom," Lucy said.

The captain of the Coast Guard cutter approached us—lean, clean-shaven, maybe fifty—and introduced himself. He made sure we were all okay and let us know there would be an ambulance at the dock to take us to a hospital. He apologized profusely that he'd been ordered to dock at the mainland while all this was going on.

"And Sergeant Marder," he said to me, "if you hadn't fired that projectile at their ship, I don't know what mayhem they would have caused. It was a stroke of genius. The Secret Service agents were badly outnumbered. Sinking the ship completely changed the dynamic. They lost their weapons in the surf. An unarmed mob is easier to arrest, so thank you."

I chuckled. "I had to improvise."

"I'm going to make sure the Marines get word of this," he said. "The commandant's going to recommend you for a medal for your heroism."

"Medals really aren't my thing," I said. "How about we just keep it to ourselves?"

CHAPTER EIGHTEEN

LUCY

Washington, DC

May 1978

"TWO PULITZER NOMINATIONS before thirty ain't bad," Bernstein joked.

"Before twenty-five," I corrected.

"Well, you had help," Woodward said.

"So did you!" I said.

From my new perch at the *Washington Post*, I'd had the distinct privilege of working with Carl Bernstein on one story and Bob Woodward on the other.

Bernstein and I exposed to the world that Bertie Lyon was the Slug Killer and that Max Lyon's former assistant Penelope Watters, who was scheduled to testify against her boss, had likely been set up by Max himself and murdered by Bertie. Their plan might have worked had the late Ashley Mars not followed her hunch.

Mom's hypothesis that the case was like Christie's ABC killer was off in one key respect: Bertie was already a killer, having slaughtered his nanny at the Lyon manse in the UK and then killed the nanny's husband, a gardener who also worked for the Lyons. Bertie had somehow avoided drawing suspicion for those murders, and there would be too much family shame in acknowledging his crimes, so the Lyon family had hoped a fresh start in the United States, along with some tranquilizers and electroshock therapy, would cure him of his homicidal impulses. But as soon as the dead women started popping up in Virginia, they knew it was him.

He never admitted it, but it was accepted as fact that after the second murder, Max invented the black person of interest and forced the newspaper to cover it to gin up newsstand sales and throw the cops off the scent. That was my theory, and I was very public—and repentant—about it.

Ivan Lyon would later testify that when the family figured out what Bertie had done to his nanny and her husband, Max threatened to have him lobotomized. In a desperate attempt to save his brother from that horrible fate, Ivan convinced Bertie to make himself useful to the family by silencing Penelope Watters. Ivan knew his father all too well; he pitched the idea, and Max was more than pleased to help them put the plan in motion.

Ivan testified that he hadn't written the fake letter purportedly from the Slug Killer threatening Bertie, and we never found out who had. Part of me suspects it was Harry or Danielle. But they never admitted anything. No one is more opaque than wealthy media families who demand transparency from everyone else.

Ivan was sentenced to ten years in prison for his part in the murders of Penelope and Ashley, but he fled to South America; Bertie was sent to a hospital for the criminally insane, where his family seemed delighted to leave him. Max and the rest of the Lyons were never even charged, though during the trials, they sold the *Sentinel* and moved to Australia.

I never spoke with Harry again. During Bertie's trial, our eyes met across a packed courtroom. He smiled at me ruefully. I'd be lying if I told you I didn't feel anything. But whatever pitter-pat I might have felt was accompanied by nausea.

With Woodward, I wrote about the storming of Pitchfork

Island. Working with Ike and using extensive interviews with Dante and Johnny Alighieri, who had stayed on the mainland, and several imprisoned members of the mob, including former Idaho governor Lucky Strong, we told the story of a skilled demagogue turning the perceived grievances of a mob into a violent insurrection. Call it a cautionary tale.

As for Ike's part of this story: as you no doubt know, in September 1977, Evel Knievel approached author Shelly Saltman outside Twentieth Century Fox studios and beat him with a baseball bat, breaking his wrists and sending him to the hospital. During his trial, Knievel expressed zero remorse and openly admitted having conducted the attack. "I am a fighter and I stand up for what I believe in," he told the judge.

"We long ago abandoned frontier justice in California," the judge replied; he sentenced Evel to six months in the county jail with three years' probation. Woodward and I were able to talk to him in his prison cell and get his take on the mob's invasion of the island, which of course he said he would never have participated in, and we ended up quoting him in the story.

"I just wanted to do a big showy outdoor protest in Washington, DC!" he said. "Peaceful!" Once he'd answered our questions, he told us that he was going to be paid twenty million dollars to jump out of a plane without a parachute at forty thousand feet into thirteen haystacks in a casino parking lot.

I'm working on another story now. In March 1978, the Veterans Administration announced that it was beginning to study whether illnesses experienced by a couple dozen veterans were possibly tied to their exposure to the defoliant Agent Orange. I'm talking to Johnny and Dante as well as a brave former helicopter pilot at death's door named Paul Reutershan, and they tell me that some kids of veterans have been born with birth defects similar to those of children in parts of Vietnam that were sprayed with the defoliant. A VA spokesman told me that Agent Orange had no lasting medical effects and that reports of birth defects were based on "North Vietnamese propaganda." I don't believe him. I'm going to get to the bottom of this. Separately, from his perch on the Senate Veterans Affairs Committee, Dad is also looking into it, with the blessing of its chairman, Senator Alan Cranston, though I haven't said a word to him about my work.

Dad also sits on the Senate Human Resources Committee, which is investigating these claims about laetrile. Despite all evidence medical and scientific, people—desperate, many of them, and my heart goes out to them—continue to believe there's a miracle cure in those apricot pits (there isn't) and that the government is denying it to them. I read in the *Sentinel* gossip pages (I know, I know) that folks worry that the great Steve McQueen, who has developed a horrible cough, has cancer and some of his dumber friends are pushing him to head south of the border for this quackery. No doubt to the hospital the Lyons built. I hope it's not true.

There was a third story that won a Pulitzer for the *Post* that year, but I didn't write it. I put a source I knew—a first-hand participant, since honorably discharged—in touch with our Pentagon reporter, Walter Pincus, who blew the lid off a disastrous foray by the U.S. Marines into Beirut, Lebanon, and the subsequent cover-up by Marine generals. It was a huge story and the main source for it insisted on going on the record, regardless of the consequences that might come his way. He's out in Montana right now spending time with a woman named Rachel, an FBI agent. Dad's going out there next weekend to fish with them on the Snake River. I couldn't be prouder of my baby brother and the man he has become.

ACKNOWLEDGMENTS AND SOURCES

First and foremost, I want to thank Christina Kovac, editor extraordinaire, who helped with plot and character and, perhaps most especially, with Lucy's voice. She was encouraging and kind, and her ideas were so smart. Her novel *The Cutaway* came out in 2017 and her next one, *Watch Us Fall*, comes out in 2024. Check them out!

Matt Klam, a dear friend and literary icon, also helped with editing and writing and was a strong supporter. Check out his books *Sam the Cat* and *Who Is Rich?* if you haven't already.

Geoff Shandler, a wonderful editor who worked on my previous nonfiction book *The Outpost*, provided some great editing help as well.

Others, upon request, lent thoughts, guidance, and expertise. U.S. veteran Henry Hughes, whom I met while writing and then filming the movie version of *The Outpost*, weighed in with some great suggestions about my invented U.S. mission in Beirut, Lebanon. Rep. Seth Moulton, D-Mass., a Marine veteran who served in Iraq, surveyed his fellow Marines on my behalf to discuss what cadence Ike might be chanting to himself in Lebanon.

Motorcycle journalist and enthusiast Mark Gardiner made Ike's love for bikes seem real and Ike's creator seem like he knows a carburetor from a kick-starter.

ACKNOWLEDGMENTS AND SOURCES

Journalist, classmate, and friend Jacqueline Keeler provided some valuable insights for me on Native American perspectives.

My friend and CNN colleague John Berman read an early draft and provided some smart notes.

My sage attorney Bob Barnett has been great throughout this process.

Little, Brown editor Judy Clain has been an enthusiastic supporter of the Marder family. My Little, Brown family also includes publicity director Sabrina Callahan, associate publicist Gabrielle Leporati, marketer Bryan Christian, production editor Pat Jalbert-Levine, designer Julianna Lee, and former editorial assistant Anna de la Rosa. Tracy Roe was a detailed and excellent copyeditor!

Obviously, this is a work of fiction, although, as I did with the novels that precede it in the series, I played with real people and events. That said, here are some details about the nonfiction elements.

Staying at my friend Jimmy Kimmel's fishing lodge in Idaho, I was inspired by his and fellow guest P.J. Clapp's love of Evel Knievel. This led me to watch the great 2015 documentary about the daredevil that Clapp produced, *Being Evel*, directed by Daniel Junge.

I also enjoyed *Evel: The High-Flying Life of Evel Knievel*, by Leigh Montville (New York: Doubleday, 2011). And although it's been scrubbed from existence as much as possible, Sheldon Saltman's *Evel Knievel on Tour* (New York: Dell, 1977) can still be found on the web.

Some Knievel quotes in the book come from his own mouth; see, for instance, Russ Ewing, "Evel Knievel, the Greatest Motorcycle Stunt Rider of All Time," *Penthouse*, May 1974. Scott Bachman published a book of Knievel quotes: *Evel Ways: A Daring Approach to Life* (Minneapolis: DARE Sports Entertainment, 1999).

Other sources for the book are below.

CHAPTER ONE

For some takes on bars in Montana, check out Ed Kemmick, "Recalling Long-Gone Bars, and Two Survivors," *Last Best News*, January 25, 2015. Peter T. White and Emory Kristof's "How Are We Using the Land?," *National Geographic* (July 1976), provided vivid imagery of the Jimtown Bar in Lame Deer; a real-life homicide at Al's Tavern in 1979 inspired some of the events described.

There is no such song as "All the Demons Are Here"; I made it up.

CHAPTER TWO

Carl Bernstein told much of his Barry Goldwater story to me and my viewers when he and Bob Woodward were on my show *The Lead* on June 17, 2022.

Other scenes were inspired by Associated Press, "Goldwater Demands Nixon Tell Full Story," May 13, 1977; Martin Schram, "Nixon and the Truth: By Carter, Baker, and Nixon," *Newsday*, May 15, 1977; and Samuel Dash, *Chief Counsel: Inside the Ervin Committee* (New York: Random House, 1976). See also John Dean, "Rituals of the Herd," *Rolling Stone*, October 7, 1976; Al Spiers, "Butz Says Liberal Press Brought On His Downfall," *Columbus (IN) Republic*, February 17, 1977; and Associated Press, "Jimmy Carter Filed UFO Sighting Report," May 1, 1977.

The Frost/Nixon interviews aired in May 1977, but in general no one should be using the events mentioned in this novel as a reliable chronological guide.

CHAPTER THREE

Viva Knievel! was a real film. From the June 2, 1977, review in *Daily Variety*: "In the most daring feat of his career, Evel Knievel leaps over a mountain of blazing clichés and a cavernous plot, somehow landing upright to the predictable cheers of his legions of fans."

The description of the Chicago press conference before Knievel's shark jump is drawn from John Lampinen, "Evel Knievel Press Event a Real Bomb," *Chicago Daily Herald*, January 26, 1977. The event itself was described in several newspapers, including "Daredevil 'Defies Death,'" *Albuquerque Journal*, January 30, 1977.

Some descriptions of life on the pit crew came from Jan Biles, "Evel Knievel Crew Members Recall Working for Legend," *Topeka Capital-Journal*, November 11, 2017.

The Ribicoff-Daley anecdote came from, among other sources, David Farber, *Chicago '68* (Chicago: University of Chicago Press, 1988).

CHAPTER FOUR

"Transcript of Questions and Answers in President Carter's Call-In," *New York Times*, March 6, 1977; Associated Press, "Cancer Patient Cited in Carter Call-In Dies," May 17, 1977.

Some of the quotes and views attributed to Max Lyon come from his nonfictional counterpart; see the documentary series *Gossip*, directed by Jenny Carchman, aired August 22, August 29, September 5, and September 12, 2021, on Showtime; and Thomas Kiernan, *Citizen Murdoch* (New York: Dodd, Mead, 1986).

There's no such place as Trinity Island or Pitchfork Island.

The inspiration for the subplot involving laetrile, aka B$_{17}$, came from Josh Levin, "The Miracle Cure," episode four of the great *Slate* podcast *One Year: 1977*, July 29, 2021, which included the tragic true story of Chad Green—though the White family in this book is fictitious. Other information came from Lee Edson, "Why Laetrile Won't Go Away," *New York Times*, November 27, 1977; Irving J. Lerner, "Laetrile: A Lesson in Cancer Quackery," *CA: A Cancer Journal for Clinicians* 31 (March/April 1981): 91–95; Donald Kennedy, "Laetrile: The Commissioner's Decision," U.S. Food and Drug Administration, 1978.

CHAPTER FIVE

The story Lucky tells about the UFO sighting comes from Allen Spraggett, "The Unexplained: UFO Over Idaho," *News Tribune*, April 17, 1977, and "'Flying Saucer' Discovery Denied," *Billings Gazette*, July 8, 1947.

Teddy Roosevelt related the fable of the beast as told to him by a "grizzled, weather-beaten old mountain hunter, named Bauman" in *The Wilderness Hunter: An Account of the Big Game of the United States and Its Chase with Horse, Hound, and Rifle* (New York: G. P. Putnam's Sons, 1893).

The reference to Black Jack's and the death of a journalist with gambling debts is of course an homage to the late great Norman Maclean's *A River Runs Through It*, and the truth of the real story of the death of Paul Maclean was covered by Richard Babcock in "A Tragedy Runs Through It" in the March–April 2021 *Dartmouth Alumni Magazine*.

See also Joan Ryan, "TV Hit Bottom with Ghoulish Knievel," *Washington Post*, February 2, 1977.

Evel's bedside excuses came from an article by Michael Sneed, "Why Knievel Filmed Shark Jump," *Chicago Tribune*, February 2, 1977.

CHAPTER SIX

For information on ridesharing, see "MIT 'Real-Time' Rideshare Research," January 24, 2009, http://ridesharechoices.scripts.mit.edu/home/histstats/.

For information on the Fleecer mountain cabin, see U.S. Forest Service, https://www.fs.usda.gov/recarea/bdnf/recarea/?recid=5700.

CHAPTER SEVEN

Information in this chapter was drawn from John Steinbeck IV, "The Importance of Being Stoned in Vietnam," *Washingtonian*, January 1, 1968; Jeremy Kuzmarov, "From Counter-Insurgency to Narco-Insurgency: Vietnam and the International War on Drugs," *Journal of Policy History* 20, no. 3 (July 2008): 344–78; Sanjay Gupta, "Vietnam, Heroin, and the Lesson of Disrupting Any Addiction," CNN.com, December 22, 2015.

CHAPTER EIGHT

Information in this chapter came from the following sources:
Cady Drell, "How Son of Sam Changed America," *Rolling*

Stone, July 29, 2016; Thomas Pugh and Vincent Cosgrove, "Victims' Hair Style a Link in 3 Killings," *New York Daily News*, March 12, 1977; Carey Winfrey, "Son of Sam," *New York Times*, August 22, 1977; Daniel Henninger, "The Sweet Life, New York, 1977," *Wall Street Journal*, December 2, 1977; James Barron, "45 Years Ago Tonight, a Blackout Struck New York City," *New York Times*, July 13, 2022.

There's no such song as "Dogs in Heat."

Roy Cohn was indeed a fixture at Studio 54 and in fact provided legal representation for its owners, Steve Rubell and Ian Schrager, when they were charged with (and ultimately convicted of) tax evasion. I recommend the documentary *Studio 54*, directed by Matt Tyrnauer, 2018. Random trivia: President Obama pardoned Schrager in 2017.

CHAPTER NINE

Information in this chapter came from Linda Deutsch, "The Elvis Presley Legacy: He Changed Your Life," *Sioux Falls Argus-Leader*, August 21, 1977; and Matthew Sewell, "'Our Lady of the Rockies': The Miraculous Story Behind Montana's 90-ft Statue of Mary," ChurchPOP.com, March 22, 2016.

CHAPTER TEN

I played with the Son of Sam timeline here. Jimmy Breslin, "Breslin to .44 Killer: GIVE UP! IT'S ONLY WAY OUT!" *New York Daily News*, June 5, 1977.

CHAPTER ELEVEN

Yes, the story of a young Bob Knievel hitchhiking to DC to protest elk policy is true! See "Plans of Elk Rancher Thwarted by Slaughter," *Great Falls Tribune*, December 15, 1961; Associated Press, "Butte Nimrod Schedules Trip," *Billings Gazette*, December 1, 1961; "Sportsmen Will Try to Halt Elk Park Kill," *Montana Standard*, November 22, 1961; and "Guide Protests Shooting of Elk," photo caption, *South Bend Tribune*, December 13, 1961.

Also see Mark Stinneford, "Former Marines Found and Bought Vintage Bikes in Lebanon," United Press International, June 24, 1984.

CHAPTER TWELVE

Information in this chapter came from Red West, Sonny West, and Dave Hebler as told to Steve Dunleavy, *Elvis: What Happened?* (New York: Ballantine, 1977). I should note that, despite Margaret's skepticism, most of the book's salacious allegations have stood the test of time.

See also Ben Fong-Torres, "Elvis Presley: Broken Heart for Sale," *Rolling Stone*, September 22, 1977; and Chet Flippo, "Will Elvis Presley See Revenge Against Media Mogul Rupert Murdoch?," CMT.com, July 14, 2011.

CHAPTER THIRTEEN

Eugene Jarecki's fantastic 2017 documentary about Elvis, *The King*, was a tremendous source of inspiration, and I must in particular credit the wise observations of Ethan Hawke in it.

See also David E. Stanley with Frank Coffey, *The Elvis Encyclopedia* (North Dighton, MA: World Publications, 2002); "Elvis Presley Hit by an Amazing Series of Crises," *San Antonio Express*, May 15, 1977; "Elvis Presley's Bodyguards Blow Whistle on Their Boss in Startling Book," *San Antonio Star*, August 14, 1977.

Marine cadence from Carol Burke, "Marching to Vietnam," *The Journal of American Folklore*, vol. 102, no. 406 (October–December, 1989).

Quotes from Shelly Saltman's previously mentioned book are verbatim.

CHAPTER FOURTEEN

The degree to which Hearst and Pulitzer were actually responsible for the U.S. entry into the Spanish-American war has been hotly debated, and it was effectively debunked by W. Joseph Campbell in *Yellow Journalism: Puncturing the Myths, Defining the Legacies* (New York: Praeger, 2001).

See also H. G. Rickover, *How the Battleship "Maine" Was Destroyed* (Washington, DC: Naval Historical Division, 1976).

William F. Buckley's comments are based on Buckley, "Future of the Republican Party," syndicated column, November 30, 1976.

Patrick Buchanan's comments are based on Buchanan, "New York's 'Night of the Animals,'" syndicated column, July 22, 1977.

The observation that it was the IRS investigating segregated religious schools that got the religious right involved in politics comes from conservative activist Richard Viguerie, quoted in Joseph Crespino, "Civil Rights and the Religious Right," in Bruce J. Schulman and Julian Zelizer, eds., *Rightward Bound: Making America Conservative in the 1970s* (Cambridge, MA: Harvard University Press, 2008).

CHAPTER EIGHTEEN

Evel really did go to LA and attack Shelly Saltman with a baseball bat, and he went to prison for it. Saltman later sued and was awarded $12.75 million in damages. See Jack Jones, "'I Stand By What I Did' Knievel Says," *Los Angeles Times*, September 22, 1977; and Associated Press, "Knievel Starts Jail Term," November 22, 1977.

According to the Congressional Research Service, the VA started getting claims from veterans related to exposure to Agent Orange in 1977. For more, see https://sgp.fas.org/crs/misc/R43790.pdf; Casey Bukro, "Illnesses May Be Tied to Vietnam Defoliant," *Chicago Tribune*, March 24, 1978; United Press International, "Suspected 'Orange' Contamination Leaves Veteran Facing Early Death," May 21, 1978.

ABOUT THE AUTHOR

Jake Tapper is the chief DC anchor and chief Washington correspondent for CNN; he hosts the weekday show *The Lead with Jake Tapper* and cohosts the Sunday public-affairs show *State of the Union*. A Dartmouth graduate and Philly native, he lives in Washington, DC, with his wife, daughter, and son.